Praise for *The Katharina Code*

Nordic Noir Thriller of the Year

Winner of the prestigious Petrona Award for Best Scandinavian Crime Novel

Longlisted for the CWA International Dagger Award

"Compelling, original, and suspenseful. *The Katharina Code* grabs you at page one and never lets go!"

Kathy Reichs, #1 *New York Times* bestselling author of the Temperance Brennan series

"A well-crafted, atmospheric, character-driven thriller—I couldn't put it down!"

Alex Dahl, bestselling author of *After She'd Gone*

"Jørn Lier Horst only gets better and better. *The Katharina Code* is a beautiful crime fiction."

Stavanger Aftenblad

"The best and most ingenious novel that Jørn Lier Horst has written thus far."

Tvedestrandsposten

"With *The Katharina Code* Jørn Lier Horst again delivers an excellent crime novel with a credible plot . . . All that remains is to declare that Jørn Lier Horst impresses again."

Østlands-Posten

"Jørn Lier Horst has truly done it this time . . . Exceptionally well-executed."

Tønsbergs Blad

"It's impossible to resist the allure of this superbly crisp suspense novel about the tangled lives of the people left behind when two women go missing. A powerful must-read."

Samantha M. Bailey, *USA Today* and #1 nationally bestselling author of *A Friend in the Dark*

"Spare prose, elegant structure, and a masterful layering of secrets and suspense. Brilliant!"

Daniel Kalla, bestselling author of *High Society*

"How lucky we are to have mastermind storyteller Jørn Lier Horst on North American shelves. *The Katharina Code* is icy Nordic noir at its best: Twisty, gripping, and with a dark ache of a cold case that won't let its protagonist go."

Roz Nay, bestselling author of *The Offing*

"Norwegian bestselling author, former policeman Jørn Lier Horst delivers yet another adept story . . . Without excessive complications, unnecessary frills and decorations in his style, [Lier Horst] writes in a bare and sober prose which one still may refer to as masculine. In the style of the genre's founder, Ed McBain."

Politiken

"It's thrilling and well-narrated . . . I look forward to reading the upcoming novels and am excited to see what old cases appear. . . . The author is an expert when it comes to characters, and I'm crazy about William Wisting as well as his family, and colleagues at the Larvik police."

Litteratursiden

"*The Katharina Code* vibrates with anticipation all the way to the finish."

Dagbladet

"I'm crazy about Jørn Lier Horst's style of writing and crime fiction, where the story and the human character traits are front and center and a theme is used as the fulcrum of the story—in this [novel] it's the theme of lies, and what they do to people."

Bogblogger.DK

Praise for Jørn Lier Horst

"Horst, a former Norwegian police detective, is often compared to Sweden's Henning Mankell for his moody, sweeping crime dramas."

The New York Times

"Jørn Lier Horst is one of the most brilliantly understated crime novelists writing today."

The Sunday Times

"Up there with the best of the Nordic crime writers."

The Times

"If you haven't already, introduce yourself to Norway's Chief Inspector William Wisting—you'll warm to him even though his patch can get pretty cold."

Jon Wise, *Sunday Sport*

"Horst invites the readers to join the investigation in a credible manner that highlights professional practices [in the police] and generates a new kind of suspense."

Bok 365

THE KATHARINA CODE

JØRN LIER HORST

Translated from the Norwegian by Anne Bruce

Published by Scribner Canada

NEW YORK   AMSTERDAM/ANTWERP   LONDON
TORONTO   SYDNEY   NEW DELHI

SCRIBNER
CANADA

An Imprint of Simon & Schuster, LLC
166 King Street East, Suite 300
Toronto, Ontario M5A 1J3

Originally published in Norway as *Katharina-koden*, 2017

Text Copyright © 2018 by Jørn Lier Horst

English Translation Copyright © by Anne Bruce, 2018

This Scribner Canada edition January 2025

SCRIBNER CANADA and colophon are trademarks
of Simon & Schuster, LLC

For information about special discounts for bulk purchases, please contact Simon & Schuster Special Sales at 1-800-268-3216 or CustomerService@simonandschuster.ca.

Interior Design by Jouve (UK), Milton Keynes

Manufactured in the United States of America

1   3   5   7   9   10   8   6   4   2

Library and Archives Canada Cataloguing in Publication
Title: The Katharina code / by Jørn Lier Horst ; translated by Anne Bruce.
Other titles: Katharina-koden. English
Names: Horst, Jørn Lier, 1970- author. | Bruce, Anne, 1952 April 22- translator
Description: Scribner Canada edition. | Translation of: Katharina-koden.
Identifiers: Canadiana (print) 20240354753 | Canadiana (ebook) 20240354761 |
ISBN 9781668076071 (softcover) | ISBN 9781668076088 (EPUB)
Subjects: LCGFT: Detective and mystery fiction. | LCGFT: Novels.
Classification: LCC PT8952.18.O77 K3813 2025 | DDC 839.823/8—dc23

ISBN 978-1-6680-7607-1
ISBN 978-1-6680-7608-8 (ebook)

THE KATHARINA CODE

I

The three cardboard boxes were stored at the bottom of the wardrobe. Wisting lifted out the largest. One corner had started to tear, so he had to be careful as he carried it into the living room.

He opened the lid and removed the top ring binder—black, with a faded label on the spine: *Katharina Haugen*. Laying it aside, he took out a red binder marked *Witnesses I* and two others of the same colour tagged *Witnesses II* and *Witnesses III*. Soon he found what he was looking for—the ring binder labelled *Kleiverveien*.

These cardboard boxes contained everything written and undertaken in the Katharina case. Strictly speaking, he should not have brought the case documents home, but he felt they did not deserve to be locked away in an archive room. Sitting there at the bottom of his wardrobe, they reminded him of the case every time he took out a shirt.

He picked up his reading glasses and sat down with the ring binder on his lap. One whole year had passed since he had last looked through it.

Kleiverveien was where Katharina had lived. The unpretentious detached house, surrounded by forest, had been photographed from various angles. In the background of one of the images it was just possible to make out the shimmering waters of Kleiver Lake. The house itself was situated on a small plateau, about a hundred metres from the road. It was brown, trimmed in white, with a green door and empty window boxes on the ledges.

Browsing through the folder of photographs was like walking through a ghost house. Katharina was gone, but her shoes were left on the floor in the porch. A pair of grey trainers, some brown leather boots and a pair of clogs, beside her husband's clumpy sandals and work boots. Three jackets hung from the row of pegs. On the chest of drawers in the hallway lay a ballpoint pen and a shopping list, an unopened letter, a newspaper and a few unaddressed flyers. A half-withered bouquet of roses lay beside an ornament. A few little memos were stuck to the mirror above the chest—one with a date and time, another with a name and phone number, and a third with three initials and a sum of money. *AML 125 kr.*

Her suitcase lay open on the bed, full of clothes, as if she had intended to be away for some time: ten pairs of socks, ten pairs of briefs, ten T-shirts, five pairs of trousers, five sweaters, five blouses and a tracksuit. There was something about the contents he had never managed to make sense of, though he could not quite put his finger on why. The selection seemed so rigid and formal, as if it had been packed by someone else, or for someone else.

He continued to peruse the photos. Five books taken from the bookcase lay on the coffee table. Wisting had read some of them himself: *Mengele Zoo*, *The Alchemist* and *The Satanic Verses*. Beside them was a photograph of Katharina with Martin Haugen, taken at a scenic viewpoint—they were standing with their arms around each other, smiling at whoever had taken the picture. The picture had been framed but had been removed from its frame and lay beside the glass.

The photographs of the kitchen were the ones that caused the greatest puzzlement. A plate with a slice of bread and butter and a glass of milk were left on the kitchen counter. The chair she usually sat in had been pushed out from the table, and on the table lay a ballpoint pen and what subsequently became known as "The Katharina Code."

Wisting squinted at the photocopy of it, which comprised a series of numbers arranged along three vertical lines. So far, no one had succeeded in deciphering its meaning.

In addition to the police's own experts, they had involved cryptologists from the military's security centre in the examination of the mysterious message, without arriving any closer to a solution. The code had also been sent to experts abroad but, to them, the paper had also seemed to hold a senseless combination of numbers.

Wisting turned the copy this way and that, as if something might change on this occasion to allow him to grasp its significance.

All of a sudden he looked up. Line had come in, but he had failed to catch what his daughter had said. He had not even registered that she had entered the room.

"Eh?" he asked, as he removed his reading glasses, leaving them hanging from a cord around his neck.

Line sat down with her daughter on her knee and began to take off the toddler's jacket and shoes, all the while peering over at the cardboard box Wisting had brought out.

"I'd forgotten tomorrow is 10 October," she repeated.

As Wisting put down the ring binder, he held out his arms to his granddaughter and lifted her on to his lap. She was no longer a baby. The helpless little creature he had held in his arms for the very first time fourteen months earlier had now developed a personality of her own. He pressed his lips to her round cheek and gave her a loud kiss. Amalie burst out laughing and tried to catch hold of his glasses with her chubby hands. Unhitching them, he laid them well out of her reach.

"Do you think there's anything in there you haven't read before?" Line asked, gesturing at the ring binder on the table.

She seemed annoyed and out of sorts.

"Is something wrong?" Wisting queried.

With a sigh, Line thrust her hand into her bag and quickly dug

3

out a yellow plastic strip. A lipstick, a ballpoint pen, a packet of chewing gum and other bits and pieces spilled out of her bag at the same time.

"I got a parking ticket," she explained, tossing it on the table before stuffing the rest of the contents back into her bag. "Seven hundred kroner."

Wisting glanced at it. "Parking in contravention of sign 372," he read out. "What is sign 372?"

"No parking."

With a broad smile, Wisting bent down and rubbed his nose on his granddaughter's cheek.

"Mummy got a fine," he said, in an affected voice.

Line rose to her feet. "I can't fathom why you still keep going through these papers," she said, heading for the kitchen. "After all these years."

"Are you going to complain?" Wisting asked. "About the parking fine?"

"There's nothing to complain about," Line answered. "I didn't see the sign. I'll just have to pay the money."

Returning with a teaspoon, she produced a yogurt from the changing bag and hoisted Amalie on to her lap.

"Have you found any more of her relatives?" Wisting asked.

Line tore off the lid of the yogurt pot. "A few fourth and fifth cousins in Bergen," she replied, flashing him a smile.

"How do you get to be a fifth cousin?" Wisting quizzed her.

"When you have four-times-great-grandparents in common," Line explained as she fed Amalie.

"And what four-times-great-grandfather are we talking about?"

"Arthur Thorsen," Line specified. "He was Mum's great-great-grandfather."

"Never heard of him," Wisting admitted.

"Born on Askøy in 1870," Line told him.

With a shake of the head, Wisting picked up the report he had been reading. "And you think *I'm* messing about with old papers?" he said jokingly.

"But what you're looking for isn't there," Line said. "You've kept this up for twenty-five years, but the answer's certainly not in those papers."

"Twenty-four," Wisting corrected her, and stood up. He knew the answer probably wasn't to be found in any of the boxes in his wardrobe, but at the same time he was convinced that at least one of the 763 names that had cropped up in the investigation material belonged to someone who knew what had happened on that October day almost twenty-four years ago.

He picked up one of the red ring binders and riffled through to a random document. A witness statement. The paper it was written on was tattered and the text faded. Wisting read the beginning of a haphazard sentence in the middle of the page and knew how it ended without having to read to the conclusion. A routine interview, it contained nothing of significance, no interesting details, but every time he read it, or any other document for that matter, he had the same idea that this time he would discover a detail he had previously overlooked, or spot a connection he had not made before.

"Are you?" Line asked, shaking him out of his thoughts.

He closed the ring binder, aware once again of missing what she had said.

"Are you tagging along with him on another trip to his cabin?" she asked.

"Who's that?" Wisting asked, even though he knew what she meant.

"Him," Line replied, with a long-suffering look at the heaps of case documents.

"I don't think so," Wisting answered.

"But you do intend to visit him tomorrow?"

Wisting nodded. It had become a habit, visiting Martin Haugen every year on 10 October. "Sorry," he said, putting down the ring binder.

He knew his behaviour changed as the anniversary approached. The old case filled his mind, pushing everything else to one side.

"What are you doing this evening?" he asked, walking towards the window. It was dark outside, and raindrops speckled the glass.

Line gave her daughter the last spoonful of yogurt. "I'm going to the gym," she replied, lowering Amalie to the floor. "I was hoping you could babysit. She doesn't like the crèche very much."

Little Amalie stood on the floor, wobbling.

"You're welcome to leave her here," Wisting said happily, clapping his hands to entice his granddaughter towards him. She toddled across and laughed loudly when Wisting caught her and lifted her up in the air.

"Careful, now," Line warned him. "She's just eaten."

Putting her back down again, Wisting headed into an adjacent room to fetch a box of toys. He poured the contents on the floor and sat down beside her.

Amalie grabbed a red wooden block and said something that Wisting could not make out.

"Thanks, Dad," Line said as she stood up. "I'll be back in a couple of hours."

She waved to them both, but Amalie was far too busy to notice her mother leave.

They sat together on the floor for ten minutes or so, but after a while Wisting's grandchild grew more interested in playing on her own.

His knee joints creaked as he got to his feet. He made for the cardboard box, took out a notepad and sat down again in the chair. As he flipped through the pages, he reached for his glasses and put them on once more.

All the information from the cases he was working on ended up in his thick blue notebook. First, the crucial facts of the case, then details, witness statements, documentation and lab results. The notebook was the case's anchor, a compendium of every single interview he had conducted and every single scrap of evidence collected. It always formed the basis for deciding the next move.

He could not understand why Line was so averse to his continued interest in this old case. Usually she was attracted to unsolved mysteries and unanswered questions. The same thirst for knowledge that had made him into a detective had turned her into a journalist. After Amalie was born she had taken up genealogical research. She was mostly keen to provide her daughter with a big family, since Amalie's father was more or less out of the picture. However, her deep-seated curiosity was another reason. He could well understand the satisfaction in uncovering new family connections and gradually creating a family tree. It was not so different from a police investigation.

The search for answers lay at the heart of everything Line had done as a journalist. As far as Line was concerned, it was not simply a matter of reporting on a news event. She wanted to know what lay behind it. This was a quality the editorial team at the *VG* newspaper regarded highly. They were eager to keep her and had extended her maternity leave in the hope that she would return to her post.

He had no desire for her to involve herself in the Katharina case, but could not understand why she was so uninterested. Maybe it was because the case had always been there. Line had been six years of age when Katharina Haugen had disappeared. She had grown accustomed to him taking out the old documents from time to time and immersing himself in them. Or perhaps it was because she, like so many others, had accepted the explanation most people had become reconciled to—that Katharina Haugen had chosen to take her own life one dark October night twenty-four years ago.

But if that were true, what had become of the body?

An alternative theory was that there had been an accident. That she had gone for a walk, fallen and been left lying unconscious. However, that simply raised more questions than answers.

Regardless of the circumstances of her disappearance, there were also other unsolved aspects to the case. These were what made Wisting take out the case files again, year after year. Such as the mysterious code on the kitchen table, the peculiar neighbour, and the business of her unidentified father. And then there were the flowers: fourteen red roses.

Amalie had scrambled to her feet and was now standing in a world of her own, clutching an armrest and chewing a brightly coloured plastic rattle.

Wisting beamed at her before locating the interview with one of the last people to see Katharina Haugen alive, a friend of hers called Mina Ruud. She and Katharina sang in the same choir and had known each other for five years. For the last few weeks, Katharina had not attended choir practice. In a phone call, she had explained to her friend that she was not feeling well, that she had no energy. So, two days before Katharina vanished, Mina had paid her a visit. True enough, her friend had looked tired and pale. Something was obviously bothering her, Mina thought, but Katharina had brushed off any questions and explained that she had started a course of vitamin tablets in the hope of feeling better. During the interview, Mina had explained that she had seen a huge change in Katharina in the course of the past year. She was usually what Mina would call a vivacious person, always happy. *Bubbly* was the word she used. But then something must have happened to change her personality. She stayed at home, seldom went out and hardly ever mixed with her friends. She became reclusive, depressed and quiet.

One paragraph in Mina Ruud's statement in particular had

drawn Wisting's attention. She believed Katharina was hiding a dark secret that she was reluctant to reveal to anyone.

Several people described Katharina Haugen as depressed before she went missing, both friends and work colleagues. A widespread perception attributed this to missing her family and friends in Austria.

Wisting skipped forward slightly and read a few other extracts from Mina Ruud's statement. He stopped abruptly at a sentence he had not lingered on before. Mina Ruud had been trying to put a date on a conversation with Katharina during which her friend told her that she had met an Austrian man two days earlier. It had been a chance encounter in a café, when he had asked her if the chair at her table was free, and Katharina had noticed his accent and asked him if he came from Austria. It had been pleasant for her to meet someone from her own country.

The investigators had committed endless resources trying to locate this man. Because of this, it had been crucial to discover when exactly the encounter had taken place. As far as Mina recalled, it had been one afternoon in the middle of August.

He read the sentence one more time: *It was afternoon in the middle of August.*

A word was missing. He had always read the sentence as if it said, *It was one afternoon in the middle of August,* but the word *one* was missed out. It was a common mistake, one he made himself sometimes. Not all the words that ran through his head ended up on the paper. On reading it through, the brain was tricked into believing that the word was there, because in fact you didn't read the sentence word for word but let your eye run across it.

This missing word was of no consequence. It changed nothing, but it made him think there might be other things in the comprehensive investigation material that he had overlooked.

He put down the report and plunged into the nearest bundle with renewed interest and enthusiasm. When anyone disappeared as Katharina had done, there were four distinct possibilities: suicide, accident, escape or some sort of crime. They had investigated all the theories, including the possibility that she had left the country without telling anyone in order to start a new life.

Wisting had never believed in the idea that Katharina had disappeared of her own free will. Even though they had no body or crime scene, he had always regarded the Katharina case as a murder investigation. No single aspect caused him to draw this conclusion but rather the sum total of circumstances. Such as the suitcase on the bed, the books removed from the bookcase and the picture taken out of its frame. And then there was the code on the kitchen table.

He picked up the photocopy and studied it once again. Three faint curved lines divided the sheet of paper and formed two columns, with a line drawn across at the bottom. The remainder consisted of a series of numbers. The number 362 was circled and noted in two instances. The same applied to 334. Similarly, the number 18 was written twice and enclosed in a square. In addition, several numbers were scattered around the paper: 206, 613, 148, 701, 404 and 49. What made the cryptic information so intriguing was that a plus sign had been drawn on one side of the paper, with the vertical line longer than the horizontal, so that it resembled a religious symbol, a cross. Time after time the black ballpoint pen had been drawn back and forth over the same symbol almost until a hole was torn in the paper.

Yet again Wisting sat looking at the cross and the numbers. This time it was as if something tugged at his subconscious—he felt as if the numbers were about to convey some sort of meaning.

He took in a deep breath and held it. Such a spark was what he was after when he took out the old case documents again, a hope that he might have learned something in the course of the year gone by—heard, seen or somehow lived through something to extend his experience in such a way that when he reread the papers he would be able to interpret the contents differently. He felt he was there now, on the brink of understanding. A response, a picture or an insignificant detail that had attached itself to his subconscious in the course of the past twelve months was about to provide him with a lead in the case.

He read the numbers aloud in an attempt to assist his brain to let something surface: "Two hundred and six, six hundred and thirteen, one hundred and forty-eight . . ."

Little Amalie mimicked him. She tried to say the same numbers and laughed at her own unsuccessful efforts.

Wisting glanced across at her. All around her mouth was completely blue, and she had a ballpoint pen in her hand. She had bitten a hole into it and the ink was running down her hand.

She gurgled and chuckled as she put the pen back in her mouth.

Wisting threw aside the papers, rushed across and snatched the pen from her fingers.

Her lips, teeth, tongue and the entire lower part of her face were stained blue. Carrying her under his arm, he dashed out to the bathroom, where he turned on the water and held her over the basin. He filled his hand with water and splashed it on her face repeatedly. Amalie began to shriek but he scooped up more water and flung it at her, into her open mouth. Amalie coughed and spluttered. Coloured water ran into the basin. Despite her protests, he continued to rinse her face until he was sure her mouth had been emptied of ink, then he sat down on the toilet seat with his granddaughter on his knee and tried to comfort her.

"It's okay," he said, struggling to sound cheerful.

Amalie calmed down a bit. Wisting coaxed his mobile phone from his pocket: he rang Accident and Emergency and gave a hurried account of what had happened.

The nurse asked for the child's name. "Ingrid Amalie Wisting," he answered, and provided her date of birth.

He heard the sound of a keyboard rattling at the other end of the line. "How much ink has she ingested?" the nurse asked.

"I don't know," Wisting admitted, carrying Amalie back into the living room. The pen was lying on the floor and had left a blue mark on the carpet.

"There's just over half the ink left," he said. "But I think most of it is probably on her clothes and hands."

"Small quantities of ink are normally perfectly harmless," the nurse reassured him. "The worst thing is if she's swallowed some pieces of plastic."

As Wisting studied the pen, he saw that the top was splintered. "What would happen then?" he asked.

"They could get caught in her throat," the nurse replied. "But it sounds as if she's fine. She might have an upset tummy, but any fragments will probably come out naturally."

Wisting thanked her and carried Amalie into the bathroom again, where he wet a flannel and tried to wash her face and fingers. This helped a little, but the blue stain stubbornly refused to disappear. He picked up her toothbrush, applied some toothpaste and made an effort to brush her tiny, discoloured teeth. Amalie protested and began to grizzle again. Now he gave up, brought her back to the living room and slumped into his chair with his granddaughter on his lap. The fear he had felt was changing to annoyance: he was furious with himself.

Amalie went on sobbing. She was probably tired and his anxiety had affected her. He stood up again and, with his granddaughter hoisted on his hip, he collected all the papers connected to the Katharina case and returned them to the box. One of the ring binders was not closed and loose papers drifted on to the table and down to the floor. He swept them up and stuffed them back into the large box, heedless of whether they became crumpled or disordered. He simply wanted it all out of the way.

Shifting Amalie to his other hip, he closed the lids on the big cardboard box and used his foot to push it alongside the wall. He sat down on the floor and studied her closely. Her clothes were ruined. She was probably growing out of them anyway, but he would have to offer to replace them.

By the time Line returned home Amalie's tears had subsided and they were both absorbed in a game of stacking wooden blocks.

She smiled when she saw them playing but froze when she noticed the blue dye around Amalie's mouth and on her clothes.

"What happened?" she asked, lifting her daughter.

"She got hold of a ballpoint pen," Wisting answered.

"Weren't you watching her?"

"She was too quick," Wisting replied.

"But you were with her, weren't you?"

"Of course," Wisting said. "But then all of a sudden she was sitting there with her face covered in ink. I think it was your pen. It must have fallen out of your bag when you showed me your parking ticket."

Line moistened her thumb and began to rub Amalie's chin.

"I phoned Accident and Emergency," Wisting explained. "Ink isn't dangerous, at least not in small quantities. A bit difficult to remove, but not harmful."

Line sighed. "I'll have to take her home and give her a bath."

She sat down on a chair and began to put a snowsuit on her daughter, while Wisting started to clear the toys from the floor.

"I can buy her some new clothes?" he offered. "Or at least pay for them."

Line shook her head. "Not at all," she said, getting to her feet. "Thanks for looking after her, anyway."

"I'm sorry," Wisting said. "I'm obviously a terrible babysitter."

Line gave him a fleeting smile. "It's perfectly okay," she said, glancing at the box of case documents. "Remember Thomas is coming home this weekend, won't you?" she said.

Thomas was her twin brother who worked as a helicopter pilot in the military, and he came home only a couple of times a year.

"I'll make pizza!" Wisting said enthusiastically.

This was something Wisting had instigated when Line and Thomas were teenagers. Every Friday when he returned home from work, he made pizza dough and Line and Thomas helped to prepare the topping. This was a practice they had continued right up until Thomas left to join the army.

"We'll be there," Line said, hugging her daughter. "Are you going to say cheerio to Grandpa, then?"

Wisting approached them and gave each a hug before accompanying them to the door. He stood gazing after them as they walked through the rain down to Line's house at the bottom of the street.

He had lied, and he realized how easy it had been to say he was with Amalie instead of admitting how engrossed he had been in the Katharina case. It wasn't only that he had lied, but he had pushed part of the blame and responsibility on to Line by claiming it was her fault that a pen had been among the toys.

Closing the door, he returned to the living room and stood looking at the cardboard box he had shoved aside.

Lies were an element of every investigation. Everyone lied. It was seldom a matter of downright untruths, but most people avoided the unvarnished truth in some way or another. They equivocated, kept quiet about particulars, exaggerated and embellished things to make them more interesting or held back circumstances that cast them in a bad light. In addition, things slipped people's minds, they remembered their experiences differently from how they had actually taken place. And instead of admitting they could not remember, they filled in the blanks with what they believed and thought must have occurred, usually based on what other people had heard or seen. In order to expose these lies, you depended on being in possession of supplementary information, making it possible to verify what had been stated.

He crouched down to retrieve the pen Amalie had been chewing. The Police Federation logo was only just visible beneath the marks left by Amalie's teeth. It was his ballpoint pen. He wondered whether he should tell Line or just let it drop. He slung it into the kitchen rubbish bin. He returned to the living room, opened the flaps on the cardboard box and extracted the case notes once again.

2

Torrents of water slashed through the darkness in front of the head-lights as Wisting reversed from the garage. The rain had intensified overnight. He had stayed up past midnight in an effort to seize the lead that had eluded him earlier that evening, but it was gone.

Glancing over his shoulder, down towards the house where his daughter lived, he spotted a light in the kitchen. He knew Amalie woke around six o'clock and hesitated momentarily behind the wheel, wondering whether he should stop to ask Line how Amalie was doing. He had plenty of time, as usual in the mornings. His working day did not begin for another hour, but she would proba-bly be struggling to get Amalie back to sleep again, and he didn't want to disturb them.

Twenty-four years ago, 10 October had been a cloudless day with a gentle, south-westerly breeze, he recalled from the reports. It had clouded over slightly in the course of the evening when the wind strength had increased and the temperature had dropped to around eight degrees Celsius. He remembered all these details as if it were yesterday.

He drove steadily through the residential area and swung to the left as he emerged on to Larviksveien, well aware that his working day would be unproductive; he would be unable to concentrate on much else, either before or after his meeting with Martin Haugen.

Katharina had disappeared once prior to this when her name had been Katharina Bauer. At the age of twenty-one, she had mounted her motorbike at home in Perg and driven out of the small Austrian town, never to return.

At that time she was fleeing a dysfunctional family with a violent, alcoholic stepfather and an unstable mother with mental-health problems. Katharina and her sister had stuck together, looking after their younger brother, but when he grew old enough to take care of himself Katharina had packed a rucksack and left.

Her journey had ended in Norway. Somewhere in that country she had a father. At least that was what her mother had told her, that her father was Norwegian. She had scant hope of finding him: all she knew was that his name was Richardt and that he had been a regular customer for a while in the restaurant where her mother worked during the summer of 1958. Subsequently he had moved on, and it was not even certain he was aware he had become a father.

To be honest, her unidentified father had not been the reason she had travelled to Norway. Above all it had been a question of running away. However, she had been curious about the country— before she left she had learned something of the geography and history of the place, and a little of the language.

She had tried to find her father after she arrived in Norway. Among the effects she left behind were lists of names and addresses of men called Richardt, spelled in different ways, but this looked like a project she had given up on several years before she went missing. Some of the names had been scored through, but more than three quarters remained. The police had been in contact with all of them. The ones crossed out confirmed they had been contacted, but that none had been the person she was seeking.

Wisting was forced to increase the speed of the windscreen wipers. Once he approached the town centre, the traffic became congested. The rainwater of the past few days had found new courses and in several places earth had been washed away and parts of the road had collapsed, causing traffic to be diverted.

In Austria, Katharina had studied to become a surveyor and land-use planner, and she had undertaken some work for the local roads authority after her arrival in Norway. With a talent for languages, she rapidly became fluent in Norwegian and had taken further qualifications at technical college. Eventually she had obtained contract work with the National Directorate of Public Roads and took part in the design and construction of a new motorway through the southern part of Telemark. This was where she had met Martin Haugen, who worked as a foreman and was one of the road workers constantly in and out of the planning office.

The traffic made slow progress as a cyclist in full rain gear picked his way through the cars.

He would visit Martin Haugen at home around twelve o'clock. They never had any fixed arrangement, but every year since Katharina disappeared, he had turned up there at the same time, and he expected Martin Haugen would be waiting for him this year too. The coffee would be ready, and the shop-bought cake would be on the table—probably a lemon-drizzle cake with icing or a raspberry Swiss roll. At first they would make small talk and then the conversation would find its way to Katharina.

Wisting had met her once. He could not recollect it himself, however, and it was not until five or six years after her disappearance that Martin Haugen had reminded him of it. It had been on 17 May, Norway's national day, he had said, showing him a newspaper clipping. Katharina and her friends in the choir had been singing during the festivities in Bøkeskogen. A photograph of them appeared in the newspaper and Wisting, who had been on duty, could be glimpsed in the background.

When the photo was published, Katharina had pointed out Wisting and told Martin that just as they were about to sing, she had found a bunch of keys. She had handed them to the policeman in the picture.

His initial reaction had been that Katharina must have mixed him up with another police officer. He had rooted out the lost-property register, leafed back through it and, to his surprise, had discovered his own note that one item, namely a bunch of keys, had been found and handed over by Katharina Haugen. So he had spoken to her, noted her name and later transferred the information into the lost-property register. When he tried to cast his mind back, he only managed to conjure up a vague recollection. Martin Haugen had also forgotten about it, until he had been tidying a drawer, found the clipping and recognized Wisting.

A car tooted behind him, wrenching Wisting from his thoughts. He crawled forward to fill the space that had opened up while his attention had drifted.

The vehicles moved more smoothly through the town-centre streets, and he reached the police station with plenty of time to switch on the coffee machine before other members of staff arrived.

No major incidents had been reported from the previous night. He divided up the most important cases for investigation, sifting out the ones where there was no basis for further action. He had a budget meeting at ten o'clock, and would go through the lists of arrears with one of the police lawyers. In addition, his input was required for the criminal-investigation department's consequence analysis regarding the planned amalgamation of the police district with neighbouring police forces, but that could wait until after his meeting with Martin Haugen.

Reclining in his office chair, he sat with his hands clasped behind his head, before leaning forward to pull out the bottom desk drawer. He had taken a copy of the newspaper's photograph from 17 May, and brought it out to examine it.

The photo was black and white. Katharina stood with a group of friends, all dressed to the nines; she was wearing a light summer dress. Her hair was long and he knew it was reddish-blonde. She had blue eyes, but there was a touch of sadness in her expression, an obvious despondency even though there was a smile on her full lips. They looked soft, he thought, as he gazed at them now. Softer than her eyes.

He did not believe she was still alive but wondered what she might have looked like now. As for himself, he had changed a lot. In the picture he was in his late twenties, slim, with dark hair only just visible under his uniform cap. His back was ramrod straight.

As far as Wisting was concerned, the Katharina case had begun on Wednesday 11 October, when her husband had reported her missing. Two detectives had travelled out to Kleiverveien to undertake the initial investigations, Wisting and Eivind Larsen. Wisting had sat in the living room with Martin Haugen while Larsen had gone through the house searching for something to indicate what had become of Katharina. Nothing found in the house or emerging from their conversation had led them closer to an answer.

Wisting stood up, crossed to the window and paused there, aware of a strange but nevertheless familiar grumbling sensation in his body. A restlessness caused by unfinished business.

The suspicion that Martin Haugen had been somehow involved in his wife's disappearance was one of the first things to be checked out. At that time, he was working on road construction in Trøndelag and living in workmen's barracks in Malvik, more than eight hours' drive from his home.

The spouse was always the initial suspect whenever anyone disappeared, but the timeline gave police no grounds for suspicion. Martin Haugen had spoken to Katharina by phone at around ten o'clock on the evening of 9 October. The telephone company confirmed a phone call at 22.06 from a pay phone in the barracks' dining room to the landline belonging to Katharina and Martin Haugen in Kleiverveien, Larvik. The conversation had lasted eight minutes and seventeen seconds. The next morning, at seven o'clock,

Martin Haugen was seated behind the controls of an excavator. There was a nine-hour window, but it would have taken him sixteen hours to make the round trip to Larvik and back.

After his shift he had tried to phone home but received no answer. Several workmates had seen him attempt to phone his wife in the course of that evening and he had given the impression of being worried. He had called friends and acquaintances, but no one had seen her. Late that evening he had asked his nearest neighbour to go to the house to investigate, but there had been no sign that she was at home. The neighbour had done a circuit of the house and peered in through the windows. Apart from spotting what looked like a handwritten note on the kitchen table, he had nothing else to report.

Just before midnight, Martin Haugen had driven home. At 8.47 on 11 October he had phoned the police to report his wife missing.

They knew no more today than they had at the time. They knew a great deal about what had *not* happened, what Katharina had *not* done, and where she had *not* gone, but nothing about why, how or where she had.

3

Wisting left his office at quarter to twelve to drive to Kleiverveien. By now it had almost stopped raining and the sky was brighter.

His relationship with Martin Haugen had changed over the years. The interactions between them had gone from being purely professional to increasingly informal. They were able to share jokes and talk about things far removed from the case. A few years ago Martin Haugen had borrowed an excavator and helped Wisting to get rid of some tree stumps in his garden. Every autumn Wisting bought a few bags of firewood from him, and before Christmas he usually showed up with a Christmas tree from the woods behind his house. They had been on fishing trips to Haugen's summer cabin, and Martin had attended Ingrid's funeral when she died. But it was not a true friendship, and never could be. Their relationship had its roots in tragic circumstances and something indefinable still caused Wisting to keep his distance. They were around the same age, and from time to time it crossed his mind that, in different circumstances, Martin Haugen could well have become one of his few good friends.

Two years after Ingrid's death Wisting had embarked on a new relationship. Although it was over now, it had been tender and loving while it lasted, and he wished it could have continued. Martin Haugen had never entered into a new relationship, even though he had been married before he met Katharina, a short-lived union with a woman eight years older than him. One of the ring binders in the case files was marked with her name: *Inger Lise Ness*. In the weeks following the disappearance it had grown bulky, but yielded no answers.

The windscreen wipers scraped the glass and Wisting turned them off.

The houses flanking the road became more scattered as he approached Kleiver, and the road grew narrower and less well maintained. He passed a market garden and a small farm. On the left-hand side he saw the old car-repair workshop and noticed that some of the wrecked cars outside had been there since the previous year.

He slowed down as he neared the intersection and the exit road where the mailbox was situated. A sign had been erected at the road verge since his last visit. A *No Entry* sign, with an exception made for permanent residents.

As Wisting drove past the sign, he glanced in the mirror at the red house across the road. Steinar Vassvik lived immediately opposite the turn-off, and Wisting spoke his name aloud now. He was the closest they had come to a suspect in the case. He was the nearest neighbour, the last person to have seen Katharina, and he had no alibi. To make matters worse, he had a previous conviction for assault.

The gravel track zigzagged through the trees. After a hundred metres Martin Haugen's house appeared. It had been given a fresh coat of paint since Wisting last visited and some of the forest around the house had been cleared. It now looked brighter and more open.

The rain had formed a puddle in the yard and Wisting parked to avoid stepping into it.

The cat rose from the doormat, arched its body and approached to inspect him.

It was not usually necessary to ring the doorbell. Martin Haugen normally came to the window when he heard a car in the yard.

Looking up at the house, Wisting let the cat curl round his legs while he waited for Martin to appear at the door.

Nothing happened.

Wisting climbed the few steps and rang the doorbell, the cat following at his heels. He heard the sound of the doorbell reverberate inside the house but nothing else.

In the tiny crack between the doorframe and the door he could see that the lock was engaged. He rang the doorbell one more time and bent down to pet the cat's wet fur.

Wisting turned his back on the door. Haugen's car was not parked in the yard, but that did not necessarily mean anything, since he usually kept the car in the garage. However, the door to the garage was locked and there were no windows to afford a view inside.

He crossed to the kitchen window and stood on tiptoe. The room was tidy, with the exception of a writing pad and pen on the table.

"Martin!" he called, hammering on the windowpane.

Something was written on the top sheet of the pad, but from where he stood it was impossible to see what it said.

The pad lay in approximately the same place as the coded message had done twenty-four years earlier. It was most likely Katharina who had written the code back then. Her fingerprints had been found on the paper.

Handwriting experts had also studied the paper, but they could not say for certain that the handwriting was Katharina's. They had made comparisons with handwriting samples from letters and other papers they knew Katharina had written. The numbers on the paper were slightly more slanted than on the reference samples, and the results were inconclusive.

Chemical analyses showed that the ink in a ballpoint pen on the kitchen worktop contained identical ingredients to the ink on the paper. The pen was a promotion for the National Directorate of Public Roads, in all likelihood one that Katharina had brought home from work, and had been manufactured in Germany in a factory producing nineteen million ballpoint pens annually. From a purely theoretical point of view, a pen other than the one lying there could also have been used.

Somewhere in the woods behind him, a solitary magpie screeched. Apart from that, he was surrounded by silence.

He walked round the house, across the damp grass on the lawn and up on to the verandah at the rear, with the cat trailing in his wake.

The garden furniture was still outside, and dead leaves were collected in wet heaps. A spade caked with earth was propped against the wall, and beside it stood a pair of Wellington boots flecked with clods of dried clay.

Wisting approached the window and peered inside. Many of the fixtures and fittings were the same as when Katharina had lived here: pine furniture and a few colourful prints on the walls. The dark leather settee was new, and on the coffee table in front of it, a partially completed construction set divulged Martin Haugen's hobby. It seemed likely to be a lorry once it had the finishing touches. On the bookshelves, previously filled with Katharina's books, a number of finished models were displayed.

The cat mewed and scratched at the verandah door. On the inside, he could see the blanket it usually claimed as its own.

The animal must be old now, Wisting thought. Martin Haugen had told him how, scrawny and with a dull, matted coat, it had slunk out of the woods one summer's evening and sidled on to the verandah where he was sitting. He had offered it his plate of leftovers, and ever since then it had made its home with him. That had been five or six years ago.

Wisting turned to face the woods, denser now than twenty-four years earlier. He could only just make out the small lake down between the spruce-tree trunks.

They had combed the woods twice in their efforts to find Katharina. First with sniffer dogs, and then with volunteers who had walked in rows at arm's length from one another. They had dredged the lake and also dispatched divers. She was nowhere to be found.

Another magpie screech broke the stillness. It flew up from one of the nearest trees, hovering and flapping its wings as it swooped and shrieked.

Wisting pulled his coat closer around his neck and returned to his car. He was taken aback that Martin Haugen was not at home. He had expected him to be here, just as he had been last year and all the years before.

He glanced up at the house before climbing into the car. Maybe Martin Haugen had just nipped out to run some errands, but Wisting doubted it. The cat was rolling on the mat in front of the door, its coat soaked through, as if it had been out all night in the rain.

4

The car bumped over potholes on the gravel track. Wisting came to a halt by the mailbox marked with Martin Haugen's name. It had been pictured in the case documents, revealing that it contained newspapers for 10 and 11 October, as well as an electricity bill. The newspaper dated 9 October was on the chest of drawers in the hallway of the house.

Martin Haugen must have had Katharina's name taken off the mailbox at some point, as it now showed only his name.

Lifting the lid, he found it empty, though that did not necessarily mean anything. It was probably too early in the day for the postman to have called, and Martin lived so far out of the way that very few delivery services would go to the bother of making the trip.

A man with a dog came walking out of the woods on a footpath further along the road. He called the dog at once and attached the lead.

Wisting returned to his car and peered at the *No Entry* sign linked to a chain that could be stretched across the track to block the route. Maybe Martin was bothered by hikers who parked their vehicles on his property. The sign itself must be something he had picked up from work. After Katharina had disappeared he had secured a job in the operations and maintenance department of the roads authority, a position that had changed somewhat over the years. Initially he had been involved in clearing vegetation, snow ploughing and removing roadkill. Gradually the practical aspects had been subcontracted to various private firms and Martin Haugen's task became more supervisory in nature, but he had always had flexible working hours and normally took 10 October off. Perhaps that had not been possible this year.

Wisting considered phoning or sending him a text but worried he might seem pushy. It would be better to call in again after work.

At the time of Katharina's disappearance mobile phones were not common, and it was before the Internet and social media. No electronic traces existed at that time to point in the direction of where she was or what had happened to her.

He glanced at the house on the other side of the road as he drove off and thought he saw Steinar Vassvik at the window. It had been difficult to obtain any kind of worthwhile statement from him. He was the type of person who did not let anyone come close, who usually answered questions mainly in words of one syllable, and who never took the initiative to change the subject in conversation. When Wisting had spoken to him, he often turned away and looked in a different direction. His answers were always evasive, and every conversation left Wisting with the distinct impression that he was withholding something. That there was something he was concealing.

Steinar Vassvik had confirmed Haugen's statement: he said he had been phoned on the afternoon of 10 October and asked to go up to the house to look for Katharina. He had done so. When he was phoned again half an hour later he had told Haugen she was not at home but it looked as if she had left a message for him on the kitchen table.

Wisting picked up his mobile and rang Line. He was still anxious about his granddaughter. Her voice sounded flat when she answered.

"How's Amalie?" he asked.

"She's a bit unsettled today," Line replied. "Whimpering a lot."

"Is she sick?"

"Well, I'm not sure. I'll just have to keep an eye on her."

"Did you manage to get rid of the blue dye?"

"Not all of it."

Wisting cleared his throat to fill the ensuing silence.

"Do you need anything?" he asked. "Do you want me to buy anything from the shop?"

"No, we'll manage," his daughter assured him.

Wisting swerved on the narrow road to avoid an approaching lorry. He apologized again and told her how dreadful he felt about it before saying goodbye.

He returned to the police station at five past one, and in the corridor bumped into Nils Hammer, who acted as Wisting's deputy.

"I've arranged a meeting for us tomorrow," Hammer said.

"What sort of meeting?"

"Somebody's coming from Kripos," Hammer explained, referring to the National Criminal Investigation Service based in Oslo.

Wisting frowned. "Who is it, then?"

"I don't know him," Hammer admitted. "Adrian Stiller?"

Wisting shook his head. The name was unfamiliar to him too. "What does he want?"

"It's to do with an old case. He wants to go down to our archives and take a look. He'll explain it all when he arrives. I arranged a meeting for nine o'clock."

Wisting entered his office and made a note on the calendar. It happened relatively often that Kripos—or kokrim, the national police squad dealing with financial crimes—investigated cases in which witnesses or other leads brought them across borders into their district.

His restlessness had returned, and he headed for the conference room, where the coffee machine was located, and poured a cup. It tasted foul on an empty stomach, but he brought it back to his office, where he pushed it aside as he picked up the phone to call Martin Haugen. It was easier to call from his office rather than standing outside his house, he thought as he let it ring. Now he could simply ask whether it was convenient for him to drop by.

After ten rings he was diverted to voicemail and hung up without leaving a message.

He took out the papers referring to the new police reforms. They claimed that fewer yet larger police districts would allow the police greater capacity and improved competence to discharge their core duties in a better, more effective fashion throughout the country. It meant that the district Wisting worked in would be joined together with Telemark in the west and Buskerud in the east. He saw obvious advantages in such a large combined criminal-investigation department, but he still lacked the willingness to change. Only a few years from retirement age, he would prefer to spend his time solving cases rather than adjusting to a future in which he would play no part.

He made an effort to bring the plans and visions down to a practical level and sketch out a picture of how the changes would impact their everyday workload. From time to time he was interrupted by phone calls, conveying enquiries and requests about urgent matters, which he could either answer or refer to the appropriate person. The section he led was just large enough for him to manage the necessary supervision.

Just before half past three it began to rain again, heavy rain that battered the windowpane. He sat for another half hour before logging out of his computer and leaving his office.

On his way back to Kleiver he hung behind the school bus, the only form of public transport in the vicinity. It made the journey twice in the morning and twice in the afternoon, stopping where the schoolkids lived or where someone waiting at the road verge gave a signal that they wanted to board. On 10 October twenty-four years ago, it had been the same driver both in the morning and the afternoon, and he had been absolutely certain that Katharina Haugen had not been one of his passengers.

The bus in front of him pulled in to the side of the road and stopped. The road was too narrow for him to overtake, so he sat waiting until it discharged a cloud of black exhaust and drove on.

Two boys wearing satchels crossed the road before he could follow.

Katharina Haugen had driven a silver Golf and a Kawasaki Z650 motorbike. She mostly used the motorbike, but both vehicles were parked in the garage when she went missing.

He slowed down and turned off in the direction of Martin Haugen's home. The rainwater had gouged deep ruts in the gravel. He bumped along the track and drove into the yard in front of the house.

No other cars were parked there.

He drove up to the same spot as last time and the cat, slightly more rumpled than a few hours ago, came running towards him when he stepped from his car. Wisting followed him to the door and rang the doorbell, not really expecting Martin Haugen to open the door.

Wisting fished out his phone and called him, but it again went to voicemail.

The cat rubbed against his legs and Wisting stood motionless, feeling a sense of anxiety begin to tie knots in his stomach. He was trained to assume that the worst had happened, but all the same he tried to come up with reasonable explanations for Martin Haugen's absence. A work seminar, overtime, another appointment. For all Wisting knew, he could have met another woman, was now living with her and had gone home to her after finishing work.

He stepped out into the rain again and dived round the corner of the house. A sweet scent of damp earth drifted from the edge of the woods. Where the lawn ended and the tangle of shrubs took over, a footpath led into the forest. It had always been there, and they had searched for Katharina all along that path. Over the years it had become increasingly overgrown, but now it looked as if it had been cleared.

The cat stood gazing at the opening into the forest while Wisting sheltered under the eaves on the verandah. He peered inside, but nothing had altered from when he had been here several hours earlier.

Just as he was about to step down again he spotted something behind one of the curtains, a small wireless video camera with the lens directed straight at the garden behind the house. If anyone sat watching somewhere, Wisting's face would have filled the screen at that very moment.

He bumped against the garden table as he took a step back. These days, they increasingly found that video recordings accompanied reports of burglaries or vandalism. The tiny cameras were of high quality, and technology had made it possible to sit anywhere in the world and watch via the Internet. When Katharina had vanished twenty-four years ago, they had collected CCTV tapes from petrol stations and other places with surveillance installed. But the recordings were grainy and it was difficult to recognize anyone. These videotapes were still stored with the case documents, but he had no idea whether they still had equipment to play them nowadays.

He walked to the next window, a room furnished as a guest room but originally intended as a child's bedroom, as Wisting had learned. Now it was used to store cardboard boxes. A few chairs were upturned on a table and a bundle of clothes was draped over the handlebars of an exercise bike. He saw a computer with a screen, a wireless mouse and a keyboard on a writing desk, and a number of model cars displayed on shelves along the wall.

The room next to this was the bedroom, with only a single quilt on the double bed. It was thrown aside, and the pillow was topsy-turvy. Apart from the fact that one person slept alone in this room, there was nothing more to read from it.

He skirted round the house and discovered another surveillance camera. In the bathroom window, fixed quite high on the wall, the camera was directed at the area in front of the entrance.

The rain increased in intensity, and he thought he heard the sound of thunder in the distance. He tried to recall what the weather forecast had predicted.

The cat darted up the steps again. Wisting strode across to the outhouse on the other side of the yard, not much more than a tool shed with room for a snowblower, a lawnmower and a pile of logs.

Rainwater cascaded from the corrugated-metal roof as he tried the door handle, but it was locked. Peering in through a side window, he caught sight of an axe on a chopping block but found it difficult to peer into the dark corners.

A layer of condensation had formed on the windscreen when he returned to the car and started the engine. Turning the heating up, he drove down the track.

On the other side of the intersection, Steinar Vassvik's garage door was drawn up and he stood beside a hefty motorbike with a screwdriver in his hand, gazing across at him.

Wisting drove across the road and got out of the car, leaving the engine idling as he hurried into the garage, seeking shelter from the rain.

Steinar Vassvik greeted him with a nod. A powerful work lamp on the ceiling threw light on his coarse features. Since they last met he had sustained a cut under his left eye that had turned into a crimson scar.

"I was up at Martin Haugen's," Wisting explained. "He's not at home."

Steinar Vassvik put down the screwdriver and grabbed a rag from the bench.

"Have you seen anything of him?" Wisting asked.

Vassvik shook his head and wiped his hands on the rag. Wisting glanced behind him, towards the sign that forbade entry.

"Have you seen anyone else there?" he added.

"There's rarely anyone hereabouts," Vassvik replied.

"When did you last see Martin Haugen?"

Steinar Vassvik shrugged. "He drives out at half past seven most mornings."

"Did he do that today?"

"Not that I noticed."

"When does he usually come home?"

Steinar Vassvik glanced at the time, and Wisting did the same. It was twenty to five.

"Before four," Vassvik answered.

Wisting nodded. "Okay," he said, turning back to his car. "Thanks anyway."

Steinar Vassvik took a couple of steps after him. "Has something happened?" he asked.

Wisting shook his head. "I'd just expected him to be at home today."

Steinar Vassvik nodded. "I see," he said. "Maybe he's at his cabin."

"Maybe so," Wisting replied.

Hovering for a moment to see whether Steinar Vassvik would add anything further, he thanked him again and dashed through the rain towards his car.

5

He did not ring Line's doorbell but let himself in and instead rapped on the connecting door between the porch and the hallway.

Line popped her head out of the kitchen and waved him in. "You're drenched," she said.

Wisting took off his jacket and draped it over the back of a kitchen chair.

"It's raining," he said, a smile on his lips, without any further explanation. "How's Amalie doing?"

"Fine. She's sleeping." Line stood up and moved to the cooker. "Would you like some soup?" she asked. "Cauliflower?"

"Yes, please."

Line switched on the hotplate. "It's just from a packet," she told him.

Sitting down, Wisting pointed at the computer on the table. "What are you working on?"

"The usual," Line answered. "Family history."

She brought out a loaf, cut two slices and buttered them generously.

"Could you check something for me?" Wisting asked.

"What's that?"

"Whether Martin Haugen is on Facebook."

Line resumed her seat at the kitchen table. "Haven't you been to his house?"

"He wasn't at home," Wisting told her. "I thought there might be something on Facebook about him being away."

Line's fingers raced across the keyboard. "Doesn't look as if he's on Facebook," she said. "Can't you phone him?"

"I've tried."

As steam rose from the pan on the hotplate, Line got to her feet and removed it from the heat. "What do you mean?" she asked, ladling out a bowl of soup for him. "Has he gone missing?"

"He's just not at home," Wisting clarified with a smile.

"Can't you track his phone or something?" Line suggested.

"It's not as simple as that," Wisting told her. "There are formalities to go through. And his family would have to report him missing first."

"Have you spoken to any of his family?"

Wisting took his first spoonful and shook his head. "His mother died a few years ago," he explained. "He has an aunt and a few uncles in Porsgrunn, but I don't think he has much contact with them."

"What about his work?"

"I can speak to them tomorrow," Wisting said. "If he's not back by then."

He lingered at the table after finishing his soup but headed home before Amalie woke.

When he entered his empty house he wondered how long it would take for anyone to initiate an official search for him if he ever went missing. Line was the person closest to him, but she was used to him being away for several days in a row for work. And he wasn't always good at telling her where he was going and when she could expect him back. However, at work they would be puzzled if he wasn't at his desk in the morning without making contact to tell them he was ill.

In the living room he stood gazing at the cardboard box with the case files. Elling Kverme had been the officer in charge of the investigation. Fifteen years older than Wisting, he had been an experienced detective. He was retired now, but Wisting ran into him occasionally, and he always brought up the Katharina case, describing it as the greatest conundrum in his entire police career.

One of the challenges had been the delayed start to the investigation. Katharina had probably been gone for more than twenty-four hours before Martin Haugen had reported her missing. After that, it took some time for them to organize the police work and switch from searching for a missing person to investigating a possible crime. The first twenty-four hours after a crime was committed were crucial—that was when they had the best opportunity to map out the appropriate way forward. After that, details slipped the minds of witnesses and facts began to blur. Now, all he had were ring binders with twenty-four-year-old information.

He took out the file marked *Steinar Vassvik* and settled down to read.

Two days after Katharina disappeared Steinar Vassvik reported to prison to serve his three-year sentence for grievous bodily harm. Late one Saturday night, after a heavy drinking session, he had ended up in an argument in the town and had attacked another man. This was his fourth conviction for drink-related misdemeanours, but this time the crime was more serious. The man he had assaulted had lain in a coma for three weeks and been left with eyesight problems and chronic headaches.

Wisting had spoken to him in prison. He turned to the old witness statement. His aim in questioning Vassvik had been threefold: firstly, to check up on Martin Haugen's account of the phone calls; secondly, to probe Vassvik's knowledge of Katharina and her activities during her last few days; and finally, to chart Vassvik's own movements around the time Katharina Haugen went missing.

Steinar Vassvik described his relationship with Katharina as a normal neighbourly one. They were on speaking terms, and usually exchanged a few pleasantries whenever they met. He spoke more often to Katharina than to Martin, but the reason for this was that Martin was living away from home on a construction site. Also, he and Katharina shared an interest in motorbikes. That was usually what they chatted about.

The last time he had seen Katharina was on Sunday 8 October when she had called in to see him with some books. This was the first time she had been inside his house. They had made an arrangement the day before, when Katharina had been out on her motorbike and stopped at Steinar Vassvik's house on her way home. This was her last bike ride before she intended to store the vehicle away for the season, and they had talked about important maintenance issues prior to winter storage. He gave some advice and offered to help her with this.

She brought the bike to him later that day, after having washed it thoroughly. In the course of their conversation Steinar Vassvik had told her he was going to jail. It was no secret—Katharina knew he had been inside before and that he had been convicted again. Steinar Vassvik had sold his car and was preparing to store his motorbike for the next three years. That was how the arrangement concerning the books had come about. Katharina thought he would need something to read while he was behind bars. The next day, when she arrived to collect her motorbike, she had brought a carrier bag filled with books, and Steinar Vassvik had chosen five of them.

Wisting put down the ring binder and picked up the photographs of the house. On the coffee table in Katharina's home lay the books that Steinar had apparently rejected—*Mengele Zoo*, *The Alchemist* and *The Satanic Verses*.

It was easy to dream up a scenario in which Steinar Vassvik was responsible for Katharina's disappearance. Sporadic contact with his neighbour's wife had developed over a period of time: they had interests in common, and she was friendly and obliging. She paid him attention and was considerate. Steinar Vassvik had little experience with women. He had lived at home with his mother until he was over thirty. When his mother had inherited the house in Kleiver from her sister, he took it over and moved in around the same time as Martin and Katharina Haugen bought the house nearby. His few relationships with women had been chance meetings in pubs. It was easy to imagine that he might have incorrectly interpreted the signals from Katharina Haugen. He was known to have a temper when he drank and this had already landed him in prison on three separate occasions. Something could have gone seriously wrong during his meeting with Katharina.

On days three, four and five of the investigation the police had concentrated their attention on Steinar Vassvik, searching for something specific to support their suspicions, such as mistakes and discrepancies in his statement or in withheld information. The problem was that he was extremely taciturn. Nevertheless, they had discovered a disparity in his account. In connection with the search on the first day, an officer from the uniformed branch had gone from door to door in the scattered settlement and asked whether anyone had seen Katharina. Steinar Vassvik claimed that she had called in at his house with some books around four o'clock on Sunday. When Wisting interrogated him in prison, five days later, he claimed that it had been seven o'clock, a difference of three hours. The difference between daylight and darkness.

If it had not been for Steinar Vassvik already being in prison, they would have considered charging him with perjury for derailing the investigation. This would have given them permission to search his house for traces of Katharina.

As things turned out, they were able to gain access anyway. A routine urine sample provided by Steinar Vassvik when he turned up to serve his prison sentence gave a positive result for THC. He had been smoking hash, and that allowed the police scope for some creativity. A charge was drawn up to give them legal access to search the house for narcotics. What they did find was eleven of Katharina's fingerprints—two on the back of a kitchen chair, three on a chest of drawers in the hallway and two on the inside of the front door. In addition, they found four prints in the garage, of which two were on Steinar Vassvik's motorbike. She had been there, just as Steinar Vassvik had said, but there was nothing to suggest his house was a crime scene.

Wisting flicked through the ring binder. Steinar Vassvik had no alibi for most of the day Katharina Haugen disappeared. He had been working as a driver on one of the council's refuse-collection trucks but had been forced to give up his job because of his imminent prison sentence. He had spent the week prior to the start of his sentence on practical business, and on Tuesday 10 October he had visited several clothing outlets in Nordbyen shopping centre to buy some clothes. The centre was brand new and boasted the latest CCTV equipment. They had clocked Steinar Vassvik in at 14.25 and followed him round the shops until he left the centre at 15.53.

The photos in the ring binder were black and white. Steinar Vassvik wore a pair of jeans, a thick sweater and heavy boots. He had thrown out all these clothes, together with most of the contents of his wardrobe. He told them this was for no other reason than that they were old and worn. Most of the investigators found this odd, but it did not give them reason to hold him on any specific grounds.

Wisting continued to browse through the pages, reading the statements given by colleagues and friends from the motorbike fraternity, but he found it difficult to concentrate. In the end he laid aside the ring binder and keyed in Martin Haugen's number. This time he was diverted immediately to his voicemail without it ringing first. He sat for a few moments, conscious of escalating anxiety. Ever since the first time he had visited Martin Haugen's house that day, he had been aware of something in the air, a fraught feeling he could not quite put into words.

6

Although unsure what to do, he felt he had to take some action. Abruptly, he rose and went out into the hallway, grabbed his jacket and clambered into his car.

The trip to the police station was faster in the evening since there was less traffic and the rain had abated.

From the car park he noticed a light in Christine Thiis's office; otherwise, that entire floor was in darkness. The police prosecutor had either forgotten to switch off her light, or else she was working late.

He let himself in and ascended the stairs to the criminal-investigation department. Christine was on her way from the photocopy room with a sheaf of papers.

"Hello!" she said, beaming with surprise when she caught sight of him. "Has something happened?"

Wisting shook his head. "I just had to check a few things," he said. It still felt premature to say anything about Martin Haugen.

"There's coffee in my office," Christine told him as she walked on.

Wisting let himself into his own office and logged on to his computer. What was it he actually believed? That Martin Haugen had disappeared in the same way his wife had done twenty-four years earlier? Before he allowed himself to jump to any conclusions, he needed to examine all the possibilities.

When his computer was ready he logged in to the intelligence system. It was used to check all the registers and databases which the police had access to, meaning that one search would find out if Martin Haugen had been mentioned anywhere on the system.

He keyed in his date of birth and ID number and obtained a limited number of hits, the most recent two years old and concerning a speeding fine. What he had half hoped to find was an entry by another police district about an accident or that he had been admitted to hospital. This would have explained everything.

He tried another search on only the name. Individuals were not always entered in the operation logs with all their personal details. This search produced a copious number of results, but they all seemed to refer to occasions when the police had been in contact with Martin Haugen about his work in the roads department—loose objects on roads, trees that had blown down and animals that had been knocked over. The last report was three weeks old and referred to a landslide of earth and stones on Highway 40.

Maybe that was why he was not at home, Wisting speculated. The downpour of the past week had caused a number of roads to collapse. Maybe he quite simply had a lot to do at work.

Since the traffic-management switchboard was manned twenty-four hours a day, he lifted the receiver and dialled a direct number which was restricted to police and other public services.

A woman answered and Wisting introduced himself.

"I'm trying to get hold of Martin Haugen," he explained, listening to the immediate sound of tapping on a keyboard.

"I can try to transfer you to his mobile phone," the woman offered.

"I have his mobile number, thanks, but I can't get through," Wisting replied. "Have you any information about where he might be?"

"No," the woman answered without consulting her keyboard. "What's it about?"

"Just a few questions about an old case," Wisting answered.

"Then surely it can wait until the morning?"

Wisting turned a deaf ear to this. "Do you have the number for someone in his department?"

The keyboard sprang to life again and Wisting noted down two names and two phone numbers.

"I can transfer you?" the woman offered.

"Yes, please."

"Then we'll try Henry Dalberg."

After a lengthy silence, when Wisting was beginning to think something had gone wrong, he heard another ringtone. Henry Dalberg answered almost at once. His voice sounded gruff and he spoke with a northern accent. Wisting explained who he was and asked whether Dalberg worked with Martin Haugen.

The man at the other end confirmed this. "Is something wrong?" he demanded.

"I'm just trying to get hold of him," Wisting explained. "Have you spoken to him today?"

"He's ill," Dalberg said.

Wisting drummed his pen on the notepad in front of him—perhaps he was in hospital after all.

"Anything serious?" he asked.

"I don't think so," Dalberg answered. "He sent me a text message yesterday morning to say he wouldn't be at work."

"What did he write?"

"Just that he wasn't feeling well and would be off for a few days. I'm not expecting to see him before Monday."

Wisting sat in silence.

"Is something wrong?" Henry Dalberg asked.

"I just haven't been able to get hold of him," Wisting said again.

He thanked Dalberg for the information and said goodbye before ringing the hospital. The woman who answered had a voice and accent similar to the woman Wisting had spoken to in the roads department. He introduced himself and informed her that it concerned the investigation of a crime.

"Is Martin Haugen one of your patients?" he asked, giving the date of birth as well.

Once again he heard the sound of fingers typing on a keyboard. "No," was the swift reply.

"Are you sure?" Wisting insisted.

"Has he been sent to Accident and Emergency?"

"I don't know," Wisting admitted.

Renewed typing on the keyboard, but the same answer.

"Is there anything else I can help you with?" the woman asked.

Wisting rounded off the conversation and made a note of the exact time. At some point or other he might have to write a report on the investigations he had conducted.

Christine appeared at the door. She had brought him a cup of coffee and set it down on his desk.

"Hammer was talking about a code," she said, "that I might be able to help you unravel."

Wisting drew the cup towards him and gave her a long look. Christine had been working in the police station for three and a half years. Probably not long enough to have heard of the Katharina case.

"What did he say?" Wisting asked her.

"Not much. I asked where you were earlier today, and he explained that you were out on an old case, and there was a code you hadn't managed to decipher. He asked me to have a word with you about it."

Wisting sipped his coffee. "It's an old missing-persons case," he said. "It was years ago. Katharina Haugen." He reached out and pulled open one of the desk drawers. "She left a note on the kitchen table," he continued, taking out a copy. "It's not certain that it has any significance," he said, handing it to her, "but it must have been one of the last things she did before she disappeared."

Christine picked up the piece of paper and studied it.

"It looks like a financial statement," she commented. "With columns for debit and credit."

Wisting agreed. This thought had occurred to him too.

Christine recited some of the numbers aloud. "Three hundred and sixty-two, three hundred and forty-four . . . CFB, CDD."

Wisting smiled, aware of what she was doing. Exchanging the numbers for letters of the alphabet.

"It doesn't mean anything," she said, sighing, after studying the paper for a while.

"I think it meant something to the person who wrote it," Wisting replied.

"You say that as if you're not sure Katharina Haugen was the one who wrote it."

"Her fingerprints are on the sheet of paper, but there are also some unidentified prints."

"What about handwriting experts?"

"They couldn't come to a conclusion."

Christine stood looking at the sheet of paper. "It's a simple code," she decided.

Wisting took a gulp of the coffee. "It's done the rounds of the Interpol system, and no one succeeded in interpreting it," he pointed out.

"By simple I mean that there aren't many characters. There are twelve numbers, and some are repeated. If every number has a meaning, then it can't be a long message."

Wisting smiled. Christine's comments expressed thoughts that had gone through his head a long time ago. "I wondered if it could be some kind of map," he suggested.

"And that the cross marks a spot," Christine added. "Maybe a grave."

Wisting shrugged—this was as good an interpretation as any.

"Do you think she's buried there?" Christine went on, pointing at the cross.

"In that case, she might have marked her own grave."

"If she committed suicide, isn't that a possibility?"

Wisting concurred.

"Have you tried to get the numbers to match map references or coordinates or something of that nature?"

"We've had a number of geographers look at it."

Christine turned the sheet over and studied it from various angles before handing it back. "What do you suppose happened to her?" she asked.

"I think somebody murdered her and hid the body," Wisting answered.

"Her husband?" Christine suggested.

"He has an alibi: he was in Trøndelag. Anyway, he lacks a motive."

Christine sat down on the empty chair. "Are there any other suspects?"

Wisting explained about Steinar Vassvik in the nearby house.

"We also spent a lot of time on Martin Haugen's ex-wife," he added.

"Had he been married before?"

"Inger Lise Ness," Wisting told her. "It didn't last long. She was eight years older than him and quite an unusual character. She could seem both sympathetic and well meaning, but behind the façade she was manipulative and vengeful. He met Katharina while they were still married."

"What made you suspect her?"

"She had found it difficult to let go of her husband and was hostile to Katharina."

"In what way?"

"She visited her, screaming that she was a whore and a witch, scratched her car, ordered goods in her name by mail order, spied on them, phoned at all hours of the day and night and stole things from their mailbox."

"I know the type," Christine said, glancing at the corridor and her own office, where case files were piled high.

"She seemed totally reckless, and at times her behaviour was really intense," Wisting went on. "Then it calmed down and things were completely quiet for the six months or so before Katharina went missing."

"Was she checked out?"

"Never completely, and she was difficult to challenge. Her behaviour was helpful and compassionate after Katharina disappeared, but behind the friendly façade her hostility continued."

"How so?"

"Two months after Katharina's disappearance, Martin Haugen began to receive porn magazines in the post. Someone had taken out subscriptions for various publications in his name. He suspected Inger Lise. We brought her in and searched her house, where we found a few of Katharina's belongings."

Christine raised her eyebrows.

"She had a separate drawer for them. Bills stolen from the mailbox, reminders and debt-collection notices, but also other bits and pieces. Underwear, a necklace, an earring, a book, perfume and a little teddy bear which had *I Love You* written on it. Martin Haugen had bought it for Katharina. It used to sit on a settee in their guest room."

"But . . ." Christine began, without being able to formulate a question.

"It all happened before Katharina disappeared," Wisting explained. "Martin Haugen recalled that around midsummer Katharina had complained that she couldn't find a book she was reading. She insisted she had left it on the bedside table, but now it was gone. Later that summer she was upset because she had lost a necklace and an earring. All the items showed up in Inger Lise's house."

"Had she been inside the house?"

"She admitted it," Wisting said. "But this was several months before Katharina went missing. The verandah door had been left unlocked. She had sneaked in and on impulse taken things that belonged to Katharina."

"Did you check her fingerprints against the code letter?"

Wisting nodded. "We didn't find any of her fingerprints in the house. Even though she denied it, she probably wore gloves and had most likely been in the house more than once."

"Does she have an alibi?"

"At least for most of the day Katharina disappeared. She was working in a children's nursery. On 10 October she was at work from seven o'clock in the morning until half past three in the afternoon. Some of her neighbours also confirmed they had seen her, but then we don't know with any certainty what time Katharina disappeared."

The phone rang in Christine's office. She excused herself and went to answer it.

Wisting turned to his computer and logged out. Before he left, he glanced at the desk calendar. At nine o'clock the following day he had a meeting with Adrian Stiller from Kripos. If he did not succeed in making contact with Martin Haugen by that time, he would get the ball rolling on an official investigation.

7

He wanted to make one last attempt to see Martin so he drove along the narrow road to Kleiver. The wind had picked up and dead leaves came swirling through the rain, sticking on the car windows before being blown away.

The tyres crunched on gravel and stones as he turned off from the asphalt road on to the track leading up to Martin Haugen's house. Everything looked so different in darkness. The surrounding trees seemed taller and the house looked more desolate and inhospitable.

He swung round into the yard and stopped in front of the house. The headlights shone through the kitchen window and lit up the empty room.

Rain beat a tattoo on the car roof. Wisting remained seated behind the wheel, pondering whether to venture outside. If Martin Haugen were at home, he would probably come to the window and look out.

He reversed a short distance, looking for fresh tyre tracks in the gravel in front of the garage, or any other sign that Martin Haugen had come home. The only change was that the cat was nowhere to be seen.

Pulling on the handbrake, he put the car into neutral and left the engine running. As he opened the door, he noticed a movement to the left of the west-facing corner of the house. The car's interior light had switched on, depriving him of his night vision, and he was unsure what he had actually seen. It could have been something plucked up by the wind, but he thought it was someone lying flat on the ground who had stood up, only twenty metres away.

He threw open the door and scrambled from the car. Something was there. "Hey!" he shouted, increasing his pace.

Whoever or whatever he had seen moved like a shadow to slip between the trees.

Wisting followed, sliding on the wet grass, and narrowly avoided falling. Twigs scraped his face and poked his side, but he swept them away and pressed on. After a hundred metres he stopped to listen, but all he could hear was the rain and the wind, and the panting of his own breath.

It was useless to continue so he returned to his car, got in behind the wheel and manoeuvred the vehicle so that the headlights illuminated the area where he had spotted something. He stepped from the car again and examined the ground but all he could see were withered leaves and dead grass. Although it was difficult to say for certain, in one small patch it looked as if the grass had been flattened. If it had been an empty cardboard box or something similar that the wind had shifted, then it must have blown some distance away.

He ran his hand through his wet hair as he headed for the front door, where he rang the doorbell. Without waiting for an answer, he tried the handle, but the door was locked. He skirted round the house to the verandah. The back door was still locked and there was no evidence of any attempted break-in.

For a moment he stood in the glow cast by the exterior light, scanning the fringes of the forest, but all he could see was darkness. He glanced at the tiny camera lens on the inside of the glass before turning on his heel and making for his car.

The vehicle jolted along the gravel track, and he turned right at the crossroads to investigate whether any cars were parked along the road. After only a kilometre he turned and drove back. The footpath that entered the woods behind Martin Haugen's house eventually led to the E18 motorway. If anyone had really wanted to approach the house unseen, they could have had a car waiting there, but he would not manage to drive all the way round in time to check. Instead he drove home, took off his sodden clothes and changed into some dry ones.

The two cardboard boxes filled with documents from the Katharina case still sat at the bottom of his wardrobe. He opened one of them and located the ring binder in which they had filed everything to do with Martin Haugen's ex-wife. He brought it through to the living room and skimmed to the photos of the drawer in Inger Lise's house. It contained several of Katharina's personal possessions, including the book that had disappeared from her bedside table, *The Honeymoon* by Knut Faldbakken.

He could not envisage Inger Lise Ness still sneaking around her ex-husband's house. She must have put Martin Haugen behind her long ago. Other more dramatic events had taken place in her life since then. She had met a new man, for one thing. A relationship that had lasted only a few months before he extricated himself. A short time afterwards, he met another woman. Inger Lise Ness had encountered them at a pavement café, where a quarrel had ensued, and she had been thrown out after physically attacking his new girlfriend. But it had not ended there. When the café closed for the night, she had followed the couple home and loitered outside, watching through the windows as they undressed each other in the living room before moving into the bedroom. Then she set fire to the house.

She had stacked cushions from the garden furniture against the wall, doused them with the lighter fuel she had found beside the barbecue, and set them alight.

A passing taxi driver discovered both her and the blaze and managed to call the fire brigade. Both occupants were rescued, but the house was extensively damaged. Inger Lise Ness was arrested that same night and later found guilty of arson.

Wisting flipped through to the specialist report provided following her psychiatric evaluation. Paranoid and psychopathic personality traits were identified, but the conclusion was that she was criminally liable and fit to plead. She had served a sentence of eighteen months.

Laying aside the documents, he crossed to the kitchen and inserted a pod in the coffee machine. While it buzzed and brewed, he peered through the window and down the street to Line's house, where a car was parked outside. The vehicle had not been there when he had driven into his own driveway earlier. It was a recent model, a BMW or perhaps an Audi—it was not so easy to distinguish different makes of modern cars. All the same, it was not a car he had ever seen on the street before and it was parked in a shadow, which made it impossible to make out whether anyone sat inside.

He picked up his phone and called her. "How's Amalie doing?" he asked.

"She's fine," Line answered.

Wisting made for the switch by the kitchen door and turned off the ceiling light. He picked up his coffee cup and moved back to the window.

No one was sitting in the car, he could see that now, but he could not bring himself to ask Line if she had a visitor.

"It was my pen," he said instead.

"It doesn't matter whose pen she chewed," Line told him. "It was an accident."

"I'm really sorry about it."

"I know that," Line reassured him.

Wisting took a gulp of coffee. "Do you have a visitor?" he eventually asked.

"No, why do you ask?"

"I'm in my kitchen," he explained, "and I noticed a car parked outside your house. I wondered whether I was disturbing you."

"I'm watching a series on TV," Line told him.

He heard her get up from the settee.

"By the way, could you look after Amalie for a few hours on Saturday?"

"Of course I can," he replied, delighted to be asked. "What are you planning?"

"A meeting at work," she answered.

"In Oslo? You're still on leave, aren't you?"

"Yes, but they're keen for me to take part in a project on a free-lance basis."

"That sounds interesting," Wisting said. "Do you know what it's about?"

"That's what we're going to discuss. I have to be there at noon. Would it be okay if I drop by with her at ten o'clock?"

"That's fine," Wisting said, smiling. "Give her a goodnight hug from me."

He said his goodbyes, raised his cup to his mouth, and stood looking down at Line's house. He had admitted his guilt in the business with the ballpoint pen and had concocted a plausible explanation for his query about a visitor. What he had really wondered was whether she had embarked on a new relationship, and whether this was her new man's car parked there.

He lowered his cup, deciding to return to the documents in the living room, but just at that moment he spotted a man striding down the street towards the parked car. It was difficult to say where he had come from. He was wearing a dark jacket with open lapels that flapped with every step he took.

The car lights flashed orange as he remotely unlocked it. He hastily opened the driver's door, and the headlights switched on when the engine fired up. The windscreen wipers pushed water from the glass, but it was still impossible to see the person at the wheel.

He noticed Line at the window of Amalie's bedroom, peeking out at the car.

Wisting tried to read the registration number, but his eyesight was too weak in the darkness and the car disappeared.

8

It was a gloomy morning. Ducking his head into the wind and rain, Wisting tramped through the puddles in front of his house as he made his way to his car.

He drove straight to the police station. En route, he attempted to call Martin Haugen, but it again went to voicemail.

He intended to drive to Haugen's house that morning to have another look round the property in daylight before setting a formal missing-persons inquiry in motion.

When he flopped down behind his desk he remembered he had a meeting with the investigator from Kripos. Hopefully this would not take longer than an hour. Whatever the subject matter, it was something he intended to delegate to Hammer.

The log for the previous night showed there had been little to do for the patrols on duty. The rain had put a damper on everything. A break-in at an office block in Lågen, a minor road accident, and a boat on the verge of sinking at the quay in the inner harbour but pumped out and saved by the crew of the fire tender. In addition, the heavy downpour had caused a landslide that had closed parts of the main road north of the town. No major tasks for the criminal-investigation department to take on, and no reports that could be linked to Martin Haugen's disappearance.

Prior to the morning meeting, he looked up Haugen's name once again in the police records. No information had been logged overnight.

At five to nine Nils Hammer popped his head round Wisting's office door. "He's here," he said.

Wisting glanced up from his paperwork. "Who?" he asked, despite being well aware what Hammer meant.

"Stiller," Hammer clarified. "The guy from Kripos."

"I'll be there in a minute," Wisting answered, looking down again at a circular from the police directorate. He could finish reading it later, but something made him want to give Hammer the impression that he was busy.

"He's from the CCG," Hammer added, before vanishing in the direction of the conference room. Wisting read another couple of paragraphs without taking in their meaning.

CCG was the acronym for the Cold Cases Group, a newly established section for investigating old, unsolved cases in which inquiries had been scaled down or had ceased completely.

He got to his feet and joined the others, to find that coffee cups had already been distributed. Christine Thiis sat at the end of the table with Nils Hammer at her side. Opposite was a slim man in a suit with short dark hair who stood up quickly when he caught sight of Wisting.

Wisting held out his hand and introduced himself.

"Adrian Stiller," the other man said. "Pleased to meet you."

Younger than Wisting had imagined, he was not much older than thirty-five, giving him, at best, twelve or thirteen years of experience as a policeman and a maximum of ten years as a detective, maybe not even that. Young investigators were turning up all the time, with various qualifications in addition to those obtained at police college. Credits and certificates qualified them for posts that had previously required experience of practical police work in order to advance through the ranks.

He produced a business card from his inside pocket. Wisting accepted it and sat down beside Hammer, staring in anticipation at the man opposite him. Smooth-shaven and well groomed, he reminded him of a business lawyer, or an FBI agent in the movies.

"Thanks for seeing me at such short notice," he said.

"How can we help you?" Wisting asked.

Adrian Stiller had a leather portfolio in front of him. He opened it and glanced down at his notes.

"Well, I work in the CCG," he began. "As well as unsolved murder cases, we work with missing-persons cases that could possibly involve homicide."

As Wisting leaned slightly across the table, Adrian Stiller fixed his eyes on him. They were steely grey but rimmed with red, as if he had been reading a lot.

"I'm here because of Martin Haugen," Stiller said. His eyes narrowed and he squinted at Wisting, as if trying to work out his reaction. "I understand you might be the person who knows him best?"

"Are you going to reopen the Katharina case?" Nils Hammer asked.

Adrian Stiller shook his head, though his eyes did not waver from Wisting.

"We're working on another case," he eventually answered. "The Krogh kidnapping."

Wisting cleared his throat. Nadia Krogh had been kidnapped in the late eighties; it was one of the most notorious cases in Norwegian crime history.

"What's the connection?" he asked.

"Fresh evidence indicates that Martin Haugen was involved," Adrian Stiller replied. "We've reopened the inquiry and we're treating it as a homicide with him as the main suspect."

9

Adrian Stiller did not move a muscle as he sat with his eyes on them all. He regarded investigation as a game of strategy that depended on positioning the pieces in the correct places and playing the right cards at the right time—even when dealing with colleagues. He was satisfied with his opening gambit.

He noticed a minuscule but distinct twitch on Wisting's face. His hand reached out for his coffee cup. The experienced investigator's hands were rough. His right thumb and forefinger were slightly discoloured, blue. He still wore a wedding ring. Through his preparation for this meeting, Stiller knew that Wisting's wife had died seven years previously, but the ring had made a depression on his finger and would probably be difficult to remove even if he wanted to.

Now Wisting drew his cup towards him and paused for a second before raising it to his mouth: clearly a diversion to conceal his surprise at the news he had just been given.

The female police prosecutor at the end of the table had no wedding ring. She sat with a blank notepad and pen pedantically aligned in front of her. A furrow had formed on her forehead, and she gazed across at Wisting with a look of concern.

The younger detective who had received him initially was less proficient than his two colleagues at hiding his incredulity. His eyes opened wide and his jaw dropped, revealing a row of teeth stained with coffee and snuff.

"Are you familiar with Martin Haugen's background?" he asked. "You know that his wife went missing?"

Adrian Stiller rose from his chair and moved to the little kitchen counter at the far end of the room, where he helped himself to a glass.

"That happened two years after the Krogh case," he told them as he filled the glass from the tap.

Wisting put down his coffee cup and leaned further across the table. Stiller had seen his face many times before, in newspapers and at press conferences broadcast on TV. It was a memorable face, rugged, with pronounced cheekbones. His greying hair was longer than it should be and fell over his large forehead. If he were married, his wife would have told him he needed a haircut.

"What sort of fresh evidence are we talking about?" Wisting demanded.

Stiller liked that question. It was straight to the point. Nevertheless, he avoided answering. Instead he wanted to run all three of them through the case.

Carrying his glass of water back to the table, he pushed aside the coffee cup the police prosecutor had laid out for him and resumed his seat.

"Nadia Krogh was the daughter of the multimillionaire Joachim Krogh," he said, even though he was aware all three of them knew the man he was referring to. "On the night of 18 September 1987, she disappeared after a teenage party in Porsgrunn and her boyfriend was promptly charged. They had quarrelled before she left the party, and he had gone after her. But three days after she vanished, a letter from the kidnappers turned up."

"They demanded three million kroner for her," Nils Hammer recollected.

Stiller produced a copy of the first letter the kidnappers had sent. He pushed it across the table, wondering which of his three colleagues would pick it up. As Wisting peered obliquely down at it, he almost imperceptibly raised his eyebrows and a tiny furrow appeared on his forehead.

The letter was like something out of a TV thriller, Stiller had thought when he saw it for the first time three weeks earlier. Letters and words cut out of a newspaper and pasted together to form sentences. It seemed childish, but the truth was that many threatening letters handed in to the police were fashioned in this way. The letter writers must all have watched the same films or read the same books. However, no matter how amateurish it appeared, there was something terrifying about it.

The communication method used by the kidnappers had never been revealed in the newspapers. Wisting seemed taken aback at its clumsy style as he gazed down at the letter, his eyes filled with astonishment and curiosity.

"The family received it on Tuesday 22 September," Stiller explained. "Three days after her abduction."

Hammer was the one who drew the letter towards him, a faraway look in his eyes. "She was never found," he reminisced, running his tongue over his upper teeth as he studied the sheet of paper.

The missive comprised twenty-one words, ninety-seven letters. Its message was simple: *We have Nadia. You can get her back. The price is three million kroner. Further instructions to follow.* The brief communication was signed *The Grey Panthers.*

Hammer handed the letter to Wisting.

"What makes you suspect Martin Haugen now?" Wisting asked.

"The letters," Stiller said, producing another document. "Another blackmail letter arrived, two days after the first one. They were both cut from the same edition of *VG*."

He put it down without saying anything else. The detectives who had originally worked on the case had tracked down the edition: it had been published on Thursday 27 August 1987 and it emerged from the report that 332,468 copies had been printed.

Wisting picked up the other letter and sat with a sheet of paper in each hand.

The second letter was devised in the same way, but this one was shorter: *Put the money in a black plastic bag behind the kiosk at Olavsberget.* This time the letter was signed *The Grey Ones.*

"The family was willing to pay. They followed the instructions, but the money was never collected. The pickup point was under surveillance for six days."

"You think Martin Haugen made these?" Wisting asked, putting down the letters. "What have you found that the investigators didn't at that time?"

"Fingerprints," Stiller told him. "The technology has advanced. We've found concealed prints which we didn't have the equipment to identify then. Also, new computer programs and more-powerful data technology have improved our search methods. The prints were crosschecked with the records, just as we do when biological traces are analysed again using new DNA procedures. This produced a match with the Katharina case, with prints found at her home. A manual search showed they belonged to her husband, Martin Haugen."

Silence filled the room. Stiller could almost feel the authority invested in the senior detective. It caused the others to remain quiet to avoid hindering his judgement.

"Do you have grounds for believing these to be genuine?" Wisting asked. "That they were written by whoever actually abducted Nadia?"

Stiller nodded but allowed Wisting to complete his objections: "Kidnapping with a ransom as its objective is a carefully planned action. Little thought seems to have gone into these letters. Usually such letters turn up less than twenty-four hours after the abduction. They normally contain a warning not to involve the police, threats about what will happen if the kidnappers' demands are not met, and also more specific details with regard to handing over the money. Finally, it seems as if they just gave up their plan and didn't do anything more about it—apart from getting rid of Nadia."

As Wisting put down the letters, he added: "These letters appeared after Nadia's boyfriend was arrested. They created enough doubt about what had happened to shift suspicion away from him. I would think this was a diversionary manoeuvre, and the letters were written by someone keen to help the boyfriend."

Stiller produced yet another document and laid it on the table, picture side down.

"The investigators in Telemark also thought along those lines after the first letter arrived, but this was enclosed with letter number two."

He turned the paper and pushed it across the table, though his colleagues had to stretch forward to see it properly.

It was a photocopy of a passport photograph. Stiller had seen the original. Stored among the case documents in his office in Brynsalléen, it was dog-eared and torn. Two children were depicted in the photo.

"Nadia and her little brother," he explained. "She had it in her purse. If the letters were sent by someone who wanted to help her boyfriend, then it must have been someone who was an accomplice or somehow implicated in the kidnapping."

Wisting reclined into his chair, his jaw working as if chewing on something. Stiller watched him struggle to find alternative explanations for the picture.

"What about the envelopes?" Wisting asked. "Did they give you anything?"

Stiller took two more photocopies from his file. "They were quite ingeniously addressed," he said, putting down the pictures produced by the crime-scene examiners.

Each of the white envelopes had an adhesive address label attached.

"It's the address of Krogh's company," Stiller elaborated. "The sender has cut them out of a telephone directory."

He saw how Wisting held the picture of one envelope up to the light and studied it intently.

"As you see, both envelopes were franked locally, as was the practice in those days. The investigators travelled throughout the entire region, checking telephone kiosks. In Vallermyrene, they found a phone book with the page listing the letter *K* torn out. The other directory was never tracked down."

"Prints?" Hammer queried.

"Lots, on the phone directory, the phone box and the envelope. Three of the prints on the phone book produced results matching petty criminals living in the vicinity. They were all eliminated from the inquiry. One fingerprint on the envelope belonged to an employee in the firm who attended to the post."

"Where on the letter was Martin Haugen's fingerprint found?" Wisting quizzed him as he picked up one of the blackmail letters again. "On the actual sheet of paper, or on the newspaper clippings?"

Stiller smiled. He liked this older investigator's ability to home in rapidly on the most essential aspects of the case.

"On the clippings," he answered. "Three instances on the first letter. Letter number two has no prints at all."

He displayed another copy of the same letter, with spots and lilac patches resulting from the chemical process it had undergone. Three points were marked in pencil where fragments of a fingerprint had been found. Above the *dia* in Nadia. At the end of the word *million*, and above the two final letters of *Panthers* in the signature.

"So this means he had read the newspaper but not necessarily constructed the letter?" Hammer said.

Stiller agreed. "If we had a direct link between him and the letters, we'd have brought him in. We've chosen a slightly more tentative approach."

His eyes latched on to Wisting and he tried to make his gaze seem amicable. It was common knowledge even outside the local police station that a friendship had developed over the years between Wisting and Haugen. Their close connection baffled him. Wisting had more than thirty years' experience in the police force. This ought to have taught him to recognize most types of people. If, through his friendship with Martin Haugen, he had failed to realize that he was a man living a lie, then this would be cause for concern. Normally he would have voiced these misgivings, but now he held them back. It would not be a wise introduction to what was likely to become a lengthy investigation with Wisting. If he were to succeed in persuading Wisting to do what he wanted him to, he should really exercise restraint.

"We need your help," he went on instead. "You're already close to him."

Wisting placed both hands on the table in front of him and intertwined his fingers. No reluctance was visible, just a professional understanding emphasized by a brief dip of his head.

"There's only one problem," he said. "Martin Haugen has gone missing."

IO

Adrian Stiller had to admit to himself that he was not prepared for this. He sat still, watching how the two others at the table turned in amazement to face Wisting, and left them to ask him what he meant.

Wisting glanced at the calendar on the wall. "Katharina Haugen disappeared on 10 October, twenty-four years ago," he explained. "I've made a habit of visiting Martin Haugen on the anniversary every year since then. I think he has appreciated that. He's always been expecting me, with coffee and cake ready. But yesterday he wasn't at home."

"He may have forgotten about it," Stiller suggested.

"He hasn't been at work either," Wisting continued. "I've tried to phone him, but he's not responding, and now it seems as if his phone has run out of charge. I visited his house a few times yesterday and tried to call him again this morning. He's gone."

"Have you checked the records?" Hammer asked.

Wisting responded: "There's nothing there. The hospitals don't have him either."

Christine Thiis turned to face Stiller. "Is it possible he's got wind of these fingerprints and knows that the case has been reopened?" she asked. "And he's done a runner?"

Stiller shook his head emphatically. "This has been kept within the CCG," he replied, turning towards Wisting. "Has he been formally reported missing?"

Wisting shook his head as he replied, "No, he has no close family."

Stiller clicked his ballpoint pen twice in succession. His first reaction had been that a disappearance created complications, but then it struck him that, on the other hand, it brought with it a number of possibilities. The fact that Martin Haugen had gone missing gave them the opportunity to legally enter and search his home. Officially, they would be looking for something to indicate what had become of him, but at the same time they could search for evidence that he was behind Nadia Krogh's kidnapping, without officially involving him as a suspect. It was doubtful whether they would find anything after so many years, but it was worth trying.

"You should initiate an official investigation," he said, directing his remark to the police prosecutor, who would have to take the formal decision.

"The Krogh case will have to wait until we know where he is, and why he's disappeared," she said.

Wisting closed his notebook, ready to leave the meeting. "I'll get an inquiry under way," he said, turning to Hammer: "Can you trace his mobile phone?"

"Of course," he answered, noting the number Wisting gave him.

"Christine can help you find a spare office," Wisting continued. "I expect you'll be here for a few days."

"Who's going to head out to his house?" Stiller asked.

Wisting gave him a long, penetrating look. "I expect you'll want to come with me," he replied. "We'll leave in quarter of an hour."

II

Twenty-five minutes passed before Wisting reached his car. Once Martin Haugen had been formally reported missing, he had made a hurried search on Adrian Stiller. He wanted to know who this Kripos investigator was and what he had done in the past. There was something about his manner that grated on Wisting. Stiller seemed preoccupied with being correct, and that gave him an overly stiff demeanour while he was also superficially pleasant and obliging. The overall impression was that there was something he was not giving away.

The records had not yielded much. Adrian Stiller was thirty-six years old and had been born in Oppegård; he now lived in Seilduksgata in Grnerløkka in Oslo. He was unmarried, with no partner registered at his address. His address history showed that he had lived in South Africa from his mid-teens until he moved home at twenty. Maybe he had acquired that golden tan down there.

The intranet gave the usual results. His name was mentioned in lists of participants in a number of different post-qualifying courses. It looked as if he had specialized in interrogation techniques and the management of investigations. The latest entry was connected with the establishment of the CCG. Wisting knew several of the other men in the group and thought it strange that they had chosen to allocate an entirely new, unfamiliar investigator to this case.

Stiller pushed back his seat before fastening his seat belt.

"He lives five minutes from the town centre," Wisting told him as he exited the car park.

Stiller nodded, as if he already knew that. He probably did. Maybe he had also driven past Kleiverveien. This is what Wisting would have done if he were keen to familiarize himself with a suspect.

"Have you been up there?" he asked. "Driven by and taken a look?"

"I've studied the map," Stiller answered.

Wisting glanced across at the policeman. That was not the question he had asked.

As he manoeuvred the car to one side to let a delivery van overtake, he decided not to pursue the topic.

"I thought I'd go through the documents in the Katharina case this afternoon," Stiller told him. "But apparently the office staff couldn't locate them in the archives. Do you know where they're stored?"

Now it was Wisting's turn to avoid the direct question. "There are three cardboard boxes," he replied, without adding any further details. "I'll see that you get them."

The traffic lights ahead in Stavernsveien changed to red, and Wisting stopped while the windscreen wipers cleared rainwater from the glass. A flock of nursery children in Wellington boots and yellow reflective vests crossed the road in front of them.

"What about the Krogh girl?" Wisting asked. "Have you photocopied the case files for me to take a look at?"

"They're digitized," Stiller replied. "You can read them on your computer. I'll make sure you get access."

The lights changed to green and the car eased forward. They drove in silence until they left town.

Stiller straightened up in the passenger seat. "What's he like?" he queried.

"Martin Haugen?"

"Yes."

Wisting gave the question some thought. "He's a quiet man."

"Still waters run deep," Stiller commented.

"Maybe *reserved* is more apt," Wisting went on. "Withdrawn. He still seems affected by what happened. At the same time, he's very good-natured."

"Withdrawn *and* good-natured?"

Wisting agreed, adding, "It's the best description I can come up with."

"Have you never thought about what that might mean?"

Wisting had given this a great deal of thought but left it to Stiller to draw a conclusion.

"He's hiding something," Stiller reckoned. "Something he's trying to smooth over by being friendly."

"He's a complex person," Wisting pointed out, without saying whether he agreed.

A spray of water from an oncoming car splashed the windscreen. At that same moment, Wisting's mobile phone rang. Slowing down until the road ahead was clear, he answered the call.

Nils Hammer's voice filled the car. "Where are you?" he asked.

"I'll be there soon," Wisting responded, turning on to the gravel track leading to Martin Haugen's house.

"I've traced his mobile phone," Hammer told him. "It looks as if it's in his house in Kleiverveien."

Wisting mulled this over. He had tried to ring Martin Haugen on multiple occasions.

"When was it last active?" he asked.

"It's active now," Hammer said. "It'll take some time before I get the data from the past few days, but the phone company has tracked it in real time, and it's either in or near his house at the moment."

"Are you saying it's in use?"

"Not necessarily in use, but it's connected to the network."

As the car bumped along the gravel track it was obvious that the rain had washed away any possible traces of other vehicles.

Wisting thanked him and hung up.

They turned into the empty yard, where Wisting sat for a minute behind the wheel before switching off the engine. The house looked just as deserted as the previous day. Or was there a change? From where he sat it looked as if the light in the extractor fan above the cooker was on. He was not sure but did not think it had been the previous evening.

He opened the car door and stepped out. Adrian Stiller did likewise. Although the rain had eased, it did not seem as if it would stop completely any time soon.

"Was this how things looked here twenty-four hours ago?" he asked, leaning over the open car door.

"More or less," Wisting told him.

He took a couple of paces towards the garage, where there seemed to be fresh tyre tracks in the gravel in front of the door.

At that moment the front door opened and Martin Haugen emerged on to the steps. The cat shot out between his legs.

"Hello," he said, gazing from Wisting to Adrian Stiller.

Wisting greeted him with a nod of relief.

"We were just calling round," Wisting explained. "I wanted to see if you were at home."

"I've been at the cabin for a few days," Martin Haugen explained. "I was trying to do something with the roof down there. It's leaking."

"I came to see you yesterday," Wisting went on. The cat rubbed against his legs.

They both knew this had been in connection with Katharina's anniversary, but neither of them mentioned it.

"I saw you had phoned," Martin said. "Do you want to come in?"

Wisting shook his head. "We were just passing," he said, heading back towards the car. "I can come round again this afternoon, if that suits?"

"Fine," Martin answered. "I'm not going anywhere."

Stiller closed the car door behind him as Wisting waved goodbye and settled into the driver's seat. Martin Haugen stared at them from the door for a moment before moving inside, shutting the cat out in the rain.

12

The garage door opposite slid up as Wisting turned on to the asphalt road.

"Steinar Vassvik," he said, waving to the man who stood there holding an oily rag. "You'll come across his name when you read the case files. He lived there at the time of Katharina's disappearance too."

"Does he have an alibi?"

Wisting shook his head. "The problem is that we don't know exactly when Katharina disappeared, but according to our timeline Vassvik was the last person to see her alive. Two days later he showed up to serve his sentence for a violent crime. He was inside for three years."

Stiller took out a packet of Fisherman's Friends, ripped off a corner and tipped a cough lozenge into his hand before tossing it into his mouth.

"Tell me about the cabin," he asked, replacing the pack in his pocket. Wisting understood where he was heading.

"Haugen's cabin?" he asked all the same.

Stiller nodded.

"It's in Bamble, bordering on Skien, an hour's drive from here," Wisting told him. "An old small farm situated in an isolated spot deep inside the forest. No running water or electricity. His grandfather renovated it during the fifties."

"I assume you searched for Katharina there?"

"Yes, but there was no reason to believe she might be there. She didn't like the place and, anyway, both her car and motorbike were still at home. To reach the cabin you have to drive several kilometres along a closed forest track, beyond a barrier. Then it's fifteen minutes' walk to the cabin. The key for both cabin and barrier were still lying in a drawer in the house."

"But you did go there?"

"I wasn't there at that time, but I've been there on fishing trips with Martin Haugen a couple of times." He felt Stiller's unspoken criticism.

Stiller crunched on the cough lozenge.

Wisting nodded pensively. "It would be a very suitable place for holding someone captive," he said.

The idea that Martin Haugen had been behind the Krogh kidnapping still seemed remote but, if it were true, then the cabin at Langen would have been an ideal spot to keep her hidden. Little more than half an hour from the place where Nadia Krogh was last seen, it was well off the beaten track.

"Do you have a theory?" he asked. "About what happened to Nadia? Why did the kidnappers go quiet?"

"Something went wrong," Stiller answered. "Maybe she tried to run away and was killed in the attempt. Maybe the kidnappers lost their nerve when it came to going through with the transaction and left her sitting somewhere to starve to death."

"Like the Charles Lindbergh case," Wisting commented.

The Lindbergh kidnapping was one of the most notorious of all time. In 1932 a two-year-old boy was taken from his bedroom on the first floor of the family home. The kidnapper left a letter with a demand for fifty thousand dollars. The money was paid, but it did not bring about a resolution. Two months later the boy was found dead. The post-mortem showed that he had died of injuries sustained in a fall, and that the kidnapper had probably dropped him from the top of the ladder used in the abduction.

Stiller shifted in his seat. "Whatever happened, we need you to get to the bottom of it," he said.

Wisting swerved to avoid a man walking his dog in the rain. "What do you mean?" he asked.

"You're the one who knows him best," Stiller replied. "We want you to try to get even closer to him. Gain his confidence and engineer a situation that encourages him to confide in you."

Wisting looked at him but did not say anything. This was what Stiller had been holding back at the meeting. Stiller and the other members of the Kripos team had dreamed up a plan in which he would play an important role.

"We've had good results in other cases," Stiller went on. "Infiltration combined with surveillance, wire-tapping and traditional investigation is an effective mix."

"He knows I'm a policeman," Wisting said. "It's not the same as sending in an agent."

"But he doesn't know you're aware of Nadia Krogh," Stiller protested, smiling for the first time. "That gives you an advantage. You can say the right things in the right places. Plant some thoughts. Press the appropriate buttons. That's something you're good at anyway. Getting people to give themselves away."

Wisting gently shook his head. He had been allocated a role he had no wish to assume. It was different in an interview room. There, you put all the facts on the table, but what Adrian Stiller was suggesting was some kind of undercover assignment that entailed misleading and deceiving someone he knew well. Someone who had almost become his friend.

"It's been cleared with your police chief," Stiller added. "I suggest you start this evening, when you've already arranged to visit him."

Wisting stopped the car outside the main police station entrance. "Were you given your own pass?" he asked.

When Stiller patted his breast pocket, Wisting motioned towards the swing doors.

"I've some business to attend to before I come in," he said. "You can tell the others Martin Haugen is no longer missing."

Stiller hesitated before putting his hand on the handle and opening the door slightly. "What do you think?" he asked.

"We can discuss that when I get back," Wisting responded.

Stiller nodded and stepped out into the rain. Veering away from the pavement, Wisting put his foot down on the accelerator.

13

Stiller was left standing in the rain, watching as the car drove off. He took shelter under the overhang above the main entrance and brought out his phone.

Leif Malm was leader of the newly established CCG section. His number was at the top of Stiller's speed-dial list, and he answered after the first ring.

"How's it going?" he demanded.

"We got off to a bit of a bad start," Stiller replied, explaining that Martin Haugen had just turned up after being AWOL.

"Is Wisting going along with it?" Malm asked.

Stiller chewed his lozenge. "I don't know yet," he answered. "He doesn't seem to like us having planned this behind his back."

"He's a sensible man," Leif Malm said. "He'll understand."

The doors into the police station slid open in front of Stiller and he entered the reception area, where he nodded to the policeman on duty before swiping his pass.

"Anyway, he's too committed," Malm went on. "He can't say no. He'd rather be involved than stand on the sidelines."

Stiller looked around to make sure he was on his own.

"What's the status with the comms surveillance?" he asked softly as he began to ascend the stairs.

"We've been allowed a fortnight," Malm replied. "It's in force from 15.00 hours."

Stiller used his pass to go through the next door. "Great," he said. "I'll phone you this afternoon."

Stiller returned the phone to his pocket, standing deep in thought for a few moments. If the phone-tapping were to give them anything, Martin Haugen would have to have acted with someone else in the kidnapping and feel compelled to make contact with the other accomplice or accomplices once Wisting pressed the right buttons.

Full comms surveillance meant they had an overview not only of who Haugen was in contact with and what he said over the phone but also via email and other electronic means of communication. Moreover, his mobile phone would function as a tracker so that they always knew exactly where he was. At least, as long as it was switched on.

Nils Hammer approached him with a mug of coffee in one hand and a bundle of papers in the other. "Back already?" he asked.

"Martin Haugen hadn't gone missing after all," Stiller said. "He'd just been at his cabin."

The burly policeman broke into a smile. "So what happens now?" he asked.

"I'd like to assemble the investigators who can be allocated to the case and hold another meeting this afternoon," Stiller answered.

"For the moment it's just Wisting and me," Nils Hammer replied.

Stiller considered two operatives very sparse provision. However, it would have to do until they got a break in the case. He was the only one from the CCG and he could not expect more in a case that, strictly speaking, was not under the jurisdiction of this police district.

"Before that I'd like to read up on the Katharina case," he went on. "Have the documents been located?"

Hammer took a slurp of coffee before shaking his head. "Ask

Bjørg Karin if she's found them," he suggested, pointing towards the admin office. "If she can't find them, they're not in the archives."

Stiller approached the triangular-shaped office. He had introduced himself to a cheerful woman at a nearby desk prior to the meeting earlier that day.

"Hammer said I should speak to you," he said. "I want to have a look at the Katharina case files."

Bjørg Karin shook her head and offered him an amiable smile. "I was down there this morning," she explained. "There's no room for a case like that in an ordinary archive box. It's probably somewhere with the other cases that get taken out now and again. I'll ask Wisting to find it for you."

Stiller was unimpressed but returned her smile.

"It's urgent," he said, heading for the office placed at his disposal.

It was the standard government-issue size with pale grey walls and an angular desk made of ash veneer with a computer on it.

As the room was stuffy, he moved to open the window. The green curtains, decorated with an indeterminate pattern, were drawn to one side and afforded an outlook to a drab wall on the opposite side of the street.

He surveyed the room. On a cork wallboard above the desk, the last investigator to use the office had left some red, green and blue drawing pins. Last year's calendar hung on the wall beside a poster with an appeal to "Say No to Drugs."

The office chair had no armrests and was covered in blue fabric, threadbare on the seat. It creaked loudly when he sat down.

The computer was slower than what he was used to. It took ages before he was even asked for his user name and password, and it looked as if it would take even longer for him to gain access to the system.

Everything was progressing more slowly than he had planned and anticipated. Irritated, he glanced at the time and saw it was

13.42. He had expected by this point that he would be familiar with all the salient aspects of the Katharina case and ready to inform the local police officers about his plans for the investigation.

The reopening of the Krogh kidnapping was the first case he had been given personal responsibility for in the CCG. It was crucial that he succeeded.

He had difficulty discerning any clear link between the two old cases, apart from the fact that they both concerned women who had gone missing. The modus operandi was different in each, and they were too dissimilar to be able to highlight any pattern or connection. As things appeared now, Martin Haugen was the only common denominator. This was interesting enough, but it also complicated matters. All the same, it pleased him as it meant the Katharina case might be solved in the cross-current, all due to him.

14

Wisting reversed his car along the driveway, as close to the front door as possible, before letting himself in and heading for the living room. His shoes left wet footprints on the floor.

The cardboard box filled with the Katharina case documents still sat with the lid open. He collected the scattered ring binders and put them back. Some of the papers were still loose, and a report slid out: a picture was attached to it with a paper clip. He picked it up and stood holding both parts in his hand.

The photograph depicted the three notes fixed to the mirror above the chest of drawers in the hallway of Katharina Haugen's home. The camera flash was reflected in the glass, and it was possible to make out the silhouette of the crime-scene technician who had taken the picture.

The report contained answers to what was hidden behind these household memos. The note with the date and time had to do with a hairdresser appointment arranged a fortnight before Katharina disappeared. Katharina had wanted to have her hair cut and coloured. The hairdresser had been able to tell them that the appointment had been cancelled a few days later. The name and phone number belonged to one of the choir members. The sum of money, a hundred and twenty-five kroner, referred to a collection for a gift for the conductor's fiftieth birthday. AML was the treasurer, Anne Marie Larsen.

This was how the police had spent the days and weeks following the disappearance. The newspapers wrote that they had "left no stone unturned." Tiny fragments of Katharina Haugen's life had been pieced together. For every answer, they came up with new questions. Why had Katharina planned to have her hair cut and coloured, and why had she cancelled the appointment?

Wisting returned the photo and report to the ring binder and carried the box out to his car. Then he climbed the stairs to the bedroom to fetch the two boxes still stored in his wardrobe. They were large and heavy, and he had to make two journeys.

When he slammed the boot lid closed he spotted Line and Amalie standing beside his car. Line was wearing a raincoat and Wellington boots and had her hood pulled over her head.

"Are you clearing things out?" she asked, adjusting the rain cover on the pram.

"I thought it was about time," Wisting answered, a smile on his lips.

"I thought maybe you'd come home to make the dough," Line said.

Wisting had no idea what she meant.

"The pizza dough," she explained. "Remember? Thomas is arriving tonight."

"Oh yes—no, I'll do that later," he said, refusing to admit he had forgotten both Thomas and the pizza. "It only needs to rise for an hour," he added, sheltering beneath the overhang above the front door. "Are you going far?" He motioned towards the pram with rainwater overflowing from its cover.

"We've been for a long walk, and now we're going home."

"See you tonight, then," Wisting said, making for the driver's door. "Pizza night!" He started the car, but then rolled down the window on the passenger side and leaned across. "There was one thing I was wondering," he said. "Do you have access to old copies of *VG*?"

Line nodded as she adjusted the hood on her rain jacket. "Why do you ask?" she queried.

Wisting was not sure how to answer. He wanted to look at the newspaper from which Martin Haugen was supposed to have cut out the letters and words but did not want to mention the threatening letter and the Krogh kidnapping.

"I just wanted to have a look at an old newspaper," he replied, nodding in the direction of the boxes in the boot, as if it had to do with them.

"You can search for it yourself," Line told him. "Everything's on the Internet. It's a paid service, but I can send you a link with a user name and password."

"That would be brilliant," he said.

He let the window slide up but waited until Line and the pram had left the courtyard before he let the car crawl forward. He knew he had a packet of white flour in the kitchen cupboard, and maybe even a few packets of dried yeast, but they were probably out of date. He also needed to surreptitiously buy cheese and the ingredients for the pizza toppings.

15

Wisting parked his vehicle at the car wash in the police station garage and found a trolley for the cardboard boxes before moving them up to the admin office.

Bjørg Karin glanced up at him from her desk.

"The Katharina case," he informed her as he set down the boxes on the floor. "Somebody from Kripos will be asking for them."

"He's already been here," Bjørg Karin told him.

"He'll be back," Wisting assured her.

The computer screen told him he had gained access to the electronic version of the Krogh case. The machine toiled as it uploaded all the documents that had been scanned in. They originated from a time when all documents were produced on typewriters. What he was looking for was, however, one of the most recent documents: the one confirming that Martin Haugen's fingerprints were linked to the crime.

He sorted the documents in chronological order, with the most recent at the top. Among the very last ones was an application to the District Court for comms surveillance. He opened the document that contained the ruling and saw it had been approved.

Further down the overview was the fingerprint report from Kripos. It ran to four pages, including photocopies of the two letters from the kidnappers. The report opened by describing how the original ransom letter from 1987 had been swabbed with a magna brush. It was still one of the most popular methods of searching for fingerprints. The report explained how in the nineties they had begun to use ninhydrin to reveal fingerprints on paper and other porous materials. Wisting was aware of how the chemical reacted with amino acids from perspiration to produce a purple stain. When the letters from the kidnappers were reexamined, this was the method that had been used. It resulted in the discovery of three fingerprints on the first letter.

The accompanying photocopies were the same as the ones Stiller had shown him earlier that day. Wisting read the first letter over again. *We have Nadia. You can get her back. The price is three million kroner. Further instructions to follow.* In three separate places, it was marked in pencil where Martin Haugen's fingerprints had been detected. The findings were incontestable.

His mobile phone buzzed with a text message. Line had sent him a user name and password for the *VG* archives. He clicked on the link and was able to log straight in.

He tested it out by searching for Nadia Krogh. The screen filled up with a row of miniature images of newspaper pages on which her name was cited. *VG* had written about her a total of eighty-nine times. The name was so unusual that he assumed all the results were connected to the kidnapping. The images were relatively poor-quality newspaper pages in black and white. The pictures lacked contrast and were indecipherable but the text was evidently searchable. Most of the coverage was from the autumn she had gone missing, but there were also a few more recent results for articles about the unsolved mystery. Or else it appeared as an example in other kidnapping cases.

He made a similar search for Katharina Haugen. That produced four hits in the capital city's newspaper. The Krogh kidnapping had obviously been of more interest to the media, as if there were something more sophisticated about a case that involved a threatening letter and a ransom demand rather than a presumed suicide.

He returned to the image with the fingerprint report. The investigators had almost certainly identified the edition of *VG* the cut-out words had come from and which kiosks had sold them. This was probably mentioned in one of the reports but Wisting wanted to try something else. He had noticed that the first letter from the kidnappers was signed *The Grey Panthers*, while in the second it had said *The Grey Ones*. The three words in *The Grey Panthers* were in bold letters and the phrase had been cut out in its entirety. So they were consecutive words in the newspaper, whereas *The Grey Ones* had been assembled from three separate words.

He went back to the *VG* archive and typed in "The Grey Panthers," in quotation marks. This produced three results. The Grey Panthers were a political organization campaigning for improved rights for retired workers. Two of the results were from December 1987, three months after Nadia Krogh was kidnapped, while the last result was from Thursday 27 August 1987, three weeks before.

Wisting clicked on the article and found *The Grey Panthers* in the caption below a picture of a man described as the Senior General.

Organizing the screen so that he had the newspaper page on one half and the letter from the kidnappers on the other, he looked from one side to the other and discovered three other words that had probably been taken from the same article. *Price, million* and *kroner.*

The fingerprints had been found on the words *Panthers* and *million*, in addition to the three final letters of the word *Nadia.*

The name was composed of two cut-outs, *Na* and *dia*. Wisting made a search on *dia* in the edition he had in front of him now—it produced several hits on *media* and one on *dialysis.*

He clicked his way back to the front page of the newspaper, where the headline stories included an armed raid in Bodø and a daredevil who had jumped from the Pulpit Rock with a parachute.

The article on page two focused on the local government election campaigns that were taking place.

At one time, twenty-six years ago, Martin Haugen had sat leafing through this same newspaper. There was no doubt about that.

He rose from his desk and went to see Bjørg Karin in the admin office. One of the boxes of the Katharina case files had been removed. Wisting opened one of the others and took out a ring binder marked *Finances*.

Katharina and Martin Haugen's personal finances had been examined in connection with the investigation, primarily to see whether Katharina could have set aside money to start a new life elsewhere, but nothing had come of it. Seen in light of the Krogh kidnapping, however, certain circumstances could have given Martin Haugen a financial motive for attempting extortion. A couple of years prior to Katharina's disappearance, they had had problems paying their mortgage. The situation had not improved when Katharina went missing and Martin Haugen had to cope alone with all the expenses, but a drop in the interest rate had ensured that he had managed to keep the house.

Nils Hammer popped his head round the office door as Wisting sat down again. "Stiller wants a meeting with us at three o'clock," he said.

Wisting glanced at his wristwatch. It was already quarter to. "Half past three," he said, opening the ring binder. The top document referred to the payout on an insurance policy in Katharina Haugen's name.

"I think it has to be three on the dot," Hammer said. "The police chief and his colleague from Telemark are coming, as well as the public prosecutor."

Wisting raised his head and sat gazing at Hammer. He understood what Stiller was up to. The presence of the police chief and public prosecutor was a means of applying pressure to Wisting to persuade him to go along with the investigation strategy devised by the CCG.

"Okay," he said, and turned his attention once more to the papers in the binder.

The insurance payment had not arrived until four years after Katharina disappeared and was part of a collective agreement in the Roads Directorate, of which Martin Haugen had not been aware. Wisting had helped him to get the money paid out, a sum of approximately one hundred thousand kroner. It was not settled until the District Court had made a legal declaration that Katharina Haugen could now be presumed dead.

He flicked back to find the papers he was actually looking for, a copy of a letter from the Sparebanken bank dealing with a default on their loan and threatening the enforced sale of the property. They had subsequently come to an agreement which ensured this did not come to pass, but the letter was dated 14 September, five days before Nadia Krogh was abducted.

Almost unconsciously, Wisting drew a timeline on a blank sheet of paper, with the dates of the kidnapping, the bank letter and the two ransom letters. What did not quite fit was that the newspaper was dated 27 August, more than three weeks prior to the abduction. Newspapers were fresh goods. They were not usually things people had lying about for weeks on end. On his visits to Martin Haugen's home he could not recollect ever seeing any stacks of newspapers. And at that time there was no notion of recycling— newspapers were burned on the fire or thrown out with the rest of the rubbish.

Twenty-six days had elapsed from the time Martin Haugen had browsed through this newspaper until the first letter appeared in Nadia Krogh's parents' house. There could be numerous explanations for why this particular newspaper had been used. It could even be that the perpetrator had picked it out of a bin somewhere.

He sat leafing through the newspaper pages on the screen, searching for plausible explanations. It might be that Martin Haugen had read the newspaper at work. He had been working on road construction outside Porsgrunn when Nadia Krogh was kidnapped. This was where he had first met Katharina, but Porsgrunn was also Nadia Krogh's home town.

He had reached the sports pages and an article about Grete Waitz, who was injured and unable to run the marathon at the World Championships in Rome, but had to thumb back through the pages. Something had caught his attention.

He read the caption on the article he had passed, studied the photograph and read the text underneath twice over. It felt as if he were looking at a blinding light that had flashed out of nowhere, but it gave him exactly what he required: the knowledge that Martin Haugen was without a doubt involved in the Krogh kidnapping.

16

Stiller followed the second hand of the clock on the conference room wall. It was forty-three seconds past three.

The public prosecutor and the two police chiefs were present, as were Christine Thiis and Nils Hammer. The only person they were waiting for was William Wisting, though it was too early to read anything into that.

The local police chief poured a cup of coffee for his colleague from Telemark. They both sat in their uniforms with their jackets on. Ivan Sundt had only held his post for a couple of years, whereas the Telemark police chief was more experienced. Agnes Kiil had recently led a major narcotics case in the media. She was present because the Krogh inquiry actually belonged to Telemark district, giving her formal responsibility, whereas Ivan Sundt was the highest authority in the police district where the investigation would take place. Both had applied for the position of head of the new, amalgamated police district, and a breakthrough in the Krogh case would lend them wind in their sails. Most likely, they would go out of their way to achieve a resolution, and even further to take credit for it.

Wisting entered the room at two minutes past the hour, closing the door behind him and greeting the police chiefs and public prosecutor with a nod.

"Apologies," he said, as he placed a bundle of papers on the table before assuming his seat.

Stiller opened the meeting before anyone else had the chance to speak. He was a guest in the police station, but this was his meeting. His case.

"Thanks for coming," he began. "Some of you had shorter notice than others, but I'm pleased to see you're all here."

He cleared his throat and shifted some documents. "As you know, the investigation into the Krogh kidnapping has been reopened. In light of new technical evidence, Martin Haugen has been accorded the status of suspect. In our journey towards a successful arrest, we intend to adopt a somewhat untraditional investigation method."

He paused to allow an opportunity for comment. The Telemark police chief seized the moment: "Personally, I'm really pleased about this development," she began. "An unsolved missing-persons case like this is a terrible burden for the family and the local community. Incidents like these provoke insecurity and speculation, and diminish confidence in the police."

The local police chief voiced his agreement, going on to address Wisting: "We're prioritizing this work from now on."

Stiller continued, giving a brief summary of the recent fingerprint report.

"However, the case does not depend on technical evidence alone," he added. "We're going to have to prompt fresh evidence, including circumstantial."

"How can we do that?" Ivan Sundt asked.

Stiller avoided meeting Wisting's eye. "Primarily through an infiltration initiative," he answered. "It's well known that Martin Haugen and William Wisting are already close friends. We intend to exploit that."

"How?" Sundt queried.

"Haugen has nursed his secret for a long time," Stiller told him. "We'll try to persuade him to unload it. This is going to be a case that is brought home through talking," he said, now fixing his eyes on Wisting. It was impossible to read anything in his facial expression.

"Do you have a detailed plan for this?" the local police chief pressed him.

Nodding, Stiller took on a meditative air to give the impression that the plan was more fully developed than was actually the case.

"Next week the reopening of the Krogh case by the CCG will be publicized. We intend to publish the ransom letters and expect a great deal of media attention. This will be our way of levering the case open. We plan to ensure that Wisting is with Haugen when the news breaks, so that we pick up his immediate reactions and make sure he is pushed in our direction."

The public prosecutor sat up in his seat. "Are you ready for this, William?"

The answer came faster and clearer than Stiller had anticipated: "Yes."

"You have no personal or ethical problems with it?"

The experienced investigator shook his head. Stiller was about to progress the meeting further but was forestalled.

"I crossed the ethical boundaries long ago," Wisting said. The room fell silent.

"When I resumed contact with Martin Haugen after the investigation of the Katharina case was suspended, it was really because I didn't believe him," he went on. "I was left with a distinct impression that he was hiding something. I thought, and still think, he knows what happened to Katharina, and I initiated conversations in an attempt to prise it out of him."

The silence continued.

"What made you think that?" Christine asked after a pause.

Wisting gave this some thought. The Katharina case felt like a piece of music with false notes, but it was difficult to put that into words for other people.

"It's really a matter of slight discrepancies," he replied. "Tiny details in his statement that sometimes change when we're chatting. Call it intuition or a gut feeling. The entire time, I've felt something doesn't tally, and I'm keen to get to the bottom of that."

Nils Hammer, a man who would not fare well at a poker table, had turned to face his colleague. "So you embarked on a fake friendship?" he summarized. "Based on a gut feeling?"

"That's how things turned out," Wisting agreed.

"But he was at your wife's funeral," Hammer reminded him.

"A lot of people were there," Wisting said.

"What's come of it?" Christine asked him.

"Nothing, apart from my suspicions being reinforced," Wisting answered.

"Fine," the police chief from Telemark broke in. "When are you going to start the ball rolling in *this* investigation, then?"

"We already have comms surveillance up and running," Stiller interjected. "Wisting is paying Haugen a visit later this afternoon, so we'll let it roll from there."

The meeting continued with the clarification of certain formalities, until the public prosecutor and two police chiefs departed.

Stiller made eye contact with Wisting. "Thanks," he said. "We couldn't have got this off the ground without you on board."

Wisting bowed his head slightly.

"You seemed doubtful this morning," Stiller added. "What made you decide to go for it?"

"*VG,*" Wisting replied.

"*VG?*" Stiller repeated in astonishment.

Wisting turned over the bundle of papers in front of him. Stiller recognized the front page of the edition used by the kidnappers to cut out words and letters.

"Martin Haugen isn't a fan of newspapers," Wisting said, pushing the transcripts across to him. "I know him. He doesn't subscribe to the local paper and I've never seen him buy any of the tabloids."

"I see," Stiller said, lifting the first sheet.

Wisting pointed to the stack of papers. "Page seventeen."

Stiller leafed through the pages. The heading on the article read *Improved Surface*. It described a new type of asphalt to be laid on the E18 motorway then being built through Telemark. This asphalt would reduce noise and produce less airborne dust.

"Second from the left," Wisting told him.

Stiller peered at the photograph of five road workers in front of a bulldozer, but it was only when he found the name in the caption underneath that he realized what he was looking at. "Martin Haugen!" he exclaimed.

Hammer and Christine sprang to their feet and came round to look.

"I thought it was strange that the ransom letter was crafted using words from a newspaper nearly four weeks old, especially when Martin Haugen neither buys nor reads newspapers, but he would definitely have bought the newspaper on the day his picture appeared in it. And then it would be natural for him not to throw it out right away but to leave it lying around."

Stiller leaned back in his chair. He could not quite fathom how the connection between Martin Haugen and the newspaper was something they had overlooked, but at the time the newspaper had been identified no suspicion had hung over Haugen. He was only a random name on page seventeen. Now he was the person everything centred upon.

Wisting stood up. "Let's get going, then," he said. "I'm off to visit Martin Haugen."

17

Wisting had forgotten where he had parked his car. He went to the outdoor car park first, before eventually finding his car in the garage extension and driving out into the rain again, this time in the direction of Kleiverveien.

He had met a multitude of liars and con artists throughout his career. People who did not tell the truth but instead served up whatever stories suited them. He had believed some and seen through others.

Experience had made it easier for him to recognize a liar. When he emerged from an interview room aware that the man inside was lying, it was usually based on gut feeling or intuition. Wisting had come to the conclusion that this actually hinged on picking up tiny discrepancies in emotional reactions. In the case of Martin Haugen, for example, a smile might come a couple of seconds too late, last a bit too long and his lips be too tight. When people told the truth, their body language, facial expressions and tone of voice were coordinated and matched what they were talking about. With Martin Haugen there was often a contradiction between what he said and the way he said it. And then of course there was everything he did not say. At an interview seminar Wisting had taken part in the lecturer had said that liars had a tendency to avoid words such as *but*, *or*, *except*, and *while*, because they had difficulty with complex thought processes. They also preferred to communicate using fewer personal pronouns. In an unconscious attempt to distance themselves from their fabricated stories, they avoided words such as *I*, *me*, and *my*. All of this applied to Martin Haugen.

He turned off the main road, drove up the bumpy gravel track and parked in the yard. Thick smoke rose from the chimney on the roof, but it was beaten back by the dampness and rain, drifting off like fog towards the edge of the forest.

Wisting took his time getting out of the car and walking up to the front door. Martin Haugen opened it before he rang the door-bell, the black cat between his legs.

"Dreadful weather," he said as he ushered Wisting inside.

Wisting hung up his jacket and followed him into the kitchen. Martin had been eating at the table. A potato and a slice of meat were left on his plate. He cleared it away and put a flask of coffee on the table.

"Sorry I wasn't at home yesterday," he said, setting out two cups. "It's so many years ago now, and the days just run into one another."

Wisting stood at the kitchen window, thinking of how he had forgotten his mother's birthday the previous year. He usually accompanied his father to her grave on that day, but it had slipped his mind completely. It was easy to forget, but he was sure there was something else behind Martin Haugen's disappearing act.

He let it pass. "It's played havoc with your track," he commented, looking out. "The rain," he added.

Haugen agreed. "I was wondering about laying asphalt," he said, producing a Swiss roll from the cupboard.

"Well, you're in the trade, after all," Wisting replied with a chuckle. He considered asking a question about different types of asphalt, to bring the conversation round to the newspaper article from 1987, but quickly dismissed it. "I noticed you have your own sign," he said instead.

"Sign?" Martin asked, unwrapping the cake.

"*No Entry*," Wisting said, pointing in the direction of the main road.

Haugen crossed to the cupboard again and took out two plates. "Perks of the job," he said with a grin. "It was lying around at work."

"Have you had problems with strangers turning up in cars?"

Haugen shook his head. "Not really," he answered, as he cut the cake into slices. "There have been a few foreign cars turning on my drive. Lithuanians and suchlike."

Wisting's thoughts turned to the surveillance cameras installed in the windows and wondered whether he should mention them. If Haugen had watched the recordings, he would know that Wisting had spotted them.

Martin beat him to it. "I installed some cameras," he said.

"I saw that," Wisting interjected quickly. "I walked round the house looking for you yesterday."

He used the subject to switch the conversation to Katharina. "Have you seen anything more of Inger Lise?" he asked.

Haugen poured coffee into the cups. "No," he replied. "It's nothing to do with her. As a matter of fact, I saw her this summer, down by the harbour. She was with a new man then."

Wisting dropped the subject. "How were things at your cabin?" he enquired instead.

Helping himself to a slice of cake, Haugen seemed not to understand the question.

"You said something about the roof leaking?" Wisting added.

"Oh yes," Martin answered, nodding and chewing the cake, seemingly playing for time. "It wasn't as bad as I'd thought, but I wanted to go down and take a look at it."

"Are you going down again?" Wisting asked.

"I'll probably have to," Martin replied.

"I could come with you?" Wisting suggested. "Then we can lay some nets, like we did last time."

Haugen took another bite of cake. A weekend at the cabin in Bamble would give Wisting the opportunity to draw confidences from him.

"I could really do with a few days away from it all at the moment," Wisting went on before Martin had a chance to brush off the suggestion. "It's nothing but stress at work these days."

As Haugen continued to chew, Wisting lifted a slice of cake on to his own plate. "Do you have any plans for next weekend?" he asked.

The mobile phone pinged with a message alert. Martin got to his feet, headed for the kitchen worktop where his phone lay and read the message. He stuffed the phone into his pocket without sending an answer.

"Next weekend?" Wisting repeated as he sat down again. Haugen's thoughts were obviously somewhere else entirely. "A trip to the cabin," he added, by way of explanation. "At the weekend."

"Yes," Martin replied. "We'll do it. We'll take a trip."

Wisting tasted the cake, noticing that Haugen seemed even less focused than usual. "There's no news," Wisting volunteered.

Martin understood what he meant. No new leads in Katharina's case.

"Did you check out that report from Sørlandet?" he asked.

Wisting nodded. It had been on the news that summer. A corpse had washed up on one of the little islands outside Portør. It was the body of a woman who had been in the water for a long time.

"I phoned them," he answered. "But they already suspected who it might be, and their suspicions proved correct. An elderly woman who disappeared around Easter."

"How do you think she'd look now?" Martin's questioning continued. "Do you think there'd be anything left of her?"

In the first few years, they had talked about Katharina as if she might still be alive but gradually the conversations about her came to assume she was dead.

"It absolutely depends on where she is," Wisting told him. "I don't think we're going to find her in the sea."

"What if she's buried somewhere?" Martin asked.

Wisting had put down his slice of cake. This was the first time Haugen had broached such things.

Clearing his throat, he felt a stab of distaste about discussing this.

"It depends on the soil conditions," he answered. "If she were buried in a graveyard, only the main bones and teeth would remain. If she's lying in a dense environment, such as clay or a peat bog, more would probably be preserved." He paused for a moment before continuing. "But if it is the case that someone has buried her, she would most likely be wrapped up, in tarpaulin or plastic. Then the clothes could also have survived."

"Have you found bodies like that?"

"On occasion."

Martin's mobile phone pinged again, but this time he ignored it. "It's the not knowing that's worst," he said. "Not knowing what happened."

Wisting made no comment. Not knowing was a recurring theme in his encounters with Martin. Eventually it had begun to sound rehearsed, and he knew how Martin wanted the conversation to go.

"No matter what has happened, I'd rather know about it," he continued. "After all, you hope in the fullness of time that some-thing will be found to provide a clue or an explanation about what took place. I've never given up that hope, but I realize it's my lot in life to carry this burden."

They changed the subject and returned to chatting about the interminable rain. Martin wanted to know how Amalie was getting on, and Wisting told him about the ink episode.

After a while Wisting stood up and thanked him for his hospitality. "I'll need to buy myself a new rod," he said, to remind Martin about their fishing trip.

Martin accompanied him to the door. "I'll bring along some steaks," Martin said. "In case the fish don't bite."

Wisting turned and shook Martin Haugen by the hand and dashed through the rain to his car. Through the rain-spattered windscreen he saw Martin take his mobile from his pocket before closing the front door.

18

Wisting swiped his pass and keyed in the four-digit code to gain entry to the CS room. Very few admission cards were authorized for the small room on the top floor of the police station. Comms surveillance was one of the police's covert investigation methods. Only a handful of staff knew what type of equipment was installed in the control room, and even fewer were trained in its use.

Hammer and Stiller turned to face him.

"He received a text message while I was there," Wisting said, glancing at the computer screen monitoring current telephone traffic.

"From a number registered to someone called Henry Dalberg," Hammer told him as he turned towards the screen. *"How are you feeling? Will we see you on Monday?"* he read out.

"A work colleague," Wisting explained. "I called and spoke to him yesterday when I couldn't get hold of Martin. He said he'd phoned in sick."

"He told us he'd been out to his cabin," Stiller reminded him.

Wisting agreed. Strictly speaking, this was the first time he had caught Martin Haugen downright lying, but that did not necessarily mean anything. He would not be the first person to tell his employer he was ill in order to take some time off.

"Another message came in, a bit later," Wisting went on.

"From the same number," Hammer said, placing his index finger on the screen: *"Should have taken a look at the revised contract with*

Bryntesen about ditch clearing. He obviously didn't respond until after you left: *I'll be back on Monday. We'll do it then.*"

"What did you talk about?" Stiller asked.

"The weather," Wisting answered, pausing slightly before adding: "We arranged to take a trip to the cabin next weekend."

He could see that Stiller was pleased. "We're working on getting a slot for the case on *Crime Scene Norway* on TV2 on Thursday, and a follow-up in the newspapers on Friday," he said. "A trip to the cabin sounds ideal."

One of the other computer screens lit up.

"He's on the Internet," Hammer explained.

A window with rolling text appeared, showing which Web pages Haugen was accessing. Another screen displayed the relevant page: the weather forecast from the Meteorological Institute.

"He's looking at the weather report on the Yr site," Stiller commented.

In the window containing rolling text, a new line appeared. The screen beside it showed the weather forecast for Malvik in South Trøndelag.

"Malvik?" Hammer said, sounding baffled. "Why on earth is he checking the weather up in Malvik? That's more than eight hours' drive from here."

"He used to live up there," Wisting told him. "At the time Katharina disappeared he was working on the construction of a tunnel and living in the workers' barracks."

"Does he still have contact with people up there?"

Wisting bit his lower lip, puzzled. "I don't think so."

"It's raining up there too," Hammer remarked ironically.

The Google home page popped up on the screen.

"We can't see what he's searching for," Hammer told his colleagues. "Only what pages he clicks on."

The text rolled up further in the little window. On the big screen the front page of the *Trønder-Avisa* newspaper showed up. Eventually Haugen clicked on a story about parts of the E6 motorway south of Stavsjøfjellet having collapsed.

"He was involved in building that road," Wisting said.

The other two nodded, and all three stood in silence for a while as the onscreen image changed: Martin Haugen was visiting the *Adresseavisen* newspaper website to read about the collapse. The road had been narrowed and traffic forced to drive at reduced speed through the affected area. It was unclear when the road would reopen for normal use.

"Can we look at the history?" Wisting asked. "See what pages he was looking at yesterday, for example?"

Hammer shook his head. "For that we need to examine his computer," he said. "What we're doing now is standing outside sniffing up the Web addresses downloaded via his broadband connection. If we want to find out what's on his computer, we'd have to hack into it. We don't have the equipment to do that remotely."

"Okay," Stiller said, grabbing his coat from the back of the chair. "We're up and running." He pointed to the screens. "It's unlikely anything exciting will happen until we start to apply some pressure. I suggest we break for the weekend. I'm returning to Oslo, but I'll be back here on Monday."

Hammer agreed and began to log out. It dawned on Wisting that he had to buy the pizza ingredients. He excused himself and dashed out of the room ahead of the other two.

19

The carrier bag split open when Wisting lifted it from the car and most of the contents spilled out on to his drive. The bag of flour burst, and the rain made the fine powder damp and sticky.

He swore under his breath as he began to pick up the groceries. He had hoped to arrive home before Thomas showed up, but his son's car was already parked in the street. Thomas had not lived at home for twelve years, but he still had a house key and was sure to have let himself in.

Wisting gathered the shopping into his arms and stumbled to the front door. Struggling to open it, he discovered that it was locked. With a groan, he set down the various items on the steps and dug out his key. Before he stepped inside he looked over his shoulder and it crossed his mind that Thomas must have gone to see Line and Amalie.

After he managed to unlock the door he dumped the shopping on the kitchen worktop, and it then struck him that he had forgotten to buy something at the supermarket. Yeast.

He crossed to the cupboard to check the packets of dried yeast. There were three sachets left. He had to use his glasses to read the date stamp and, as he had thought, they had expired almost four months earlier. He decided he might get away with using two sachets instead of the one the recipe called for.

He took out the baking bowl, threw the dough ingredients

together and left it to rise before making a start on frying the minced-beef topping.

Thomas arrived with Line and Amalie while he was cooking. He dried his hands on his apron and gave all three a hug. Thomas had grown too old for hugs while at junior high school but a few years ago he had been the one to greet Wisting with a warm embrace again. That had been after his first tour of duty in Afghanistan. He had undertaken seven tours altogether, handling medical helicopter evacuations. Despite not fighting on the ground, he had witnessed more than most the impact of war on its victims.

"I brought you a present," Thomas said, tossing a parcel across to him.

It was a bundle of cloth inside a plastic bag. Wisting unrolled it and saw it was one of the Norwegian Army's khaki-coloured T-shirts. *Captain Wisting* was embroidered in black thread on the left side of the chest.

Captain was Thomas's military rank. A squadron leader, his responsibilities included air support for the police and the military's own Special Forces. It made Wisting feel very proud.

He thanked his son as he held the T-shirt up in front of himself to see whether it would fit.

"I'm not too sure this will be such a success," he said, lifting the tea towel off the bowl where the pizza dough was rising.

"Why not?" Line asked. Approaching him, she peered down into the bowl with Amalie on her hip. The dough had risen slightly, but far from sufficiently.

"It's been set aside for almost an hour," Wisting told her. "But I used yeast that was out of date."

"It'll probably be okay," Thomas said. "I like a thin base."

Wisting shrugged as he divided the dough in two. Line carried

Amalie into the living room, leaving Thomas in the kitchen while Wisting laid the dough on some greaseproof paper.

"There's beer in the fridge," he said as he began to roll out the dough.

Thomas grabbed a bottle for each of them. "Have you solved the code yet?" he asked.

"The Katharina code?" Wisting said, smiling, and shook his head.

A few years ago he had allowed Thomas to try to unravel the code. They had been talking about navigation and how people had found their way before the use of GPS. Thomas had shared Wisting's view that the numbers were reference points on a map, but they were not something he recognized from cartography or navigation.

Line popped her head round the kitchen door. "What are you two talking about?" she wanted to know.

"Nothing of any interest to you," Wisting joked.

"The Katharina case," Thomas told her.

"He's finally taken the case documents back to the police station," Line said, disappearing into the living room again.

"Maybe it was about time," Thomas suggested.

"Maybe so," Wisting replied with a smile, as he poured the sauce on to the pizza bases.

"Why does that case mean so much to you?" Thomas asked him.

All of a sudden, Wisting felt a sense of guilt. The world was so much vaster than his police district. Thomas had engaged in military service in a part of the world which was more brutal and ruthless on a scale far greater than he could possibly imagine. Despite countless individuals meeting their doom, very few in the Western world showed as much as a scintilla of concern.

"Is it wrong of me, do you think?" he asked, aware of sounding defensive. "That I spend so much time on a single case, a single person?"

Thomas shook his head. "I was just curious about why," he said.

Wisting wondered whether he should explain that the case had become a kind of obsession for him, one he was unable to let go.

"I just don't like leaving a job unfinished," he answered simply, sprinkling grated cheese over the pizzas.

Thomas nodded as if he recognized the feeling.

Line returned to the kitchen again, and the conversation moved on. "Have you remembered you're looking after Amalie tomorrow?" she asked.

"Of course," Wisting replied. "I'm old, but I'm not senile."

The pizzas appeared on the table half an hour later. The bases were dry and hard, but neither Thomas nor Line made any complaint.

"How are things?" Line asked her brother.

She was really asking whether he had a girlfriend. He had never had a long-term relationship. The army was to blame for that—he had served in the military in numerous locations before being stationed at the Rygge airbase.

The rolling tours of duty in Afghanistan had lasted for more than four years and taken up much of his twenties.

Thomas deflected her by asking her the same question.

Line had put one lengthy relationship behind her, with a Danish man of her own age called Tommy Kvanter, but he was not Amalie's father. He was an American who worked for the FBI and had only been in Norway for a few weeks, working on a case, when he had met Line.

Line, too, wriggled out of the question. "How long are you staying?" she asked instead.

"Until Tuesday," was her brother's response. He was in the habit of meeting up with old schoolfriends when he came home.

After he'd eaten Wisting lifted Amalie on to his lap. He was sitting with the three people who meant the most to him in his life but nevertheless could not quite manage to concentrate on the conversation around the table. His thoughts kept being diverted. He was dwelling on death and on the Katharina code. A cross was a symbol of death. If Katharina had been the one who had left behind the coded message on the kitchen table, it did not seem to convey any meaning. Unless it was about Nadia Krogh, and the code revealed where she was.

20

A new entry system had been installed to access the *VG* building, and Line had to seek help from the security guard to negotiate the locked gates before being told to upgrade her pass.

Once past the barriers, she lined up behind a group of unfamiliar people waiting for the lift. They stood aside to let people leave before crowding into the confined space. Line, with plenty of time to spare, waited for the next one. However, it was just as packed and stopped twice before she reached the fifth floor.

She cast her mind back to the occasion when she had entered the editorial offices for the very first time. Her hands had been clammy and her head aching after a sleepless night. The clocks on the wall showing the time in New York, Tokyo and other major cities in the world were one of the things she remembered most. Her only experience as a journalist had been a temporary post at her local newspaper. She felt like an inexperienced trainee and thought the job would be far too much for her. But the simple fact of entering the huge editorial office had done something to her and she quickly adapted to the demands of the environment. In *VG*, the prevailing culture was that only the best was good enough, and from the very first moment the bosses had told her how they wanted her to work. There was not so much talk of knowledge and experience but more about skills and abilities. This included far more than being able to master the technology and create headlines. Skills and abilities were also a matter of something else:

focus, strategy and attitude. It had not taken her long to establish her place and she filled her role with more aplomb than could ever have been expected of her.

Hoisting her bag further on to her shoulder, she headed for the coffee machine and searched for a cup. One of the sports journalists approached, though Line could not remember his name.

"Have we run out of cups?" she asked.

The sports journalist gave her a sympathetic smile. "The plastic cups have been done away with," he said, pointing at the cupboard beneath the worktop. "You'll have to borrow one of those mugs."

"Cutbacks?" Line asked as she took out a porcelain mug.

"Respect for the environment," her colleague explained, putting a Thermos mug to the machine.

Line waited for her turn and selected coffee with milk. The machine rumbled, belching out steam while slowly filling her mug. She carried it into the open-plan office, where the rows of desks were sparsely populated, since it was Saturday. However, she spotted a number of familiar faces, and she smiled and said hello. Her usual seat was empty, but a box of snuff and half-empty cola can beside a stack of scrap paper told her it was in use.

Harald Skoglund rose from his place by the window, came across to her and gave her a hug. They had worked together on several assignments.

"Are you back?" he asked her.

"Not entirely," Line answered. "They want me to do some feature articles, on a freelance basis." She glanced at the glass walls of the office belonging to the head of the news section. "Isn't Sandersen here?" she asked.

"He's in a meeting," Skoglund told her, pointing in the direction of the staircase leading to the floor above.

"What about Frost?"

"He is too."

Line suddenly wondered whether she had got the time wrong. These were the two people she had arranged to meet.

Still carrying her mug, she trudged upstairs. The conference rooms also boasted glass walls. From the top of the stairs she saw Frost and Sandersen ensconced inside the nearest one, sitting with a man Line did not know. He was wearing a dark suit and looked like a lawyer.

She busied herself with her mobile phone, anticipating that they would catch sight of her. Behind her, Daniel Leanger, one of the youngest journalists in the crime section, jogged up the stairs.

"Hi!" he said, giving her a hug. "So you're early too?"

He spotted her confusion. "Looks like we're going to be working together," Daniel added.

Line peered into the conference room. None of the three men sitting inside had noticed them.

"Do you know what this is about?" she asked.

"I've been working on the project for a couple of weeks, but I'm not allowed to say anything," Daniel replied, and was prevented from providing any further explanation. Sandersen had noticed them and appeared at the door.

"Come in!" he said.

Line was given a fresh round of hugs. She then walked round the table to offer a greeting to the man in the dark suit.

"Adrian Stiller," he introduced himself, taking her hand. "Kripos."

Line's curiosity was piqued. She had met many police officers, including Kripos investigators, but never in the newspaper offices, and certainly never in a meeting with the editorial chiefs. Her eyes flitted from him to Frost and Sandersen on the opposite side of the table.

She put down her bag and mug and took a seat.

"Stiller is the reason we're all here," Sandersen said by way of introduction. "He works in the newly established Cold Cases Group at Kripos. They have just reopened a case they're keen to investigate in cooperation with us."

Line took out her notepad.

"The Krogh kidnapping," Frost said, sliding the front page of an old newspaper across the table.

Boyfriend Released was the headline above a picture of a girl in her late teens with a full backcombed hairstyle. The subheading beneath the photograph read *Ransom Money Demanded for Nadia.*

21

Stiller sized up Wisting's daughter. The sight of the old newspaper ignited a spark of curiosity in her big blue eyes. Her hair was still slightly damp from being out in the rain. Longer than in the pictures he'd seen of her when he'd done his preliminary research, it fell forward over her face as she leaned over the newspaper. While she read, she tucked the stray locks behind her ear.

"The short version is that Kripos wants us to write about this case," the chief editor said. "And we'd like you to be the one to do it."

"I'm not familiar with it," Line said. "I was only about five years old at the time."

Stiller leaned across the table, closer to Line. Close enough to catch a faint whiff of her perfume, some kind of flower from the lily family.

"That's a good starting point," he said. "Look at the case with the fresh eyes of a journalist."

Line moistened her lips with her tongue. "Why this case?" she asked.

"It deserves an answer," Stiller responded.

This reply failed to satisfy Line. "I mean, what's the reason for opening it again? Have you somehow obtained new information?"

Stiller offered her a disarming smile. He knew she was smart. She'd come straight to the point, but he was not willing to tell her about the new fingerprint evidence. Not yet.

"That's where we hope a series of articles in *VG* can play a part. We want renewed attention focused on the case, in the hope that someone who knows something will choose to speak up."

Line glanced across at her two bosses. "But surely we need to have something new to write about?" she said.

"We'll have that," Sandersen told her. "Including publication of the ransom letters."

Stiller opened the leather portfolio in front of him and produced the two photocopies of the letters.

"The kidnapper is one of our readers," Sandersen continued. "He's cut these out of our newspaper."

Line picked up the two letters, holding one in each hand. "Will we have exclusive access to police information?" she asked.

Stiller agreed. "We're dependent on public interest," he explained. "But at the same time we need to retain a certain control in order to have the best possible impact. So it's entirely natural to release this by some means or other. You'll have access to all the original case documents."

"All of them?"

Stiller agreed again. "They're digitized and searchable," he said. "What's important for us when the case is brought to light again is that it's done with consideration for the relatives and others involved. According to your bosses here, you have the necessary empathy for that."

"Have the relatives been informed?" Line asked.

Stiller gave her yet another enticing offer: "Yes, and the boy-friend is willing to give an interview. At first he was suspected of killing her, but he was released when the kidnappers' letters turned up. He has never spoken to any journalist about it."

"What about the rest of the family?" Daniel asked. "Her younger brother, for example?"

Stiller said that he had outlined the plan to them but they had made it clear they had no desire to speak to the press. "Not all the pieces are in place as yet," he replied.

Sandersen cleared his throat. "Let's clarify a couple of things," he said, turning to face Line. "First of all, are you interested?"

"Yes, but how in-depth have you considered making it?"

It was Joachim Frost, the chief editor, who answered: "The idea is to reignite the old case by running a series devoted to the Krogh kidnapping. Of course, this depends on how the case progresses, but we thought it could run weekly for six weeks, focusing on a different point each week. First an overview of the case, then the ransom letters, an introduction to Nadia Krogh and the boyfriend interview, a look at the old investigation and finally a police angle from Stiller. At least, that's how we've sketched things out, but of course you'll have a free hand to give other things a whirl too."

Sandersen took over: "Daniel Leanger is here to produce a podcast, but we're keen for you to be the voice of the story."

Line's eyebrows shot up on her forehead. "A podcast?"

"A radio documentary," Frost clarified, as if the terminology might be unfamiliar. "We already have advertising in place. Daniel, could you give us some idea of how you intend to tackle it?"

"It will be a multimedia presentation of the whole story," he explained. "With graphics and animation, but the podcast will be the most important element. We were thinking you could talk about the approach to each week's instalment. What investigations you've undertaken, what your thoughts are, recordings of conversations you've had—quite simply take the listener with you on the job, out into the field on research."

Sandersen spoke up again: "Are you interested?" His voice had grown insistent.

Line raised her pen to her mouth and chewed it as she mulled things over.

"You could work from home," Sandersen went on. "Nadia Krogh lived in Porsgrunn, and that's only half an hour or so from you."

Stiller filled his glass with water from a carafe on the table. Line turned towards him. "Is there a suspect?" she asked.

Stiller put the glass to his mouth. Although this was a question he had hoped would not be posed, he relished it as evidence of her incisiveness. Line resembled her father, homing straight in on the essential points. Playing for time before answering, he swallowed and put down his glass. "Yes," he said finally, aware of how surprised the chief editor and news editor appeared. "I don't want to say anything further about that now, but our plan is for the media coverage to play a part in exposing him and lead to an arrest. You'll have it first, but it really depends on having the first article in print on Friday."

"Friday?" Line asked. "As in this coming Friday? I don't know—"

The chief editor interrupted her, obviously keen not to lose this opportunity. "Daniel, you've been working on this for a fortnight already," he said. "Is it possible to have the first instalment completed by Friday?"

"The conceptual graphics and layout are almost ready. The initial round will be a presentation of the facts in the case. I've already put that together, and made a start on the script for the podcast."

"So the answer is yes?"

"Yes."

The chief editor turned to Line. "Are you with us?"

"Yes, I'm with you," she replied, without a moment's hesitation, unable to resist the challenge.

22

Daniel Leanger had managed to transform one of the smallest conference rooms in the building into a lockable workroom. Line had followed him into the makeshift office. A huge map of parts of Grenland hung on the wall—Porsgrunn, Skien and Bamble. Various pictures were also displayed: press photographs from the official search but also images taken from the police investigation, including two different portraits of Nadia and several photos taken at a teenage party.

"She disappeared after a house party here," Daniel explained, pointing to a picture of a standard brown-varnished Norwegian detached house with a basement and a pitched roof. "She quarrelled with her boyfriend and left. He followed her, but never set eyes on her again."

Line sat down. "I'm not entirely comfortable with the assignment," she said. "We're being used. That Kripos guy is trying to steer the story."

"That's really the point, don't you think, for him to decide the angle?"

"I guess so," Line said, with a smile. "But there's something more to it. Why won't he tell us who the suspect is?"

"But he was quite open about that," Daniel interjected. "The investigation is going in a particular direction, but they don't want to share that with us yet. I think that's okay. Then we avoid being influenced by it."

Line reluctantly agreed.

"He was the one who asked for you, you know," Daniel added.

"What do you mean?"

"I understood Kripos virtually made it a condition that you would be the one to work on this."

"Why was that?"

Daniel shrugged. "Maybe he has a hidden agenda?" he suggested with a grin. "Maybe he's seen photos of you."

Line pulled a face.

"He's probably read your previous articles," Daniel said. "Like a lot of people."

He picked up a state-of-the-art recording device from the desk.

"You'll have to learn to use this," he said, handing it to her. "It's what we use to make the podcast."

Line took it from him and peered sceptically at it. She liked to write, when she could take time to formulate what she wanted to say, changing the words and amending the sentences. This was something completely different, but she had listened to a number of interesting podcasts lately and liked the medium and the format as well as the oral presentation.

"Would you like to hear our theme tune?" Daniel asked. Without waiting for a response, he flipped the lid of his laptop and played a sound file. "You have to hear it more than once," he said when Line did not come out with any immediate reaction. "It has energy—not too much, but just enough to create the right mood."

Line fixed her eyes on the map as she listened to the theme tune again. The picture of the brown house where Nadia Krogh had been last seen was attached with a drawing pin placed almost exactly in the middle. "Have you been down there?" she asked.

"I thought we could go together at the beginning of the week," Daniel answered, lowering the volume of the music. "That would let you spend a couple of days familiarizing yourself with the material before we go at it full throttle."

Line leaned back in her chair. She had been on maternity leave for sixteen months and still had eight months left. Living on her own with Amalie, she had decided to stay in Stavern. She wanted to use her maternity leave to settle down and earn money as a freelance writer, outside the capital city. She felt ready to be a roving news reporter, but this was something entirely different. This was something she was really keen to do. She was compelled by the mystery. Line really was her father's daughter.

23

Stiller let himself into the apartment on the top floor of the massive block of flats in Grnerløkka.

Game on! was what passed through his mind. He spoke the words aloud as well.

His shoes echoed on the newly laid floor tiles in the hallway. Kicking them off, he flung his jacket over the coat stand and smiled with satisfaction at his reflection in the large mirror.

Investigation was often compared to a jigsaw puzzle. However, this was not the kind of puzzle he had set up. The clue lay in the name—it became too trivial. He liked games where the stakes were higher. So far he had manoeuvred the investigation in exactly the direction he wanted it to proceed.

He took a glass from the kitchen cupboard and filled it with water from the dispenser on the fridge door. While he drank it he used his mobile phone to switch on some mellow electronica to drown out the sound of the lashing rain outside.

He wondered how the old detective in Larvik would react when he learned his daughter was involved. She would surely tell him she was going to write about the Krogh case, but Wisting couldn't tell her that he was also involved in the secret investigation. He was too professional for that.

The music on the loudspeaker grew darker and more melodic as it followed him from one room to the other. The apartment was too big for him. It comprised what had originally been two loft apartments, but when his father had bought the entire old apartment block he had combined them and offered it to him as a sort of caretaker flat. However, others attended to the supervision of the rental apartments.

The three boxes of Katharina case papers sat on the coffee table. On Monday he would have to make sure a start was made on scanning the documents so that the whole case could be digitized, but browsing through old papers brought a very special feeling. A feeling he savoured.

He sat down, hoisted his feet on to the table and reached for the nearest ring binder. The traces of Wisting's work were evident. Coloured sticky notes with keywords protruded here and there, individual words were underlined in the documents and there were occasional marks in the margin.

He chose the black ring binder that contained the police documents. Most of them held information about the investigations that had been carried out but had failed to produce any results. There were reports about dredging and diving, door-to-door questioning and passenger lists of traffic from abroad. Some of the reports had pictures attached with paper clips. One of the photographs showed a bouquet of roses on the chest of drawers in the hallway. The flowers were withered and had no packaging around the stalks, as if some time had passed before they were placed in water. It emerged from the report that they were fourteen blooms of the genus Acapella. These were imported from the Netherlands and sold in six shops in the town. They were sold in bunches of seven, and the bouquet on the chest of drawers in Katharina's home had most likely comprised two bunches. The investigators had not succeeded in identifying where the flowers had been sold or who had bought them.

The rain battered against the windows. Stiller laid back his head. Had Katharina received the roses from someone, or had she bought them herself? In that case, did she intend to keep them or give them away? Women sometimes bought flowers for themselves, but seldom roses, and the suitcase on the bed was packed as if she intended to be away for some time.

He straightened up again and looked at the picture fastened to the next report. The clothes were neatly folded and looked as if they had been placed carefully inside the case to make best use of the available space. Wisting had scribbled on a yellow note: *Planned?*

Stiller agreed. It looked as if she had planned to travel, otherwise she would have thrown the clothes together more haphazardly. There was also something slightly odd about the contents of the suitcase. The report listed ten pairs of socks, ten pairs of briefs, five bras, ten T-shirts, five pairs of trousers, five sweaters, five blouses and a tracksuit. It all seemed so rigid, and gave no indication of the intended destination. All the same, why had she not taken the suitcase with her when she left, if she had gone voluntarily? Nothing in the photographs indicated that she might have been forced out of the house against her will, and there was no evidence of a fight. No furniture knocked over or items torn down, as was usual at a crime scene where there had been resistance. The rugs were tidily in place and the shoes on the floor in the porch neatly arranged in pairs.

And then there was the code, the mysterious note found on the kitchen table. Kripos held a copy, and he had already spent hours studying it. Some kind of pattern with various combinations of numbers and a cross. One line on the cross was slightly longer than the other, so that it resembled a religious symbol. Also, its placement on the paper did not seem random. The X, or cross, marked a spot. Regarded from the viewpoint of Martin Haugen's involvement in the old kidnapping case, he could not shake off the thought that this had something to do with Nadia Krogh.

He grew none the wiser after scrutinizing the coded message this time either, and eventually laid the photocopy aside. In order to gain an overview of the Katharina case he would have to work systematically through the material. In other words, he would have to start at the beginning.

24

The microwave oven emitted a high-pitched signal and Wisting was afraid it would wake Amalie. He took out the slice of pizza, carried it with him into the living room and moved gingerly across to the settee. Lying on her side, she was covered with a blanket, her dummy in her mouth and half her face buried in a soft blanket.

He had arranged two chairs with their backs to the settee to prevent her from falling off if she grew restless or began to stir, but there seemed no danger of that.

Wisting sat down in the armchair on the other side of the coffee table, weighing up whether to switch on the TV. Instead he opened the tablet Thomas had bought him for Christmas. He had grown accustomed to using it for reading the news.

He logged on to the *VG* archives and searched for Nadia Krogh. The first mention was nothing more than an announcement describing how an official search had been set in motion. The next day her face was on the front page. After a fruitless search, an investigation had been initiated, on the assumption that a crime had been committed. According to the article, it did not seem as if the police knew anything more. The investigation leader, Gaute Fallet, a man unknown to Wisting, was quoted. They were keen to find witnesses who had noticed anything in a residential area in Stridsklev where Nadia Krogh had last been seen. It was presumed she had intended to walk home to her parents' house in Heistad, and it was primarily along that route where police were interested in sightings.

Then came the news that her boyfriend had been charged and remanded in custody. The background was that he had denied following Nadia when she left the party after their argument, whereas several other partygoers had stated that he had indeed followed her and not returned. In court, at the custody hearing, he had admitted pursuing her in an attempt to catch up and talk to her, but he had lost sight of her. She had vanished, even though she had not had much more than a minute's head start on him.

He glanced up from the tablet and across at his granddaughter to see her still sleeping soundly. Wisting returned to the newspaper articles. The kidnappers' letters had led to a number of front-page stories. The media had learned of the letters only after the kidnappers had failed to pick up the ransom money. And if it had not been for the letters resulting in the boyfriend having to be released, it was far from certain the situation would have been publicized at all.

In the following days, various stories were printed, but none that revealed anything new. Then all went quiet. The Krogh kidnapping disappeared from news coverage, but three years later an interview with Nadia's mother appeared. She spoke of the uncertainty she had lived with and how Nadia was in her thoughts all the time. Her entire life was on hold, and even her grief had to be held in abeyance until she was given answers.

Wisting wished Thomas could have read it in order to gain some insight into what made him refuse to give up on his cases. Nadia Krogh's mother could not even bear to look at photographs of her daughter. It was too painful.

Martin Haugen had told him he felt the same way. He had taken down all the photographs of Katharina.

He read on. Hannah Krogh tried to describe her loss and the uncertainty. *"You hope that eventually the police will find something and uncover a clue,"* she told the newspaper, *"so that we can have an explanation for what happened. I haven't given up on it, but it seems to be my lot in life to carry this burden of uncertainty."*

Wisting read the extract one more time as an uncomfortable feeling welled up inside him. Martin Haugen had spoken about that same lot in life, only yesterday. It could easily be that he had reasoned things out in the same way as Nadia's mother, but it wasn't only the business of one's lot in life. Martin had repeated the same thing so many times that Wisting recognized the wording when he spoke about how he hoped the police would find something and come up with a clue.

His immediate thought was that Martin Haugen must have read this interview and imitated Hannah Krogh's pattern of reactions after Katharina disappeared. Wisting's pulse pounded in his neck and a cold shiver ran up his spine, all the way to the roots of his hair, but he did not have time to absorb it properly. Amalie began to wriggle about on the settee, and immediately started to whimper.

Wisting lifted her up, found a rattle and let her play with it on his lap while he continued to read about Hannah Krogh's inconsolable loss. *"If Nadia had been on a ship that had gone down and never been found, then at least I would have some kind of certainty,"* she said.

Martin Haugen had also talked about certainty.

He heard a noise at the front door. Amalie stopped playing with her rattle and sat listening.

"Hello!" Line shouted into the house.

"We're in here," Wisting answered.

He put down the tablet and lowered his granddaughter to the floor. Her legs were slightly unsteady and he held her by the arms until her mother appeared.

Line lifted her daughter and soon had her smiling and laughing. "Did it go well?" she asked.

"She's just woken up," Wisting replied, pointing to the impro-vised bed at one end of the settee.

"Where's Thomas?"

"Out for a coffee. He's meeting up with Jonny and Rolf."

As if this jolted his memory, he got to his feet and carried his empty cup through to the kitchen. "How did you get on?" he asked.

"Fine," Line replied, following him into the kitchen. "They want me to write about an old, unsolved kidnapping case."

Wisting wheeled round to face her. "What case?"

"The Krogh kidnapping in Porsgrunn in 1987," Line told him. "Are you familiar with it?"

Wisting turned to the coffee machine and inserted his cup. "I remember it," he said. "Why are you writing about it now?" he asked, keeping his back turned.

"The case is being reopened. I'm going to do a series of feature articles that will run in parallel with the police investigation."

Wisting kept busy with the coffee machine. An uncomfortable premonition had begun to stir inside him.

"How did you find out that the case is being reopened?" he asked over his shoulder.

"We're working in cooperation with Kripos," Line explained. "The initiative has come from them." She was seated at the kitchen table and had begun to put on her daughter's snowsuit. "Do you know a Kripos investigator called Adrian Stiller?" she asked. "He was at the meeting."

He felt himself blushing, and kept his back turned. "I know who he is," he said, before steering the conversation in a different direc-tion: "Have you agreed to do it?"

"I couldn't really say no," she replied. "After all, it's exactly the kind of thing I love doing. We're going to make a podcast as well."

Wisting concentrated his attention on his cup of coffee. Although he was annoyed, he tried to remain calm. Admittedly, Stiller had said they were working to get the Krogh kidnapping publicized in the media, but nothing about this. He must be aware of who Line was, but perhaps he had not known that the editors would pick Line to work on the story.

"We have a few Stillers in our family, actually," Line went on. "Do you think we might be related?"

Still unable to rely on either his voice or facial expression, Wisting took a long swig of coffee from his cup.

"I've never heard of it," he said, after swallowing. "Is that on Mum's side?"

Line put a hat on her daughter's head. "I don't recall," she answered, tying the cord under her chin. "Maybe they could take a look at the Katharina case too?"

Wisting, lost in his own thoughts, had not followed what she said. "Who?" he asked.

"The Cold Cases Group," Line said, as she stood up. "Maybe they can look at the Katharina case when they're finished with this one."

"Maybe," Wisting replied. He was about to say something, but held it back and stood watching as she left.

25

On Monday morning, when Wisting woke, there was a message from Stiller which had been sent at 2.23 a.m. It said he would start the day at Kripos and come to Larvik at lunchtime—which suited Wisting very well. The police chief had indicated that the investigation into Martin Haugen should be a top priority, but he still had a department to lead. Nils Hammer operated as his second in command, but he would have more than enough to do in the comms surveillance room for the foreseeable future.

The weather was fine when he left home but had not managed to dry the streets, and dark clouds threatened more rain to come.

The weekend had been quiet, so his routine tasks were completed by ten o'clock. He spent the next hour working on the consequence analysis for the new, extended police district. Nevertheless, he felt the points he made were mere platitudes. Larger departments would provide strengthened specialist expertise and improved opportunities for the development of knowledge and experience. However, he was basically opposed to the change. He liked small units and the local knowledge that accompanied them, but at the same time he understood that a pooled investigation team would make the police more efficient and provide a resource that could get to grips with really serious crimes.

Stiller showed up just after eleven o'clock. Wisting had no idea how long he had been standing in the doorway when he caught sight of him.

"Have you read the comms surveillance data?" he asked, glancing in the direction of the secret room above them.

"We wanted to wait for you," Wisting answered.

"Okay, then," Stiller said. "Shall we get on with it now?"

"Wait a minute," Wisting said. "We need to discuss something else first. Have a seat."

Stiller sat down on the vacant chair. "Close the door," Wisting requested.

Stiller turned and shut the door before sitting down again. "Is this about your daughter?" he asked.

Wisting was taken aback that Stiller had broached the subject first.

"I heard you met her on Saturday," he said.

Stiller was suddenly wary. "Did you tell her about the connection to the Katharina case?"

"Of course not," Wisting replied.

"This business of the fingerprints on the ransom letters is strictly confidential," Stiller went on, as if Wisting had not been aware of this. "Apart from that, *VG* will have access to all the Krogh files. They're planning to run a sort of feature series."

"I know that," Wisting commented.

"Lovely girl, by the way," Stiller said. "I'm pleased *VG* have chosen her to write the story. I've read other things she's written. She's really talented."

"You don't think that might pose something of a problem?" Wisting asked. "At some point she's going to find out about the suspicions against Martin Haugen."

"That's been cleared by the public prosecutor. It's not a problem for him. Will it be a problem for you?"

Wisting considered this. "I'll have to lie to her," he said. "Keep things back when she asks questions. Sooner or later she'll realize I've been investigating the case she's writing about all along, without telling her about it."

"Is that a problem for you?" Stiller asked again, but did not leave Wisting sufficient time to answer. "Line's a professional," he said. "She'll understand the situation."

Wisting knew Stiller was right. He and Line had been involved in similar situations before when her role as a journalist had brought her centre stage in cases he was investigating, and they had emerged from them relatively unscathed.

"The first instalment will be printed on Friday," Stiller went on. "By then you and Haugen will be sitting in the car en route to the cabin. You'll have to make sure you drive into a petrol station and buy a copy of *VG* so that you have something to talk about on the journey."

He flashed a smile, obviously satisfied with the arrangement, before getting to his feet.

"Shall we go and check what Haugen's been up to over the weekend?"

With a nod, Wisting rose from his office chair. They located Hammer and headed to the CS room.

"We'll tackle the phone first," Hammer said. "It looks as if there's not been much traffic."

A short list of telephone numbers appeared on the screen, sorted in chronological order according to date and time and divided into outgoing and incoming calls. The system had performed an automatic search in Directory Enquiries so that all the numbers were identified.

On Friday evening Martin had rung the Pizza Bakery. An hour later he had been called by a number used for telephone sales. That conversation had lasted only five seconds. On Saturday morning Martin had phoned a number registered to Even Vomma in Kilebygda.

"Play that one," Wisting said.

Hammer pressed a few buttons and the loudspeakers began to

crackle. They heard a ringtone and a man with a broad dialect answered.

"Hello, this is Even."

Martin Haugen introduced himself.

"I have a cabin at Eikedokkheia near Langen," he added.

"I know who you are," the other man confirmed. "I was thinking of going there next weekend."

Pause.

"I haven't been there for a while," Martin continued. "What's the track like?"

"Well, I haven't been along there since the rain, but I brought out some timber on the Gisholt side last month. There wasn't a problem then, and there shouldn't be a problem now. The track is fairly solid, you know."

"Great. Is it the same key for the barrier?"

"The lock was broken a couple of years ago, or was it three? Someone had smashed it to pieces. Probably poachers, or something of the sort. But I sent you a new key at the time, didn't I?"

"Oh yes," Martin assured him. "I just wanted to know if the same thing might have happened again."

"Not as far as I know," the other man said. "In that case, it'll be lying open, anyway, so there won't be a problem."

"Okay, then. What's the fishing like these days?"

"The same as usual."

The two men exchanged a few pleasantries before winding up their conversation.

"Lies," Stiller said firmly, turning to Wisting. "I was with you in the car when he told you he'd been to the cabin to repair the roof. Unless he has more than one cabin, he lied to you."

"He's only got the one cabin," Wisting said. "So why would he lie?"

Hammer turned to face them. "I have difficulty believing this has anything to do with the Krogh kidnapping, or the Katharina case, for that matter," he said. "After all, he can't know the investigation is up and running again."

"But he's been up to something he doesn't want to tell us about," Wisting said.

Hammer turned to the screens again. There were only two further conversations. The next one was an incoming call from Kirsten Solum in Porsgrunn, which began with Martin Haugen answering and giving his name.

"Hello, Martin," said the voice at the other end. "This is Aunt Kirsten."

"Hello."

"How are you doing?"

"Fine."

What followed were more pleasantries before Kirsten Solum revealed her reason for phoning:

"It's Uncle Reidar's birthday soon," she said. "He'll be seventy-five. We were planning to celebrate it at home here."

"At the weekend?" Martin asked. It seemed from his tone of voice that he was beginning to take some interest.

"Not this weekend," Aunt Kirsten explained. "Saturday 26 at five o'clock."

Haugen's interest immediately waned.

"It would be lovely if you could come," his aunt continued.

The conversation ended with Martin thanking her for the invitation and promising to show up.

The final conversation was a call to a man in Sandefjord. They heard Haugen introduce himself.

"I'm calling about the model-building sets you've advertised on Finn," he said, referring to the Norwegian online site for classified ads.

"I see," the other man answered.

"You haven't sold them?"

"I've had a couple of calls, but they're still here," he confirmed.

The upshot of the conversation was that Martin Haugen agreed to purchase a plastic building set for a Scania T142 eight-wheeled tow truck and a Peterbilt 359 conventional big rig truck. He arranged to come and collect them that same evening.

"Has that always been a hobby of his?" Stiller asked. "Model building?"

"He has a huge collection," Wisting replied. "I think it was something he took up when he was living in workers' barracks, to pass the time in the evenings."

Stiller shrugged but made no further comment. "Check the Internet log," he requested.

Hammer switched to another system. This showed that Martin Haugen had visited various online newspaper sites, and also that he had spent hours browsing through Finn.no. In addition to various model-building sets, he had looked at cars and motorbikes.

"He's preoccupied with that road up in Trøndelag," Hammer said, calling up a screenshot from an Internet address Haugen had visited. It was a new article in the *Adresseavisen* newspaper about the road collapse, now including an interview with some roads chief or other.

Stiller discovered something else further down the log. The Web address revealed what the page was about: *http://research.no/body/effects-death-hasonbody.*

Hammer opened the page to find a popular-science article about research into what happens after death, from the first few hours of post-mortem lividity and rigor mortis to decay and decomposition.

Stiller swore aloud as he opened and clenched his fists. "That's very revealing," he remarked, swearing again.

Wisting was used to looking at a case from a variety of points of view. "It doesn't necessarily mean anything," he said.

"Doesn't mean anything?" Stiller erupted. "The guy has searched for information about the decomposition of bodies!" He pointed further down the log, where there were clearly several searches on the same topic.

"Oddly enough, he asked me about the same thing when I was with him on Friday," Wisting said. "He was obsessed about whether or not it would be at all possible to find Katharina, and whether there would be anything left of her after so many years."

"It's obvious it's preying on his mind," Stiller said. "He has buried her, and now he's wondering if he should still be afraid of her turning up again."

"You're forgetting he has an alibi," Hammer said.

"Not as far as Nadia Krogh is concerned." Stiller brushed him off as he turned to face Wisting. "At what point in the conversation did this crop up?"

Wisting cast his mind back. "He was wondering if we had investigated a body found recently in Sørlandet, a woman who had been washed ashore," he explained. "That had made him wonder what Katharina would look like if she were found now."

"Okay," Stiller said, making a dismissive gesture with his hand. "But was this before or after you had arranged to go on a fishing trip?"

"After," Wisting answered, realizing where Stiller was heading. "You think Nadia Krogh is buried down there, beside the cabin?"

"What goes on inside our heads is a perpetual series of chain reactions," Stiller said. "One thought leads to another. And Martin Haugen obviously doesn't like the thought of you going down to his cabin to dig for worms."

"Regardless, we should really have a tracker on him to follow his movements, in addition to the trace on his phone," Hammer said. "If he's wondering whether there's anything left of her, there's only one way he can find out, and that's by digging her up."

26

A car drew to a halt in the street outside Line's house, a compact, black Audi. Daniel Leanger craned over the steering wheel and peered out through the windscreen. Line waved to him from her kitchen window to let him know he had arrived at the right place and that she was ready.

"She's just fallen asleep," Line said to Thomas as she showed him a jar of baby food.

Thomas had ended up being Amalie's babysitter. She had hoped to persuade her friend Sofie to do it. She was at home full-time and had a daughter only a few months older than Amalie, but she had an appointment with a lawyer in Oslo who was still trying to reach a settlement with her ex-partner.

"How long do you think she'll sleep, then?" Thomas asked her.

"Until she wakes," Line said with a smile. "An hour or an hour and a half."

Thomas had zero experience of children but had practised both changing nappies and feeding Amalie the previous day. He could fly helicopters, and so it could not be beyond his capabilities to look after his niece for a few hours.

"Phone me if anything crops up," Line said, as she disappeared out of the door.

"Have you got to grips with the case?" Daniel asked, once she was settled in the passenger seat.

"Yes, and there are a few things puzzling me, one of them being the woman we're going to visit now, the one who organized the party . . ."

Daniel interrupted her. "Wait," he said, pointing at the podcast equipment. "We'll discuss that once we have the recorder running."

"Not everything that crosses my mind will be suitable for broadcast," Line warned him.

"We'll edit it, of course," Daniel said, as he turned into the main road. "I just want it to be as authentic as possible."

Instead of talking about the details of the story and their thoughts on it, they discussed how to divide the instalments and what should be included in the various articles.

They had three interview appointments. The first was with Liv Hovet, a classmate of Nadia Krogh who had held the party after which Nadia had disappeared. Afterwards, they were to talk to the man in charge of the local Red Cross branch, who had taken part in the official search. Their third appointment was with Kittil Nystrand, a police officer who was a member of the surveillance team that had kept watch over the spot where the ransom money had been left.

"The policeman couldn't manage today," Daniel told her. "You'll have to contact him later in the week, but I've made an appointment with the Grey Panther instead."

"The Grey Panther?" Line repeated, her mind shifting to the signature on the kidnappers' letter.

"The Senior General," Daniel explained. "Vidar Arntzen—he lives in Skien now. It'll only be a short detour."

Line recognized the name from the case documents. It had not been made public that the letters from the kidnappers had been signed *The Grey Panthers* and *The Grey Ones*. The police had followed it up and interviewed the leader of the pensioners' organization, almost grasping at straws, since they had nothing else to go on.

"I thought that could be the title of the second episode, where we reveal what the letter from the kidnappers said," Daniel went on. "*The Grey Panthers.*"

"How old is he now?" she asked. "If he was the Senior General at that time, I mean."

"Ninety-three, but he remembers the whole business. He said it was the only time in his entire life he'd had the police at his door."

"We'll have to report on how the letters were sent as well," Line said. "That the kidnappers had removed the Krogh family's address from telephone directories."

"I tried to get hold of the secretary who opened the letter, but she's dead," Daniel told her. "And the telephone kiosk is gone."

"Maybe we can find one of the people whose fingerprints were discovered on the telephone directory?" Line suggested. "There were three of them. Their names are given in the police reports."

"Good idea," Daniel said.

"If they're willing to come forward," Line added. "After all, there must have been a reason their fingerprints were listed in police files."

"If not, we can try to get hold of the postman," Daniel said. "We have his name too. The police took his fingerprints to eliminate his prints from the envelope."

He followed the final directions from the GPS and swung into a typical seventies residential area with spacious gardens and detached houses, all very similar in style and construction but subsequently added to with contrasting extensions.

He stopped at a row of rubbish bins by the roadside but left the engine running. "There," he said, pointing at a house almost hidden behind a tall cedar hedge thirty metres ahead of them.

"We're early," Line said, looking at her watch.

"We're not ready yet, though," Daniel told her.

He picked up the recording equipment and handed Line the

microphone. "You have to say where we are and what we're planning to do," he said.

Line had thought through how she would tackle this and had an idea about what she was going to say. She took her notebook from her bag and placed it on her lap, together with printouts of some of the police documents.

"We'll do a soundcheck," Daniel said, asking her to count to five.

The equipment was working, and Daniel asked her to begin.

"We're in Glimmerveien in Stridsklev in Porsgrunn," she said, imagining what it would be like to listen to the broadcast. "We, that is Daniel Leanger and me, Line Wisting," she explained. "We're the ones making this podcast, and we're here because this is where Nadia Krogh was seen for the very last time."

She paused for effect.

"We're sitting in the car, looking at the house thirty metres away from us where Liv Hovet lives. She also lived here twenty-six years ago. At that time she was the youngest daughter in the family: now she has taken over the house and stays here with her husband and children. On Friday 18 September 1987 she was alone at home and had invited a few friends to a party. One of them was her best friend, Nadia Krogh. We have come to talk to her about what actually happened that night." She lowered the microphone.

"Good," Daniel commented. "You need to tell the listeners what it looks like here as well. That's quite important. After all, this is the nearest we get to a crime scene."

Line raised the microphone again. "The house is situated on the outskirts of a residential area, close to the edge of the forest," she explained. "The trees are bare, and we can just make out the blue waters of the Eidanger Fjord, located barely a kilometre below us. Nadia left the party at about half past eleven that night. She said she was going home. Her most natural route would have been to walk towards us, where we are parked now. Then she would eventually have reached the main road, where she could either have walked the five kilometres home to Heistad, waited for a bus or tried to hitchhike. But nobody knows what became of her. That's what we are going to try to find out."

Daniel Leanger nodded in satisfaction and drove up to the house. "Leave the recording device running," he told her.

The branches of a massive fruit tree stretched out above the hedge into the street. Two birds pecking at a suet ball held in a net flew off and disappeared when the car doors slammed shut.

Line could hear the faint rumble of traffic from the E18 that passed somewhere behind the forest. She thought this was something she should have mentioned in her podcast commentary, as part of her description of the surroundings, but shrugged off the idea.

Daniel rang the doorbell. He was the one who had made the interview appointment. Line held the microphone discreetly in her right hand, to capture the sound of the doorbell and the initial meeting.

Liv Hovet was pale, tall and slim with short, dark hair. She had prepared for the meeting and set a table in the living room. As expected, she was sceptical when she spotted the recording equipment, even though Daniel had already warned her of this when they had spoken on the phone.

"We're only going to use short extracts," he clarified. "It will be much the same as in a written interview in which we highlight what is said." He attached a microphone to her blouse and checked the sound with her before handing the interview over to Line.

"Who was Nadia Krogh?" Line began.

The old friend rolled her eyes as if she had no idea where to start.

"Nadia was Nadia," she answered. "She was always cheerful and interested but not particularly modest. She talked a lot and usually said exactly what she thought and felt. Sometimes it just kind of blurted out of her—if she thought someone was wearing a horrible sweater or something like that. She was brutally honest about everything."

Line nodded, reluctant to break in with any comments or questions.

"And then she was smart," Liv Hovet continued. "She did well at school. Nadia talked of studying business law so that she could work in her father's firm."

The description matched what Line had read in the police documents. Liv Hovet had also thought that Nadia was spoiled, jealous and a flirt, but Line didn't want to include this in the first interview. Perhaps she would use it when summing up at the end.

"And of course she was so pretty," her classmate rounded off. "But I'm sure you already know that. You'll have seen the photographs."

Line agreed. "Can you tell me about the evening she went missing?" she asked.

The woman facing her rubbed her palms on the armrests of her chair. "My parents were going to our summer cottage," she began. "I was given permission to have some friends over. Ten or twelve people, but more than that turned up. Twenty-something."

Line knew there had been thirty-two partygoers, according to the case documents. The police had spoken to all of them.

"Most of them were from our class, but there were also a few older boys. Including Robert."

Robert was Robert Gran, Nadia's boyfriend. He was one year older than her and had a car and a driving licence.

"Really, nothing in particular happened," Liv Hovet went on. "We chatted, danced and drank, just like every other party, but there was a bit of drama between Nadia and Robert."

"What happened?"

Liv Hovet shrugged slightly. "Nadia came to me, on the verge of tears, and it wasn't so easy to make out what she was saying. She was drunk and everything was sort of incoherent, but it was something about Robert and Eva. They'd gone out before, at junior high school, and now they were huddled together in the bathroom."

She turned her head and looked out into the hallway, where the bathroom was situated.

"Nothing had happened in there; at least that was what they said afterwards. Nevertheless, Nadia stomped off. I don't really know any more. A lot of people arrived, there was loud music and everything was a bit out of control. I should probably have tried to persuade her to stay or gone after her, but somebody had just broken a picture. I think it was Olav. He'd bumped into it and it had fallen off the wall. The glass and frame were smashed, and I was more concerned about that."

While she spoke, Liv Hovet had moved her hands from the armrests and placed them protectively on her knee. "I don't really know anything more than that," she concluded. "The next day Nadia's mother phoned, asking for her, and then there were lots of comings and goings. With the police and all that."

"Did you say any more to Robert about it?" Line asked.

Liv Hovet shook her head. "I spoke to him when Nadia left, and said he should really go after her, but after that I didn't speak to him at all. I've hardly seen him since, and I'm not sure I'd even recognize him now."

"But he did go after her that night?"

"I didn't see him go," Liv Hovet explained. "And anyway, he didn't leave right away, but the others said he did."

Line asked a few more questions to catch some of the atmosphere on that night and managed to conjure a picture of a teenage party most people would find familiar.

"What do you think happened to Nadia?" she probed.

"At first we thought there had been an accident," she answered. "That she had walked through the forest and broken a leg or something, but then they didn't find any trace of her there. So I wondered if she had hitchhiked, or if she had started to walk home and someone had stopped to offer her a lift." She sat for a moment pondering what she had said. "Anyway, I never believed what the police did in the beginning, that Robert had gone after her and killed her. And then the letters arrived. They had to mean that someone had followed her, that they had been standing waiting outside here, ready to kidnap her."

Line left her words hanging in the air.

"Do you have any pictures of you and Nadia together?" she asked after a lull. "A class photograph, for example?"

She continued to wear the microphone as they followed her into a guest bedroom. Liv Hovet knelt down in front of a cupboard and took out an album. "Here she is," she said, after flicking through it for a moment or two.

It was a picture of the leavers' class at junior high school. Liv Hovet pointed at a girl in the second row. The photo had been taken more than two years before Nadia had gone missing, but she was easy to recognize.

"Could we borrow it?" Line asked.

Liv Hovet agreed and removed the picture from the album. "There should be a few more here," she said, leafing further through. "One where she's with Robert as well."

"Can I take a picture of you?" Line asked, as she searched through her bag.

Liv Hovet looked up. "Of me?"

"Yes, now, while you're looking through the album."

She had already produced her camera from her bag, and Liv Hovet made no objection.

In the end they left with five different photographs of Nadia

Krogh. She was pictured with her boyfriend in one of them, and it looked as if they were both laughing at something, Nadia with her mouth open and her chin thrust forward. Something about the light may have been what made Robert's eyes look extra dark and almost sombre, despite the smile on his lips.

*

"Shall we get something to eat before we meet up with the guy from the Red Cross?" Daniel suggested once they were back in the car again.

Now hungry, Line agreed. They drove into Porsgrunn and found a restaurant open for lunch in Storgata. Line ordered a fish-and-seafood salad, while Daniel decided on a burger.

"We'll have to edit out the bit where she talks about Eva being with Robert in the bathroom," Daniel said. "I've spoken to her, and she's not willing to participate or be named."

"But we must include it some way or other," Line said. "I can read from her police interview and call her something else. She says nothing happened in the bathroom, anyway. They just talked."

"Robert Gran says the same," Daniel said.

The food arrived at the table.

"Maybe we should find another voice for the commentary too," Line suggested as she began to tuck in. "Someone distanced from the police investigation but who can say something authoritative about how the local community reacted."

Daniel agreed. "A clergyman or the mayor, or someone along those lines," he suggested, as he munched his burger. "Maybe we can find someone who was a local politician at the time but is still well known today. That would be good! Or some other celebrity. That hotel guy, for instance, Petter Stordalen? He's from hereabouts and probably remembers the case."

"I don't think we should drag in any celebrities," Line told him. "I was thinking more of a local journalist who covered the story at the time."

They discussed various angles and possibilities and agreed what was crucial in the initial coverage was a chronological review of the facts, though more questions came up than answers.

Someone who could help to outline a picture of what had taken place in the period after Nadia went missing was Realf Tveten of the Red Cross. He met them in the organization's local premises and had unearthed the log of the official search in 1987. In addition, there were several maps with areas gradually shaded in as the search progressed.

"I was well aware of who her parents were," he said, "Joachim and Margareta Krogh. Of course, everyone knew who Joachim was, but I knew him from school. A great guy. Down to earth. Not at all arrogant or high and mighty, even though his family had money."

"When did you learn that Nadia was missing?" Line asked, to bring the conversation back to the missing girl.

"The police phoned about two o'clock on the Saturday," Realf Tveten replied. "By then they had already searched with police dogs, but they wanted to conduct a more systematic search. I set in motion an alert system to bring in the volunteers. Half an hour later I had established a control centre."

He referred to the log before continuing. "We concentrated on the neighbourhood, scoured gardens, under redcurrant bushes, in playhouses, sheds and garages. It's happened before, that someone under the influence lies down somewhere to find shelter. At that time it wasn't cold or bad weather, but she had been drinking and could have felt unwell. She could have lain down some place, thrown up and choked on her own vomit. That was a possibility."

Line glanced across at the recording equipment in Daniel's hand and saw the LED strip move to the rhythm of Realf Tveten's deep voice. The slightly vibrating tone was easy on the ear.

"As soon as I had more feet on the ground, we extended the search to include the forest behind the house." He took out one of the maps and pointed. "It was hilly terrain, steep and stony. She could have fallen and knocked herself unconscious."

Line took out her camera and snapped a picture of the table in front of them. This would provide a striking image, with the maps and their shaded areas.

Realf Tveten produced a larger rolled-up map. "The party was here," he explained, pointing. "But the Krogh family lives here. It was reasonable to assume she had decided to head for home. In reality there are three main routes. She could walk down to the old E18 and follow it all the way home to Heistad. Then she'd also have the possibility of jumping on a bus. Or else she could have gone along the new E18 that was under construction at the time, but it was dark and deserted. The shortest way would probably have been to walk through the residential area and come out at Lundedal, even though that meant she'd also have to use some of the forest paths."

The three routes were marked with red lines on the map.

"We conducted searches along all three of these routes. Our thinking was she might have been knocked down by a car and left lying in a ditch, but that brought no results either. Nor was there anything to indicate there had been any such accident."

Daniel Leanger broke in. "So what do you think happened to her?" he asked.

Realf Tveten leaned back in his chair. "I've taken part in countless searches," he said. "In the mountains, in the forest, at sea and in towns. Most people are found. Generally, they're no longer alive, but they are found—whether they've met with an accident or committed suicide, or been killed by someone else for that matter, they're eventually found. If we don't find them, then a hunter or a hiker does. So I've always believed someone took her away in a car and drove off with her."

"The kidnappers," Line broke in.

"The question is what happened afterwards," Realf Tveten said. "What happened to Nadia, and why did they never collect the ransom money?"

*

Their conversation with the man from the Red Cross had taken longer than Line had estimated. As soon as they were back in the car, she phoned Thomas to ask how things were going.

"Everything's fine," Thomas reassured her. "I'm teaching her how to use the iPad."

"The iPad?"

"I've bought her a few apps," Thomas explained. "She's sitting on my knee, tapping the screen and laughing. She's very enthusiastic, and is managing to do it. It's educational."

Line had not allowed Amalie to play with her iPad, and it was not long since she had let her watch TV for the first time. Her feeling was that putting children in front of a screen provided artificial stimulus and was only an excuse to give the parents a break.

"Has she eaten, though?" she asked.

"We've eaten and changed her nappy, so everything's okay," her brother assured her before Amalie began to babble and demand attention.

Line said goodbye to them both and said she thought she would be home in a couple of hours.

Daniel had entered Vidar Arntzen's address on his GPS. "The Grey Panther," he said, as he began to follow the onscreen instructions.

"Does he live alone?" Line asked.

"In a collective," Daniel answered.

"A collective?" Line repeated in surprise.

"A shared residential complex is probably the right description," Daniel said, grinning. "It's one of the things he worked on when he was the Senior General," he explained. "He and a group of people the same age got together and built housing for seniors."

Line read through the police documents. Vidar Arntzen had recently retired, following a long career as an architect, when two police officers in civilian clothes stopped at his door one day and demanded to know if he had been involved in a plot to kidnap a seventeen-year-old girl. She took note of the brief summary and thought she could read it out into the podcast later. It would provide an excellent introduction to the meeting with the old man.

They passed a sign with directions to Henrik Ibsen's childhood home before they turned off and drove up in front of a massive wooden building, idyllically situated with a river in the background. Wet, dead leaves from a huge farmyard tree blanketed most of the courtyard.

Line splashed into a puddle when she stepped from the car. She quickly darted ahead but felt cold water squelching in her shoes.

"Vidar Arntzen lived in Oslo at the time," Daniel told her. "This was probably an old family farm."

They walked into an entrance resembling a reception area with no staff and found a panel of doorbells. Vidar Arntzen must have seen them arrive because he appeared almost at once when they rang the bell. He was tall and thin with a wiry beard and carried a little document folder tucked under his arm. It seemed there was nothing wrong with either his mind or his hearing as he took them on a brief guided tour of the building and explained all about the facilities.

"State of the art, every aspect of it," he told them. "This offers health and well-being for people getting on in years who don't want to live in detached houses with big gardens. You should write about it in your newspaper. Politicians should consider how, from a statistical point of view, this kind of residential arrangement encourages the elderly to be independent."

He ushered them into a common room, where they sat down at one end of a long table.

"Is there any news of the girl?" he asked as Daniel attached a microphone to him.

"Nothing apart from the police are reopening the case," he said. "Maybe they'll discover something now that didn't come to light at the time."

"After so many years," the old man muttered, shaking his head. "They couldn't have had many clues then anyway, since they came to me."

"Why did the police come to you?" Line asked, once Daniel had checked that the sound was acceptable.

"I don't know how much I can tell you," Arntzen replied. "The police told me what we had discussed was a secret part of the investigation and I was bound by rules of confidentiality."

"That was a long time ago," Line reminded him. "We've been given copies of all the police documents, so they have in a sense lifted the confidentiality rule."

"So you know about the Grey Panthers?"

"That's why we've come," she said.

"Well, at that time I'd just joined a few other pensioners and started up an organization for old people, to improve pension rights. Our name was the Senior Association, but we were known as the Grey Panthers, exactly the same alias that Nadia Krogh's kidnappers gave themselves."

"What did the police want?"

"They came to me because we had been mentioned in the press

but, after all, *grey panthers* is a common expression, a description used for old people who are still healthy and active. We didn't have anything to do with the kidnapping, and the police were well aware of that."

Line glanced across at Daniel. So far it was a short story, briefly told, and she was unsure whether it was suitable for use. It was rather lacking in content.

"Could you tell us what happened when they turned up?" she asked, in an effort to approach it from a different angle.

"Nothing more than that happened," the old man answered with a shrug. "There were two of them. They arrived and asked me if I was Vidar Arntzen and showed me their ID. Of course, I'd read about Nadia Krogh in the newspapers. Most people had, but I had no idea what the police wanted with me. It was a shock, I can tell you."

"Why was it secret, what they were talking about?"

"Because of the Grey Panthers," Arntzen explained. "They didn't want journalists or anyone else to know that pensioners were behind it all."

It took some time for Line to understand his reasoning. She herself had thought it was a random nickname cut out of a news article about the Senior Association. But it dawned on her that Vidar Arntzen probably knew nothing about how the letters had been pieced together and that he had placed more significance on the signature than she had and interpreted it differently.

"Did they show you the letter from the kidnappers?" she asked.

Vidar Arntzen shook his head. "They didn't tell me what it said, only that it was signed *The Grey Panthers*."

"I'd like to show it to you," Line said, taking out her laptop, on which all the case documents were stored.

His curiosity roused, the old man leaned across the table. Line spent some time logging in. There was a police report stating that the newspaper used by the kidnappers was the edition of *VG* for Thursday 27 August 1987, and *The Grey Panthers* had been cut out of an article on page eleven.

Locating the correct picture file, she brought the first letter up onscreen and turned the laptop towards Vidar on the opposite side of the table. He fumbled to take out a pair of glasses and moved his lips as he read it.

"They've cut the words *The Grey Panthers* out of a newspaper interview with you," Line told him.

Vidar Arntzen sat deep in thought. "So that was why they were so interested in the newspaper," he said, taking off his glasses again.

"What newspaper?"

"I had saved the newspaper," Arntzen explained. "I had it lying out when the police paid me a visit. It was open at the page with the interview because I'd been showing it to Aspaker from the local council—he'd been with me the day before."

Line closed her laptop.

"But then they saw that my copy of the newspaper was intact," Vidar Arntzen went on. "So there must have been someone else who'd saved the same newspaper."

Line mulled over what he had said. This was a point she had not considered and not seen mentioned in the police documents. Nadia's family had received the letter from the kidnappers on 22 September, while the newspaper used had been dated 27 August. Someone had saved it for some reason.

Daniel wrapped up the interview. He switched off the recorder and tried to explain to the old man how he could listen to the finished programme, but Vidar had difficulty grasping what he was saying.

Line thanked him for the interview and told him it would also be printed in the newspaper.

Outside, it was still raining, and the wind had picked up.

27

The wind blew the rain sideways against the office window and reverberated through the room. A steady beat.

Wisting was bowed over his desk. He had located a map on which Martin Haugen's cabin was marked and was struggling to match the numbers in the code to various points on the terrain. He managed to get two of the numbers to tally with two mountain peaks, but that meant next to nothing. This was not where the solution lay.

Adrian Stiller arrived to speak to him. "I'm bringing down a technician tomorrow who'll attach a transmitter to his car," he said, referring to Martin Haugen. "It'll be more stable and precise than following his phone. As soon as it's in place and we're sure we know where he is, we'll go in and search the house."

"A clandestine search," Wisting commented.

"He's hiding something, and I want to find out more about him before you start to apply pressure," Stiller explained as he sat down. "If he gets the slightest whiff of suspicion that we're after him, he would have time to dispose of evidence. I don't want that to happen."

"What do you think he might have at home that would give him away?" Wisting asked.

"I want to look at his computer and see what he has saved there," Stiller answered.

"That'll be a challenge," Wisting said. "He has CCTV installed."

Stiller raised his eyebrows as Wisting went on to tell him about the two cameras.

"That makes it even more interesting," Stiller said. "What about an alarm?"

"No alarm."

"Good. The cameras suggest he does have secrets in there."

Although Wisting had come to the same conclusion, he made no comment. Martin Haugen clearly felt he had to protect himself from something other than Lithuanian migrant workers.

Stiller stood up abruptly and crossed to the window. "I'm staying down there," he said after a while, pointing down to the new hotel at Sanden. "The Farris Bad." Then he changed the subject. "Have you had any contact with Katharina's family?" he asked, his back turned to Wisting.

"In Austria?"

"Yes."

"I spoke to her sister a few years after her disappearance," Wisting said. "In connection with Katharina being formally declared dead."

Stiller swivelled round. "Are they alike?" he asked.

"I've only seen photographs of her," Wisting told him. "They don't have the same father, but they look similar. Why do you ask?"

"I've hired a firm in London to create an illustration of what Nadia Krogh might look like today," Stiller said. "You know, based on biometric facial data and suchlike."

Wisting nodded. He was familiar with the technology but had never used it before.

"The idea is that we'll use it on *Crime Scene Norway* on Thursday," Stiller added. "But I'm not certain it will be a true likeness. No matter what data programs they use, in the end it's only an approximation. It would have been easier with Katharina. We'd have had something more specific to go on."

"Have you seen the sketch?" Wisting asked.

"I'll receive it tomorrow."

Wisting leaned back in his chair. "Does that mean you think Nadia may be alive?" he asked.

"No," was the forthright response. "It's just to have something to show on TV, to generate interest. *VG* will have the ransom letters and the TV will have the face."

He headed for the door. "Katharina is different from Nadia," he said. "She seems competent. She'd broken with her family before and travelled to a new country to start a new life. She could have done so again. Wiser and more resourceful than the first time she left."

28

Line enjoyed the final hours of the day, when Amalie had sunk into a deep sleep. Usually she spent them reading or working on family-history research, but now she was seated on the settee with her laptop perched on her knee, writing. Now and then she stopped to listen for sounds from the child's bedroom, but all that could be heard was the constant rain.

In her text, she alternated between the content of the police documents, the contemporary newspaper accounts from 1987 and her own notes from the interviews she had conducted in tandem with Daniel. He had sent her the sound files but was now in Oslo editing the content for the first podcast.

She was on a roll. In the opening article it was a matter of presenting the facts, briefly and concisely, but in a compelling way, to make the reader want to follow the story over the next few weeks. What she lacked was a slightly authoritative view of the case. She had arranged an appointment with a journalist on the *Porsgrunns Dagblad* newspaper who had covered the whole story at the time and was still working at the newspaper. The problem was that he wanted to write about the story before hers had gone to print. This was not ideal, but a local newspaper such as *Porsgrunns Dagblad* was not a serious competitor and the journalist did not have the same access to material that she had.

She read through what she had written, even though it provisionally comprised fragments to be fleshed out later. As things stood, she was simply a tool of the police and all the information had been collected in advance. In order to intrigue readers and podcast listeners, she would have to make something more of it, something that would create momentum and involvement. She would have to try to find some aspect the police had overlooked or had interpreted incorrectly. A clue she could follow up, perhaps. From experience, she knew something usually cropped up once a story had gone to print. Readers sometimes preferred to speak to the press rather than the police about what they knew, but she felt impatient and restless.

29

Wisting reheated the leftover pizza in the microwave. It had been stored in the fridge since Friday evening, but it looked fine.

"Would you like some pizza?" he called through to Thomas in the living room.

"I ate at Line's," he answered, walking through to the kitchen.

Wisting took out the pizza and sat down, with Thomas in the seat opposite him.

"Why do you do it?" Thomas asked.

Wisting laid his fork down on the slice of pizza. It had gone soft in the microwave. "What do you mean?" he asked, cutting off a piece.

"Working on these cases, the very worst cases. Murder and so on."

Wisting reflected on this as he ate his pizza. He was occasionally faced with this question. People wondered whether he lay awake at night because of his job. Sometimes he had sleepless nights because a case was weighing heavily at the back of his mind, but then that was for professional reasons. He would run through details in pursuit of something that had been overlooked.

"I enjoy it," he replied. "I like to think I contribute to bringing about justice. When someone takes another person's life, they have to know someone will come after them and hold them accountable. If no one did this job, then we'd have a society where the rights of the strongest would prevail."

Thomas listened without making any comment.

"What's more, I think it's exciting," Wisting added. "I could easily have said I became a policeman because I wanted to make the world a better place, to make a difference, but when all is said and done, it's really because of a fascination with serious crimes."

"Isn't that . . ." Thomas was searching for the right word. ". . . callous, in a way?"

"I could have become a traffic cop," Wisting said, smiling, "but I didn't want that. I wanted to try to understand the incomprehensible. How one human can take another human's life. It's a bit like a clergyman who ends up working in a hospital, among the dying. He could have chosen to work with weddings and christenings instead. Or why some doctors choose to work in a unit with children suffering from cancer. It's difficult and painful, but maybe that's where they find some meaning in what they do."

"I met a girl a couple of months ago," Thomas said. "It was getting serious."

Wisting resumed eating. Thomas had not said anything about a girlfriend.

"At first she didn't appreciate what my job involved. When she did, she couldn't understand how I could do such a job. In her eyes I was still part of the military and mixed up in brutal wars. I tried to tell her what motivated me, but I couldn't do it."

Wisting was lost for words.

"I tried to tell her it was about keeping the world safe and secure," Thomas went on. "But it's just like what you were saying. I enjoy it, both in an everyday sense and in contributing to something greater. I can't imagine ever doing anything else—flying commercial flights, for instance."

"Maybe it's just something that's part of our makeup," Wisting suggested. "I think your sister has it too."

Thomas stood up.

"Are you leaving tomorrow?" Wisting asked.

"No," Thomas replied. "Line's working on a major story. I'm going to stay here all week to look after Amalie."

30

The hotel was partly built over the shore and the sea. Stiller had been allocated a room overlooking the water with a small balcony. He stepped outside and stood, inhaling the tang of seaweed and salty air. In the inner part of the harbour a man was out walking a big black dog. He saw them in the light of a streetlamp. Cold, frothy white surf pitched against the jetty on which they were standing, showering them in sea spray.

He lingered on the balcony until the man and his dog disappeared, moving beyond the yellow circle of lamplight.

He had put a bag with six cans of beer in it down on the balcony floor, and there were three left. The air temperature kept them relatively cool. He cracked open another can and carried it in with him to his computer. Hopefully, it would help make him sleepy. He slept badly, and even worse in a hotel.

The new face of Nadia Krogh filled the computer screen. The drawing had arrived just before nine o'clock. Admittedly, it was no later than eight in London, but this probably meant someone had spent a lot of time reaching the best possible result.

He opened his can of beer and settled into the seat. As far as Stiller was concerned, it was immaterial what Nadia looked like. Some computer nerd or other could almost certainly have come up with a passable likeness in his teenage bedroom for a far cheaper price.

He poured the contents of the can into a glass and glanced up at the screen again.

This could well be what she would have looked like if she were still alive, he thought as he took a gulp from his glass. However, he had no confidence that making it public would bring them any benefit. The sketch was simply a prop to help move the case forward.

He shifted his gaze to the mirror on the wall above the writing desk. His eyes had started to become puffy and he could see a spatter of red specks on the whites.

The first time he had experienced problems sleeping had been while he was living with his parents in South Africa. The reason was not difficult to trace. It had been because of Julie Ann. But regardless of whether he could link it to what had happened there, it did not cure his insomnia.

In the beginning, he had simply tossed and turned for an hour or two after going to bed, but eventually the insomnia developed and deteriorated. He had tried various medications that had given him a few hours of sleep but did not leave him feeling rested. Then, after six months or so, it had all passed and he was sleeping normally once more. Since then, insomnia had overtaken him at regular intervals. Now it had been more than six months since he had slept all through the night.

He closed the image of Nadia Krogh and sent it to the chief editor he had been in contact with about Thursday's programme. Then he concentrated on Martin Haugen, a man he could not quite fathom. There was nothing in the old investigation documents to indicate what sort of person he really was. He appeared to be a fairly anonymous character, living alone and not socially active. His circle of acquaintances seemed restricted to work colleagues and a few elderly relatives. In time, the comms surveillance would possibly help to sketch out a better picture of who he was, as would the search of his home. But, in the meantime, it seemed as if something overshadowed his existence, holding him back and preventing him from living life to the full.

Adrian Stiller took another swig of beer. He was familiar with that kind of person, people with secrets darker than the deep sea. These were the secrets he liked to unearth.

31

"Anything new?" Wisting asked as he closed the door of the CS room behind him.

"Porn," Hammer answered, pointing to the screen. "Looks like he subscribes to something. He was looking at it last night. We can't pull up the mirror images of the pages behind the pay wall, but the login page tells you all you need to know."

"Extreme XXX," Wisting read aloud. The pages appeared to cover topics such as restraint, sadism and masochism.

"I don't know what to make of it," Hammer said.

"It makes you think, anyway," Adrian Stiller commented, rubbing his eyes. He seemed tired and out of sorts.

"Any phone calls?"

"Nothing."

"What about emails?"

"Only incoming spam."

"Anything else?"

"It's possible he's planning to go on holiday. He's been browsing through expensive, exotic travel destinations, but hasn't booked anything."

Stiller looked at the time. "The technicians are on their way," he said. "They'll drive into the roads department offices in Tønsberg and fix a tracking device to his vehicle. Then we'll be able to track him on a screen as well."

"Isn't that risky?" Wisting asked. "In broad daylight, in an open car park outside his work?"

"They'll have a look at where his pickup's parked, but it's the best opportunity," Stiller said. "At home he keeps his vehicle parked in the garage. Anyway, it only takes a second. It won't be easy for anyone to spot it or know what's going on."

Wisting agreed. "And once it's done?" he asked.

"I've legal permission to conduct a covert search," Stiller told him. "The technicians are coming here with equipment to read Haugen's hard drive."

"How will we get inside?"

"We've got that sorted," Stiller assured him. "It won't be a problem."

"Let's hope not," Wisting said, before returning to his own office.

Covert searches were not an everyday occurrence. As a rule, the police visited the person concerned with a warrant and then the search took place in the accused's presence. Or else it was done after the person had been remanded in custody. Only twice before had Wisting taken part in a clandestine house search.

*

At six minutes past twelve Adrian Stiller poked his head round Wisting's office door.

"We're all set," he said. "We're swinging into action now."

This was short notice, but Wisting stood up and followed Adrian Stiller down to the police garage, where a grimy white delivery van with a Lithuanian number plate was parked. A magnetic sign with a hammer-and-saw logo was displayed on the side.

"Creative," Wisting commented.

Presuming the man behind the wheel to be one of the technicians, he greeted him with a nod. Nils Hammer was already seated behind him in the cargo hold. Wisting clambered in and said hello to the other colleague from the Kripos technical section. Adrian Stiller jumped in after him and drew the sliding doors closed before the van drove from the garage building.

"Did it go okay?" Wisting asked them, referring to the tracker they had attached to Martin Haugen's pickup.

"No problems," the technician answered, holding up a tablet with the image of a map displayed on it. In the centre was a red dot at the far edge of an open area Wisting understood to be a car park.

"I'll set it up for you in the comms room afterwards, so you can keep a close eye on him," the technician said.

The smoked windows in the rear of the van made the grey skies look even darker and more threatening.

Everyone in the vehicle jolted forward when the driver dropped the van into a lower gear to drive up the steep ascent to Kleiver. Adrian Stiller was on his phone and exchanged a few brief words with someone before wrapping up the conversation. He lifted his right arm to his face.

"All set," he said into a tiny microphone on his wrist.

The man behind the wheel adjusted the almost invisible plug in his ear and gave a thumbs-up to the window separating the cabin from the cargo space.

"We've switched off the electricity," Stiller explained. "So the cameras won't work."

As the wheels gripped the gravel track leading to the house, grit rattled in the wheel arches. The van tilted, and Wisting planted one hand on the roof to keep his balance.

The driver swung into the extensive yard and parked side on to the house. Wisting moved position to peer outside. Without electricity, Martin Haugen's home looked even more desolate than when he had been here the previous week.

They remained seated and let the driver go out and up to the front door. He rang the doorbell and took a step back.

"You need repair?" Stiller joked, in broken English.

No response from the house. The driver stepped up to the door and produced something resembling a cup from his jacket pocket. He placed it over the cylinder lock and, in less than a minute, the door was open.

"Is there any movement on his part?" Wisting asked, glancing at the technician.

He checked the tablet. "Cooling his heels."

Drawing open the side door, Adrian Stiller handed out gloves and rubber overshoes. The technician who had picked the lock on the door trudged through the house while the others were still waiting in the hallway.

"All clear," he said, in final confirmation that the house was empty.

Wisting let the others go in front. The floor in the passageway creaked under their feet.

"Two computers," said the man who had already scouted through the house. "Desktop computer in the guest bedroom, laptop in the living room."

He pointed at the latter, on the coffee table in front of the TV set. The other technician sat down and opened a suitcase. He took out his own laptop, an external hard drive, a battery pack and various cables.

"Will this take long?" Wisting asked.

"It depends," he replied. "First we have to link up, and then it's a matter of how much data he has stored. It can easily take an hour or so."

"An hour," Wisting repeated, glancing through the window. Although it was no longer raining, water dripped steadily from the trees.

One corner of the living room was used as a home office. A few invoices and bundles of papers were stacked on the desk, and several ring binders marked by years were arranged on a shelf on the wall. Adrian Stiller began to skim through them, while Hammer disappeared into the bedroom.

Wisting made for the kitchen, where a chest of drawers was positioned against the wall by the window. It was behind Martin Haugen's usual chair, and he could reach it by twisting round.

On top of the chest of drawers was a radio, beside a number of advertising leaflets from various supermarket chains and a few copies of *Vi Menn*, a popular lifestyle magazine for men. Wisting knew Martin kept his wallet and keys in the top drawer. He opened it and peered inside. On one side lay an old mobile phone and charger, several ballpoint pens, a mini-stapler, a tube of superglue, a pair of scissors and a notebook containing no notes.

"We've got something here!" Nils Hammer shouted from elsewhere in the house.

As Wisting padded into the living room, Hammer emerged from the bedroom brandishing an old newspaper. Wisting recognized the story. It was the *VG* interview with Nadia Krogh's mother, in which she talked about the loss of her daughter.

"Isn't this a bit unusual?" Hammer asked.

Stiller agreed. "Photograph and document it," he instructed.

"It was at the bottom of a drawer," Hammer told them.

"Put it back in the same place."

Hammer nodded and returned to the bedroom. Wisting resumed his search of the chest of drawers in the kitchen. In drawer number two he found a bundle of letters. Wisting lifted them up and discovered a passport underneath. He put the bundle of letters aside on the kitchen table and picked up the passport. It belonged to Martin Haugen and had been issued on 10 October. That was only five days ago, and coincided with the anniversary of Katharina's disappearance. The passport application had been speedily processed. This meant he had applied at the beginning of the previous week and probably had the passport sent yesterday or just before the weekend. He had not mentioned any travel plans.

Wisting returned the passport to the bottom of the drawer and riffled through the bundle of letters. There were letters from the tax office, the insurance company and the bank. He thumbed through them systematically to ensure he did not tamper with the order in which they had been filed.

At the bottom of the bundle was a white envelope with no recipient's name or address.

Wisting laid the other letters to one side, opened the unmarked envelope and drew out the sheet of paper from inside. Even before he had withdrawn it completely, adrenaline was pumping through his body. The sight of the contents made him breathless, hitting him like a hammer blow to the chest and making him feel dizzy.

"Stiller," he said with a gulp, but he had not spoken loudly enough. He steadied himself by taking a step to one side, using the chair back for support, and called out again. "Stiller!"

When Adrian Stiller arrived, Wisting held out the contents of the envelope, four words on one sheet.

I know about it.

Each letter of the short message was cut from a newspaper and pasted in place like the letters from Nadia Krogh's kidnappers. The similarity was impossible to ignore. Someone knew about Martin Haugen and Nadia Krogh.

"It was in the drawer," Wisting explained, pointing at the chest. Stiller asked to see the envelope.

"Unaddressed," Wisting told him.

Stiller held the envelope up to the light from the window. "There's a tiny hole in it," he said.

Wisting peered at the sheet of paper in his hand and found a corresponding pinprick-sized puncture in it. Both drew the same conclusion that the anonymous letter had been pinned to the door.

"It doesn't look very old," Stiller said.

"Difficult to say," Wisting responded, though he did agree. "This could have something to do with his CCTV cameras. He probably put them up after he received this."

Hammer also entered the room. He swore aloud when he saw the letter.

Wisting struggled to collect his thoughts. The sender obviously wanted Martin Haugen to understand that someone knew what he had done.

"It's a confirmation," Stiller said, fixing his eyes on Wisting. "Don't you think he would have told you about this letter if he were innocent?" he asked. "If he had no idea what it was all about?"

Wisting agreed.

"We have a dilemma," Hammer said.

"How's that?"

"The sender clearly knows what Martin Haugen has done," he began to explain. "There could be fingerprints or biological traces on the letter that will allow us to discover who the sender is, but in order to do that we'd have to take it with us. And then Haugen would realize somebody's been here."

Wisting let Hammer hold the letter as he disentangled an evidence bag from his pocket. "We'll take it with us," he said firmly. "We'll take the risk that he has no intention of removing it from the drawer for a while, and if he does take it into his head to look for it, we'll just have to hope he thinks he's mislaid it." He took out another evidence bag for the envelope.

"It raises a few questions, though," Hammer commented. "How the letters from the kidnappers were pieced together is something that hasn't been made public. In other words, only the police, the kidnapper and whoever sent this letter know."

"Nadia's family knows too," Stiller reminded him. "In the course of the twenty-odd years that have gone by, it could have been discussed, and last week *VG* were told of it."

"But none of them knows Haugen has cropped up as a suspect because of fresh fingerprint tests," Hammer persisted.

Adrian Stiller shrugged. "It's possible we're drawing too hasty a conclusion," he said. "The note could be about something else entirely. Perhaps the sender knows about something else. Or it could even be that Haugen has concocted it himself, that he's got a new plan on the go."

Wisting did not believe any of these options. "I saw a man here last week," he said. "I was here late one evening, on the anniversary of Katharina's disappearance. He tried to hide but retreated into the forest when he clocked that I had spotted him."

"Did you notice if there was an envelope on the door?"

Wisting shook his head doubtfully before heading out into the hallway again. He opened the front door and stood in front of it. In the middle, beneath the small pane of textured glass, he found a tiny hole made by a drawing pin or something similar used to affix the letter to the door.

"It wasn't here on Thursday," he decided.

"Fine," Stiller said, taking charge of the two evidence bags. "I'll get the boys to take these in with them and deposit them at the lab, and then we'll see if they give us anything."

Wisting returned to the kitchen, replaced the remaining letters in the drawer and opened drawer number three, which held magazines and a pile of Christmas cards. Wisting flicked through them. They were from Martin Haugen's aunt and uncle in Porsgrunn, and said the same every festive season: a few brief words and wishing Haugen Merry Christmas and Happy New Year. In between, there were also a few envelopes with birthday greetings from them.

They bore silent witness to the limited circle of Martin Haugen's friends.

The further down the pile he went, the stiffer and more yellowed grew the papers. Towards the bottom of the pile he found an envelope different in style from the others, almost entirely square. When he took out the card, he found himself standing with a picture of Line and Thomas in his hand. It was a thank-you card for the money he had given them for their confirmation. This had been fifteen years ago, but it was lying in a hoard that had barely increased with each passing year.

It suddenly felt extremely invasive to be rooting around in another person's kitchen drawers. Line and Thomas had received presents from family and friends on the occasion of their confirmation. Martin Haugen had gained a place in that circle.

He replaced the bundle of greetings cards and slid back the drawer.

Wisting spent the next half hour delving into all the other drawers and cupboards, laboriously examining the contents of a blue jug on the windowsill and a bowl on top of the fridge. The technician in the living room finished working on the laptop computer and headed into the guest bedroom to copy the data from the desktop machine in there.

On top of the row of cupboards above the kitchen worktop six large porcelain mugs decorated with wise and witty mottos were displayed. Wisting stood on his tiptoes and lifted down one with the text *Your best time is now—remember to enjoy your coffee.* It left a greasy layer of congealing dust that fell into the kitchen sink. He pushed the gunk into his back pocket to avoid leaving any traces.

The mug contained a handful of foreign coins. He put it back and carefully brought down mug number two. *Life is long— happiness is coffee.* A key lay at the bottom of this mug, and Wisting used two fingers to retrieve it. The metal was sticky and attached itself to his disposable gloves: it had obviously been there for ages, gathering grease from cooking fumes. Although it bore no marks, its shape and size suggested it could be for a door or a large padlock.

He put it back in place and looked inside the next mug. This one was empty, as were the remaining three.

"On the move!"

He heard a shout from the guest bedroom.

The investigators gathered round the man who held the tablet. Wisting watched as the red dot moved south along the E18.

"The connection is down," the man with the technical equipment told them. "He started driving seventeen minutes ago."

Wisting glanced at his watch. Martin Haugen still had two hours left of his working day, but the red dot on the screen was heading in their direction.

"Then he'll be here in less than ten minutes," Hammer reckoned.

The image on the technician's laptop showed it was busy transferring data from Martin Haugen's computer.

"How much time until you're finished?" Stiller asked.

"I need those ten minutes," the technician answered.

"Okay," Stiller said. "Is your tracking data secure? Are we one hundred per cent in real time now?"

The technician confirmed this.

"Then you stop when the vehicle turns off from the E18." He wheeled round to face Wisting and Hammer. "We'll make sure everything's exactly as it was when we arrived, and we haven't left anything behind—gloves, evidence bags or anything else. Then we'll move out to the van."

Wisting returned to the kitchen and took a look around. Everything appeared undisturbed. He went out to the van and sat inside with Hammer, leaving Stiller standing in the doorway. When Wisting checked the time, four minutes had elapsed. The next minute moved at a snail's pace, and then another. After seven minutes the driver showed up at the door. He strode across the yard, sat behind the wheel and started the engine before returning with the device for locking the door. At last the man with the suitcase and computer equipment emerged.

A dark shadow slid across the house wall. "The cat!" Wisting groaned.

It crept up the steps and sneaked in just as the door was closing. Wisting leapt from the van and dashed across to the house.

The cat had left wet pawprints, as had the technician who chased after it. Wisting followed them into the living room. "Puss, puss, puss," he called, without seeing anything of the cat.

He crouched down, inspected underneath the table and caught sight of a pair of eyes behind the settee. The cat slipped out as he approached and dashed into the kitchen.

Wisting and the technician followed. The cat did a round of the chair legs before settling in the middle of the space beneath the table.

Wisting tried to coax the cat towards him, but it seemed uninterested. The technician moved quietly towards it, but it proved impossible to catch and darted out into the living room again.

They carried on chasing him until Wisting managed to launch himself at the animal. The cat thrashed about in his arms as he carried it outside. The technician knelt down to wipe the damp patches on the floor in the hallway with his jacket sleeve. Then he shut the front door and used his device to lock it. Wisting let go of the cat and jumped back into the cargo hold, letting the side door slam shut. With Stiller now in the passenger seat, the driver leapt in behind the wheel and got the van moving.

"Position?" Adrian Stiller asked.

"Still on the E18," replied the man with the tracking equipment. "He hasn't turned off but is continuing along the road."

"So he's not on his way home, after all?"

The technician shook his head. "He's on his way to Telemark."

As the van juddered on to the main road, Wisting cast a glance at Steinar Vassvik's house, but saw no sign of the neighbour.

"Did we get everything we needed?" Adrian Stiller asked.

The man with the IT equipment confirmed this. "Two hard drives. I'll set up copies this afternoon that you can all access and have a look at."

When Wisting asked to see the tablet tracking Martin Haugen's pickup, the technician handed it to him. The red dot had passed the regional boundary between Vestfold and Telemark.

32

Line looked down at the speedometer. She had a tendency to slow down when lost in her own thoughts, as she was now. The needle hovered on 90 kph. A large pickup truck that had pulled out and drawn up alongside accelerated and overtook her, even though she increased her speed.

She had two interview appointments—one with Geir Inge Hansen at *Porsgrunns Dagblad*, and the other with police officer Kittil Nystrand, whose shift would start at four o'clock.

Yet another vehicle passed her, even though she was observing the speed limit. She kept a steady pace until she turned off from the E18, heading for Porsgrunn. The newspaper offices were in Jernbanegata, and she found the address without using her satnav, a grey, dismal building opposite the railway station. All the guest parking bays were occupied, but Line found a vacant spot in the nearest side street where she could park for two hours free of charge.

She was almost half an hour early and took out the recording gear to compose an introduction.

"We're on our way into the editorial offices of *Porsgrunns Dagblad*, or simply *PD*, as they say in these parts," she began, thinking it appropriate to use the pronoun *we*, even though Daniel was not with her. She and the listeners were *we*.

"*PD* is a small local newspaper covering the Porsgrunn and Bamble area. It comes out five days a week and has a circulation of just over three thousand. Geir Inge Hansen has worked here as a journalist for more than forty years and has covered all sorts of stories, both major and minor. The story he has written most about is the one concerning Nadia Krogh."

She stopped the recorder and stowed it in her bag. She was delighted to have found Geir Inge Hansen, who had seemed enthusiastic when she spoke to him on the phone. The last time he had written about Nadia Krogh had been one year ago, on the twenty-fifth anniversary of the case. Hansen seemed pleased the local paper had already shown renewed interest in the topic, and was keen to know what had happened to make *VG* decide to run the story now. She had avoided telling him that a new investigation had been initiated. This news would be made public on Friday. Instead she had said something vague about an emphasis on the podcast.

There were still twenty minutes until the appointment. She killed some of the waiting minutes by reading through the statements given to the police by Nadia's boyfriend, Robert Gran. Adrian Stiller had arranged contact and she was to meet him on Saturday—she was on tenterhooks about what he might have to tell her. He had given three different statements to the police about what had happened on the night Nadia had gone missing, so it was not difficult to appreciate why suspicion had been directed at him. She would have to ask him questions both difficult and critical.

At five to two she stepped from the car and strolled to the newspaper building, where a man stood at the entrance with a mug of coffee in one hand and a cigarette in the other. Line had seen photographs of Geir Inge Hansen on the Internet and easily recognized him.

The man at the front door had obviously undertaken similar research. He smiled at her and took one last drag of his cigarette before stubbing it out in an ashtray.

Line switched on the recorder again as she approached him. Her hand seemed small in his when they shook hands.

"Welcome to *PD*," said the experienced journalist. "Let's go up."

She followed him upstairs to the first floor and they passed through a kitchenette, where Geir Inge Hansen refilled his coffee mug. Line accepted a glass of water and continued after him into a cramped, stuffy office.

Line sat down in the visitor's chair while Geir Inge Hansen tidied the desk between them.

"The Krogh kidnapping," he said, as if clarifying the topic for himself. "I've been a journalist for forty-two years, but I've never been interviewed before."

Line smiled. Journalists interviewing journalists usually added little news value to a story.

"Do you remember when you first heard of the case?" she asked.

Geir Inge Hansen replied, "It wasn't a kidnapping at that point, but a missing-persons case—of the kind that is pretty common: a teenager who hasn't come home from a party. When the search was set in motion it became something of interest to us. People get inquisitive when they see the police, the Red Cross and volunteers out and about."

He cast a glance at the recorder, as if it prevented him from expressing some of the thoughts in his head.

"The police got started early," he said, all the same. "Maybe it had something to do with it being Joachim Krogh who had raised the alarm, but probably also because it fairly quickly became clear she had not spent the night with her boyfriend or her best mate. Quite the opposite—she had left the party early. Something must have happened."

The old journalist paused again. "Of course, it was a dramatic development when her boyfriend was charged," he went on. "Firstly, for having given a false statement and later for murder. I'd never come across anything like it before. I remember the remand hearing. I've never seen so many press folk gathered in one place. Robert Gran was led in and seemed virtually unmoved by everything going on around him. He seemed so cold. Cynical. Stared straight ahead with those dark eyes of his."

A mobile phone rang. Geir Inge Hansen took it out of his pocket, checked the display and flicked it off.

"Then the great turnaround came about," he continued. "Nearly a fortnight after the girl's disappearance the police called a press conference. We thought it meant one of two things. Either the boyfriend had confessed, or they'd found the body. Or both. But that wasn't it at all. The police chief opened the meeting by saying that over the past week the police had been in touch with people who claimed they had abducted Nadia Krogh and demanded a ransom for her release. No one had seen that coming. The room fell totally silent, as if after an explosion. And then the cameras began to click."

The journalist on the opposite side of the desk raised his coffee mug and took a loud slurp. "The rest of the story, you're familiar with," he said. "Her boyfriend was released. Nadia was never found."

"What did people think about what had happened?" she asked.

"In my opinion, people didn't know what to think," Geir Inge Hansen replied. "At first, of course, it created fear, that a young girl was missing. Then the arrest brought some kind of relief, but caused shock. When this business of the kidnapping became known, I think people were confused. Joachim Krogh, Nadia's father, was a controversial figure. He still is. Lots of people thought it might have something to do with him. He was in the midst of a business reorganization and had just closed down the timber factory when it happened. Some folk thought the kidnapping could have been revenge by a former employee. Almost a hundred people were made redundant, workers who had been there all their lives, some for several generations. But if that were the case, the outcome was different from what was expected. The kidnapping had stirred people's sympathy, and no one blamed Joachim Krogh for the industrial closure after what had happened to his daughter. On the contrary, politicians and trade unionists kept their heads down. However, there were some who claimed Joachim Krogh used the situation to his financial advantage. They speculated that the money demanded for Nadia was such small change in comparison to what he had made, but no one felt they could protest or oppose a grieving father."

Geir Inge Hansen went on to describe how he had covered the story. He had been there when the divers searched in Eidanger Fjord and when they dug up the forest looking for a body, after a clairvoyant claimed that Nadia had been killed and buried. People also became convinced that they had seen her alive in another town or country. The mystery had grown out of all proportion.

By the end of the interview Line had quotes and ideas she could use and had identified people who could contribute.

She reassured herself that the interview had been saved before switching off the recorder. Geir Inge Hansen got to his feet to accompany her out.

"I still think it was the boyfriend," he said.

"Why's that?"

"Call it a hunch," Geir Inge Hansen answered. "There's something about that guy. Something not quite right."

"What about the ransom letters?" Line quizzed him. "After all, they were sent while he was in custody."

"Anyone at all could have sent those letters," Geir Inge Hansen said.

"Not anyone at all, surely?" Line objected. "Not Robert Gran?"

"But somebody who wanted to help him could easily have done it," the local journalist pointed out. "As soon as Robert Gran was freed, nothing more was heard from the kidnappers."

"A photograph was enclosed with the letters," Line interjected. "A picture of Nadia and her little brother that she had in her purse when she disappeared."

Geir Inge Hansen shrugged and smiled. "I expect you're right," he said. "It can't have been just anybody who sent those letters. It must have been an accomplice. Someone who knew what had happened to Nadia and where she was."

Line regretted having turned off the recorder, but this was probably why Geir Inge Hansen had dared to express his personal views on the case.

He took out a cigarette, inserted it in the corner of his mouth and followed her downstairs.

"Who would have wanted to help him, then?" Line asked, once they were standing outside.

"I've no idea," Geir Inge Hansen admitted as he lit his cigarette. "What I do know is that Robert still lives at home with his mother."

These last words rang in her ears as she headed back to her car.

Now she had acquired a fresh perspective prior to her meeting with Nadia's boyfriend.

This thought evaporated as soon as she returned to her car. A yellow ticket on the front windscreen made her swear out loud. Yet another parking fine.

This was her second in a week. She flopped down behind the wheel and tossed the yellow ticket on to the passenger seat, annoyed, discouraged and frustrated. Switching on the ignition, she stepped too hard on the accelerator and the tyres squealed as she reversed out of the parking bay.

On her way to meet Kittil Nystrand, she phoned Thomas. He

told her he and Amalie were having a good time. As of New Year, she would no longer be dependent on having someone look after Amalie whenever she was working, as she had been allocated a nursery place.

She was early once again. Kittil Nystrand was due to start work at four and had arranged to meet her at half past. On the whole, the weather had been fine all day, but now the rain had started again.

Line turned on the recorder while the engine idled and the windscreen wipers cleared away the water.

"I'm at Olavsberget Camping in Porsgrunn," she said. "It's out of season so the campsite is closed: there's just a faint light in the shower block and in the dome above the yellow kiosk in front of the entrance. Twenty-six years ago, three million kroner was stashed in a bin bag behind this kiosk. We'll find out more about this shortly, when we meet Police Sergeant Kittil Nystrand."

The patrol car arrived on the scene just as she finished speaking, almost ten minutes early. It drove alongside her and the window slid down.

"Are you the person I'm due to meet?" the driver asked. His gruff voice suited his appearance—short, bristly hair, prominent cheeks and a strong chin. "Will you come over to me?" he asked.

Thanking him, Line picked up her equipment and transferred to the police car. She had previously alerted him to the fact that she would be recording their conversation and that parts of it might be used in the podcast.

Line embarked on her questions. "Tell us about your role in the case."

"I worked in the Drugs Squad at that point," the policeman began. "We were a separate group that undertook surveillance activities. One afternoon we were called into the section leader's office. It was a Thursday. We were given a brief rundown of the situation. Nadia

Krogh had been abducted by kidnappers and the family had received a ransom demand. The payment was to take place here, in a black bin bag hidden behind the kiosk. We were told to come out and move into position before Joachim Krogh turned up with the money."

"What was the actual plan?" Line asked.

"Joachim Krogh wanted to pay up for his daughter. Our job was to keep our eyes on the money. We were not to intervene in any way, just keep a lookout. Of course, the risk was that some nosy parker would come along and start rummaging through the bag."

A message was announced on his police radio. Kittil Nystrand turned down the volume.

"The people who worked here didn't have a clue about it," he went on. "We told the owner that we were conducting a surveillance operation in connection with a narcotics case. You see, the E18 went directly past here at that time so there was a great deal of traffic, and a lot of coming and going. The plan was to let them take the money and then follow them. We had reinforcements from Oslo and three surveillance groups altogether. Two on the ground for twelve-hour shifts, and one resting. Eighteen men, both in cars and on motorbikes. In addition, we had a plane standing by at Geiteryggen airport. I was sitting in a van camouflaged as a plumber's vehicle, just about where we're parked right now."

"And what happened?" Line asked.

"Nothing," the policeman said with a sigh. "The problem really was that no particular time had been stipulated in the letter from the kidnappers. It simply stated where the money should be left. It was never collected, and there was no further communication from them. After that weekend we reduced the manpower, and towards the end of the week the entire operation was called off. We took the money and returned to base."

A lorry passed on the road and Line waited until the noise had died out. "Have you been involved in anything similar, before or since?" she asked.

"No."

"Do you have any thoughts about what was actually going on?"

"Plenty," the policeman answered. "But none to provide any clue about what really happened."

33

The tracker image had appeared on one of the screens in the CS room. The red dot showed Martin Haugen's pickup at a standstill just outside Porsgrunn, only a few hundred metres after he had turned off the E18.

Hammer replaced the map image with an aerial view. The vehicle was parked in an industrial area. The most obvious feature of the scene was an extensive sandpit. It was becoming overgrown again and in the aerial photograph it looked like a scar on the landscape.

"He's parked outside a retail unit," Hammer said, checking the address. "Monter Building Supplies. What's he doing there?"

"Nadia Krogh disappeared a few kilometres from there," Stiller reminded them, pointing at the screen. "They searched for her in that sandpit."

"Has there been any phone activity?" Wisting asked.

"No, but triangulation shows the phone is located in the same place as the pickup," Hammer told him.

"We should have had him followed," Stiller said. "Then we could have watched what he's doing."

"Maybe he's buying a spade?" Hammer suggested.

At that split second, the red dot began to move. The three men in the room stood in silence, watching the vehicle continue towards Porsgrunn. It drove through the town centre and across the bridge to Vestsiden before taking the road heading west.

"He's going to his cabin," Wisting said.

Hammer swung his chair round to face him. "Isn't that suspicious?" he asked. "After all, he hasn't been there for ages, and now all of a sudden he leaves work early to take a trip out to his cabin."

Wisting refrained from answering and instead sat down on a vacant chair.

The red dot progressed through Kilebygda and after ten minutes turned off from the main road and came to a halt.

"The barrier," Wisting said.

Hammer zoomed in on the aerial image, and they could see a narrow ribbon of track snaking through the forest. The red dot was now advancing more slowly, and it stopped after another ten minutes.

"That's the cabin," Wisting told them, indicating a building located beside an elongated lake. "The track doesn't go all the way up to it. He has to walk the final stretch."

"Do you have the coordinates?" Stiller asked.

Hammer placed the cursor in the centre of the picture to trigger a read-out of the degrees of latitude and longitude.

"I'll ring the helicopter service," Stiller said, locating a saved number on his mobile phone. "We currently have electronic surveillance on a person of interest in connection with a homicide case," he explained on the phone. "Is it possible to obtain assistance in the form of a fly-past to find out what the suspect is doing?"

The response sounded positive. Stiller provided the coordinates.

"Could we have photographs?" he asked, making a note of what was being said before rounding off the conversation.

"Are they able to do it?" Hammer enquired.

"They were in the process of winding up an assignment in Agder," he explained. "Now they're just going to refuel at Kjevik and attend to it on their way back to base. They'll be above him in three quarters of an hour."

"And we'll get live images?"

Stiller tore a sheet of paper from his notepad and handed it to Hammer. "If you log in here," he said.

Hammer opened a new window on the screen where they could stream a live video from the helicopter. All three sat staring at the blank screen.

"I think he took both of them," Hammer said, digging a box of snuff from his pocket. "Nadia and Katharina. Two missing-persons cases with one common denominator—Martin Haugen."

Wisting had run through the same thoughts himself but had not arrived at the same conclusion. Martin Haugen had been in a different part of the country, eight hours away, when Katharina disappeared.

They sat swapping thoughts and ideas, but he believed the theories underpinning any connection were fanciful and the alleged motives absurd.

The screen burst into life with video images from the helicopter. After some interference, they were looking down at an angle into a forest. Rain covered the picture with shades of grey and details on the ground were difficult to make out.

When Stiller's phone rang with a call from the helicopter, he switched to loudspeaker.

"We'll be above the subject in around two minutes," the pilot clarified, speaking above the constant buzz of background noise in the cockpit. "Approaching from south-south-east, at a height of six hundred metres, going down to five hundred, but we have to maintain that altitude to avoid being identified. I'm assuming that's a factor?"

"Absolutely," Stiller confirmed. "Can you zoom in closer with the camera?"

"We'll lock the camera on to the target when we have it in our sights," the pilot explained. "Then we'll zoom in closer."

The phone line was momentarily disturbed by electrical interference before the pilot returned.

"Sixty seconds," he announced.

The camera image rotated vertically to point ahead of the helicopter.

"Forty seconds."

A long lake appeared at the right-hand side of the picture as a target sight swept across the land.

"Do you have visual?" the pilot asked. Stiller answered in the affirmative.

When a building appeared in a forest clearing, the camera image latched on to it, and zoomed in closer. The rain made the surroundings blurred and grey.

"Looks like movement on the roof," the pilot reported.

"That's him!" Hammer exclaimed, pointing at the screen.

The picture became a closeup. They could see a ladder propped up against the cabin wall and someone standing on the roof. He stopped what he was doing to raise one hand to his forehead and peer up at the helicopter.

The picture grew smaller and smaller and, ultimately, both man and cabin were swallowed up by the spruce trees.

"Would you like one more fly-past?" the pilot asked.

Wisting shook his head. Stiller thanked the helicopter crew for their help and hung up.

Hammer rewound the recording to freeze the image of the man on the cabin roof.

"That wasn't very exciting," he said.

"It depends how you look at it," Stiller told him.

Wisting agreed. "He claimed he'd repaired the roof last week," he said. "We know that wasn't true." He pointed at the still image. "He's trying to cover his tracks, to make sure he's not caught out when I go with him to the cabin at the weekend."

34

Line had kitted out a workroom for herself in the basement, but she rarely used it, preferring instead to lie on the settee with her laptop on her knee and her notes spread out across the table and the floor. When curled up there, she had no need to use the baby alarm in case Amalie woke up.

Thomas was sitting in an armchair watching a documentary on TV. This did not disturb either her or Amalie, who was sleeping with the bedroom door open.

Work on the podcast and the series of articles had progressed both faster and more smoothly than she had envisaged. Tomorrow she was going into Oslo to interview Adrian Stiller at Kripos, and then she would visit her editors to present her work. After which she had only one day left to perfect everything.

In front of her was the material on Nadia's boyfriend, Robert Gran. Adrian Stiller had sent her an email with contact information and background details, probably more than the police should hand over, but she was grateful, as it was verified information which would save her time.

As Geir Inge Hansen had told her, Robert Gran lived at home with his mother. The address was given as Slottsbrugata, a mere stone's throw from the centre of Porsgrunn. He hadn't always lived there, however, and had two children with two different women he had lived with at various times. Names, dates of birth and addresses were given for them too. According to the final change of address, it looked as if the last relationship had ended three years earlier and he had subsequently moved to his mother's home.

His parents had separated a couple of years after the Krogh kidnapping and his father had remarried. His name and address were also listed. However, his mother had remained single.

Robert Gran was one year older than Nadia. They had been together since she had enrolled at upper high school when he had been in the second year. Now he was forty-four and worked as a logistics operator in a building-supplies firm. His annual income was also listed.

The police had interviewed him for the first time on the Saturday afternoon at 1.45, about fourteen hours after Nadia had left the party. He explained that he had been drunk and had not taken in much of what had happened. Nadia had been annoyed because he had been talking to another girl, and he eventually realized that she had walked out. He was questioned again at eight o'clock in the evening and confronted with the information that people had seen him standing in the hallway arguing with Nadia. They said the altercation had ended with her turning her back on him, grabbing her jacket from a peg on the wall and storming out. Several people had seen him rush out after her only a few minutes later. He denied he had followed her and said he had been too intoxicated to remember anything. Other partygoers, however, insisted that he had drunk next to nothing. By the end of the interview he had gone from being a witness to being charged with having given false testimony and taken into custody. On Monday morning he was brought before the court for a remand hearing. He now changed his story, claiming he had pursued Nadia to talk to her but had not succeeded in catching up with her. Instead of returning to the party, he had headed for home.

Thomas rose from his chair at her side and padded through to the kitchen with an empty glass. "Would you like anything?" he asked, but she shook her head.

Adrian Stiller had attached a recent photograph to his email. It was marked *not for publication*, and probably intended to help her recognize Robert Gran when she met him. He was a good-looking man, even though his expression in the picture seemed morose and serious. There *was* something about his eyes. They were dark and gave the impression of hiding something.

Her initial impression had been that the photo was taken from passport records, but there was something about the height and width that did not tally, and it dawned on her that it was most probably obtained from police photo files but trimmed to exclude the file number in the bottom corner.

35

Stiller opened the balcony door in his hotel room to let in some fresh air. The extra hard drive linked to his laptop had made the room stale and stifling.

He hovered in the doorway as the brisk sea air wafted over his face.

The hard drive contained two folders, mirror images of Martin Haugen's computers. The laptop in the living room was the one most in use, but it contained no personal files. The desktop computer, connected to the two CCTV cameras, was far more interesting. Haugen had installed the cameras on Monday of the previous week and had set them up in such a way that the recorder switched on as soon as movement was detected. Occasionally the cat triggered the recording, but once Stiller had managed to sort through them they showed brief film sequences of Martin Haugen coming and going. On Thursday there were recordings of William Wisting. He had been there three times in total and had been filmed at both the front and rear of the house. The next sequence was of Martin Haugen returning home. The time in the top-right-hand corner showed that it had been 3.47, early on Friday morning. Thereafter it showed himself and Wisting when they had visited later that day.

He retraced his steps to the desk but left the door open a crack. The red dot of the tracker on Haugen's vehicle was moving again. He had been at the cabin until after dark and then the marker had slowly begun to travel along the forest track and back towards

Larvik. For the past half hour it had been at a standstill in Vallermyrene outside Porsgrunn. The map showed a snack bar located there. Martin Haugen had stopped for something to eat and was heading for home.

The surveillance cameras had helped them draw a simple timeline. Martin Haugen had left his house on Wednesday at 11.23 and returned home in the small hours of Friday, forty hours later. Before he left he had ordered a new passport and bought CCTV cameras. It was easy to draw the conclusion that the anonymous letter had provoked all this. *I know about it.* Clearly this had terrified Haugen. Stiller revelled in that thought. Frightened people did irrational things.

He rubbed his eyes, aware of how exhausted he was. Last night he had slept for three hours, and he doubted he would manage more tonight, even though his eyelids were heavy. It was a long time since he had discovered that being tired was not the same as being sleepy.

He sat looking at the tablet and the moving red dot. After twenty minutes or so it stopped outside the house at Kleiver.

Stiller took out his mobile phone and sent a message to Wisting, informing him that Martin Haugen had arrived home.

36

His mobile phone buzzed again and Wisting picked it up: yet another message from Adrian Stiller, slightly longer this time. He had examined the mirror images of Martin's computers, and the most interesting aspect had been the surveillance cameras, which showed Martin had been absent from the house for forty hours.

Wisting gave a brief *OK* in reply and rose from his chair in the living room to head for the kitchen. He felt restless and began to clear the kitchen worktop, where Thomas had forgotten to put away the breadboard and knife.

Martin Haugen had left his house for reasons he was unwilling to share with anyone, and had lied about the reason for his absence, both to his work colleagues and to him.

The surveillance gave them a complete overview of where Martin Haugen was at any time but did not tell them where he had been last week. However, there was one way to find out.

Pulling his phone from his pocket, he wrote a message to Stiller: *Traffic data from last week.*

Stiller was bound to understand this simple message. The historic traffic data on the mobile phone would be able to tell them who Martin had been in contact with and where he had been during that day and a half.

The response was rapid: *I'm on it.*

In all likelihood, those four little words had compelled Martin to act. *I know about it.* The anonymous message was similar to the ones in the Krogh kidnapping and must have been troubling to receive.

But who sent it and what did they know?

Wisting returned to the living room. He had brought the ring binder marked *Inger Lise Ness* home from work with him. She was perhaps the person who had known Martin Haugen best. They had lived together for a number of years before Martin met Katharina, but everything she had said to the police had been assessed in the light of her mental condition.

One of the things that had caused the greatest problem for Katharina and Martin was that she stole their post. This meant that they had neglected to pay bills and led to payment defaults and debt-recovery proceedings. Wisting picked up the document listing the various belongings of Katharina that were found in the chest of drawers at Inger Lise Ness's home. There was a letter from their insurance company, dated 21 September 1987, the Monday after Nadia had gone missing. This suggested that Inger Lise Ness had been rummaging in Martin Haugen's mailbox while the kidnappers held Nadia.

When questioned, she admitted the harassment and police believed her actions had been motivated by anger and frustration towards Martin Haugen. *You don't know what he's really like*, she was quoted as saying. *You don't know what he's done. You don't know what I know.* At the time, these statements were seen as attempts at self-justification and shifting blame. Now there was reason to wonder whether she really had known something.

37

The section for old, unsolved cases was situated on the sixth floor of the Kripos building in the east end of Oslo. Adrian Stiller had not yet managed to furnish his office. It was empty, apart from a few shelves with individual ring binders on them, an office desk with a computer and an office chair.

He had not spent very many hours in that chair. His work in the CC group mainly took place out in the police districts, where these unsolved cases had taken place. If it had not been for his interview appointment with Line Wisting, he would not have been here today either. Naturally, it would have been easier and more practical for them both to meet in Larvik, but it was best that she remained unaware of his presence in the town.

At five to twelve a call came from reception to say Line had arrived, and he went down to meet her. She stood with a bag slung over her shoulder and a recording device in her hand. Although he knew it was switched on, he ignored it as he greeted her and welcomed her to Kripos.

She held the recorder in front of her to allow it to catch the sound of his pass being swiped through the reader and the code being keyed in. When the door shut behind them she paused the machine.

"How's it going?" he asked, as they waited for the lift.

"Fine," Line assured him. "Most of it's in place. I just need a few words from you about the reasons for reopening the Krogh case."

The lift doors slid open and they stepped inside. He stood so close to her that he could smell her faint, slightly sweet fragrance, which automatically turned his thoughts to summer.

On the way to his office he fetched a carafe of water and two glasses from the kitchenette. He offered her coffee, but she declined. They continued to his office and sat down.

She seemed efficient: her notepad was out and the recorder running again even before he had managed to fill the glasses.

"Why have you decided to reopen the Krogh case?" she asked.

Although Stiller was prepared for this question, he was loath to disclose the real reason: that they had found Martin Haugen's fingerprints on the letter from the kidnappers. This was a card he was disinclined to play until a later stage in the game.

"The Krogh kidnapping is unusual," he said instead. "It's a case without parallel in Norwegian criminal history, and has been an unlanced boil for the police, the relatives and an entire local community."

This was claptrap, a politician's answer, words of the type rattled off by police chiefs before him, and Line Wisting was obviously far from satisfied.

"What makes it unusual?" she pressed him.

"Kidnapping cases of this kind are out of the ordinary," he replied. "Rare. We have to go to other countries and other continents to find anything comparable."

"Could that be the reason it hasn't been solved?" Line ploughed on with her questions. "That the police here don't have the competence to deal with it?"

Stiller now had to tread warily. Regardless of his own opinion of the work previously undertaken, the head of Kripos had made it clear that the CC group must never criticize colleagues for their efforts in these old cases.

"The Krogh inquiry had top priority when it took place," he reassured her. "The most competent officers were assigned to it. The challenge was the same as in all missing-persons cases—that there is no crime scene to examine."

The conversation continued. He explained how the Cold Cases Group had been formed and organized, and how the police were now in possession of constantly improving techniques and tools to help them solve difficult cases.

"But even though scientific evidence and DNA are important, it's often fresh information from somebody who knows something that leads to a resolution," he pointed out. "The right person might start to talk."

This seemed a suitable concluding remark. He was happy with it himself and motioned towards the recorder to signal that she should switch it off.

"Do you know who that person is?" she asked, with the recorder still running.

He said nothing. Line let the silence build for a few seconds for dramatic effect, before she turned off the recorder and replaced it in her bag, as if to indicate that his answer, if forthcoming, would be off the record, quite literally.

"You must have something more," she went on when he did not respond. "Waiting for the right person to start talking sounds like a flimsy investigation strategy."

"It's maybe more a matter of *persuading* the right person to talk," he corrected her, flashing a smile.

"Do you intend to speak to Robert Gran again?" she asked. "Her boyfriend?"

"We already have done."

"I've an appointment to interview him on Saturday," Line told him.

"Yes, I was the one who arranged it," Stiller reminded her.

"I know," Line replied. "I was wondering whether there's anything about him I should be aware of."

"Such as what?"

"Well, does he have a criminal record?"

Stiller nodded.

"What has he done?"

"Things that weren't very honourable." Reluctantly, he told her: "He's been convicted of assault."

"Who did he assault?"

"His ex-partner. There's a restraining order in force at present."

He watched as thoughts raced through the journalist's head, as if she were now forced to sort through surfacing questions and choose what to say first.

"Doesn't that cast the whole case in a new light?" she asked. "I mean, violence against his partner. What he has done surely turns him into a prime suspect?"

She was pointing out the obvious, but this was not where their focus lay. The investigation was aimed in an entirely different direction.

"You have to remember you're wading through troubled waters," he said. "The guilty party is out there somewhere. You must be aware that the job you've taken on could mean that one day you'll be standing face to face with him. I'll understand if you'd prefer to withdraw from the interview."

Line Wisting shook her head. "I don't want to do that," she answered. "I just want to know as much as possible in advance." She pushed back her chair and stood up but did not move from the spot. "Is he your suspect?" she demanded. "Is he the target of the new investigation?"

Stiller hesitated to deny this, pausing for long enough to ensure that she would harbour doubts about whether or not he was telling the truth.

"We're on our way towards something," he said. "If we're lucky, I might be able to reveal something next week, in time for the next article. But right now it's too early."

She appeared satisfied now that she had secured the promise of more information.

38

From his office window, Wisting could see Inger Lise Ness's home, a flat in a block of four in Kirkestredet, directly beside the railway line. As the crow flies, the distance was no more than six hundred metres.

He needed a pretext to speak to her. An anonymous letter was just her style, but if she really knew something, her plans probably did not include telling the police about it. He would have to feel his way forward and so needed an excuse. And he had found one.

According to the record of offences, she had recently been found guilty of criminal deception. After being unemployed for a lengthy period, she had obtained work in a shop but had declared fewer working hours in her notification to NAV, the employment office, than was the case. Over a six-month period she had been paid almost one hundred thousand kroner more in unemployment benefits than she was entitled to. The punishment was ninety days' imprisonment, and she was now on the waiting list to serve her sentence.

He picked up the phone, dialled the number for Kriminalomsorgen, the Criminal Justice Social Work Service, and got through to a caseworker he already knew.

"I'm looking for a favour," he said.

"What's that?"

"It's in connection with a convicted person called Inger Lise

Ness," he explained. "I'd like her to be moved up the prison waiting list."

"We should be able to manage that," the caseworker said, and the line went quiet as he tapped on his computer keyboard.

"There's a vacancy in Sandefjord in three weeks," he offered. "Would that do?"

"That's excellent," Wisting answered. "What I'd like is for you to send me the summons so that I can deliver it in person."

"It's usually sent in the post," the caseworker told him.

"Send it to my address and I'll deliver it and make sure she turns up at the specified time."

Inger Lise Ness would hardly react to a plain-clothes policeman arriving to hand over the summons in person.

"All the same to me," the caseworker replied. "She should receive an information booklet as well. If I send them today, they should be with you tomorrow."

Wisting thanked him and supplied his address.

39

The security system made no objection to letting her pass. The green light lit up and an electronic click sounded, and with no fuss she was inside.

The Krogh kidnapping was the kind of story not to be discussed anywhere other than in closed editorial meetings. It was an assignment that only a select few in the newspaper offices should know of before it went to print. However, it was also the kind of story that caused rumours to fly, and it seemed as if everyone knew about it and was desperate to know more.

Line replied politely but dismissively to the questions she was bombarded with and hurried upstairs to the room they had been allocated, where Daniel was waiting. She knew he had been working on the project for longer than she had but she was still impressed by how rapidly everything had fallen into place. Most of it was now ready for publication. All that was left to do was the final editing of the podcast and to put the finishing touches to the first article. They hoped to publish on Friday morning in the *VG* newspaper and in *VG+*, which was formatted for iPads. They could add to the online newspaper during the course of the day. The podcast would be available from two o'clock in the afternoon, which was in forty-eight hours' time. Then work would begin on the next episode.

Everything about the Krogh kidnapping would be gathered on

a single Internet page. It had been given a visually appealing look, with a collage of old documents, images and newspaper cuttings.

Line leafed through some of the printouts of police documents. "I don't know if I believe this kidnapping yarn," she said.

"What makes you doubt it?"

"Because the kidnappers simply gave up. They sent two letters and explained where the money should be left, but they never made any attempt to collect it. It seems as if they just gave up."

"Maybe they got cold feet?"

"Maybe, but it just looks a bit half-hearted."

"In what way?"

"I've looked at some other classic kidnapping cases, mostly American—the son of Frank Sinatra, Charles Lindbergh junior—but also a few in France and Germany. What repeatedly happens is that the letters from the kidnappers contain detailed instructions and warnings about not contacting the police. The ones who took Nadia used only one sentence—*Put the money in a black plastic bag behind the kiosk at Olavsberget.*"

"They had enclosed a photograph," Daniel reminded her.

Line had a copy of it in front of her, a picture of Nadia and her younger brother taken in a photo booth in which they were sitting with their heads close together to make room for the two of them. The situation had clearly caused them both to erupt with laughter. The picture had been in the purse she always carried with her in her handbag.

"It doesn't really prove anything," Line insisted.

"It was enough for the police to release her boyfriend."

"The ransom letters may have been a diversionary tactic," Line pointed out. "In order to free him."

Daniel held up his hand. "Save it!" he said. "The letters are the next episode. Now, we have to go into the studio and stitch this together."

They headed in, and Daniel sat down at the control console. Line took a seat in front of the microphone, spreading the script sheets out across the desk.

"I'm not sure what words to use when describing the evening she disappeared," she said.

Daniel glanced up. "What do you mean?"

"Should I say 'the evening she disappeared' or 'the evening she was kidnapped'? 'When she was taken' or 'when she went missing'?"

Daniel reflected on this for a moment or two. "The evening she disappeared," he decided. "After all, it's accurate and it's what seems most natural to you."

Speaking into the microphone to unknown listeners was easier than she had imagined. Despite having a script, she spoke freely and felt that her voice sounded suitably relaxed and spontaneous.

All the time she was speaking, her thoughts returned to the picture of Nadia and her little brother.

She lifted her gaze from the script and fixed it on the microphone in front of her.

"There's one question that's going to become crucial in this podcast," she heard herself say. "I haven't yet asked it of any of the people I've interviewed so far, because I didn't think it was important. The police have asked this question of Liv Hovet, among others: she was one of the last people to see Nadia on 18 September 1987. The question is, was she carrying anything? Did she have anything with her when she left? Or, to be more specific, did she take her bag with her when she stormed out of the party in Glimmerveien?

"The investigators had probably asked about that as a matter of simple routine, one of the points they had to go through, in the same way that everyone at the party was asked what kind of clothes

Nadia was wearing on the night she went missing. They received different answers about the handbag. Why that question was so important is something you'll learn in the next episode of *The Nadia Krogh Mystery*."

40

Line flopped down on the settee, exhausted. It had been a long day and she was pleased to have Thomas there. He had already put Amalie to bed when she arrived home, and had prepared food for her, a chicken sandwich with bacon and Brie.

"Did you know we're related to that TV chef?" she asked, cutting off a piece.

"Which one?" Thomas said, smirking, with his hand on the remote control. "Jamie Oliver?"

"No, the Norwegian one. Hellstrøm."

Thomas did not seem too delighted at the news.

"Not directly related," Line corrected herself. "But one of our great-great-grandmother's sisters was married to his great-grandfather's brother."

Thomas looked as if he was trying to work this out, but ended up giving a shrug before concentrating all his attention on the TV.

Line ate half the sandwich before wrapping the rest in cling film to put in the fridge.

A strip of photographs from a photo booth was suspended from the fridge door, showing three versions of Thomas and Amalie. In the first one, Amalie was smiling happily and almost looking directly at the camera lens, but by the last one she had obviously grown impatient.

"Did you take some photos?" she shouted through to the living room.

206

"Yes," Thomas replied cheerfully. "I kept the best one for myself."

Line opened the fridge and put her plate inside. "Where did you find one of those photo booths?" she asked.

"At the shopping centre," Thomas told her. "It wasn't actually a booth but a toy train that took photos as we rode on it."

Line sat down on the settee again. "Thanks," she said, glancing at her brother. "For being so good with her."

Thomas nodded in acknowledgement—he was engrossed in the TV programme again. Like their father, he was not particularly good at accepting praise.

She took out her laptop to make some amendments to her article, a few minor details her editor had suggested; they would not take long. However, instead of opening the document, she located the family-history program and searched for "Stiller."

There were three results for Stiller in her own extended family, belonging to a branch emanating from a four-times-great-grandfather. His sister married an Anders Stiller in Mysen in 1862 and they had two sons, Ole and Lars. According to the source reference, the information came from digitized parish records. She decided to take a closer look when she had time.

"Isn't that the story you're working on?" Thomas asked from his chair in front of the TV.

Line looked across at the screen and caught a mention of Nadia Krogh's name and a glimpse of her face. "What was that?" she asked, even though she saw it.

"A trailer for *Crime Scene Norway*, tomorrow," Thomas clarified. "They're going to cover the Krogh kidnapping."

Line sat bolt upright and put the laptop on the coffee table. "They can't do that!" she protested.

Thomas just stared at her. Line took out her phone and keyed in Frost's number.

He answered in his usual fashion, brusque and surly.

"Weren't we to have the Krogh kidnapping story as an exclusive?" she asked.

"Yes, of course."

"TV2 are running a trailer on it right now," Line told him. "They're covering it on *Crime Scene Norway* tomorrow night."

The chief editor swore at the other end of the line. "Adrian Stiller," he said, cursing again. "He's playing both ends against the middle. That wasn't the agreement."

"What was the agreement?" Line pressed him.

The line was silent before Frost swore again. "We were to get the ransom letters," he said, "exclusive disclosure, but we didn't have an agreement about exclusive access to the story itself. I took it for granted we would get first crack at everything."

Now it was Line's turn to swear. "What do we do?" she asked. "Shall we expedite it? Print the story tomorrow? I can have the article ready in an hour."

"No," Frost said firmly. "We've got another spread planned for tomorrow. We do as planned, but we'll write a news item saying that the Krogh kidnapping case has been reopened and we're bringing out a podcast with exclusive material on Friday. We'll use the TV2 programme as a teaser for our own story. Can you have something ready for me in three quarters of an hour?"

"Okay, that'll be fine," Line assured him. "Will you talk to him?"

"With whom?"

"Stiller, so we don't get any more surprises? Or would you prefer me to do it?"

"I'll do it. The two of you have to stay friends."

They ended their conversation. Aware that Amalie had begun to whimper in the bedroom, Thomas got to his feet. "I'll see to her," he said.

With an expression of thanks, Line drew the laptop towards her.

41

Adrian Stiller had assembled the local police personnel—William Wisting, Nils Hammer and Christine Thiis—in one of the smaller conference rooms. The door was closed, and the exterior red light was lit.

Hammer, standing by the window, lowered the venetian blinds. "What's the weather forecast for tomorrow?" he enquired.

Wisting sat down. "It'll probably go on raining," he answered. "Why do you ask?"

"You're the one who's going on a fishing trip," Hammer commented.

"It's good," Christine told them. "Lightly overcast and dry all weekend. Sunny periods."

Adrian Stiller sat at one end of the table, waiting for the others to take their places. Finally, Hammer joined them.

"It all kicks off today," Stiller said. "TV2 has the Krogh kidnapping as their main feature on *Crime Scene Norway* tonight. It's being broadcast live. I'll be in the studio." He turned to face Wisting. "Can you be at home with Haugen then? I'd like to know his immediate reaction."

"That would seem a bit unusual," Wisting broke in. "And suspicious."

Stiller took out a timetable. "I've drawn up a plan for it," he explained, reading aloud: "At 20.15, you'll send him a text message to say you're working late, but wonder if you can call in on your way home to discuss the fishing trip."

Wisting nodded.

"The TV broadcast starts at 21.40. You'll have to arrive at Martin Haugen's a few minutes before that."

"What if he's not watching TV?" Hammer interjected.

Stiller had not finished speaking and continued without pausing. "The item about Nadia Krogh will be sixteen minutes into the broadcast, at 21.56. As soon as it comes up, Hammer will send you a message asking you to watch TV2." Crouching down, he took a mobile phone from his briefcase and passed it across the table. "Use this phone," he said to Hammer before fixing his gaze on Wisting. "You'll have to store the number as *Line* on your phone, so it looks as if it's your daughter who's asking you to watch it. That should be enough for him to switch the TV to the right channel."

He glanced at Hammer before concentrating on Wisting once more. "You can tell Martin Haugen your daughter is working on the Krogh kidnapping for *VG*. Tell him you remember the case and ask if he does too."

Stiller could see Wisting felt uncomfortable with the plan. He grabbed a ballpoint pen and pushed his chair away from the table, as if distancing himself from the scheme. "You'll be equipped with a hidden microphone," he went on. "A microscopic recording device you'll have with you all weekend, voice-activated and with a storage capacity of forty-eight hours. The battery time is double that, so once it's attached you won't need to give it another thought."

Wisting, obviously nervous, began to fiddle with his pen.

"Tomorrow we'll apply more pressure. When you're talking to him tonight, it's crucial you both agree to use your car. We'll put a tracker and a bug on it so we can sit and listen to what's being said. Once you're on your way, you'll have to call into a petrol station and buy a copy of *VG*. When you're halfway to the cabin, 'Line' will send you a text message with a link to the podcast, so you can listen to it in the car. It lasts thirty-four minutes, so you won't manage to hear it all before you get there. A couple of hours later, 'Line' will send you another text and ask you what you thought of it. This will give you an excuse to listen to the rest and discuss with Haugen what he made of it."

Nils Hammer was the one to break the silence. "And that'll make him confess?" he asked sceptically.

"It'll raise the Krogh kidnapping as a topic of conversation," Stiller replied. "Investigation is fifty per cent psychology. Sometimes it's not evidence we need, but to get the suspect entangled in a net he can't find his way out of."

Wisting sat mutely as Stiller handed out copies of the schedule. "There are a lot of details here," he commented. "A lot to go wrong."

"Relax," Stiller cautioned. "It's a matter of setting his thoughts in motion and making him feel vulnerable and insecure. If we make things unbearable for him, he'll be easier to crack when the time is ripe. He has to be made to understand that carrying a big, dark secret is worse than what awaits him if he confesses."

42

The computer screen in the CS room showed abnormally high activity. While they had been sitting in their meeting, seven outgoing calls had been registered to seven different telephone numbers.

Rolling his chair up to the desk, Hammer played the first one: a man, resident in Sandefjord.

Martin Haugen introduced himself.

"It's about the air pistol you have for sale on Finn," he began.

Wisting glanced at the screen showing the computer traffic.

"He's still at work," Stiller said. "He must have used a computer there."

The recorded conversation ended with an arrangement for Martin Haugen to visit the seller's home between four and six o'clock to look at the air pistol.

"What does he want with an air gun?" Stiller asked.

Hammer went into Finn.no and tried to do a search on the phone number Martin Haugen had called, but that proved unsuccessful. The name of the seller was not searchable either. Instead he searched for air pistols in Sandefjord. This produced four results: he opened each individual advert and found the name of the correct seller in the third instance. In the photograph, the weapon looked like a real gun. The text of the advertisement stated that it was a copy of a Swiss SIG and used twelve-gram CO_2 cartridges.

Wisting had his own ideas, but none of the three men in the room said anything.

Hammer played the next recording, another, similar conversation. Martin Haugen arranged to inspect another air pistol. They listened to four more recordings, all about the prospective purchase of air pistols.

"He's running scared," Hammer commented. "He doesn't have a licence to buy a real gun and doesn't know where to go to get an illegal one. He's resorting to the next best option. Something he can use to threaten and frighten someone."

On one of the screens, the red dot showing Haugen's pickup suddenly began to move on the map.

"He's out driving," Hammer said.

All three followed the marker as it progressed out on to the main road in the direction of Tønsberg.

"He's not going home," Wisting said.

"He's probably gone out to buy an air pistol," Stiller told him.

Hammer played another conversation. This one also concerned an air pistol, as did the final one. Martin Haugen made appointments with all of them to look at the pistols between four and six that evening, apart from one person who would not be home until the following day.

The red dot had stopped. Hammer checked the address but it told them nothing except that the location was in the centre of town.

"None of the gun sellers lives there," he said, consulting his notes.

Wisting looked at the clock. "It's also too early," he said.

They sat staring at the red dot for ten minutes or so, though nothing happened. In the row of cabinets behind the computer screens, electronics buzzed and hummed. The air in the small room grew increasingly hot and stuffy.

"We should have had someone follow him," Stiller groaned.

Wisting gave a loud sigh as he headed for the door. "Let me know if anything interesting happens," he said.

He went downstairs to his office, where he thought for a while, drumming his fingers on the back of his chair. Despite his misgivings, he was beginning to look forward to this fishing trip.

43

It was half past six and still raining outside. Wisting had spent the last few hours completing the consequence analysis report about the imminent reorganization, as well as eating leftovers from the fridge in the canteen. The report was not as detailed or as comprehensive as he had anticipated.

Adrian Stiller came to see him, having changed both his shirt and jacket and put on a tie. Although his eyes were still red-ringed, his enthusiasm ensured he seemed neither tired nor weary.

"I'll have to be off now," he said. "To TV2."

Wisting wished him luck.

"Are you going to wear that this evening?" he asked, pointing at Wisting's shirt.

"Why do you ask?"

Without replying, Stiller crossed to the desk and set down a little cardboard box.

"Have you worn a bug before?" he asked.

"So long ago that we used a cassette recorder and there was only just room for it in my inside pocket."

"This is the very latest," Stiller told him, opening the box, which contained three items: a tiny tube of glue, a roll of Velcro and a microscopic black chip, which Wisting understood to be the actual recorder.

"All you need to think about is turning it on," he said, showing him how the recorder switched on and off by pushing a minuscule button. "Even though it's small and innocuous-looking, it's important to attach it somewhere it'll be concealed," he added.

He picked up a pair of scissors from the pencil holder on the desk, snipped off a strip of Velcro and asked Wisting to stand up. "Textile glue," he explained as he removed the tube from the box and pressed out a few drops on the reverse of the Velcro. "Stand still," he said, fixing the Velcro to the inside of Wisting's shirt pocket.

"Velcro?" he asked doubtfully.

"NASA uses it," Stiller reassured him. "Press!"

Wisting put his hand to his chest and firmly squeezed the tiny strip.

"Martin Haugen has been to the bank," Stiller told him as they waited for the textile glue to dry. "He was at DNB in the centre of Tønsberg four hours ago and withdrew a substantial sum of money."

Wisting's thoughts turned to the red dot they had watched four hours earlier.

"I've initiated financial surveillance on him," Stiller continued. "I'll be notified if there are any irregular movements in his account."

"How much?" Wisting asked.

"Twenty-five thousand kroner," Stiller told him, gesturing to Wisting that he could now remove his hand. "That's the maximum he can take out without notice."

"Did he give any reason?"

Stiller picked the recorder out of the box. It had a fleece backing which stuck to the Velcro strip. "He claimed he was thinking of buying a car," he said, giving the recorder to Wisting.

Wisting fixed the recorder to the inside of his shirt pocket.

"You'll have to prepare the clothes you're taking with you on the trip, so that you're ready to wear it all the time," Stiller said.

"Won't there be too much interference, from clothes rubbing?"

"Minimal. Anyway, that can be filtered out."

Nils Hammer came in and closed the door behind him.

"Can you see it?" Stiller asked, giving Wisting a meaningful look.

"What?" Hammer asked.

"The microphone."

Hammer scrutinized Wisting closely but had to shake his head. Wisting tore the recorder from his shirt pocket and showed it to him.

"No cables, no LEDs," Stiller clarified.

Taking the tiny chip between his fingers, Hammer examined it before handing it back. "Martin Haugen has bought a Walther CP88 air pistol," he said, explaining how he had followed the man's movements to five addresses. "The final two appointments were cancelled by text. He had obviously found what he was looking for."

"How much did it cost?" Wisting asked.

"One thousand seven hundred, if he paid the advertised price."

He handed Wisting a printout of the advert. The air pistol, in a blue plastic case, looked like a real gun. Anyone with the muzzle pointed at him would not be able to tell the difference. The magazine took eight shots, and the gun had been sold with five hundred steel pellets. It would certainly sting to be hit by one, but for self-defence purposes it was more suitable for threatening rather than causing injury.

"I need to rush now," Adrian Stiller said as he strode towards the door. "The Krogh case will be covered in the first half. I'll leave at the commercial break and I reckon I'll be back here just before midnight. Can we meet up then for a debrief?"

Wisting was about to suggest that they could discuss whatever came up on the phone and wait until the following day for a face-to-face meeting but abandoned the idea. Instead he gave Stiller a nod of confirmation.

44

It was now ten past eight, and Wisting let himself into the CS room, where Nils Hammer sat, reading a magazine. There was no movement on any of the screens.

"Is he at home?" Wisting asked.

"His vehicle's there, at least."

"Any other signs of life?"

"He was on the Internet an hour ago, checking various online newspapers."

Wisting took out his phone and began to write a text message: *Working late today. Would it be okay for me to drop in around half past nine?*

"We'll follow Stiller's schedule," he said, sitting down to wait until 20.15.

Hammer shot a warning look at Wisting's breast pocket, where the recorder was in place, to avoid him making any unfavourable remarks about Stiller.

Three minutes later he pressed Send. Immediately afterwards, the incoming text message popped up on the main screen in front of them, with information about the time, the base station it had been sent through and other technical data, the significance of which was lost on Wisting.

Half a minute passed before the text rolled up to include Martin Haugen's response: *That suits fine.*

At the same time, Wisting's phone buzzed.

"Step one completed," Hammer said with a wry grin.

*

At 21.38 Wisting swung on to the bumpy gravel track leading to Martin Haugen's house. The headlights swept across the building before Martin Haugen's face appeared at the kitchen window, as if he had been sitting waiting for him.

Wisting looked down at the recorder in his breast pocket before stepping from the car and striding across to the entrance. He heard the lock being turned just before the door opened wide.

"Come in!" Martin welcomed him.

The cat stood between his legs, peering out.

"I just thought we could have a quick chat about tomorrow," Wisting said, closing the door behind him.

He followed Haugen into the kitchen. The sound of the TV in the living room, evidently tuned to a foreign channel, carried out to them.

"When do we plan to leave?" Wisting asked. "It would be good to get there before dark."

"Then we should leave about four," Martin said, taking two cups from the cupboard. "We probably ought to stop and do some shopping en route as well."

"Four is fine for me," Wisting told him. "I can leave work a bit early."

Martin placed the cups on the table. "Me too," he said, filling them with coffee from the machine.

"I thought we might take my car," Wisting continued. "Then we can avoid having our luggage lying in the back of your pickup."

Martin shook his head as he returned the coffee pot to the hot plate. "We have to take my pickup," he said. "The road is pretty impassable after all the rain. Yours doesn't have enough clearance."

Wisting could not argue with that.

*

Amalie was lying on her back, sleeping soundly. Her little lips were slightly dry and parted and her breathing was even and quiet.

Line could stand for ages, just looking at her. Now she closed the door carefully and returned to her seat in front of the TV in the living room.

"Turn the volume up," she said to Thomas when *Crime Scene Norway* began.

The presenter opened by welcoming viewers. She knew him; he was a competent crime journalist with an extensive network of contacts, good sources and a thorough grasp of the stories he worked on.

The evening's content was introduced. They were going to take a closer look at a new life-threatening type of synthetic narcotics, a series of snack-bar robberies, a brutal burglary in the home of an elderly woman and a group of travelling criminals who had specialized in breaking into electrical-goods shops.

"We are also going to examine one of the most controversial kidnapping cases in Norwegian crime history," he went on. "In 1987, seventeen-year-old Nadia Krogh was abducted by unknown perpetrators who demanded a ransom of three million kroner. The money was delivered to the arranged site but never collected and no one has seen Nadia since. Now it's possible that a fresh investigation and modern forensic methods will provide an answer."

Line reclined into her chair. It was a suitably dramatic introduction, but superficially executed.

"With me in the studio, as usual, I have our expert panel," the presenter continued, introducing two men and one woman who stood beside a table. Line had seen the programme several times before and was familiar with their background. A retired investigator, a former prosecutor and a defence lawyer.

The presenter carried on. "First, though, we'll follow up on last week's cases," he said, shifting across to the uniformed police officer responsible for the tip-offs that flooded in to the programme.

Line stood up and went to the kitchen for something to drink.

*

Wisting, having adjusted his message signal to the highest volume level, sipped his coffee slowly to avoid draining the cup before Hammer's text arrived.

"I checked the weather forecast," he said, mostly for the sake of having something to say. "Apparently, the weather's going to improve slightly."

"About time," Martin responded. "It's been pretty miserable lately."

The cat sat at his feet. Wisting was about to say something, but his mobile phone vibrated and buzzed in his pocket. He took it out and held it up to read the message. "Hmm," he said, contorting his face into an expression of concern to encourage Martin Haugen to ask him what was wrong.

Instead, Martin turned away politely before getting up to fetch more coffee.

"It's from Line," Wisting explained as Martin refilled the coffee cups. "*Watch TV2*, she says."

He glanced into the living room, as if to make Martin Haugen appreciate how keen he was to do as his daughter suggested.

Without a word, Martin Haugen put down the coffee pot and moved into the living room, with Wisting following behind. Martin found the remote control and tuned it to the right channel.

*

Stiller had been shown to a spot in the TV studio where he should stand. A small piece of tape on the floor marked where to place his right foot.

221

A pre-recorded feature about Nadia Krogh was played, with a map giving viewers the geographical location. A timeline spooled back to September 1987, and old press photographs and newspaper reports slid across the screen while a reporter relayed the facts.

The studio manager counted down to the end of the item before signalling to the presenter with an exaggerated hand movement.

The presenter looked straight at the camera and began to speak. "With us in the studio today we have Chief Inspector Adrian Stiller from the new section at Kripos devoted to unsolved cases." He turned to face Stiller. "So, Chief Inspector Stiller, why has the investigation into this old kidnapping case been reopened?"

Stiller met his gaze unflinchingly. "Because this is a case with potential to be solved," he replied, concentrating on keeping his voice steady. "The solution probably lies within the existing investigation material."

Pausing, he glanced across at the so-called expert panel to let his absolute certainty sink in with both them and the viewers. He had grounds for his assertion. The fingerprint belonging to Martin Haugen had been there all the time, and when they took up that part of the case the following week the experts would have to agree with him.

"How do you tackle such material?" was the presenter's follow-up question.

"Both technically and tactically," Stiller explained. "All the impounded evidence is reexamined, using new technology and up-to-date methods."

"With DNA in mind?" the presenter interrupted.

"Among other things," Stiller confirmed. "It's a matter of fresh analysis conducted with present-day technology."

The presenter held up a finger to indicate how much time was left. "What about the tactical investigation?"

"We have digitized all the written information from the original case," Stiller told him. "Now we're picking out the various incidents piece by piece and linking them together with the aid of a modern computer program in order to form a new picture of what might have taken place."

"Have you discovered anything so far?"

This was a question that had not been posed in the preparatory run-through. The presenter was improvising but Stiller did not let it faze him.

"The work has only just begun," he answered.

The presenter checked the cards in his hand. "What about fresh information?" he continued, returning to the agreed order of questions.

"That's why we're here," Stiller said. "Bringing old cases into the light of day always leads to some development. We're convinced somebody knows something." He wanted to look into the camera to address this last comment directly to Martin Haugen, who, hopefully, was watching this with Wisting, but instead contented himself with repeating those three words: "Somebody knows something. Maybe it was difficult to come forward twenty-six years ago, but now things might be different. The passage of time may have made it easier."

"In what way?"

"Someone could have been in a relationship that made them choose to stay silent, but their situation nowadays may have totally changed."

"So the time aspect doesn't have to be a drawback, then?" the presenter asked.

"Not necessarily," Stiller replied. "This also applies to the tactical investigation work. Time can also help there. Because even though a case is thoroughly investigated at the time it was current, we're now able to examine the evidence with fresh eyes and come up with new questions."

The presenter placed one question card behind the others and shifted his feet, as if to indicate an imminent change of subject.

"So, can you countenance the possibility of Nadia Krogh still being alive?" he asked.

"We're going to great lengths to look into that," Stiller said. "It's precisely why we've obtained expert assistance to create a virtual portrait of how Nadia Krogh might look today."

*

Wisting stood in the living room in front of the TV, slightly behind and to the side of Martin Haugen, who was staring silently at the screen.

"Line's writing about this case," he explained, taking a gulp of coffee from the cup he had carried with him from the kitchen. "She's been working on it for a while—it's a whole series of articles. The first one will be published tomorrow. I bet she's not very happy that TV2 have stolen a march on her."

Martin reached out his hand to grab the nearest chair back, as if he needed support.

"They're making a podcast too," Wisting added.

They continued to stand in silence, watching the programme. "Do you remember when it happened?" Wisting eventually asked.

"Yes, vaguely," Martin answered, turning to face him. "Were you involved in the case?"

Wisting shook his head. On the screen, Adrian Stiller went on talking.

Martin looked pale. Wisting tried to read his body language. His hand was still curled round the chair back, and there was an almost imperceptible quiver at the corner of his mouth.

"I'm not really a fan of these TV programmes," Wisting said, and saw that Martin was nodding in agreement.

This was not actually true. Although he did not watch the programme often, he did like it. The format gave viewers insight into how the police worked and had been shown to make a helpful contribution to solving crimes, but he was keen to demonstrate that he was on the same side as Martin Haugen. This would be important for the weekend they were about to spend together.

"It's cynical and speculative," he added, taking another slurp of coffee.

Martin Haugen released the chair back and crossed his arms. His breathing had become laboured.

"It's entertainment," Wisting continued. "I don't think that sort of thing should be made into entertainment."

As Martin Haugen turned towards him, Wisting thought he could detect something in his eyes, something tugging and twisting inside him. Then it was gone.

"So, will I pick you up at four o'clock tomorrow?" Haugen asked.

*

Line slouched forward in her chair in front of the TV, following every single word Adrian Stiller said. He was in heavy makeup, perhaps an ineffective attempt to conceal the slightly tired expression on his face.

Until now, nothing had emerged that she had not already included in her article. On the contrary, the run-through on TV was simple and superficial. *VG* readers would receive a great deal more.

"So, can you countenance the possibility of Nadia Krogh still being alive?" the presenter asked.

Stiller nodded, as if this question had been prearranged.

"We're going to great lengths to look into that," he said. "It's precisely why we've obtained expert assistance to create a virtual portrait of how Nadia Krogh might look today."

Line opened her mouth to object. Adrian Stiller had not mentioned anything about this.

The presenter turned to face the camera. "And now we can exclusively show the police's depiction of how Nadia Krogh might look today," he said, before a pencil sketch expanded to fill the entire TV screen.

Line put her face in her hands and groaned. At the same time, the screen split into two: the left half showed a youthful picture of Nadia Krogh while on the right the speculative present-day image was projected.

"Tell us how you've gone about creating this sketch," the presenter requested.

Adrian Stiller began to explain, but Line was no longer listening. In the hours ahead, prior to her own article being printed, the "then" and "now" pictures of Nadia would have spread to all the major online newspapers. The impact of her story would be completely lost.

*

Martin Haugen was on his way back to the kitchen, leaving the TV set switched on. The crime experts were now discussing their opinions of the old kidnapping case.

"Or should we try to leave a bit earlier?" Martin asked, seemingly entirely unaffected by the TV programme.

"Four o'clock is fine," Wisting said, following him from the living room.

As his phone began to ring, he picked it up and saw it said *Line* on the display. This must be something important, he thought, since it was not part of the plan for Hammer to call.

He stood in the doorway, some distance from Martin, to ensure he could not hear Nils Hammer's gruff tones.

When he answered he was taken aback to hear Line's voice. "Are you at home?" she asked.

"I'm on my way home," he replied, crossing to the kitchen worktop, where he put down his empty cup. "I've just dropped in at Martin Haugen's. Why do you ask?"

"I wondered if you'd been watching TV," she said. "About the Krogh kidnapping."

"We saw it here," Wisting confirmed. "Was it a disappointment for you?"

"I'd envisaged having exclusive rights to the Krogh story," Line answered. "That would have brought us more readers, and listeners. This has let some of the air out of the tyres, you might say."

"Don't you think it might do the opposite?" Wisting asked. "That there will be greater interest, and readers will want to find out more?"

"Maybe," Line responded. "I just think it was very devious of that Kripos guy, Stiller. He's known about this the whole time but hasn't said a word. Instead, he let us believe we'd have exclusive rights to the story. It's exactly as if he's planning something."

"What have your editors said?" Wisting asked, to avoid commenting.

"I've tried to phone Frost, but I can't get hold of him. I'll try again. Will you drop in to see me afterwards?"

"I will do," Wisting promised.

Martin Haugen had sat down again.

"It was Line," Wisting told him, returning his phone to his pocket.

"I caught that," Martin said, smiling.

Wisting remained on his feet. "She was pretty upset," he explained. "That's how it goes with journalists. They want to be first off the blocks with everything. Now she's been beaten before she's even started."

"How is she doing, apart from that?" Martin asked him.

"Reasonably well," Wisting said. "She's working freelance now. It's a tough market and increasingly badly paid."

"I haven't seen her for a long time," Martin remarked.

Wisting glanced at the kitchen drawer where he knew the thank-you card from her confirmation lay. He was on the point of suggesting Martin Haugen should call in some day so that he could meet Amalie but found he could not bring himself to say it.

"Thomas has been home this past week," he said instead. "He's been babysitting Amalie while Line's been working on this story."

He headed for the door and Martin stood up to see him out. "You must give them my regards," he said.

"I'll do that," Wisting said, though he was well aware he would do nothing of the kind.

Martin hovered in the doorway as Wisting crossed the yard to his car. "See you tomorrow, then, four o'clock sharp," he called after him.

45

The bulb was gone in the streetlamp outside Line's house. He would have to report it to the council in the morning.

Parking beside the fence, he removed the recorder from his breast pocket, switched it off and put it on the central console. He left the car and walked to the front door, which was unlocked, so he opened it without ringing the doorbell. Thomas was still here. His shoes were on the floor. Wisting flipped off his own and tapped lightly on the doorframe leading into the hallway before stepping inside.

Thomas had the remote control in his hand and Line sat with the laptop on her knee. She looked up and waved him in.

"Have you spoken to anyone?" Wisting asked.

"Yes, I have," Line answered. "There's no crisis."

Thomas rolled his eyes. "It was full-blown crisis here not so long ago," he commented.

"I just don't like to be taken for a fool," Line said. "He could have shown his hand."

"Police work's not a game of cards where you show your hand," Wisting told her as he sat down. "That probably applies to journalists too."

"Apparently, we're related to him," Thomas broke in. "Line's found some great-great character from Mysen whose name is Stiller."

"If he has any more tricks up his sleeve, I'm going to hit back," Line said.

"How can you do that?"

"I'll write that they have a suspect."

Wisting's eyes were drawn towards the TV.

"Have they?" Thomas asked, straightening up in his chair.

"He told me the first time I met him, and confirmed it when I interviewed him," Line said.

"Who is it?" Thomas demanded.

"Well, he didn't tell me that, but he said we'd be the first to know."

Onscreen, two doctors were discussing a rare illness. Wisting pretended to be engrossed in what they were saying.

Thomas turned to face him. "Do you believe they have a suspect, or did he just say it for effect?" he asked.

Wisting got to his feet. He had no wish to cover for Adrian Stiller. "If he says so, then they probably have," he replied, moving towards the door. "But I don't think you should write about it."

"Are you leaving already?" Line asked.

Thomas had also stood up. "I'm off too," he said.

"I'm not going straight home," Wisting explained. "I have to call in at work again."

"Has something happened?" Line asked inquisitively.

He gazed at her, searching for a suitable response. "If there has, then you'll be the first to know about it," he said with a grin.

*

Nils Hammer stood at the staff entrance in the police station's back yard, opening the door as Wisting parked. He waited and ushered Wisting through ahead of him.

"What do you think of Stiller?" he asked.

"He seems determined," Wisting replied. "A real go-getter."

"I spoke to a colleague who worked with him in the Emergency Squad a few years ago," Hammer said. "He said much the same thing. Determined and results-orientated, but his methods occasionally leave something to be desired."

They stood waiting for the lift. "In what way?" Wisting asked.

Hammer waited until the doors had closed behind them. "They were driving in an unmarked vehicle with a video system on the E18, measuring average speeds," Hammer explained. "One day he placed a red L plate on the rear of the police car so no one would be suspicious. You know yourself how everybody pulls out and overtakes any car with a learner driver."

"Untraditional and creative," Wisting said.

"And totally against the regulations," Hammer added. "There were a few more incidents too, where he pushed up the speed of other drivers and invited them to take part in a race. He applied to another section before an internal inquiry could be held."

The lift doors slid open, revealing the corridor in the criminal-investigation department shrouded in darkness, with only a rectangle of light spilling out from the office Stiller used. He popped his head round the door when he heard footsteps in the passageway. Wisting noticed he wasn't wearing his tie.

"Did you see the programme?" Stiller asked.

"It all went according to plan," Wisting confirmed.

"How did Haugen react?" Stiller pressed him.

"A bit difficult to make out," Wisting said. "But he did seem uncomfortable."

"In what way?"

"It stunned him, somehow. He stood still, watching, and then he pulled himself together."

"It doesn't sound as if it was *that* difficult to make out," Stiller said. "Shall we go up to the comms room?"

Wisting agreed and moved off. "But it doesn't need to mean

anything," he said. "From an objective point of view, it could simply be a natural reaction. The feature could have reminded him of when Katharina disappeared."

Stiller took out a pack of Fisherman's Friend lozenges. "You don't honestly believe that?" he said, smiling, as he held out the packet to Wisting. "Do you have the recording?"

Wisting took a lozenge, fished out the little recorder from his shirt pocket and handed it to Stiller.

Stiller offered the pack to Hammer but he shook his head and took out his snuffbox instead. "Did you get any tip-offs?" Hammer asked.

"Loads," Stiller answered. "Releasing such a drawing at peak broadcasting time opens the floodgates for a stream of tip-offs. People have seen her everywhere."

"Anything of interest?" Hammer again asked.

Stiller shook his head. "Nothing that useful."

Wisting wondered whether he should mention Line's reaction to the TV programme but dropped the idea. Although he appreciated Stiller's creativity, he did not like the way the man was manipulating his daughter.

Hammer swiped his pass, keyed in the code and held the door open for the others. The hum of computer fans and a loud electronic whine filled the cramped surveillance room. Wisting and Stiller remained on their feet while Hammer sat down and activated the screens.

"No phone conversations or text messages," he reported. "But he's been active on the Internet."

The log of Martin Haugen's Internet traffic in the past few hours filled the screen: row after row of various online addresses. It was obvious he had searched for two keywords: *Nadia Krogh*.

Clenching his fist, Stiller pummelled it triumphantly on the chair back. "Yes," he said. "Now we're making headway!"

46

The hotel room was in darkness. Adrian Stiller sat wearing earphones in front of the window, listening to the audio file of the meeting between Wisting and Haugen. A freighter was entering the fjord, its high prow turning slowly into the container harbour.

This was the second time he had listened to the conversation between the two. Occasionally, Wisting's shirt scraped against the microphone, which meant that the recording had to be filtered, but one part was clearer than all the rest. Their conversation about Wisting's daughter. Martin Haugen asked how Line was getting on. It sounded like a genuine question, not just a polite remark. Wisting told him how difficult it was to succeed as a freelance. Maybe he could make use of it somehow. Line had worked hard on the Krogh story and had been upset when it was trounced before publication. He could let Wisting play on his daughter's setback and allow sympathy to become a factor.

It was past one o'clock. He considered whether to change his clothes and go down to the hotel gym, run for an hour or so on the treadmill and then take a bath afterwards. Maybe that would help him sleep.

He stood up and glanced at his computer. He had read countless articles about sleep disturbance, but many of these contradicted one another. Some called insomnia a symptom, while others called it an illness. There was myriad advice on what to do but, as far as

Stiller could understand from the articles, researchers were not even certain what insomnia really was.

He knew he should stop playing the amateur researcher and instead seek professional help, but that was difficult. Doctors demanded answers to so many questions. Anyway, he was able to manage. He was managing fine. At least he was no longer plagued by nightmares.

He went into the bathroom, flicked on the light and blinked at the mirror. Who belonged to this face staring back at him? Who possessed those disreputable features? With a furrowed forehead, he stood dwelling on how his life had not always been this.

47

Adrian Stiller was unaware that he was lying with his eyes open until a faint bluish glow lit up his hotel room. He twisted his head round towards the bedside table. His phone had not sounded an alert, but there was a message on the screen. The bed creaked as he turned on his side and picked it up. It was a warning from the tracker on Martin Haugen's pickup: the vehicle was on the move.

Stiller swung his legs off the bed. A few taps on the keyboard took him into the program. He took several seconds to find his bearings on the little patch of map. The red dot had left Kleiverveien.

He sat following it until it moved out on to the E18, where it headed west.

Four minutes later, Stiller was seated in his own car. Martin Haugen was 14.7 kilometres ahead of him, en route to Porsgrunn. There was a possibility this might lead him to Nadia Krogh's body, but it could also be that Haugen had simply been called out in connection with his work.

He did not really believe the latter.

He checked the dashboard clock before calling Wisting. It had just turned 2 a.m.

Wisting answered at once.

"Haugen's out driving," Stiller told him, dispensing with an introduction. "He's on his way to Porsgrunn."

"Where are you?" Wisting demanded.

"I'm a few kilometres behind him."

"Do you need support?"

"It depends what he's up to."

"I'll drive to the police station," Wisting told him. "I'll read the comms info and see if there's anything to tell us his intentions."

"Great stuff," Stiller said in appreciation. "I can't keep track of him while I'm speaking on the phone."

"Okay," Wisting said at the other end. "I'll contact you when I've got something."

The call was disconnected and the map reappeared on the display. The distance between him and Haugen had decreased to 13.8 kilometres.

The motorway was almost deserted at this time of night. Encountering only the occasional lorry, he kept his speed high. The distance between him and Martin Haugen diminished, but it was unlikely he would catch up with him.

With a glance in his rear-view mirror, he changed lane and overtook an articulated truck. When he was 11.3 kilometres ahead, Haugen passed the exit road for Porsgrunn and continued driving westwards. Stiller stepped on the accelerator. The road was wet with rain, but the weather was fine and visibility good. The powerful engine on his car thrummed continuously. The onboard computer showed that he could drive 326 kilometres before his petrol tank was empty. He did not expect them to be driving much further.

He looked alternately at the dashboard clock and the figures indicating the distance between him and Martin Haugen's vehicle. If they both maintained the same speed, he would catch up with him in a little less than twelve minutes.

All of a sudden the red dot turned off the motorway. The distance declined more rapidly, probably because of the lower speed limit where Martin Haugen was now driving.

Stiller was not familiar with this neck of the woods. He picked up his mobile phone from the passenger seat beside him, dropped his speed somewhat and drove with one hand on the steering wheel as he checked the map. It looked as if Haugen was on his way to a village called Heistad. He recognized the place name as the neighbourhood where Nadia Krogh had lived.

Six minutes later Stiller took the same turn-off. The red dot had stopped at what appeared to be a residential area. The map disappeared from the display when Wisting phoned.

"There's one outgoing call," he reported. "To Hannah Krogh."

Stiller's jaw dropped, but he refrained from saying anything.

"The call was disconnected as soon as she answered," Wisting continued. "She only managed to give her name."

"She and Joachim Krogh live in Heistad, don't they?" Stiller asked.

"He looked up the phone number and address on the Internet," Wisting told him.

"He's there now."

"How far away are you?"

"Three or four minutes."

"Do you need backup?"

"It depends what he's doing. What do you think?"

There was silence at the other end.

"Maybe he has something to tell them," Stiller suggested.

"In the middle of the night?"

"That doesn't matter so much if what he has to say is important." Stiller needed the map for directions. "Get into your car," he said, "and come here!"

He broke off contact and accessed the map again. The red dot was at a standstill on the same spot. Stiller found a spur road that led into the neighbourhood. Three minutes later he parked his car three hundred metres away and turned off the ignition. According to the map, only a grove of trees separated him from Martin Hau-gen. He adjusted the level of detail on the map and saw a dotted line through the trees. A footpath.

He stepped out of the car, familiarized himself with his sur-roundings, and found his way to the well-trodden path. Darkness closed in around him as he walked between the trees but after a while he could distinguish light from the houses on the other side.

Haugen's pickup was parked with its front wheels off the road and its bonnet facing an enormous property with a paved court-yard, a wrought-iron fence and a gate. The house itself was two-storeyed, with bay windows, high gables and dark panorama windows. There was no one to be seen. No sign of life.

From where he stood, he could not see inside the pickup. He would have to go back into the woods again and try to look at it from further along the road.

When he had emerged to take up a different position, he could see someone sitting behind the wheel. Martin Haugen's face was faintly illuminated by the nearby streetlamp. He sat motionless, with his eyes trained on the Krogh family's house. It was 2.41 and he had been sitting there for nine minutes.

Stiller lingered in the darkness, waiting, though he did not quite know what he was waiting for. After five minutes he withdrew into the trees and called Wisting.

"He's sitting in his pickup outside the Krogh house," he told him.

"I see," Wisting replied, sounding preoccupied.

Stiller explained where his colleague could leave his car and how to find his way through the woods.

"I'll be there in ten minutes," Wisting said.

Stiller switched off the sound on his mobile phone and tucked it into his pocket so that he would feel the vibration if anyone rang.

Then he crept out on to the road again. Martin Haugen was still sitting in the same place. The distance between them was forty metres.

A light came on in a house further along the street. Haugen shifted position slightly; enough for Stiller to know he was awake.

Two minutes later the light was switched off and directly afterwards a rustle behind him signalled Wisting's arrival.

"He's just been sitting there," Stiller whispered, checking his watch. "Nearly half an hour has gone by."

Wisting produced a small pair of binoculars and raised them to his eyes without saying a word.

Stiller leaned against a tree trunk.

Twenty minutes passed without anything happening. Stiller looked at his watch again. "Almost an hour now," he said.

At that moment the pickup door opened and Martin Haugen climbed out. He stood beside his vehicle with his face turned to the house.

"What do we do if he goes in?" Stiller whispered.

Wisting did not answer.

Martin Haugen crossed the street and stood in the lamplight in front of the gate. Suddenly he turned on his heel and returned to his pickup, jumped inside and started the engine. Stiller and Wisting hunkered down until the vehicle had driven off.

They rushed back through the trees and returned to their cars. They stood, following Haugen's movements, until he swung on to the E18, on his way home again.

"I think he's on the brink," Stiller said, turning to face Wisting. "I think he wanted to tell them what he did with Nadia."

Wisting remained silent, but Stiller could see he was thinking along the same lines.

"I think he just needs a little push," Stiller went on. "And you're the one to give it to him."

48

"He just sat there?" Hammer asked.

Wisting pulled up a chair to the conference table and gave him an exhausted look over his coffee cup. "For almost an hour," he said.

"Then it'll probably be early to bed for you tonight," Hammer joked.

Adrian Stiller stood beside the worktop, spooning white powder from a packet into a glass of water. "Where is he now?" he asked, glancing from Hammer in the direction of the comms surveillance room.

"At work."

"We have to take his pickup, by the way," Wisting said. "The track up to the cabin is too rough. He's coming to collect me at four o'clock."

Stiller stirred the glass with a fork before downing the cloudy drink with a grimace on his face. "Okay," he said. "We'll also give you two recorders to cover Saturday. They both normally have sufficient talking time and battery life, but you must have a backup."

Christine Thiis sat listening to them. "Shouldn't we have arranged some kind of physical protection for you?" she asked, with a fleeting look at Wisting. "You're going to be entirely on your own with him."

"I have been lots of times before," Wisting commented.

"But not tasked with trying to force something out of him," Christine pointed out.

"The police helicopter's half an hour away," Stiller said. "Make sure you've got plenty of juice in your mobile phone so you can send a message if anything untoward happens." He headed to his briefcase at the door and crouched over it. "I have something for you," he said, producing a bottle of cognac. "Have a good trip."

Wisting took it from him; it was a bottle of Hennessy.

"Does Haugen drink cognac?" Christine asked.

"It's his favourite brand," Hammer said. "He has a half-empty bottle at home."

"Anyway, he's sure to want to taste this one," Stiller said. "It's a limited edition and cost nearly four thousand kroner. You'll have to make up a story about receiving it as a gift or something."

"When will you be home again?" Hammer asked.

Wisting shrugged. "We haven't made any fixed arrangement," he answered. "Around four on Sunday, I expect."

"Forty-eight hours," Stiller said. "A lot can happen in forty-eight hours."

49

Amalie was stretched out on her tummy in the playpen, captivated by a rattle. From time to time she shook it energetically, before stopping to scrutinize it carefully once again.

Line sat on the settee, reading the first instalment published on the Internet. The news desk had used the digitally manipulated image of Nadia Krogh as clickbait. Her article was unchanged, but the photo had been incorporated into an info box detailing what Nadia Krogh might look like now. The picture was credited to the police and TV2.

The entire feature on TV2 irritated her. She thought Stiller must have been behind it all, just as he had arranged for the publication of her story. TV2 could have put their oar in next week and the programme would have been helped along by the newspaper coverage. Readers would have been drawn to watch the TV input.

She found his name in her contacts list and called him. Anyway, she was keen to find out if the programme had led to any tip-offs.

The number rang out with no one answering.

She sent a text message instead, referring to *Crime Scene Norway* and asking if there had been any new developments in the case. This was what she would have to concentrate on from now on. The series of articles and the podcast would have to elicit something new and somehow lead to an answer about what had happened to Nadia Krogh.

50

The post was distributed at the police station at half past nine. Wisting went to the photocopy room and emptied his pigeonhole of the usual bundle of new documents about current criminal cases, various circulars and letters that had been returned. Within the bundle he also found a large envelope from the Criminal Justice Social Work Service. He laid everything else aside and opened it. It contained a letter for Inger Lise Ness with information about where and when she should arrive to serve her prison sentence. In addition, there was an information booklet with practical details about what she could and could not bring with her, rules about visits, phone time, academic and leisure opportunities, and various programmes available in prison.

He took the envelope and went down to his car. It looked as if the weather forecast had been correct. It had stopped raining, the wind had turned and the clouds had scattered. He could even see patches of blue sky.

Visiting Martin Haugen's former wife had been an impulse, and now it seemed a pretty crazy idea. He did not know what he hoped to achieve, and would have to play things by ear. But that was what this entire case was like, anyway: because there was little of substance, it was a matter of finding the right buttons to push.

The name was on a plate above the doorbell: Inger Lise Ness. No other name beside it.

He could not hear anything from inside when he pressed the

doorbell. He waited for a moment and tried again, but concluded that the bell was out of order and rapped his knuckles on the door.

Something was shouted from inside. Wisting was unsure whether it was *come in*, and went on waiting. Immediately afterwards Inger Lise Ness appeared at the door. She was eight years older than Martin Haugen, and the age difference now seemed even greater. Her hair had turned grey since the last time Wisting had seen her, and it looked as if all the air had gone out of her somehow. Her face was wrinkled and there were bags under her eyes.

"I'm from the police," Wisting told her.

"I know who you are," the woman replied.

"Can I come in?" he asked.

"What's it about?"

"I've got some papers for you," Wisting explained. "A prison summons."

Inger Lise Ness sighed loudly as she ushered him in. They sat in the kitchen. Wisting told her where and when to turn up and asked her to sign a tear-off strip from the summons.

"Can't I bring my knitting?" she asked, studying the information brochure.

"Not if it's not on the list," Wisting said.

"Three outdoor jackets," Inger Lise Ness read out. "Why would I need three outdoor jackets in jail?"

With a shrug, Wisting tucked the signed part of the summons into his folder.

"And a prayer mat," she went on. "I can bring a prayer mat, but I can't bring my knitting."

Wisting got to his feet, unsure of how to steer the conversation towards the real purpose of his visit. "Do you see anything of Martin Haugen these days?" he asked.

Inger Lise Ness seemed taken aback by the question, even though Martin was one of the few things they had in common.

"Why would I?" she asked, putting down the brochure. "I'm finished with all that. It was a long time ago."

"She's never been found," Wisting commented.

"That doesn't really bother me," she answered, touching a hand to her wrinkled neck.

Wisting struggled to interpret the expression on her face, but all he could make out was some sort of amazement at how the old case had suddenly become the topic of conversation.

"We're considering reopening the investigation," Wisting told her. "Going through the whole case and talking to everyone again."

Inger Lise Ness did not utter a word.

"I think someone knows something that hasn't come out yet," Wisting went on.

Once again he tried to see if what he had said might have provoked some kind of reaction in the woman facing him, but found nothing.

"Don't come to me," she warned him.

"You said at the time we didn't know what he was really like," Wisting continued.

"Who?"

"Martin Haugen. You said in an interview that we didn't know what he was really like."

Inger Lise Ness had stood up and was beginning to make for the door, as if eager to get rid of her visitor. "That could well be," she said.

Wisting followed her to the front door. "What *is* he like?" he asked. "Really?"

"I don't know," she replied. "It's just one of those things you say. It was a long time ago, and I no longer know him. Don't have any interest in him either."

Wisting tried one more throw of the dice. "But you knew him then?"

"I'm finished with him," Inger Lise Ness said. "It took a long time and cost me more than it should have, but it's all over between me and Martin Haugen."

He got no further than that and thanked her for her time, even though he still had no idea what he had actually hoped to achieve by this visit.

51

His rucksack, made of green nylon fabric, was about thirty years old and he recalled how expensive it had seemed when they had paid for it. That had been when Thomas and Line were little and they had spent Sundays on hiking trips, into the forest, up the mountain or along the coastal path. Now it was hanging in the storeroom, unused since the last time he had accompanied Martin Haugen to his cabin, five or six years ago. The sleeping bag and fishing gear had been stowed in the same place, and he ferreted them all out.

Martin Haugen's cabin was primitive, with no running water or electricity. Water had to be fetched from a stream, and food had to be heated on a cast-iron woodstove. Everything was demanding, but relaxing at the same time. You forgot all about time and gained some distance from whatever otherwise occupied your thoughts. However, this trip would be totally different and was going to demand a great deal of him.

He would mostly wear the same clothes all weekend but packed two pairs of thick socks, two pairs of underpants, a warm sweater, a pair of jogging trousers and two extra T-shirts. The only opportunity to wash would be in a bowl with warm water from a kettle.

He changed into a pair of hiking trousers and attached a knife to his belt, put on a long-sleeved singlet and chose a checked woollen shirt with two breast pockets. Before he put it on he brought out the bugging equipment and sat at the kitchen table to fasten some Velcro inside his shirt pocket. After some reflection, he attached some to the inside of each jacket sleeve as well.

Thomas came down from his room upstairs. "When are you leaving?" he asked.

"I'm getting picked up at four o'clock," Wisting said. "What about you?"

"I'm heading off on Saturday afternoon," he replied. "Line's going to interview the guy who was Nadia Krogh's boyfriend tomorrow. I'm going to take care of Amalie."

"It's been great having you at home," Wisting said. "Both for me and for Line."

Thomas made no comment on that. "She's a bit stressed out at the moment," he said. "She got another parking fine."

"The first one's lying over there," Wisting told him, indicating the kitchen shelf where he usually left his own bills.

"She's probably already paid it," Thomas said. He crossed to the shelf and took out the yellow plastic strip. "I'll take it down to her anyway," he added.

As Thomas disappeared out of the door Wisting headed for the bathroom to find his toiletry bag. Before he stuffed it into his rucksack he brought out his travel shaver and a small bottle of shampoo. Unnecessary to carry more than the essentials, he thought, and it occurred to him that he ought to take some matches. He found two boxes and slid them into the side pocket of his rucksack.

Last of all, he packed the bottle of cognac from Adrian Stiller, tucking it between his sleeping bag and his thick sweater to protect it.

He stood staring vacantly at the packed rucksack. Something had triggered a thought process, something to do with Katharina Haugen, but the specifics eluded him. Like the next line in an old song, it was almost there, but not quite. He thought through everything he had done in the course of the day in an effort to conjure up whatever had seized hold of his thoughts, leading them on to a trajectory he had been unable to see through to the end.

At last his train of thought began to make connections and it came to him. Not like a sudden revelation, more of a slow dawning; a realization of what had gone through Katharina Haugen's head in those final days before she went missing.

He took a few paces towards the bedroom to consult the old documents in the wardrobe before it struck him that they were no longer there. Instead he took out his phone and rang Nils Hammer.

"I need some help," he said, without further explanation. "Could you go into Stiller's office and locate document 04.11 from the Katharina case files, scan pages six and seven and send them to me?"

"Document 04.11?" Hammer repeated.

Wisting knew the numbers of the main documents by heart. "It's a folder of photographs," he explained, looking at the time. It was quarter to four. "I need it right away."

He then phoned the Criminal Justice Social Work Service, but received no answer. The staff must have gone home for the day. Instead he called Directory Enquiries and was transferred to the women's prison in Sandefjord.

Introducing himself, he explained he had a rather unusual question and emphasized the urgency of the matter. "An information booklet has been produced for people convicted of crime and waiting to serve their prison sentence," he said. "Do you have access to one of those?"

"It's not in front of me, but I know the booklet you mean."

"Could you take a photo of the page listing private effects allowed in the cells?"

The woman at the other end sounded bewildered but agreed to send him what he requested.

The image file from Nils Hammer came in. He did not bother looking at it but called the operator again, this time asking to be connected to Steinar Vassvik in Kleiverveien.

The phone rang for some time before Steinar Vassvik answered.

Wisting sat down and focused all his attention on sounding as calm as possible. "It's twenty-four years since Katharina disappeared," he said, grabbing a pen with his free hand. "I've been having a look at the files and gone through some of the old reports."

"I see."

"A straightforward supplementary question has cropped up," Wisting told him.

"I see," Vassvik said again.

"It says in your statement that you borrowed some books from her the day before she went missing."

"I didn't borrow them," Vassvik said. "She said I could keep them. I still have them, in fact, if there's a problem."

"It says she was carrying a bag of books, but you chose five of them," Wisting continued, quoting from memory.

"That's right."

"Why precisely five?" Wisting asked.

"That was what was allowed," Steinar Vassvik answered. "I was going into jail, and that was all I was allowed. Five books."

"Did Katharina speak to you about it?"

"What do you mean?"

Wisting glanced at the time again. It was now five to four. Martin Haugen could arrive at any moment. In order to obtain all the answers he needed, he would have to be blunt. "Did you receive a list from the prison of what you were permitted to take with you?" he asked.

"Yes."

"Did Katharina see that list?"

"I was in the middle of packing when she was here," Vassvik explained.

"Did she see the list?"

"Yes."

Wisting's phone buzzed again. "Thanks," he said. "That was all I wanted to know."

He rounded off their conversation and opened Nils Hammer's message. On page six of the folder of illustrations there was a photograph of Katharina Haugen's suitcase open on her bed. He zoomed in on part of the picture by dragging two fingers over the screen. The suitcase was meticulously packed. He recollected the description from the report. Ten pairs of socks, ten pairs of briefs, five bras, ten T-shirts, five pairs of trousers, five sweaters, five blouses and a tracksuit.

He located the picture that had arrived from the women's prison in Sandefjord. The total items of clothing on the list in the information brochure corresponded with the contents of the suitcase. True enough, the number of books was restricted to five. On the second-to-last line, moreover, Wisting spotted what finally convinced him of Katharina Haugen's purpose in packing: it was permissible to bring one personal photograph, without glass or frame.

Wisting returned to the picture in the folder of illustrations. On page seven, he saw a photo of the coffee table, where five books were stacked, and beside them lay a photograph of Katharina and Martin together with the frame in which it had been enclosed.

Katharina had packed in preparation to go into prison.

Initially, he felt confused by this breakthrough. One part of the mystery had been solved, but at the same time it unleashed a series of other questions. He knew with certainty that Katharina had not been convicted of any crime, and had to gather his thoughts to arrive at any understanding of how this all weaved together. But it did fit with the bigger picture. Her friends in the choir had said her personality had changed and she had become depressed, as if something were weighing on her mind.

Before he could bring this train of thought to a satisfactory conclusion he heard an engine revving outside his house and a car horn blaring twice.

52

Martin Haugen had opened the tailgate of his pickup to let Wisting push his rucksack under the tarpaulin, along with his fishing gear.

"Wait a minute," Wisting said, as he hurried back to the front door and rushed inside.

He had attached the recorder to the inside of his right jacket sleeve, in the same way that officers in the security service hid the microphones linked to their comms equipment. He simply wanted to satisfy himself it was in position before settling inside the vehicle. The little switch showed a green spot, and the spare recorder was safely tucked in his inside pocket.

He dashed out again, this time locking the door behind him. "I just had to check I'd switched off the coffee machine," he said, smiling, as he clambered inside.

Martin Haugen jumped in behind the wheel. He laughed off Wisting's forgetfulness but, other than that, his face was difficult to read.

"A lot to do at work today?" Martin Haugen asked.

"No more than usual," Wisting answered. "We're about to go through another reorganization."

He explained about the merger of police districts and what it would mean for his own day-to-day work. Martin Haugen listened without showing any particular interest. As they sat in silence, Wisting felt anxiety creep through his body. He would have liked to have reported his discovery and how it shed light on Katharina's disappearance.

"Damn," he said, taking his mobile phone from his pocket. "I just need to send a message to someone at work." He located Hammer's number. "Something slipped my mind," he excused himself. "It's always a bit stressful on Friday afternoons." He held the phone in such a way that Martin could not possibly catch sight of his writing.

Sitting in the pickup with MH, he began, even though Hammer was probably ensconced in the comms surveillance room following the red dot on the onscreen map. *Check the pictures you sent me and compare them with this*, he ended, attaching the list of permissible belongings when going into prison.

Then he began another message: *I think Katharina had decided to turn herself in to the police. She was preparing to go to jail.*

He sat with the phone in his hand, waiting for a response. The asphalt on the motorway to Telemark was rough, and the vibration it created was transmitted through the springs into the seat.

"Are you going to lay new asphalt here anytime soon?" he asked.

"Next summer," Martin replied.

"That's your job, isn't it?" Wisting quizzed him. "You decide when it's time to lay new asphalt."

"I'm not really the one who decides," Martin told him, "but I report wear and tear."

"How often do you have to lay it?"

"It depends entirely on the weight bearing," Martin said. "The amount of heavy transport, studded tyres, and things like that."

Wisting glanced down at his jacket sleeve where the recorder was concealed. For an outsider listening to the recording, this would seem a trivial conversation, but he had a direction and a motive for asking.

"Does it also depend on the asphalt?" he asked, with the *VG* newspaper article of 27 August 1987 at the back of his mind, the one in the newspaper used by the kidnappers to make the ransom letter.

"That's obvious. There have been huge improvements in road surfaces as well," he replied, launching into an explanation of alloys and durability.

Wisting wondered whether he should pursue this line of discussion but decided to leave it. That was enough for the moment. He had planted something in Martin Haugen's mind that would pop up in his thoughts again on the day they confronted him with the evidence that his fingerprints had been found on the letter from the kidnappers.

His phone buzzed again: a message from Hammer. *In that case I can only think of one crime she might have committed*, he wrote. *Nadia Krogh.*

Wisting switched off the display as soon as he had read it so that it turned black. Hammer had put his own thoughts into words. In the course of the last hour he had formed a hypothesis that Katharina and Martin Haugen had worked together on the abduction of Nadia Krogh but something had gone wrong. Conscience had eaten away at Katharina and in the end got the better of her. She had decided to give herself up to the police and was ready to go to prison for what she had done. However, this also meant dragging Martin Haugen down with her. That was where the motive lay. The only chance of ensuring that Katharina did not expose them was to make sure she disappeared. There was only one problem with this theory. Martin Haugen had an alibi— Wisting had checked it countless times. Martin Haugen had been on a construction site eight hours away when Katharina had vanished.

"Bad news?" Haugen asked from the driver's seat.

Wisting peered down at his phone. "Nothing I can help with at the moment," he replied. He leaned forward to the windscreen and looked up. The sky above them was almost completely blue, with only a few scattered clouds. "We're lucky with the weather, at least," he said.

"It'll be too late to lay nets tonight," Martin pointed out. "But I thought we could try to spear some fish—there's a couple of fishing gaffs at the cabin."

Wisting had never tried that before but knew you had to row out in darkness to a shallow spawning ground with a powerful lamp in the bow and impale the fish that were paralysed by the light. The method was apparently so effective it was prohibited by law in order to conserve fish.

"Is that legal?" he asked.

"Are you in the fisheries police now?" Martin asked, laughing. "I just thought we could catch a couple of fish so we have something for supper. It would be fun to try. I haven't done it since I was a young lad."

Wisting joined in the laughter as he agreed, and Martin changed the subject by pointing out a road sign. "Katharina set that one up," he said.

Wisting glimpsed it just before they passed by. It read *Porsgrund*, with directions to take the next exit road to the right.

"It's still there," Martin Haugen said with a smile. "I laugh every time I see it. Katharina wasn't so good at spelling. There was a Swede working in the signs workshop and he didn't notice the mistake either. When it was discovered, they both protested and insisted it should be like that. All the sanitary-ware in the toilets had *Porsgrunds Porselænsfabrik* on them, after all. The sign stayed put. Now it's been there for more than twenty-five years."

Wisting had driven this stretch of road many times. He had noticed the spelling error but hadn't given it much thought. Porsgrund was the old way of writing the name.

Martin Haugen followed the sign's directions and turned off from the E18. "Shall we do some shopping over there?" he asked, pointing at a Meny supermarket.

Wisting nodded. "What do we need?" he asked.

"Eggs and bacon, at the very least," Martin replied.

53

Stiller watched as the red dot on the map moved into a retail park and drew to a halt.

"Stocking up on provisions," Hammer told him.

Stiller turned back to the screen of his own laptop, which was perched on his knee. "I've received the traffic data from his phone," he said, "for the past ninety days. There's nothing out of the ordinary to notice about who he's been speaking to—he uses it mostly in connection with his work—but it does tell us where he was last week."

"Where was that?"

"In Malvik," Stiller clarified. "He has three unanswered calls in that period. All three from Wisting, and all three bounced off a base station in Malvik."

"The weather forecast," Hammer commented. "He checked the weather forecast for Malvik a number of times. The rain had caused flooding up there, and parts of the E6 collapsed. Maybe he wanted to go up and take a look. After all, he was one of the ones in charge when the road was built."

Stiller had come to the same conclusion. "But why lie about it?" he wondered. "He must have had a reason for going up there."

"Are there no phone conversations that can be linked to his trip? No appointments or anything like that?"

"He sends a text message to a work colleague when he passes

Lillehammer just after eight o'clock in the morning of 10 October, and after that it's only Wisting trying to get in touch with him."

"Lillehammer at eight o'clock?" Hammer reiterated. "He must have left home in the middle of the night, then."

Stiller passed no comment. Instead, he scrolled up and down the list of calls on Haugen's mobile phone, as if it might contain something revealing. Lack of sleep had made him lose focus and he had difficulty collecting his thoughts. Excusing himself, he got to his feet and walked to the door. "I'll be back in a minute."

He descended the stairs to the office he was using and took out a packet of caffeine powder, something he had got hold of when he was living in South Africa. It was not sold in Norway, but he had brought some back with him the last time he had visited his father.

He carried the empty glass on his desk through to the toilet and filled it with water, then tore open the packet to pour the powder straight into his mouth before washing it down with cold water.

He did not consume the powder to stay awake—he would do that anyway—but lack of sleep affected his concentration. He stood waiting for the stimulant to take effect, aware it would happen gradually.

His phone rang, and he saw that Malm was calling. He was probably in his office in Oslo, keen for an update on the situation prior to going home for the weekend. Stiller drained the glass before answering.

"How are things?" Malm asked. This was how he began almost every phone conversation.

"Going according to plan," Stiller replied. "They're on their way to the cabin, but we don't have any surveillance on them and probably won't hear how things have worked out before Sunday."

"Should we have bugged the cabin?" Malm asked.

Stiller began to climb the stairs to the third floor. "It was a judgement call. The plan was to have one in Wisting's car, if nowhere else, but it wasn't suitable for driving on the forest track. He does have a recording device to make sure we secure any evidence."

He knocked on the door of the CS room for Hammer to open up from the inside.

"And the last risk assessment?" Malm asked.

"It's still estimated to be low," Stiller assured him.

Hammer opened the door. The red dot on the screen was still in the same place.

"Have a good weekend, then," Malm said, ending the conversation.

Stiller sat down, now aware of the caffeine flooding his bloodstream. He closed his eyes for a second to compose himself. "Can you check criminal records for Emil Slettaker?" he asked when he opened them again.

Hammer turned towards him. "Who's that?"

"The guy Haugen bought the air pistol from."

Nils Hammer nodded as if he remembered the name and put his hands on the keyboard. He searched for an address in the Population Register to find the date of birth and ID number for the correct Emil Slettaker before copying and pasting the eleven digits into criminal records and pressing Enter.

"There are a few things here," he said. "But only minor offences."

Stiller craned his neck forward to the screen, where he saw several traffic violations, a few minor drugs infringements, a couple of cases of common assault and two breaches of the gun laws.

He did not like what he saw.

"What about the first guy Haugen called about the air pistol?" he asked.

Hammer returned to the log and located the name and phone number of all the people Haugen had contacted in his pursuit of an air pistol.

"Gunnar Fischer," he said aloud before looking Fischer up. "The only thing I can find is that he reported a break-in two years ago. Looks like it had to do with Sandefjord Paintball Club. He's listed as the chairman there."

Stiller screwed up his eyes and blinked once or twice at the screen. "Okay," he said. "Find Emil Slettaker's phone number in his advert."

Hammer passed it to him.

As Stiller dialled the number, he switched the phone to loud-speaker. They sat listening to the ringtone.

"Emil Slettaker," they finally heard from the other end.

"Stein Arnesen here," Stiller bluffed, glancing at the screen. "I'm phoning about the Walther air pistol you have advertised online. Is it still for sale?"

"Yes."

He and Hammer exchanged looks.

"I can give you a thousand for it," Stiller offered.

"Fifteen hundred," the other man said, in an effort to meet him halfway.

"Sorry, I've the option of another one," Stiller said, disconnecting the call before the other man had time to lower his price any further.

Hammer stared thoughtfully at him. "I thought Haugen had bought that pistol," he said.

Stiller made no response. "Let me see the advert from the guy at the Paintball Club," he said. "Gunnar Fischer."

Hammer did as requested and Stiller dialled the number. When the man answered immediately, Stiller assumed an authoritative voice.

"Am I speaking to Gunnar Fischer of the Sandefjord Paintball Club?" he asked. The other man confirmed this, and Stiller gave his name.

"I'm calling from the special section at Kripos," he said, well aware that this sounded extremely formal.

"We're investigating the man who visited you yesterday around five o'clock to purchase an air pistol you have advertised on Finn."

A brief pause ensued before the man at the other end verified this. "That's possible," he answered.

Stiller remained silent in an effort to coerce information from him.

"He was here yesterday afternoon," Fischer continued. "I don't know his name, but I have his number stored on my phone."

"Can you tell me about your meeting?" Stiller asked.

"He actually wasn't interested in the air pistol," Fischer explained. "When he turned up here, he wondered if I had any other guns. Real guns. He probably thought I was interested in weapons, since I have a few adverts online, but I told him in no uncertain terms that this was far from the case. I don't have any guns of that nature either."

"Fine," Stiller said, about to hang up.

"What do I do now?" Fischer asked.

"Nothing," Stiller replied. "We'll send someone to you after the weekend to take a formal statement from you, but it's important you don't contact this man. Don't think of phoning him or anything."

"Of course not," the man at the other end assured him before the conversation finished.

Stiller put down the phone and turned to face Hammer. "Get hold of the police lawyer," he said. "We need a search-and-arrest warrant for Emil Slettaker. We need to find out what sort of gun Martin Haugen has armed himself with."

54

The shopping trolley soon filled up—bread, sausages and baked beans as well as eggs and bacon and a couple of large steaks in case they didn't catch any fish. Peanuts and two six-packs of beer. When they reached the checkout, they had loaded so much that Wisting was unsure whether there would be enough space in their rucksacks.

The newspaper rack had no copies of *VG* left. Wisting peered across at the neighbouring checkout, but it was empty too, and the same also applied to the other checkouts.

"Have you sold out of *VG*?" he asked.

"We have been for a while," the young girl behind the conveyor belt told him. "Plastic bags?"

"I'll pay," Martin Haugen offered, taking out his wallet. "Then we can square things up later."

Thanking him, Wisting put the shopping into plastic bags and carried them out to the pickup. "Could you drive over to the petrol station?" he asked, pointing across the street. "I must try to get a copy of *VG*. Line's writing about Nadia Krogh today."

The display racks outside the petrol station were also empty. Martin Haugen parked between the pumps as Wisting headed inside to discover the same was true of the indoor racks.

"It's not so strange, really," he said as he returned to his seat in the pickup. "After all, she lived around here." He pulled on his seatbelt. "Do you remember it?" he asked. "You worked here at the time, didn't you?"

Martin Haugen swivelled round, glanced out of the side window and let a moped pass before manoeuvring the vehicle out from the station.

"Everyone was talking about it," he replied. "The police searched the workers' barracks and trekked along the ditches beside the new road with sniffer dogs."

"Did you live in the barracks here?" Wisting asked.

"No, Katharina and I commuted every day. She worked in the construction office and, since I'd been made foreman, I worked only dayshifts."

"Getting evenings off was the best thing about becoming a chief inspector," Wisting commented. "What about weekends? Did you have every weekend off too?"

Nadia Krogh had gone missing the night before Saturday 19 September 1987, and he doubted whether it would be possible to lay hands on work rotas from that time.

"On the whole," Martin answered. "Unless we'd fallen behind schedule."

"What did Katharina do, then, if you had to work overtime? As she must have worked office hours, surely?"

"If it was pre-planned, she took her motorbike so we could travel independently. If not, she always had something to do in the office, or else she travelled home with a friend."

Wisting nodded. After Katharina arrived in Norway, she had lived in Porsgrunn and eventually obtained a job in the planning office for the construction of the new motorway. This was where she had met Martin Haugen. He had the names of several of her friends from Porsgrunn somewhere in the investigation documents. They had been interviewed after Katharina disappeared, but it had not led to anything. What they had in common was that their contact with Katharina had gradually diminished after she moved in with Martin. Her closest friend thought the last time she had spoken to Katharina had been on the phone four months prior to her disappearance. However, now the case had taken a different turn, maybe her friends could say something about how Katharina had behaved at the time Nadia Krogh was abducted.

"Was one of them called Ellen?" Wisting asked. "I think I spoke to a couple of them in connection with the investigation."

"That could be right, yes," Martin said.

If they had used Wisting's car, Hammer and Stiller would have been able to sit in the comms surveillance room, listening to live coverage of their conversation. They would have had the same thought as Wisting and taken out the statements given by those old friends. He wondered if he should send a text message but decided against it.

"How long is it since the road was completed?" he asked instead, casting a glance out of the rear window, towards the motorway.

"It was done in stages. I finished here in 1988 and started work on the E6 up in Trøndelag."

"They said on the news that it was closed," Wisting said. "All this rain has caused the road to collapse. At least, one lane of the motorway."

Martin Haugen braked hard and turned off the road into another petrol station. "Do you want to check if they've got the newspaper here?" he asked, drawing up between the petrol pumps and the shop.

Wisting jumped out and dashed inside to find a couple of copies left. Line's story was on the front page. They had used a 1980s photo of Nadia Krogh and chosen the simple headline *Nadia Krogh Mystery*.

Picking the newspaper from the stand, he placed it on the counter and paid.

Martin Haugen was waiting with the engine running. Wisting opened the newspaper while they drove. The story ran to three pages, and there was a small photo of Line beside her name, together with a younger journalist called Daniel Leanger. The main illustration was a map showing where Nadia Krogh had disappeared and where she had lived. A picture of the house where the party had been held was inserted, as was a photograph of the classmate who lived there. On the third page, a photo of Adrian Stiller appeared. At the foot of the page a reference was made to the podcast and the next article in the series, which would deal with the letters from the kidnappers.

"Does it look good?" Martin Haugen asked, without taking his eyes off the road.

Wisting folded the newspaper. "I'll read it at the cabin tonight," he said.

They drove for a stretch in silence. Martin turned up the volume on the car radio and changed the channel until he found a song he liked. Wisting leaned back in his seat, waiting for a message from Hammer—pretending to be Line—asking him to listen to the podcast. The arrangement was that this would happen when they had driven about halfway. Wisting had consulted the map with Hammer and decided this would be approximately when they passed the bridge to Vestsiden in Porsgrunn. However, that had been five minutes ago.

They now had Volls Fjord on their left-hand side, where a flock of seagulls circled around a boat. Martin, resting his left arm on the side window, concentrated on the road ahead. They had caught up with a lorry driving at a snail's pace. The road was too narrow and twisting to overtake it, and they lagged some distance behind.

After a couple of kilometres the lorry drew into the verge. Martin grabbed the wheel with both hands and sped past.

At last the phone buzzed and Wisting took it out. He had placed a full stop at the end of Line's name so he could see at a glance when it was from Hammer.

"It's from Line," he said, turning to face Martin. "She wants me to listen to the podcast she's made. Is that okay with you?"

Martin turned down the car radio. "I don't know how these things work," he said.

"Me neither," Wisting replied.

He clicked on the link in the message and switched on the phone's loudspeaker function. Martin turned off the car radio. Following some instrumental music, Line's voice filled the compartment.

They sat listening as Martin swung off towards Kilebygda, and soon forest flanked both sides of the road.

It was odd to listen to Line's voice like this. She had a good speaking voice, bright and breezy, with a note of seriousness. She began by giving a rough outline of the story before sketching a verbal portrait of Nadia Krogh and promising listeners she would do her utmost to discover what had happened to her.

The story was well constructed and journalistically methodical, with a steeply escalating sense of drama and tension.

Martin Haugen held both hands firmly on the steering wheel. No reaction could be read on his face. After less than ten minutes he turned off from the main road and up to the barrier closing off the rutted forest track. He put the pickup in neutral and pulled on the handbrake.

"I can do it," Wisting offered.

Pausing the podcast, he took the key from Martin and leapt out.

"It's a bit tricky," Martin warned him.

Wisting fumbled with the key in the padlock but managed to prise it open and raise the barrier so that Haugen could drive through. Afterwards, he lowered it and put the padlock back in place before returning to the pickup.

The track was in dreadful condition, and gravel crunched as the vehicle was buffeted by the washboard surface beneath the tyres before crashing down into a crater. Wisting switched off his phone and let Martin Haugen negotiate his way forward. In some places he had to move to the far edge of the track to avoid bumps. Branches scraped across the bodywork, and Wisting was glad they had not taken his car.

The pickup lurched forward and hit another pothole. Martin Haugen gave it full throttle. With wheels spinning, the pickup juddered towards the ditch on Wisting's side before the tyres gripped and the vehicle righted itself.

"When my grandfather took over the place, there was no vehicle access," Martin explained. "In those days they reached it by boat. Materials were dragged in across the ice."

After a few more kilometres the track divided in two. Wisting vaguely recognized the area from the last time he had been here. Martin Haugen drove to the left, though the track seemed almost impassable. Virtually all the gravel was washed away, and the track was made up of compacted earth in which rainwater had gouged deep furrows.

"It improves at the top of the hill," Martin reassured him.

He was right. After cresting the summit the track descended again. Most of the rainwater had drained into a stream that ran parallel to the track. One kilometre later they had reached a sizeable turning place. A number of decaying logs were left from the time the track had been laid for the extraction of timber.

The space was overgrown with weeds that brushed against the undercarriage as Martin turned the pickup and reversed to park alongside a footpath.

As Wisting took his newspaper and jumped out, the dense trees surrounding them rustled in the breeze.

Martin accompanied him to the rear of the pickup and opened the tailgate. They split the food between them and quickly filled their rucksacks. In the end, the lightest foodstuffs were placed in a plastic bag that Martin offered to carry. They slung the rucksacks on their backs and set off.

55

The paperwork proceeded swiftly—it had been easy to convince Christine Thiis that Emil Slettaker might have sold an illegal weapon to Martin Haugen. She had decided to have him taken into custody and his house searched for more guns. Nils Hammer had arranged for officers to carry out these instructions.

Two patrol cars drove up in front of his house. Four men got out and strode up to the door. Adrian Stiller was sitting in a car on the opposite side of the street and watched as Emil Slettaker opened the door to them. The largest policeman handed him a sheet of paper, and the man at the door read it through while something was explained to him. He then put on his shoes and jacket before being handcuffed and led to one of the police vehicles.

Stiller headed over to them and asked them to postpone driving him away.

Inside the house, uniformed officers were already busy looking for guns. Room by room, the house was systematically searched.

The house showed signs that Emil Slettaker lived alone. The furnishings were simple but practical. In the kitchen, the cooker was switched on. Stiller peered at the oven door and spotted two large baked potatoes in tin foil inside. He flicked off the oven and turned towards the kitchen worktop, where a substantial steak lay in wait. In the living room, the TV was tuned to a sports channel.

"Change of plan," one of the police officers commented. Another emerged from a room at the end of a passageway.

"Found anything?" Stiller asked.

"An air pistol," the policeman answered, holding it up to him. It was the gun advertised on the Internet.

"Okay, keep going," Stiller said.

He went outside again to sit in the back seat of the patrol car beside Emil Slettaker. The handcuffs behind Slettaker's back made his sitting position uncomfortable. As he wriggled about, he gave Stiller a quizzical look. His initial surprise had changed to anger: he was cursing and demanding to know what was going on.

"I switched off your oven," Stiller, unruffled, told him.

The man swore again, claiming he had not done anything wrong and insisting they would not find anything in his home.

"Listen to me for a minute," Stiller said.

"Who the hell are you?" the man asked.

Stiller gave his name. "I work in a special section at Kripos," he said, knowing this sounded better than explaining that he worked in the section for unsolved cases.

Emil Slettaker clammed up.

"I don't give a shit if your steak lies in there and goes off over the weekend," he went on. "I don't give a shit if there's a football match you're going to miss tonight. I don't give a shit about you. I'm only interested in one thing and one thing only. What kind of gun did you sell to the guy who visited you from 17.34 to 17.49 yesterday?"

He had the times from the tracker on the pickup and felt this would make Slettaker believe the police knew more than was actually the case.

Stiller looked across at the house, where the policeman in the doorway was signalling they had found nothing further. "I need that information right now," he insisted. The man still kept his mouth shut.

"I don't give a shit about you," Stiller repeated. "But as soon as you've answered my question I'm going to remove those handcuffs and let you go back to your kitchen to cook that steak. But I need that information right now."

Emil Slettaker gulped. "He wanted an air pistol," he began.

Stiller moved closer. "He did not," he said through gritted teeth. "That was just an excuse to make contact with you. What did he leave with?"

Emil Slettaker gazed up at his house and back at Stiller. "A Glock 34," he replied.

"In working order?"

"Yes, a competition model with an extended barrel."

"Ammunition?"

"Yes, two rounds in the magazine. It takes seventeen cartridges."

Stiller waited.

"He also took a pack of fifty cartridges."

"What did he pay?"

"Twenty thousand kroner."

"Where's the money now?"

"In the living room, inside a DVD case."

"Excellent. We'll take that with us."

Stiller got out, skirted the car and opened the rear door. Emil Slettaker scrambled out. One of the uniformed officers approached and produced the key for the handcuffs.

"What's all this about?" Emil Slettaker demanded. "Is it something to do with terrorism, or what?"

Stiller did not answer.

"What happens now?" He continued firing questions.

"We're finished with you, but you'll hear from the local police in due course," Stiller replied.

The other man merely nodded as he looked around to see if any of his neighbours had been watching what was going on.

"I'm going to tell them you cooperated with us, and that will make your sentence a lot more lenient. What's important is that you do not in any way, shape or form try to get in touch with the man you sold the gun to." Stiller looked him straight in the eye. "Do you understand?" he asked. "It will make things much worse for you."

When Emil Slettaker agreed Stiller turned his back on him and strode across to his own car.

56

After walking for ten minutes Wisting spotted the grey roof between the trees ahead of them. The cabin was situated on a level expanse of ground. Wisting was familiar with the history of the place. It had been a croft, a sparse little farm owned by one of the major land-owning farmers in the area. Martin Haugen's predecessors had made their home there until the early years of the twentieth century. At its height, four adults and nine children had lived there. They had owned a couple of cows, as well as several goats, pigs and hens.

Martin's grandfather was the last person to be born in the forest. He had bought the property after the war and renovated the log cabin.

Two other buildings had been located there, a hay barn and a byre. Apparently, the hay barn had burned down and overgrown stones were all that was left of it. Half of the byre had collapsed during a heavy snowfall, but the other half with the outside toilet and wood store still remained.

The weather bars and bargeboards had been removed on the south side of the roof. The old ones lay on the ground and had been replaced by lighter wood.

Martin Haugen went straight to the door, unlocked it and ushered Wisting inside.

The cabin consisted of a kitchen, living room and two bedrooms with bunk beds. Wisting ducked his head beneath the low doorway and headed for the bedroom he had used last time. He put down his rucksack and heard Martin do the same in the adjacent room.

From the window in the living room he could see Langen. Evening mist had settled over the lake so he could barely make out the forest on the other side. In the middle of the old hayfield down by the waterside there was an ancient apple tree, stripped of leaves, but a few small apples were still hanging from its branches.

Martin emerged from his bedroom with two cans of beer and handed one to Wisting. "I suggest we light the stove and have something to eat first," he said, opening his can.

Wisting agreed and accompanied him out to the woodshed. The axe lay on top of the chopping block, immediately inside the door. Martin put down his can of beer, picked up the axe and began to split some logs for kindling.

Wisting remained outside. He stood back from the doorway to allow daylight in. The dense forest, looming silently around them, hemmed them in completely. When he turned to face the lake again he saw the still surface disturbed by a pair of ducks swimming side by side. Apart from the sound of axe blows in the woodshed, all was absolutely silent.

When the noise stopped he went into the woodshed and picked up an armful of firewood, carrying the logs across the yard and loading them into the box on the kitchen floor. Martin was immediately behind him, holding a load of wood in one arm and a fishing gaff in the other. It resembled a hayfork, but the prongs had barbs to prevent the speared fish from slipping off. The tips of the three prongs were shiny, as if they had been recently sharpened.

"We should launch the rowing boat as well, so it can swell a bit in the water," he said, setting aside the spear before dropping the logs into the firewood box.

Wisting hunkered down and opened the door of the stove. "Is it a while since you had the boat on the water, then?" he asked, as he threw in some wood chippings.

"Last year," Martin answered, handing him a box of matches. "You'll have to do some bailing."

Wisting lit the stove and the flames quickly caught hold. He waited until they had reached a sufficient pitch for him to throw in one or two bigger logs and then shut the door. They took their cans of beer with them down to the lake.

The rowing boat was overturned on two tree trunks and covered with a tarpaulin. Dead leaves had collected in the folds.

They tugged off the tarpaulin and stood gazing at the old rowing boat. The flat keel had been coated with tar and seemed intact. Together, they managed to tip it over. The water level was high after all the rain, and it was easy to push it out. Martin took the rope from the bow and tied it to a tree before heaving in the oars and throwing in a small red plastic bucket to be used as a scoop. Some drops of water trickled from a crack in the stern, but the timber would draw water and, in the course of a few hours, expand to block any small gaps.

Dusk had crept up on them as they worked. When they returned to the cabin they could no longer see as far as the water's edge.

Martin threw a log into the stove before placing the frying pan on top.

"Shall we just have some sausages?" he suggested, as he dropped in a knob of butter that slowly began to melt.

Wisting, happy to go along with this, lit a paraffin lamp. It shed a soft light into the room, causing the table and chairs to cast long shadows.

Slowly but surely the cramped cabin became cosy. Wisting took off his jacket and hung it over the back of a chair. He took the newspaper from the bag and sat down to read Line's article. Martin put the sausages in the pan and flipped them over as they cooked.

"What do you think happened?" Wisting asked, looking up from the newspaper.

Martin Haugen picked up his can of beer and took a swig. "What do you mean?" he said.

"To Nadia Krogh," Wisting explained. "It's an unusual case."

Fiddling with the ring on top of the can, Martin raised one corner of his mouth into a smile. "I've no idea," he replied.

Wisting held the newspaper page with the digitally manipulated picture halfway up to him. "I don't think she's still alive, at any rate," he said. "Something happened to her."

"She was kidnapped," Martin commented. He turned the sausages as they sizzled in the pan and said something about unpredictable people.

Wisting asked him to repeat what he'd said.

"It's not easy to know when you're dealing with unpredictable people," Martin said.

"You're right, in a way," Wisting agreed, folding the newspaper. "That is to say, I don't think the person or persons behind it are unpredictable, in an unstable or mentally ill sense, or that their plan was for Nadia Krogh to die."

This was bait. Not something Martin would nibble at once but something that could wait, ripening, slowly sinking into his mind, something that in the end would make it easier for him to confess what he had done.

Naturally, Wisting had devised a strategy for the fishing trip, in just the same way as he would when entering an interview room. His hypothesis was that Martin Haugen had killed Nadia Krogh and a ripple effect had led to Katharina suffering the same fate. Everything Wisting said in their conversations would be rooted in this theory, and all the answers Martin gave would be interpreted in accordance with this theory. In his head, he had a whole list of topics he intended to raise to make Martin's thoughts churn. Opening the possibility that Nadia Krogh's death had not necessarily been a deliberate act was only an early ploy.

"Very few murderers are like that," Wisting went on. "Very few I have met are cold, cynical or calculating. Hardly any of them ever imagined they would end up as killers, but that's how things turned out. And they were not insane at the moment of committing the crime. Not before, or even after."

The smoke from the frying pan combined with the reek of paraffin. Martin turned his head away from the stove and waved his hand. Wisting could see his words had made some impact. Nothing that would be picked up on the recording, but something Wisting felt provided confirmation he was moving in the right direction. Martin Haugen was already demonstrating classic signs of insecurity. He avoided eye contact, smiled at inappropriate times and moved his hands constantly.

"Usually it's people who've landed in an extreme situation, totally on the edge of what they can control and tolerate," Wisting went on. "It ends by murder being committed in the heat of the moment, in desperation, or in rage."

Martin withdrew the frying pan from the stove. "I think they're ready," he said.

"They look tasty," Wisting replied.

Martin pulled out a kitchen drawer, pushed it back again, opened another and took out a bread knife. Wisting found the loaf they had bought earlier and handed it to him. Martin put it down on the breadboard, cut two slices and laid a sausage on each of them.

"There's some mustard somewhere in here," he said, opening one of the cupboard doors.

He found some and passed it to Wisting. He could not read the date stamp in the faint light but squeezed a ribbon of mustard out anyway before folding the bread around the sausage.

They ate in silence as the wood crackled in the stove. Martin opened the door and pushed another couple of logs into the embers.

57

The figures were not good. The main article about Nadia Krogh had been on the Internet since twelve o'clock. There had been two separate references on the front page, but so far fewer than a hundred thousand had ventured to read it. The online newspaper had a daily readership of 1.5 million, which meant that fewer than ten per cent had been drawn to the story. The target was two hundred thousand—this would indicate a successful article. Hopefully, traffic would increase in the course of the evening.

It would take longer to achieve high figures for the podcast. They could only measure the readers who had listened to it via the online newspaper pages, and that was barely twelve hundred. As a starting point, this was a catastrophically low figure but she had been prepared for that. The popularity of a podcast spread like ripples on water. The potential lay in more and more people discovering it and taking an interest, and eventually subsequent programmes would attract a host of listeners.

Amalie sat in the playpen, but she was bored and had started whining for food. Line shot her a smile. "Okay, then," she said. "Let's go and eat."

Perching on the edge of her chair, she picked up her mobile phone and checked Twitter. A surprising number of tweets had been posted about Nadia Krogh, but most of these were comments on the TV2 programme and from people who had shared the picture of what she would look like today.

She laid aside her phone, took Amalie through to the kitchen and sat her in her high chair while she spread a slice of bread with liver pâté. Dividing it into four quarters, she tied a bib on Amalie before putting the plate down in front of her. Then she spread a slice for herself and ate with her.

After they had eaten, she gave Amalie a bath and put her down for a nap. She fell asleep almost at once, and Line settled on the settee with her laptop again.

The readership figures had grown by nearly ten thousand in the past hour. This was promising, but now she had to concentrate on the next article. Publishing the original letters from the kidnappers would certainly have an impact on the click statistics.

She had the letters, as well as the interviews with the policeman who had monitored the ransom money and the Grey Panther whose name had been used by the kidnappers. But she would really like something more, something new.

She had noticed two things in particular in the material she had collected. One was the explanation the Senior General gave about "Grey Panthers" referring to older people who were still fit and active. The other was what the *Porsgrunns Dagblad* journalist had mentioned about the possibility of revenge as a motive for the kidnapping. Nadia's father had just closed down the timber factory when she disappeared. Many people had been laid off, people who had worked there all their lives. Old folk.

The theory was far-fetched—she should really forget about it and instead focus her attention on Robert Gran, who had been Nadia's boyfriend. She would have to prepare for their interview tomorrow but, nonetheless, she sat browsing through the digital edition of the newspaper the kidnappers had used. She stopped at the page with the picture of Vidar Arntzen. He had pointed out that the paper had been a good three weeks out of date when the ransom letter had been contrived and she sat mulling over why someone had used that specific edition of the newspaper.

The most obvious answer was that it was a random paper that the kidnappers had plucked out of a bundle. In all likelihood, she would have asked herself the same question if it had been the copy from the day before or the day after and the kidnappers had called themselves the Red Dogs instead, or the Black Cats, for that matter.

She scanned through the pages, back and forth, but in the end she changed the image on the screen.

58

Martin Haugen pushed another two logs into the stove before grabbing the fishing gaff. "Shall we give it a go?" he asked.

Wisting lifted his jacket from the back of the chair and shrugged it on. "I'll take the light," he said, taking hold of the paraffin lamp.

Outside, it was a starry night and the moon was rising above the treetops. Now and again, water squelched beneath their boots as they trudged towards the boat. The air was cold and damp.

The bottom of the boat had taken in surprisingly little water after having been kept dry for a year or so. Wisting clambered on board and sat down on the stern thwart with the paraffin lamp by his side. He then began to bail, while Martin untied the mooring rope and pushed the boat out.

Water lapped against the hull. Martin Haugen and Wisting were now face to face. Haugen braced his feet, arched his back and rowed away from shore. In the faint glow of the paraffin lamp, he looked emaciated and old.

For a second Wisting felt he could see himself in the man sitting opposite him. He too had been worn down by the passage of time. Years had gone by while he was absorbed in his work, and he wished he had experienced more days like this. He knew the contentment it brought, taking part in the simple pleasure of fishing: the silence, the darkness and the anticipation.

"There's a spawning stream on the other side," Martin said, rowing a few strokes with one oar to turn the boat round.

The boat glided slowly forward, water dripping from the oar blades each time Martin Haugen raised them to make another stroke. From time to time he twisted round to check his direction in the darkness.

As Wisting went on bailing, his thoughts turned to the night Katharina Haugen had disappeared. They possessed very few facts, but they did provide Martin Haugen with an alibi.

When the scoop scraped the bottom of the boat, Wisting threw out the last splash of water and put it aside.

"How deep is it?" he asked, peering down into the murky depths.

"About sixty metres at the deepest point," Martin told him, "but not here in the bay. It's no more than ten or twelve metres."

They were approaching the edge of the forest on the opposite side, silhouetted against the clear, starlit sky.

Martin raised the oars and they listened intently as the boat drifted slowly onward. They could hear water trickling in a stream slightly to their left.

The oars broke the surface of the water when Martin dipped them again and adjusted his course.

"Go to the bow," he whispered, as if his voice might scare off the fish.

First picking up the paraffin lamp, Wisting slipped past Martin and crouched in the bow of the boat. They had almost reached the shore by now. The forest was particularly dense here, all the way down to the water's edge, making the darkness close in tightly around them.

The paraffin lamp had a metal shield to direct the light straight down to the water and avoid dazzling him.

"Do you see anything?" Martin asked.

Wisting turned up the wick to expand the flame and stretched out towards the water to hold the lamp just above the surface. "Just the sandy bed," he reported.

Martin rowed another stroke, steering them closer to the course of the stream. A shadow flitted past along the lake bed.

"Fish!" Wisting exclaimed.

Martin guided them even closer to land. The sandy bed rasped against the keel, but the current from the stream rapidly pushed them out into deeper water again.

"We'll have to tie up," he said.

Wisting set the paraffin lamp down on a thwart before taking hold of the rope and jumping ashore as soon as Martin had manoeuvred them alongside. He moored the boat and leapt aboard again. The rowing boat drifted a couple of metres from land until the rope tightened when it came to rest.

Martin drew in the oars, picked up the fishing gaff and got to his feet. As the boat rocked, Wisting grabbed the paraffin lamp to avoid it toppling.

Martin moved forward in the boat, knelt down and hung over the gunwale with the gaff raised, ready to strike. Wisting stretched out beside him with the lamp. The bed, less than half a metre below them, comprised sand and pebbles. The current from the stream agitated a number of brown aquatic plants.

At the outermost edge of the circle of light something stirred. Wisting leaned further forward but his movement frightened off the fish.

They lay quietly, side by side. Martin lowered the fishing gaff a bit further, with the three prongs poised underneath the water. When the dark body of a fish came gliding into the circle of light and then stopped, Martin struck without hesitation. The water was too turbulent to see if he had speared the fish but when he pulled back the fish was thrashing about on the gaff. Its belly was reddish-orange, while its back had a greenish glimmer.

Martin quickly tugged it off, snapped its neck and lobbed it to the bottom of the boat. "Five hundred grams," he reckoned, wiping fish blood from his hands. "We'll need another couple before we have enough for supper."

He leaned out over the gunwale again. It did not take long for another fish to appear. This time he missed. The same happened with the next one, but then he achieved success and pulled up another Arctic char almost one and a half times the size of the first one.

He pulled it off the gaff, broke the neck and threw it beside the other fish before directing the gaff at Wisting. "Would you like a go?"

Wisting took the gaff and handed Martin the paraffin lamp. For a while Wisting forgot everything else as he concentrated totally on what was happening on the lake bed.

The snout of a big Arctic char appeared, sliding slowly towards the centre of the light. Holding his breath, Wisting's grip tightened on the gaff in his hand. He thrust it forward. His hand and arm disappeared under the water until he felt the gaff hit the bottom. When he pulled it out he realized he had missed.

Martin chuckled and encouraged him to try again.

The churned-up silt from the sandy bed quickly settled again. The unsuccessful attempt had left Wisting wet to the top of his arm. Although he was dripping and disturbing the clear surface, it was not enough to frighten the fish. Fairly quickly, two small char appeared. Their blank, black eyes stared up at the light, and then they scurried off and disappeared, as if something had alarmed them.

Another fish made an appearance from the shadow cast by the boat, its slim body gleaming in the light. Curling its tail, it slithered under the gaff.

Wisting lost no time striking, and this time knew he had nailed it. He pulled up the gaff and saw the fish caught on one of the prongs. This one was bigger than the other two, and its belly was even redder.

He swung the gaff up towards Martin, who jerked the fish off, snapped its neck and threw it on to the bottom of the boat.

They continued for a while longer, hauling up another couple of Arctic char ready to spawn before they agreed to call it a day.

As Martin picked up the oars it dawned on Wisting that the arm that had been in the water was the one with the recording equipment.

Cautiously, he used his fingers to feel the inside of his jacket sleeve. The little chip was still attached to the Velcro, but he doubted whether it would still be working. Thankfully, their conversations had not contained anything that could be used against Martin. He would have to activate the other recording device as soon as he had the chance.

When the boat reached the shore Martin drew in the oars and jumped out, dragging the boat further up and mooring it before Wisting followed him.

They rinsed and washed the fish at the water's edge before heading up to the cabin. Martin got the stove going again while Wisting lit some more paraffin lamps and a couple of candles. He took one with him into his bedroom, stripped off his wet clothes and changed into some dry ones. He located the other recorder and attached it to his shirt pocket.

When he walked into the kitchen again potatoes were boiling in a pot and the fish were ready for cooking.

Martin passed him a can of beer and drank his own. Wisting sat down on a stool, his thoughts drifting back to Katharina and Nadia Krogh. There had to be a connection between these two cases. The fact that Martin could not have been directly involved in Katharina's disappearance opened up other possibilities. Katharina could have been behind the kidnapping on her own, or she could have been working with another person altogether.

He realized Martin was watching him.

"Have you ever wanted to disappear?" Martin asked. The potato water was bubbling on the wood stove.

"Not for good," Wisting replied, wondering where Martin was planning to go with this question. "Maybe when a case has reached deadlock or a reporter asks a tricky question I occasionally wish I could just hand everything over to someone else, but not otherwise. Have you?"

"Sometimes I wish I could take off and start over again, in a different place, without having to drag all my problems with me."

"Where would you go, then?" Wisting asked.

"I don't know," Martin answered. "Probably back in time and start again, without making the same mistakes."

"What mistakes have you made?"

Martin's eyes were fixed somewhere in the darkness, beyond the light shed by the paraffin lamp.

"Inger Lise was a mistake," he replied. "I should never have married her."

Wisting pulled a smile. "I can't disagree with that," he said.

"Apart from that, it's probably more the sum total of many small mistakes," Martin continued. "I'm more than halfway through my life and I haven't accomplished anything. I've nothing to look back on. No family, I haven't travelled anywhere, I haven't experienced much, and I've had the same job for more than thirty years."

"The same as me," Wisting commented.

"But you have an interesting job—your everyday life is stimulating."

The tiny kitchen fell silent. Martin took a log from the firewood box and tossed it into the stove.

"Do you think your relationship with Katharina was a mistake?" Wisting probed.

Martin took a deep breath before exhaling slowly through clenched teeth. "Marrying her was the only thing I ever did right. Things just didn't work out the way we had planned," he said.

Wisting refrained from speaking. It felt as if Martin had more to say.

"Sometimes I think she regretted being with me," he went on. "That maybe she just moved on in life, simply disappeared, the way she had disappeared from her homeland. That was what she was like. The most important thing for her was to leave the past behind. The entire time, she was putting distance between herself and her past. I can't do the same. I'm marking time. Still on hold."

For a moment the conversation was tinged with regret and despondency, and Wisting glimpsed a possibility of steering it forward to some kind of admission, or at least to let Martin understand that settling accounts was what was required in order for him to move on in life. Before Wisting had the chance to seize his opportunity Martin stood up and put the frying pan on the stove.

"What did we do with the butter?" he asked, looking around.

"It's in the bag outside," Wisting reminded him.

Martin walked to the door and brought in one of the shopping bags that had been left suspended from a hook on the outside wall to keep them cool. He dropped a generous knob into the pan. It sputtered as the butter quickly melted.

The cleaned fish were on the worktop. Martin made a few slashes in the skin on either side of them. As soon as the butter had browned, he laid them in the pan and seasoned them with salt and pepper.

"I don't think she chose to disappear," Wisting said. "I think someone is responsible for her no longer being alive."

The fish sizzled in the pan, but Martin remained silent.

"I haven't given up on the idea of finding that person," Wisting added.

Martin drank from the can of beer and used a fork to prod one of the fish in the black frying pan.

Wisting leaned forward a little on his stool. "Most likely he's someone just like you and me," he said. "I'm speaking from experience. When I started in the police I regarded these things as more black and white—I thought there were good people and evil people—but eventually I came to realize it's more complicated than that."

Martin turned the fish; the skin had turned brown and crisp.

"I've experienced enough to understand that all humans are capable of killing, if circumstances force them into it," Wisting went on. "It's about people ending up under such pressure that, in the end, it's the only way out.

"I believe all people are actually able to take another person's life, as long as there's a reason for it," he continued.

This statement ought to provoke a comment. Martin Haugen ought to protest and ask what Katharina had done wrong to make her deserve her fate. Instead of saying anything, he took out a knife and pierced one of the potatoes. "I think they're ready," he said, drawing the pot aside. "Could you go outside and pour the water out?"

"My point is that you can be a decent person even though you've done something seriously wrong," Wisting said, getting to his feet. "Everyone has occasionally done something that impacted on others. We can't pigeonhole people as nice or nasty, good or evil. It's not either/or."

He lifted a couple of pot holders and carried the steaming pan outside, walking a few paces away from the cabin wall to stand looking through the window at Martin on the inside, unsure whether his words had accomplished anything. It was really a matter of paving the way for him to confess.

Once he was back inside, the fish were lying on plates and Martin was stirring crème fraîche in the frying pan to make a sauce.

They each carried a plate into the living room and sat opposite each other at the table.

The potatoes were a bit hard and could have been cooked a fraction longer. The fish, however, was perfect.

"Tastes good," Wisting said. His phone buzzed.

"I've switched mine off," Martin said. "I think that's one of the best aspects of being here." He surveyed the room. "At home I usually sit and eat in front of the TV, but here I'm completely unplugged."

Smiling, Wisting checked his display. It was from Line with a full stop. "It's from Line," he said apologetically.

Just wanted to wish you a good trip, Hammer wrote. *The weather forecast is fine all weekend. Say hi to Martin!*

It was a code. They had prearranged that, if Hammer or Stiller had an important message for him, they would first send a text saying something about the weather, a warning that the next message would contain something it was crucial Martin did not see.

"I'll just send a short reply," he said, writing *Have a good weekend yourself* in response.

He sat cradling the phone in his hand. The new message arrived so quickly he surmised it must have been already composed: *MH has a live weapon. Illegal Glock 34 with ammunition.*

Martin extracted a fishbone from his mouth. Wisting glanced up at him then back to his phone. He had no idea how Hammer and Stiller had found this information but imagined it must have something to do with the air pistols. Anyway, it meant Martin Haugen felt under pressure and was afraid of something.

"She's wondering if I've listened to the podcast," Wisting said, deleting the message. "She wants to know what I think. Could we listen to the rest of it?"

Martin nodded, and Wisting started the playback again.

He tried to study Martin's reactions as he listened to the podcast. Not until near the end of the broadcast did he notice something that could be construed as a nervous tic. Line was speaking about Nadia Krogh's handbag, and about whether she had taken it with her when she left the party. Martin Haugen fumbled with his cutlery and his fork fell from his hand on to the floor. His chair scraped as he pushed it back to stoop down. Line was already talking about the next episode, which would deal with the letters from the kidnappers. And then the programme was over.

As Wisting switched off the recording, he noticed he had twenty-one per cent battery power left. Things had been so hectic before his departure he had forgotten to charge it. The playback on loudspeaker had used up a lot of juice.

"What do you think?" he asked.

"She's smart," Martin answered.

"I have to send another text," Wisting said. "About her podcast. Do you think she got close to Nadia Krogh?"

Martin pushed his empty plate aside. "I guess so," he replied.

"Enough to make you curious about how she disappeared?" Wisting went on.

Martin took a gulp of beer. The can was empty and he crumpled it in his hand. "It's a bit strange, really," he said. "It makes me think about Katharina." He rose from his chair and pointed at Wisting's can of beer. "Do you want another one?"

"Yes, please," Wisting said.

Martin moved through the kitchen and out on to the steps. The light from the paraffin lamp flickered in the draught when he opened the door. On his return, he threw more logs into the stove.

Wisting drained off the rest of his beer and picked up the new can Martin pushed across to him when he sat down.

"I've always wanted to be able to tell you one day what happened to Katharina," he said. "But we've not even managed to find a suspect, let alone a motive for why anyone would do her harm. But I do believe what that detective said about Nadia Krogh on TV last night. Somebody knows what took place."

Foam spurted from the hole when he cracked open the can of beer.

"A murder inquiry isn't just about searching for a killer," he added. "It's also about delving into the circumstances that might force a person to commit homicide."

He lifted the can to his mouth, leaving Martin the opportunity to say something.

"Have you thought about what it might be?" he asked when Martin stayed silent. "The reason someone took her?"

It was a bold question. Their conversation had taken on an intimacy that would have been impossible ten years before, or fifteen, but their regular meetings had drawn them closer together and opened up the possibility for Wisting to ask such questions.

"I'd rather not think about it," Martin answered. "There are so many crazies out there. People who rape and murder and dispose of bodies. You tracked down that Caveman a few years ago, didn't you? How many women did he abduct and kill?"

Wisting nodded. A sexual motive was the most likely. The Caveman had been a topic of several conversations with Martin. He was a serial killer on the run from the USA who had arrived in Norway in 1990 and so could not possibly have any connection with the Katharina case.

"Another possibility has crossed my mind," Wisting said.

"What's that?"

Wisting hesitated before going on. He was keen to steer the conversation on to the idea that Katharina had been preparing to hand herself in to the police and serve time in prison.

"Revenge," he said, planning the forward trajectory of the conversation in his head.

Silence fell between them again, as if Martin had to chew over what Wisting had said.

"Could she have done something for which someone was seeking revenge?" Wisting asked.

Martin shook his head. "What on earth could that have been?" he demanded. "I would have known about it, anyway."

"You're probably right," Wisting agreed. "But something's been bugging me, one of the things I haven't found an explanation for until now."

"What's that?"

"Her suitcase."

"What about it?"

"Bear in mind it's just a theory," Wisting told him, "but I think she might have been packing to go into prison."

No reaction was forthcoming from Martin.

"She had packed a specific number of clothes," Wisting continued. "The contents match what is allowed when you're called up to serve a prison sentence. She'd seen the list when she paid a visit to Steinar Vassvik. She knew what was permitted and what was not, and also how many different items of clothing you could take."

They sat in the light of the paraffin lamp, on either side of the table, looking each other in the eye, almost like in an interview room. If their roles had been defined, with Wisting the investigator and Martin the suspect, this would be the point at which to throw out an adversarial line and assert that Martin must have known what Katharina had done. The way they were sitting now, it was enough to let Martin understand that Wisting was only a few steps away from the truth.

"She had taken out a photograph of the two of you as well, and removed it from the frame," Wisting added. "Exactly as described in the prison brochure: one picture with no glass or frame."

Martin shook his head half-heartedly, as if he felt compelled to protest.

"It could also explain the flowers," Wisting said, referring to the fourteen red roses lying on the chest of drawers in the hallway. "She could have bought them herself to give to someone by way of apology."

"No," Martin stated firmly. "Don't you think I would have known about it, if there was anything of that nature going on?"

"But there was something," Wisting insisted. "Her friends in the choir said she was dispirited and depressed."

"Not that I noticed," Martin said dismissively. "They didn't know her like I did. We've talked about this before. She wasn't depressed. Nothing was bothering her. She was even laughing when we last talked on the phone, just as she always did."

If they had been seated in an interview room, Wisting would have pressed him harder and confronted him with the fact that everything had not been as usual. For some reason or other she had packed her suitcase, for some reason or other there was a bouquet of roses in the hallway, for some reason or other she had scribbled a code and left it in the kitchen, and for some reason or other she had disappeared without a trace.

Instead of berating Martin with inconsistencies he stood up and made for the kitchen. "I'll put on some coffee," he said.

He filled the coffee pot with water from the bucket and placed it on the stove before going outside to take a leak.

The moon lit up the landscape sufficiently for him to find his way to the edge of the forest, where he stood with his back to the cabin. The temperature had dropped a couple of notches and hot steam rose from his urine.

He turned round and walked back, but stopped a few metres from the cabin wall. The light from the windows had taken on a coppery glow, and he could see Martin Haugen inside. He was on his feet, heading towards his bedroom with a candle in his hand. Wisting moved aside to see what he was doing.

Martin set down the candle on the bedside table and hunched over his rucksack. He stood with his back to the window and, in the faint light, it was difficult to make out what he was up to. It looked like he was taking clothes from his bag in order to change. He pulled his shirt out of his trousers, then picked up the candle and left the room.

Wisting made straight for the door. The water in the coffee pot was boiling when he reentered and he spooned in coffee powder before taking the pot and two cups through to the living room.

"I brought some chocolate with me," Martin said, indicating a bag on the table.

Wisting put down the coffee pot and cups. "I brought something too," he said cheerfully, then disappeared into his bedroom.

He unwrapped the bottle of cognac from his woollen sweater and carried it through. "It's a limited edition," Wisting told Martin as he placed the bottle on the table. "Have you tasted it before?"

Martin shook his head. "It's a bit beyond my price range," he said ruefully.

"Mine too," Wisting said, twisting the cork to break the seal. "I received it as a present from a bus driver in Risør."

The cork loosened with a dull report. Wisting raised the neck of the bottle to his nose and sniffed. The strong aroma of spices tickled his nostrils.

"His daughter was one of the Caveman's victims," Wisting continued. "She had been missing for more than six years when we found her body in a well at Tanum. Her father was so grateful to know the truth about what had happened that he gave me this."

"I didn't think the police were allowed to accept gifts," Martin said.

"I couldn't really turn him down," Wisting replied. "He had lost his only daughter."

He went into the kitchen and brought back two tumblers. "These will have to do," he said, pouring half a glass each.

Martin picked up a tumbler and raised it halfway to his nose to smell it.

"Hilde, her name was," Wisting told him, replacing the cork in the bottle. "Hilde Jansen. She was only twenty."

Martin swirled his glass attentively before sniffing again.

"I promised him the very first toast would be to her," Wisting said, raising his glass to look at Martin's face distorted through it.

Martin clinked his glass against Wisting's before they both sipped the expensive drink.

Wisting wondered whether Stiller had used his own money to buy the bottle of cognac or whether it had been claimed on expenses from the Kripos budget. Irrespective of that, he was slightly surprised at himself at how easy it had been to fabricate a lie about the origins of the cognac. He had constructed the story as a parallel to that of Nadia Krogh.

Admittedly, he had been involved in recovering Hilde Jansen's body from the bottom of an old well. Her father had been extremely grateful and had brought an expensive bouquet of flowers when he had met up with Wisting. It was easier to tell a lie when there were elements of truth within it.

The coffee was ready for drinking, and Wisting poured it into their cups.

"Did it say anything about the mother?" Martin asked, peering into his cup.

Wisting put down the coffee pot. "What do you mean?" he asked.

"In Line's newspaper article," Martin explained. "Did it say anything about Nadia Krogh's mother? She must have the worst of it."

Avoiding eye contact with Martin, Wisting cast his mind back to the old newspaper interview Martin had saved, supposedly to copy her emotions. Something in it must have had an effect on him.

"No," he replied, shaking his head. "I don't think she's ever agreed to be interviewed," he added in an effort to provoke a reaction.

Martin Haugen tasted the coffee.

"Line told me Nadia's father has a gift waiting for her if she ever returns home," Wisting went on when Martin said nothing further. "Her grandmother had bought it for Nadia in Paris. It was intended as a birthday present, but then she disappeared. Her grandmother left it for Nadia to open when she came back. She died the year her grandchild would have turned twenty-seven, and the gift is still there, waiting for her."

Martin put down his cognac glass and drew the coffee cup towards him. "Is Line writing about that?" he asked.

"It's all part of the story," Wisting said.

"What's in the parcel?"

Wisting took a piece of chocolate from the bag on the table. "No one knows," he answered. "I think the parcel is a sort of symbol of the entire case. The answer is inside, well wrapped up."

Martin exchanged his coffee cup for his cognac glass. "You investigators seem so certain that solutions exist," he said, his tumbler nestling on his lap. "But what if there are no longer any answers? What if all the people who knew anything are dead, like Nadia's grandmother?"

"There's still somebody who knows, if only we dig deep enough," Wisting told him. "The shop assistant in Paris, the customer who stood behind her, a fellow passenger she chatted with on the plane, a friend she met when she came home and spoke about her trip. There's always somebody who knows."

Martin took a generous mouthful of cognac. "Can we talk about something else?" he suggested.

Wisting had no desire to change the subject. Martin was beginning to feel the pressure. There was something in the air between them—it felt like when a balloon is blown to full capacity and could burst at any moment. He was keen to continue, but that would be lacking in respect. Moreover, it was difficult to know what would happen when Martin reached breaking point.

"Of course," he said instead. "Let's talk about something pleasant."

"What will you do when you retire?" Martin asked.

Wisting drank some of his cognac. "I thought we were going to talk about something pleasant!" he joked, before taking another swig. "I'm going to work until I'm sixty. It's another five years until then. After that, I don't know. Maybe spend more time on things like this." He waved his hand expansively. "Fishing."

The conversation swung from politics to TV programmes to the weather. They worked their way down the bottle of cognac and soon it was half empty. Wisting began to feel intoxicated, and noticed the same in Martin. He was more loquacious and occasionally stumbled over his sentences.

"I need to go out for a piss," Martin said.

"I'll come too," Wisting said.

As they walked out together to the edge of the forest, silence closed in around them. A stream trickled somewhere in the distance, and a faint rustling swept through the treetops. When

Martin began to take a leak beside him, Wisting threw his head back and gazed up at the night sky. A plane flying east blinked above them.

"Have you heard of Charles Lindbergh?" Wisting asked, in an attempt to turn the conversation back to its starting point.

Martin seemed unsure.

"American pilot," Wisting explained, as he relieved himself. "He was the first man to fly solo over the Atlantic, from New York to Paris, in 1927. It took thirty-three and a half hours. A hotel owner in London had promised a reward of twenty-five thousand dollars to the first man to achieve it. That's around three hundred and fifty thousand dollars in today's money, almost three million kroner. It made him both rich and famous. He earned just as much from the books he wrote, and even more for various personal appearances."

Fastening his fly, he took a few steps towards the cabin and wiped his hands on the dew-soaked grass.

"Five years later his son was kidnapped," Wisting went on, glancing again at the plane in the sky. "He vanished from his upstairs bedroom. The kidnappers left a letter demanding a ransom of fifty thousand dollars, and a ladder propped up on the outside wall. The money was paid, but they didn't get their son back. Ten weeks later, he was found. The investigation concluded that he had died from injuries caused in a fall and that the kidnapper had probably dropped him from the top of the ladder when he climbed out of the window. Almost half of the ransom money was found in a German man's home and, though he denied having anything to do with the crime, he was convicted and executed in the electric chair."

They walked together back to the cabin.

"It was an accident," Wisting added. "If the German had just told the truth, he would probably have avoided the death penalty." He sat down at the table again. "I think something similar may have happened to Nadia Krogh," he said. "Something happened, something unplanned and irreversible."

Martin stood looking at him. Something of the tense atmosphere had returned. "You're right," he said, lifting his cognac glass. "It was probably an accident."

"What kind of accident, though?" Wisting quizzed him.

Martin drained the cognac. "I don't know," he answered, sounding unconcerned. "You're probably right, but now I think I'll hit the hay."

He put down his tumbler and headed towards the bedroom. "Good night," he said, as he closed the door behind him.

Wisting could feel it too. It was late now and, what's more, the combination of fresh air and alcohol had a certain effect on the body.

He cleared the table, found his toothbrush and went outside to brush his teeth in the stream before going to bed.

He lay stretched out on his back in an attempt to sum up the evening, but had made no progress when his mobile phone gave a loud buzz. A text message. Wisting reached for his trousers, draped over the chair, and dug out the phone. The display illuminated the room. It was from Line with a full stop.

Just wanted to say goodnight. You're so lucky with the weather. The starry sky must be really beautiful where you are.

A weather report.

Wisting switched off the sound on the phone and sent a brief text: *Gone to bed.*

The next message arrived almost instantly: *The electricity is off again. Can't find it in the house.*

It was a half-coded message but perfectly clear to Wisting. Hammer and Stiller had entered Martin's house again and the gun was not there. This meant he had brought it with him.

He deleted the message. From the other side of the wall he heard a sound. Martin had obviously not yet fallen asleep. A door opened, and he heard footsteps on the floor. The door on the woodstove creaked metallically as it was opened, and logs were placed inside. He was again aware of the sound of a ladle in the water bucket, but also another sound he could not quite identify, before the padding footsteps returned to the bedroom.

Wisting waited a while before crawling gingerly from his sleeping bag. He placed a chair in front of the door and dumped his rucksack on it to make sure he would wake if anyone entered.

59

Wisting tossed and turned in his sleeping bag and could hear Martin doing the same on the other side of the wall. The bed was hard, and narrower than what he was used to, but it was his thoughts that kept him awake. He began to feel increasingly positive about his theory that Katharina had been suffering from a guilty conscience and had been preparing to turn herself in. The basis for this theory was that she had been responsible for Nadia Krogh's death. He could get everything to fit, even the code on the kitchen table. Before she gave herself up she had written down reference points on a map that showed where Nadia Krogh's body was hidden. One or two explanatory sentences from Katharina would probably make it easy to decipher all those lines and numbers.

He was not entirely sure how all these thoughts stacked up, but suddenly the possible meaning of it all came to him in a flash.

The bed creaked as he sat up, and he pulled the chair with the rucksack towards him and fumbled for the box of matches in the side pocket. He lit the candle and took out a piece of paper and a pencil.

He had spent so many hours studying the sheet of paper with the code that he had no problem reconstructing it from memory. Once he had sketched it out, he grew utterly certain. He had found the solution.

60

The light in the hotel room was switched off. Adrian Stiller lay on his back in bed with his hands folded over his chest. He concentrated on his breathing, how the quilt rose each time he inhaled and fell when he exhaled. How the air moved in through his nostrils and out again. His thoughts drifted until he found something to focus on, a word he could repeat to himself, over and over again. On this occasion he ended up with Tugela Falls in South Africa, picturing in his mind's eye the waterfall with its nine-hundred-metre drop from Mont-Aux-Sources.

Tugela.

In the innermost recesses of his mind he pronounced the name the way the local inhabitants did, deep and resonant, almost like a mantra.

A kind of self-taught meditation, without incense, tinkling bells, flickering candles or spiritual music, it brought him some sort of inner peace and sometimes helped him to sleep.

The phone rang on his bedside table.

Stiller stretched out to grab hold of it. The time was 2.37 a.m., he noticed, and the caller was Nils Hammer.

"Were you asleep?" Hammer asked.

"Almost."

"Wisting thinks he's solved the Katharina code," Hammer continued. "He knows where Nadia Krogh is."

Stiller sat bolt upright. "Where?" he asked.

"He sent me a text message," Hammer explained without answering the question. "He believes that Katharina Haugen, though not necessarily Martin Haugen, killed Nadia. The code refers to a map showing where the body is buried. She sketched it out to make it easier to explain things when she handed herself in."

"Where?" Stiller repeated.

"Somewhere along the E18," Hammer replied. "The new motorway was being constructed when Nadia disappeared. Katharina worked in the planning office. Wisting is convinced she had drawn a stretch of the road. The number eighteen is the road number. European route eighteen."

Stiller got up and walked to the desk. He flipped open the lid of his laptop, where he had a digital copy of the Katharina code, but could already picture in his head how the number eighteen was inscribed twice, with a square drawn around it.

"What about all the other numbers?" he asked.

"They are sign numbers."

"What kind of sign numbers?"

"Every sign is allocated its own number. The number 362, for example, is the speed limit. Katharina worked on sign plans. She knew all these numbers."

Stiller now had the code on his screen, and the parallel lines looked like a stretch of road. On either side there was a circle with the number 362 inside, just as a motorway would be marked with speed-limit signs.

"What is 334?" he asked.

"No overtaking," Hammer answered.

"And 701?"

"All signs beginning with seven are directional signs."

"What are they?"

"Signs with information about place names, giving notice of exit roads and suchlike. The square yellow signs."

Stiller mulled this over as he stared at the cross at the side of the road. "How long is the stretch of road that was being built when Nadia went missing?" he asked.

"I don't know. Maybe ten kilometres."

"And somewhere along that road there's a combination of signs that will tell us where Nadia Krogh is." He glanced at the clock in the corner of his computer screen. It was now almost three. "Can we meet up at nine o'clock?" he asked.

"Nine is perfect."

They rounded off their conversation. Stiller sat for a while in front of the computer screen before standing up to pull on his trousers and the rest of his clothes. He headed down to the basement car park, and five minutes later he was sitting in his car en route west along the E18.

61

Wisting must have woken up at daylight. There were no curtains at the window, and the sun was rising above the forest. The rays hit him directly in the face.

His body was stiff and uncooperative. He wriggled about to catch hold of his mobile phone. No new messages. It was quarter to nine and there was fourteen per cent battery charge left.

He switched it off completely to save power.

The solution to the Katharina code felt just as clear as it had done during the night. Immediately before he had fallen asleep it had occurred to him that Line's parking tickets were what had been gnawing at the back of his mind. The sign she had contravened had been quoted by number. He wondered whether he should come up with a pretext to cut short the fishing trip and go home, but he had an objective to fulfil that weekend. The Katharina code had remained unsolved for twenty-four years. It could wait another two days.

He crept out of his sleeping bag and planted his feet firmly on the floor. The room was chilly and he hauled on his socks, trousers and shirt, with a sweater on top. Then he headed for the kitchen to fire up the stove before taking the bucket out to the stream for fresh water.

He heard his own footsteps on the grass, as well as the stream gurgling and the occasional chirping of birds. Apart from that, the place was silent, a type of silence quite different from a total absence of sound. The noises he heard did not disturb him. It was the human-made hubbub of civilization that was truly disturbing. This kind of stillness sharpened his wits and clarified his thoughts.

He felt twinges in his back when he crouched down to fill the bucket. Somewhere in the forest on the other side a branch snapped. He stood waiting to see if an animal would emerge, but saw nothing so turned on his heel and returned to the cabin. Smoke from the chimney was drifting slowly down to the lake.

When he entered, Martin Haugen was also up and about. "Good morning," Wisting greeted him with a smile.

Martin reciprocated in similar style. "Did you sleep well?" he asked.

"Not really," Wisting admitted. "I'm not used to that hard foam mattress."

He rinsed out the coffee pot and filled it with clean water as Martin cleared the top of the stove.

"It's going to be a lovely day," Martin said, peering out of the window. "We'll be able to lay the nets sometime this morning."

They ate breakfast and drank their coffee. Wisting put everything to do with Katharina and Nadia to the back of his mind. The night before, the momentum had been with him, in the flickering glow of the paraffin lamp. But Martin had been on his guard. He was probably well aware of the fates that had befallen Nadia and Katharina and had been living a lie for the past twenty-six years. Every encounter with Wisting must have involved uneasy play-acting, like walking through a minefield. Martin Haugen had remained single after Katharina's disappearance, and his life was focused on avoiding a misstep. It was difficult to maintain really close contact with anyone when, all the time, you had to make sure you did not give yourself away.

After breakfast they rowed out and laid two nets, one by the mouth of the stream and the other immediately ahead of the nearest promontory. When they returned ashore they filled a Thermos and brought their fishing rods down to the lake. They followed an overgrown path until they found a rocky headland, where they positioned themselves at some distance from each other.

Martin Haugen was first to cast his line. It drew an arc in the air before breaking the surface of the water.

Wisting took out a seven-gram Toby, a light, silver lure with dark patches and a touch of red. He loosened the hasp on the reel, held the line firmly with his index finger as he guided the rod diagonally behind him and cast his line. It swished through the rod rings, and the lure followed the direction of the fishing rod, soaring obliquely until it reached the zenith and curved down to the water surface, like a swooping insect.

He let it settle a little before reeling in and casting the line again.

They fished in silence. Neither of them was rewarded with as much as a nibble.

After half an hour Martin Haugen reeled in again and changed his lure. Wisting followed suit.

The sun rose higher in the sky and started to radiate heat. Flies and other insects began to stir. Suddenly the silence was broken by a fish leaping: Wisting caught the gleam of the brass-coloured belly before ripples spread through the water.

Martin reeled in quickly and flicked his silver lure in the direction of the leaping fish, but the fish refused to bite.

After another half hour without a nibble, Martin Haugen slung his fishing bag over his shoulder and grasped his rod. "I'm going to try a bit further along," he said.

Wisting gave him a nod. Martin disappeared into the forest and emerged at a point fifty metres away, on the other side of a shallow inlet dotted with rushes and water lilies.

This gave Wisting the chance he had been waiting for. He laid down his fishing rod and motioned to Martin that he would be back soon before trekking through the forest to return to the cabin.

Martin's rucksack was propped up against the wall beneath the window in his bedroom. Wisting squeezed it in an effort to identify the hard contours of a gun. However, he could not feel anything and took the rucksack into the living room to keep an eye on the field down by the lake as he went through it more systematically. Removing the clothes one by one as he placed them on the table, he quickly ascertained there was no gun inside, or anything else of interest.

He carried the rucksack back to the bedroom and returned it to its original spot. Then he rummaged through the bed and the rest of the room without finding anything. If Martin Haugen had brought a gun with him, it was either hidden in the pickup or else he had it on his person.

The door to Wisting's room was ajar. He stepped inside and switched on his mobile phone to find the battery capacity reduced to ten per cent.

He had no new messages, but made use of the opportunity while he was alone to give Hammer a call.

"I must be quick," he said when Nils Hammer answered. "I don't have much juice left. Is there any news?"

"Your theory about the road signs might well add up," Hammer told him. "Stiller thinks he's located a place to fit the code. We're going for a site inspection with the roads authority at three o'clock."

"Excellent."

"What about you?" Hammer asked. "Are you comfortable being there?"

"It's going well."

"Are you getting anything out of it?"

"Nothing apart from fish as yet," Wisting answered. "I'll check my phone every hour and a half, but at some point I'm going to run out of power."

"I'll let you know if anything new turns up at this end," Hammer said, hanging up.

The brief exchange had cost him one per cent battery charge. Wisting walked through the living room as he switched off his phone. All of a sudden he realized Martin Haugen was standing in the kitchen doorway.

"I had to phone home," he said, stuffing his mobile in his pocket as he tried to remember the conversation and whether anything revealing had been mentioned.

"Is everything okay?" Martin asked.

He could not have heard more than the very last part, which had not contained anything compromising.

"Line's been to the doctor's with Amalie," he lied. "She seems to have an upset tummy."

Martin stood motionless, as if weighing up the story. "That sort of thing's not much fun," he said. He pulled out a kitchen drawer and removed a roll of tin foil. "I caught a little brown trout after you left. If we get more, I thought we could build a bonfire and cook them in the embers."

"That's a good idea," Wisting replied, more relaxed now.

"Anyway, you can always borrow my phone," Martin offered. "If you run out of juice."

62

Line did not like to arrive late. She always erred on the side of caution when calculating her journey time. This meant she was more than half an hour early for her meeting with Nadia Krogh's ex-boyfriend.

She drove slowly past the house where he lived. It was small and rectangular, with tiny windows. At one time it may have been creamy yellow, but now it was grimy and grubby with black mould on the exterior cladding.

Two cats chased each other through the overgrown garden and disappeared round the back. It looked as if Robert Gran possibly lived by himself in the basement. At least, there were steps leading down at the gable wall of the house. A trailer piled with rubbish was parked alongside the railings, in front of a motorbike covered in a tarpaulin. In addition, a BMW with broad wheel arches stood in the driveway.

She drove on and found a patch of gravel at the end of the street where she could linger until twelve o'clock. Picking up her notepad, she revised her questions. By way of introduction she would ask him to repeat what had taken place on the night Nadia disappeared. She was also interested in hearing his theory of what might have happened to Nadia. At some point she must also confront him with the different statements he had given, causing the police to focus their suspicions on him.

She used her mobile phone to check the readership figures for yesterday's article. Almost a hundred and eighty thousand people had accessed it now. Hopefully, even more would read the story in which they published the ransom letters.

The figures for the podcast had also increased. They had now passed ten thousand, and the graphs showed a steady growth in numbers.

Often comments and tip-offs were forthcoming in the wake of major articles. The Internet page was designed in such a way that readers could send messages direct to the journalist, but so far she had not received anything of interest. She checked her email again and spotted a response to a message she had sent to an Internet forum for family-history research, asking for descendants of brothers Ole and Lars Stiller, born in Mysen in the late 1800s. A local researcher was able to tell her they were sons of Anders and Gerda Stiller, but she already had that information. Gerda's maiden name was Svensson, and she came from Røros: she was connected to Line's family. However, she had been looking for descendants and the sender had no information about those.

There would be at least four generations between Adrian Stiller and the branch of her family. It would probably be easier to work her way backwards. She had asked one of the researchers at the newspaper to try to find Stiller's closest family in the Population Register but had not heard anything. They probably guessed this was not directly linked to her newspaper work so did not regard it as a priority.

After half an hour she got her recording equipment ready, drove back and swung into the untidy yard. She sat behind the wheel reading out her introduction: "Robert Gran was Nadia Krogh's boyfriend. The suspicion that he had something to do with her disappearance spread rapidly. He was arrested but police failed to build a case against him and so he was released. He has never been willing to talk about what happened. Until now."

She left the recorder running as she opened the car door.

A dark head emerged from the exterior basement staircase at the side of the house. Although he was slightly thinner than in the photograph she had received from Adrian Stiller, Line recognized the man.

"Hi, are you Robert Gran?" she asked, all the same.

Confirming this, the man approached her. Their handshake let her know how cold his hands were.

Line thanked him for agreeing to talk to her and showed him the recorder. "Is it okay to use this?" she asked, explaining about the podcast.

"I listened to it yesterday," Robert Gran told her as he led her down the steps to the basement flat.

"What did you think?" Line asked.

Robert Gran shrugged. "I don't know," he answered. "It's kind of strange to listen to it. A bit too close to home, you might say."

Line expressed her understanding and let the recorder run. "I'm just living here temporarily," he said apologetically.

He ushered her in and said she could keep her shoes on before giving her a brief explanation that he had separated from his girl-friend a short time ago, after spending a number of years together.

"Who lives upstairs?" Line asked, even though she knew.

"My mother," Robert Gran replied. "She's away at the moment. In Spain."

The apartment was dingy and cramped, and rather nondescript. They sat down at a dining table in the kitchenette, where two glasses and a bottle of cola were already laid out.

"Would you like some?" Robert Gran asked, unscrewing the lid.

Line shook her head. "Maybe some water," she said, placing the recorder in the centre of the table.

Robert Gran took her glass to the sink and let the water run for a while before filling it. Line waited until he had sat down again before telling him more about the series of articles and saying how keen she was to hear his side of the story.

"How did you and Nadia meet?" she asked, taking out her notepad.

"We went to the same school," Robert Gran told her. "We were at the same parties and knew the same people. Even though we were very different, we shared the same interests. We hit it off."

"How long were you together?"

"Just over a year, even though it was a bit off and on for a while. Her parents made things slightly difficult."

"In what way?"

"You know who her father is," he said. "They probably thought I wasn't good enough for her or something. My father worked in his factory."

"So your parents knew one another?"

Robert Gran shook his head. "There were a lot of employees—I don't think he knew who my dad was. Or maybe he did and that was why he was sacked."

Line let her pen rest in her hand. "Your dad was fired?"

"Downsizing, they called it. He was one of the first to go."

"Have you spoken to Nadia's parents since she disappeared?" Line asked.

"No. I haven't spoken to anyone."

Line could detect an undertone of bitterness in his voice, or perhaps some kind of aggression.

"Or maybe it's that nobody has spoken to me," he corrected himself. "I've moved around a bit, lived in other towns. Now I'm back. Most people had forgotten all about it, but then you lot brought it up again."

"It's the police who have reopened the case," Line pointed out.

"I know that," Robert Gran said. "An investigator from Kripos thought it would be smart for me to be interviewed. To show I've got nothing to hide."

"Yes, we're trying to shed light on the case from various viewpoints," she said. "Can you tell me about the night it happened?"

Robert Gran filled his glass with cola and took a sip before speaking. What he said was broadly similar to the version he had recounted in court while he was remanded in custody, but by then he had already given two other versions.

"What caused the police to direct their suspicions at you?" she asked.

"Don't they always do that?" Robert Gran said. "Suspect the boyfriend?"

"Often, yes," Line replied. "But you were remanded in custody."

"They made a song and dance about something really insignificant. They thought I had lied."

"Didn't you?" Line asked, but regretted it right away. This was early in the interview, a bit too early to get under the interviewee's skin, and she saw his hackles rise.

"I'd been drinking," he answered. "Some details had slipped my mind."

Line considered asking him what he meant by "details," but decided instead that she could edit the podcast later and mention his three different statements. It was entirely possible that a fourth version of what had actually taken place also existed.

She could return to this towards the end of the interview so instead moved on to another angle. "There's one thing I'm not quite clear about," she said. "When Nadia left the party, did she take her bag with her?"

The answer came swiftly: "Yes."

Line changed position in her seat.

"Are you saying yes because she always had her bag with her, or because you specifically remember that?"

"She always had her bag with her, but I also remember it. She took her jacket from the peg and pulled it on before picking up her bag and leaving."

"What did she have in her bag?"

"Her purse, with a picture of herself and her younger brother."

Line jotted this down, mainly to gain some thinking time. Robert Gran had gone straight to the evidence that had freed him. The kidnappers had been in possession of Nadia's bag, and they had enclosed the picture of her and her brother with the second ransom letter.

"What else?" Line probed.

"The usual stuff," Robert Gran replied. "Makeup and chewing gum, keys. It wasn't very big, so there wasn't room for much."

He lifted his glass and took a drink. "He's the one who's the boss now, you know," he added.

Line had no idea what he meant.

"Malte Krogh," Robert Gran explained. "Nadia's younger brother—he's head of the business now. He was only eleven at that time." He took another swig of cola. "I was with them when the picture was taken," he went on. "He was only ten then. Nadia was looking after him, and we took him with us into town. She was so good with him, and I remember thinking she would make a good mother."

Line glanced at the recorder. This was a personal snippet of information that would enhance the story.

"It's flashing," Robert Gran said.

He was correct. A red LED was blinking at regular intervals. "I might have some batteries," he said, about to stand up.

"It has a built-in battery," Line explained with a heavy sigh. "I thought I had charged it."

She lost no time carrying on, and asked Robert Gran to tell her about how the years had been since Nadia disappeared. He spoke about missing her and the psychological damage it had caused, but this sounded rehearsed and did not really elicit much sympathy from her.

"What do you think happened to her?" she asked, while the recorder was still working.

Robert Gran replied that he had given this a great deal of thought but had not reached any conclusion. "It seemed both unintentional and yet somehow planned at the same time," he said. "I can't imagine anyone hanging about outside the house in Glimmerveien waiting for her. Kidnapping is the sort of thing that happens in big cities, and really only in films."

He stopped, seemingly to review his thoughts.

"But I think somebody took her," he said, as if to give a direct answer to her question. "Somebody local. Somebody from around here."

"Somebody she knew?" Line suggested.

Robert Gran paused, thinking over the question. He shook his head. "In that case, it would have been somebody I knew too, and I can't imagine that."

Line wanted him to explain why he thought it had been someone from the local area, but the light on the recorder cut out.

63

The house was empty when Line arrived home.

Thomas had not mentioned anything about the plans he and Amalie had for the day. She thought of phoning him to find out where they were but dropped the idea. Instead she sat down at her laptop, connected the recording device and downloaded the interview with Robert Gran. She listened to it all, comparing it with her notes and redrafting parts she would use in her article.

Around the middle of the conversation she noticed something Robert Gran said which she had not attached much significance to at the time. She got to her feet, padded through to the kitchen again and stood in front of the fridge. The strip of photographs of Amalie and Thomas was attached with a fridge magnet in the shape of a ladybird. She slipped it off and stood with the three small pictures in her hand.

The full impact of what Robert Gran had said dawned on her. She had read the police documents from the Krogh kidnapping for days on end now, but they had not mentioned anything about this.

Outside, Thomas came sauntering along the street with Amalie hoisted on his shoulders. Her neck was bare. Even though the sun was shining, there was still a distinct chill in the air.

Thomas changed his pace and began to trot like a horse. Amalie held on tight and Line could hear her laughing.

She dashed into the living room, bent over her laptop and clicked into the folder marked *Krogh case files*.

When the front door opened Amalie was still laughing uproariously.

Line opened the file with the picture of Nadia and her little brother, and it unfolded on the screen. This version had come from the crime-scene technicians, who had placed the original photo on a grey background and set a tape measure down beside it before taking the photograph. The ransom letters had been photographed in the same way.

Line had spent time studying the picture. They were going to publish it in the next article, and many of their readers would probably feel the same sense of closeness as Line did when she looked into Nadia Krogh's eyes. This time she was not so focused on the motif itself but on the white edge around it. It was apparently right-angled but when she studied it more carefully it did not seem perfectly straight.

Out in the hallway she could hear Thomas helping Amalie take off her shoes.

With the aid of the cropping tool, she placed the marker in the top-left corner and drew the mouse diagonally across to the bottom-right corner until the whole image was highlighted. This confirmed her suspicions. The lower edge was not quite straight; it deviated by about a millimetre from left to right, as if someone had cut the picture with scissors. There must be three more pictures of Nadia and her young brother.

"Mummy!" Amalie called out, toddling across the floor towards her.

Line got up to greet her daughter and swept her up for a hug. "Have you been out for a walk?"

"We've been to the playground," Thomas told her.

"Have you eaten?"

Thomas shook his head. "She's probably getting a bit hungry."

The Katharina Code

"Then let's eat," Line said, carrying her daughter through to the kitchen and seating her in her high chair.

Line's thoughts were somewhere else entirely throughout the meal. She was desperate to return to her work, and knew Amalie would have an hour's nap after she had eaten.

"When are you leaving?" she asked, glancing across at her brother.

"This afternoon," he answered. "I've got training next week."

"It's been wonderful having you here," Line said. "Both for Amalie and for me."

It looked as if Amalie had eaten her fill: she was playing with her food now rather than eating it. Line took her through to the bathroom, where she washed her and changed her nappy. She gave her her dummy and a soft comfort blanket before tucking her up in bed.

"Almost half of all kidnapping cases are fake," Thomas said when she returned to the kitchen table. He stood up and carried his plate to the dishwasher. "It was a guy from the FBI who said that in a documentary," he explained. "Victims often stage their own kidnapping, either with others or by themselves."

"I've thought about that," Line said. "But I can't make it fit Nadia Krogh's case. There are so many extraneous circumstances."

Thomas was heading for the door. "I'm just going up to Dad's house," he said.

"I need to work," Line told him. "Drop in before you leave."

She waited until the door shut behind him before sitting in front of her laptop again. She took yet another minute to study the picture of Nadia and her little brother before picking up her phone to call Robert Gran.

He answered at once.

"There was just one thing I wondered whether I'd understood correctly," Line said.

"Yes?"

"You said you'd been with Nadia and her little brother when the picture was taken."

"That's right."

"I know it was a long time ago," Line said, "but do you remember anything more about it? It looks as if it was from a photo booth."

"Yes, it was at the railway station. They went behind one of those curtains."

"Can you remember how many pictures you took?"

The line went quiet. Either he was thinking it over or else he was undecided.

"Four," he replied. "But it was really only the first one that was any good. The flash lit up once, and they thought they were finished. They were on their way out of the booth when it flashed again, so they tried to clamber back in. The last picture wasn't too bad either."

As Line's eyes moved to the recorder, she regretted not connecting it to the phone to allow her to record the conversation. "What happened to the other pictures?" she asked.

"I think Malte got them. Nadia kept one and had it in her purse."

"And that was the first one on the strip?"

"It was the best one."

"Did she cut it off?"

"What do you mean?"

"How did she separate that one picture from the others? Did she use scissors?"

"I don't know. I don't remember. I think she did it at home. I'm not sure if I was there then."

Line thanked him and rushed to end the call before it entered Robert Gran's head to ask her why she wanted to know.

If there were two pictures of Nadia and her young brother, it opened a possibility that the picture in the ransom letter was not from her purse but was the last one on the strip. This would fit with something she would raise as a problem in the next article. Why had the kidnappers chosen to send the photograph, rather than her ID card or one of the other personal belongings from her handbag? Or even her necklace?

She puffed out her cheeks and exhaled. Robert Gran's explanation had punctured her argument. Nadia Krogh had kept the first, top picture in the strip, identical to the one in the police evidence material. Right-angled at the top, it was slightly skewed along the base. There was no reason to believe it had not come from Nadia's purse. Nevertheless, the excitement she had felt was something she would describe in the next podcast.

She played through the rest of her interview with Robert Gran. It stopped abruptly when the recorder ran out of power, but she decided to use it like that and provide an explanation to the listeners. It would provide extra authenticity.

She jumped thirty seconds back and listened to the conclusion once again. She had asked Robert Gran what he thought had happened to Nadia.

"I think somebody took her," he replied. "Somebody local. Somebody from around here."

At that point the recording ended.

She repeated his words to herself and attempted to find other grounds for the perpetrator having a local connection.

Somebody from around here meant someone from the same town. From Porsgrunn. The only thing, from a purely objective viewpoint, to support this theory was that the letters from the kidnappers bore local postmarks. In addition, Krogh's address had been torn out of a local phone directory. The newspaper used to fashion the letter had national coverage but was of course sold and read locally.

She sat pondering why the kidnappers had used that particular copy of *VG* from 27 August. The only reason for saving a newspaper was that it contained something you wanted to keep—something you were interested in, or about someone you knew.

She logged in to the newspaper archive and located the edition the kidnappers had used before opening the search field and typing in one word. *Porsgrunn*.

It produced one result. On page seventeen, there was an article of local interest.

Before she clicked into it she automatically lifted her pen, as if she knew what she was about to see would be something she must not let slip through her fingers.

The article was about the new motorway under construction at that time. A new type of asphalt would produce less airborne dust and noise. The word *Porsgrunn* was highlighted twice to show the search parameters. Line put her pen to her mouth as she studied the photograph: five roadworkers in front of a road-building machine, their names listed beneath the picture. One of them produced a spark of interest. She knew the man second from the left: it was Martin Haugen.

64

Stiller had driven his car as far out on the hard shoulder as possible and flicked on his emergency light. He had located the spot overnight. Now he had returned with Nils Hammer and they were standing with the Katharina code spread out on the bonnet. The solution seemed obvious. The columns on the sheet of paper formed two motorway lanes. The line across the foot of the columns was a local road that crossed the motorway on a bridge, more than a hundred metres behind them.

"Sign 334," he said, pointing to the signs on both sides of the road prohibiting overtaking. "And 148," he went on, indicating the triangular sign warning of two-way traffic.

Further ahead were two signs specifying the speed limit, one stating that this was a major road, another highlighting a lay-by coming up, and a yellow one drawing attention to exit road number 49. Everything matched.

A lorry thundered past, fluttering the papers. Stiller turned his back and pointed to the earth bank beside the road.

"The cross marks a spot in this area," he said.

Nils Hammer had brought a road map with him. "Glimmerveien is straight up that hill," he said, raising his hand towards the trees behind where Katharina had marked a cross. "We're only a few hundred metres from the place where Nadia Krogh was last seen."

Stiller took a few paces towards the ditch and climbed the embankment on the other side. Somewhere beneath his feet, Nadia Krogh lay buried. He thought he could feel her presence.

"The motorway was under construction at that time," Hammer added.

Stiller took out a Fisherman's Friend and dropped it into his mouth. Martin Haugen had been involved in building this road. Logical connections began to materialize. He held up Katharina's sketch and compared it with the terrain. "It's a pretty imprecise blueprint, though," he said, chewing his lozenge. "We may have to dig up a fair amount of soil."

"We can try ground-penetrating radar first," Hammer suggested. "To investigate what it looks like under the slope."

Stiller shook his head.

"I don't want to wait," he said. "I want to do this now, while Martin Haugen is out of the way at the cabin, with no access to radio or TV."

"What about a cadaver dog?" Hammer asked. "That would save time."

Stiller kicked up some turf with the toe of his shoe. They no longer had any true cadaver dogs in Norway, but there were sniffer dogs trained in molecular searches for human remains.

"I'm afraid twenty-six years might be too long for that," he said. "But it's worth a try."

One of the Public Roads Directorate's yellow work vehicles drew up behind the unmarked police car. The driver switched on the warning light on the roof and came out to meet them.

Stiller greeted him with a wave of his hand. This was probably the engineer he had asked to conduct a site inspection. His face looked creased and stern, as if he found the situation disagreeable.

They exchanged brief pleasantries before the engineer's eyes scanned the road verge. "You think she's buried in there," he said thoughtfully.

Stiller had already taken him into his confidence. There was no reason not to disclose in advance what this was about or why they were here.

"We have a sketch," he said, showing the man from the roads authority the paper marked with the cross and explaining what the numbers represented.

The man consulted the paper while alternately measuring and studying the topography.

"What do you think?" Stiller asked when the engineer made no comment.

"I think she'll be somewhere here," the man said, his hand making a circular motion in the area where Stiller had been standing.

"It's as good a place as any to start," Stiller agreed.

The engineer handed back the sketch. "I was in charge of the project when we constructed the road here in the eighties," he said, waiting until a wide load with a tail of cars behind it had passed before continuing. "I live in Bamble, and when the road was finished I drove along here nearly every day, to and from work. A few months after the road had opened I noticed flowers lying on the verge here, as sometimes happens in places where someone has died in a road accident or something. It annoyed me, because the road was built to be safe for traffic, and we hadn't had any accidents, so I drove back, stopped and got rid of them."

"Flowers?" Stiller repeated, a note of surprise in his voice.

"Red roses," the man told him. "Like on a grave."

"Where were they placed?" Hammer asked.

"It's a long time ago, but they were somewhere around here." He pointed to the same area again. "Two months later, another bunch of flowers appeared," he went on. "I removed them too, but it continued. I don't know how many bunches of flowers I disposed of before it stopped."

Stiller took out his packet of Fisherman's Friends and took another lozenge, without offering them to the others.

"When was it that this business with the flowers stopped?" he asked. The engineer pulled a face, suggesting it was difficult to estimate.

"It continued for a couple of years, anyway," he said.

Stiller moved the lozenge around in his mouth.

"Can you come back with digging equipment?" he asked, his eyes fixed on the engineer.

"Most of the machines and crew are tied up, but we'll manage something. When were you proposing to do it?"

"Now," Stiller replied.

"Now?" the engineer said, taken aback. "That's not possible."

"Why not?"

"If we're going to dig here, we have to close the road and redirect the traffic. It requires planning."

"You must already have a plan in place for that?" Stiller asked. "It's no different from what happens if there's an accident, surely?"

"This is work that demands planning," the engineer broke in. "We must wait at least until tonight to cause minimum disruption to road users."

"I can wait until tonight," Stiller told him. "Can you be here with the necessary equipment at ten o'clock?"

"I'll have to call people out on overtime," the engineer said.

"It'll come from our budget," Stiller reassured him. "Ten o'clock."

"Ten o'clock it is, then," the man from the roads authority agreed.

Stiller felt his mobile phone vibrate in his pocket. When he took it out he saw it was from a saved number: Line Wisting.

65

It sounded as if Adrian Stiller was outdoors somewhere. When he introduced himself his name was drowned out by the rumble of a heavy lorry.

Line shifted the phone to her other ear and checked the recorder was operating. "Do you have a few minutes?" she asked.

"Fire away," Stiller said.

A car door slammed at the other end of the line and the background noise disappeared.

"I'm working on the next article and a new podcast, and a name's come up that I found interesting," Line said, spelling things out more explicitly than perhaps necessary. She hoped the recording of the conversation might be used.

"I've searched through the old police documents, and it's not mentioned there," she went on. "All the same, I was wondering if it was a name you're familiar with."

Adrian Stiller seemed impatient. "What's the name?" he asked.

"Martin Haugen."

Over the phone line she could hear the sound of a lozenge being crunched, followed by a lengthy silence.

"Where did you pick that up?" Stiller demanded.

Line glanced at the recorder again. She did not want to mention her father to the listeners but could stop the recording here when editing. Stiller's silence was revealing. She was definitely on to something.

"It came up in a case Dad's been working on with the police here in Larvik," Line explained. "Martin Haugen's wife disappeared in 1989. She was never found. Haugen was working on the construction of the new motorway outside Porsgrunn when Nadia went missing."

The line was silent again. When she spoke the words aloud she heard for herself how far-fetched any connection between the two cases seemed. She would have liked to speak to her father about it before calling the Kripos investigator but he was not answering his phone.

"I'm a bit busy right now," Stiller finally said. "I'll have to ring you back." Then he hung up.

66

Five small trout were the final result of three hours at the lake. Before they built a bonfire to cook them, they changed the lures for hooks and worms. The fishing rods lay on aquatic weeds on the shore with their lines cast and red cork floats bobbing on the water.

Martin had washed the fish. Now he sat beside the bonfire, sprinkling them with salt before packing each in tin foil with a generous portion of butter on the belly.

Wisting produced his mobile phone and switched it on. Eight per cent charge. He wondered whether the startup process used just as much power as when he simply kept it on standby. Regardless, he would run out of juice overnight.

A message from Line with a full stop awaited him: *Looks like the weather will stay fine all weekend.*

Yes, but the big fish hasn't taken the bait yet, he wrote back, glancing across at Martin Haugen.

The amateurish coded language was borderline comical, he thought. This was how they usually wrote messages to informants and sources. Only the sender and recipient understood the meaning from the context, but any third party would still find it suspicious.

Forget about fish was the response. *We're going out digging tonight.*

"Is everything okay?" Martin asked as he shaped a hollow in the mound of embers.

Wisting had almost forgotten his own lie about checking how

Amalie was after her visit to the doctor's. "Yes, fine, thanks," he said, smiling.

Martin Haugen stashed the five packets of fish in the cavity and used a stick to rake embers over them. "They have to sit there for ten minutes or so," he said, looking at his watch.

Wisting glanced across at his fishing rod; the water rippled in tiny waves around the cork. It looked like a nibble, but then the water settled again.

The air was hot from the sun and the flames of the fire. Wisting took off his jacket and laid it between them, to let the microphone inside catch their voices more easily. Martin Haugen kept his jacket on, and it was impossible to see if he had a gun hidden underneath it.

"It's peaceful here," Wisting said, mostly for the sake of saying something.

"My family set up home here in the eighteenth century," Martin told him. "They lived here for more than two hundred and fifty years, but now I'm the end of the line. After me, there's nobody to carry on the family tradition."

Wisting's thoughts turned to his grandchild and the joy of knowing that his life had left its mark.

"I think I'd like my ashes to be scattered here," Martin continued. One of the pine logs crackled noisily on the fire. He used a stick to rake more embers over the packets of fish. "I wouldn't like to lie on my own in a grave nobody will ever tend, anyway," he said, getting to his feet. He walked over to the fishing rods, pulled up the line and checked the worm was still in place before casting again. The red float moved slightly as the worm sank and the line straightened out.

Wisting said nothing. He had a plot in the churchyard waiting for him. On Ingrid's gravestone an empty space below her name indicated where his own would one day be engraved.

"Will you arrange it?" Martin asked him as he sat down again.

"What?"

"The business with the ashes?"

Wisting smiled. "You should really write it down," he suggested. "Make a will."

On the other side of the lake a flock of crows took off. Wisting put his hand to his forehead to block the sun. It was obvious something had frightened them off. One of the crows held its wings close to its body and swooped down into the trees, while the others flew away.

The solitary crow rose again, flapping its wings, and screeched loudly before launching another attack.

"Why is it doing that, do you think?" Martin asked.

"I don't know," Wisting answered. "There's clearly something in the forest over there."

"Yes, but why does one choose to attack, while the others fly off?"

"Maybe it has something to protect or defend," Wisting suggested. "A nest with fledglings in it, or something."

Martin shook his head. "Crows nest in springtime," he said. "I think they're just different. It's a matter of contrasting instincts. A frightened horse usually runs away, but a dog adopts an attack position and bares its teeth. I think it's the same with human beings too; we hold inherited primeval instincts that mean, when we're threatened, some choose to attack while others decide to flee. We can't consciously choose or control it."

Wisting tried to interpret what Martin said, in light of his suspicions. It might be understood as an attempt to justify what he had done.

"Have you seen those funny home videos on TV?" Martin went on. "When somebody hides in a dustbin or something and they jump out to scare a pal or a workmate?"

Wisting smiled.

"As a rule, it's hilarious because the person who's frightened dashes off and runs for a door or something to try to escape, but sometimes the guy who's scared automatically pulls out a fist and throws a punch. Their brain has reacted differently. Nine out of ten automatically choose to run away, but one in ten reacts by resorting to violence."

Wisting did not believe this had anything to do with an inherited disposition to counterattack; he believed it was a reflex reaction guided by learned behavioural patterns. Some had been brought up with violence and confrontation and had learned this was the most common type of reaction.

"That's why there are provisions in criminal law for self-defence and the principle of necessity," he replied, instead of arguing against Martin. "You can't be punished for something you've done to defend yourself or to ward off an attack. You can kill in order to avoid being killed yourself."

The crow on the other side of the lake launched an attack for the third time.

"Have you encountered that?" Martin asked. "Someone who's gone free on the grounds of self-defence?"

"It has happened," Wisting replied, and went on to tell him about a woman who had hit her husband on the head with a hammer while he lay on top of her, trying to strangle her.

"But do you think human instincts exist so we can't be held accountable for our own actions?" Martin asked.

"Absolutely," Wisting lied. He did not believe people were governed by their instincts. "I think that's what happens when someone says that everything went black for them. There comes a point when you can no longer control yourself or know what you're doing."

"Have you come across that as well?"

Wisting nodded. "In a legal sense, it is known as involuntary lack of capacity, or being unconscious at the time of the act," he told Martin, glancing down at his jacket sleeve, where he knew the recorder was running. He was balancing on an ethical tightrope regarding how far he could go to manipulate a confession from Martin. The responses he gave were deliberately misleading. Instincts did not impair consciousness, and he had never heard of a defence built on anything of the kind. Actions that ended up in the courts were often driven by urges and desires some people found difficult to control, but not just by instincts.

Martin grabbed another stick and began to lift the packets of fish out of the embers. "What type of person are you?" he asked.

A light breeze blew bonfire smoke towards Wisting. "What do you mean?" he asked, turning away from the wind.

"Do you flee, or do you go on the attack?"

The smoke from the bonfire stung Wisting's eyes. "I don't know," he answered honestly. "If someone leapt out of a rubbish bin to scare me, I think I would jump out of the way, but I don't know what's actually deep-seated within me. I've never been in a situation where I've been put to the test."

The smoke drifted away again and he was able to look Martin Haugen in the eye. "Have you?" he asked.

Martin Haugen leaned forward slightly, as if about to say something. Then his eyes slid away, past Wisting.

"You've got a bite!" he said, pointing at the lake, where Wisting's float had submerged.

67

Adrian Stiller drove past William Wisting's house and parked in the street outside Line's. He knew the way. He had been here before. The first night he had been in town and unable to sleep, he had driven around and stopped in this precise spot. From where he was parked, he could see into Line's kitchen, and up to her father's house.

On that occasion his visit had not served any purpose but was simply a matter of wanting to be one step ahead and being keen to get to know both Wisting and his daughter as best he could.

This time he sat behind the wheel with his eyes closed to compose himself. His thoughts drifted to the roses the man from the roads authority had talked about and the bouquet on the chest of drawers in the hallway of Martin Haugen's home. How simple explanations could often be when you eventually came across them. Katharina had bought the roses for Nadia.

He had no idea how Line had stumbled upon Martin Haugen, but he had to assure himself that her knowledge did not have the potential to destroy the case.

His mobile phone caused him to open his eyes again. He was unsure how long he had been sitting behind the steering wheel. He had not fallen into a deep sleep but the short nap had sharpened his senses.

Nils Hammer was at the other end when he answered. "I've got hold of a cadaver dog," he said.

"Great stuff," Stiller replied, stepping out of the car. A face looked down at him from Wisting's kitchen window: probably his son, who was home for a few days. "Send it to South Trøndelag," he requested.

"Trøndelag?" Hammer queried.

"To Malvik," Stiller specified. "Wasn't that where the road collapsed last week?"

Hammer was silent. Stiller realized he was trying to figure it out.

"There's a pattern here," he went on. "I know Martin Haugen has an alibi for his wife's disappearance, but if he buried Nadia at the roadside here, then he could also have got rid of his wife's body in the same way while working up there. I don't know how he managed it, but there's a reason for Haugen driving up there last week and then telling lies about it. I want the landslip area searched."

68

Her father must have run out of power for his mobile phone. She had tried to call him several times, with no response.

The way Adrian Stiller had reacted when she mentioned Martin Haugen's name on the phone had provided all the confirmation she needed. In the course of the past hour she had grown even more certain she was on to something. She had found a map on the Internet. The road Martin Haugen had been involved in constructing was situated only a few hundred metres from the location of the party Nadia had attended before she went missing.

She would wait until after Adrian Stiller had contacted her before sharing her thoughts with Daniel Leanger and the others at *VG*, but she was convinced Martin Haugen was the man at the centre of the new investigation. In her own head she pictured Nadia lying buried somewhere deep beneath the durable asphalt referred to in the newspaper, and she was not keen on the idea of her father being alone with him. Her anxiety transferred to Amalie, who was fretting and restless.

She had never really liked Martin Haugen, although she could not put her finger on why. Even though she had only met him a few times, it was as if she could scent something, something negative. She could not understand why her father had maintained a relationship with him after the case went cold.

The thought that Martin Haugen's wife had also disappeared was starting to simmer at the back of her mind when she heard a car door slam outside. She went to the bedroom window and peered out. It was Adrian Stiller. He was talking on a mobile phone and gesticulating with his free hand. She had thought he was in Oslo. He had promised to phone back, and the fact he was now standing outside her house made her anxious.

Returning to the living room, she picked up the recorder and switched it on in time to catch the doorbell ring.

Stiller appeared weary, almost exhausted, standing there on the steps. His complexion was pale, with dark shadows under his eyes, and his lips were cracked and dry.

"Is something wrong?" she asked.

Stiller's eyes fell on the recorder in her hand. "I was in the neighbourhood," he replied, following her into the living room.

They sat on opposite sides of the coffee table. Line put down the recorder and lifted Amalie up beside her on the settee. "Is it about Martin Haugen?" she asked. "Is he the kidnapper?"

"What makes you think that?" Stiller queried.

There was something disarming about his question, something that made her feel self-conscious.

"Is he your suspect?" she asked again, rather than explaining why she had arrived at this conclusion. "He's a friend of Dad's. They're on a fishing trip together this weekend."

"Switch off the recorder," Stiller said.

Line did as he requested.

"I'm working with your father on this," Stiller continued. "It's an unusual case, and the fishing trip is part of the investigation."

Although Line did not quite understand, it seemed that Adrian Stiller had no intention of elaborating.

"But you believe Martin Haugen kidnapped and killed Nadia Krogh?" Line asked.

"We're going to dig for her body tonight," Stiller said.

"Tonight? Where?"

"Not far from where she disappeared," Stiller explained. "We're going to close the E18."

"Are you going to dig up the whole E18?"

Stiller shook his head. "We've a good idea where she is buried," he told her. "We have a map."

"A map?" Line repeated.

Adrian Stiller looked again at the recorder and refrained from responding. "I'd like you to come with us tonight, when we dig her up," he said instead.

69

They pulled in the nets at twilight. It was cold once the sun had gone down, and Wisting's fingers grew numb from picking fish out of the sodden nets.

The result was thirty-seven Arctic char, four trout and six perch, between the two nets they had set out.

They rinsed, washed and dried them on land, and filleted the largest fish.

For supper they would eat the steaks they had brought. The fish were dry-cured in order to take them home. Following Martin's instructions, Wisting spread some fish on the base of a bucket before scattering coarse salt and some sugar over them. Layer by layer, they filled the bucket and finally pressed down the lid.

Wisting attended to the steaks, and it was almost ten o'clock by the time the sizeable chunks of meat were in the frying pan.

He used a fork to poke and prod the meat, and looked across at Martin, who sat immersed in his thoughts, cradling a can of beer in his lap as he stared into the flames. He was softening up, Wisting thought. Their conversations had broken down the barriers. He just had to be led the last part of the way; even though he had everything to lose by talking about his crimes, it must also be difficult for him to be alone with his secrets.

Tiny pinpricks of blood began to seep from the steaks, and he used the fork to turn them over.

He glanced across at Martin again, keen to know what the man was thinking. Everyone had a need to share their innermost thoughts with someone. For ordinary folk, this was a case of talking about problems at work, in their marriage or about an illness. For a murderer, it was a matter of being willing to talk about things that would lead to many years in prison. Moving close to another person on that basis depended on finding the right emotional connection and building a bridge.

Martin leaned back in his chair, folded his hands over his beer can and looked up at him. "Have you always suspected me?" he asked.

70

Line looked in on Amalie and found her fast asleep. Thomas sat with the remote control in front of the TV. "Thanks," she said, yet again. He had postponed his journey home to look after Amalie.

"No problem," he assured her.

"She'll probably sleep all night," Line said.

She had packed the equipment she required in a large bag: laptop, camera, recorder and a pair of binoculars, in addition to a pen and some paper. Thomas stood up, lifted the bag and followed her out to the car.

"Good luck!" he said, beaming, while he stowed her belongings on the rear seat.

"Thanks," she said, and clambered in.

He closed the car door behind her and stood waiting. In the mirror, she noticed him turn and head inside just as she drove round the corner.

Adrian Stiller told her not to make any further attempts to phone her father. She had no idea what was going on at Martin Haugen's cabin, but Stiller reassured her they were in regular contact with him and that Haugen knew nothing of what was going on.

She wondered how involved her father had been in the Krogh kidnapping investigation when she told him she would be writing about it for the newspaper. His reaction had at least implied that he was unaware of the planned cooperation between *VG* and Kripos.

They had set up a conference call—Daniel Leanger, Sandersen

(the news editor), and herself—to discuss the situation. According to their timetable, the next article and podcast would come out in less than a week, and they had intended to cover the story for a period of six weeks. Now everything would have to be accelerated. She had already written a news item stating that the police had embarked on a search for Nadia Krogh's body and that the E18 was closed while the search was in progress. This would be published online as soon as she had a photograph of the roadblock and the diversion.

Daniel was also driving down from Oslo, but would not arrive for another couple of hours. She would be the only journalist on the scene when news of the police operation broke.

There was no sign of the roadblock as she approached the Porsgrunn exit road. She turned off and into a petrol station while traffic continued as usual along the E18. Two vehicles from the roads authority were parked on the forecourt. One had a trailer with a massive arrangement of lights and a sign for diverting traffic. In addition, there was a patrol car from the local police station with a female police officer behind the wheel. Line stepped out and walked across to her.

The policewoman rolled down her window.

"Hi," Line said, introducing herself. "I've arranged with Adrian Stiller of Kripos to be here when you close the E18."

The woman behind the wheel nodded in confirmation. "Then you should tag along with us now," she said, indicating a man in working clothes who was emerging from the petrol station with a beaker of coffee in his hand. "We're setting off in a second or two."

Line sat in her car again and joined the end of the little convoy as it began to move. Flashing orange warning lights illuminated the darkness. The roads crew efficiently set up the roadblock vehicle and directed traffic to a diverted route.

On the policewoman's instructions, Line drove past and parked her car at the verge before grabbing her camera and jumping out.

Oncoming traffic ceased, signalling that traffic had also been stopped at the other end. The police car drove forward and parked across the carriageway to make certain the road was also physically blocked. Line walked partway along the road to open up some distance between her and the roadblock.

This would be a striking image, with the harsh orange light against the dark background.

The policewoman emerged from the patrol car and exchanged a few words with the man from the Roads Directorate.

Lifting her camera again, Line made every effort to ensure the reflective strips on the uniform did not spoil the composition.

While she clicked through the photos she had taken, two lorries arrived, one with an excavator on the cargo bed. Two police patrol cars followed behind them. When the policewoman got into her car and reversed to the side to allow them to pass, Line took a series of photographs. As soon as the excavator had gone by, she chose three and sent them straight to the news desk from her camera as she hurried back to her own vehicle.

She had been on maternity leave for almost eighteen months and during that time had not worked as a journalist, apart from one or two freelance assignments. Now she was conscious of how much she had missed it. She had missed being on the scene, in the midst of unfolding events.

71

A thud came from the wood stove as one of the logs inside tumbled and fell. Martin Haugen rose from his chair, opened the stove door and removed the potatoes baking inside before inserting another log.

Wisting realized he had suspected Martin Haugen from day one. The suspicion had always been at the back of his mind and had never faded through twenty-four years, even though Martin had been almost seven hundred kilometres away when Katharina disappeared.

"I'd be lying if I said no," Wisting replied. "It's a textbook example. The answer most often lies with some close relation or other."

Martin sat down again. "But you never said anything?" he queried.

"You must have known that you were investigated," Wisting said. "That we charted your movements and confirmed you were in Malvik when she went missing?"

"Yes, of course," Martin said. "But we've never spoken about it."

Wisting prodded the meat in the pan. The steaks would soon be ready. "Should we have talked about it?" he asked.

"What would you have done if you'd found out it was me?"

Wisting was searching for the right answer.

"You're one of the few friends I have," Martin went on, as Wisting pondered what to say. "Would you have thrown me in prison?"

"I would have given you the number of a good lawyer," Wisting replied, feigning concentration on the steaks. "And made sure you received a fair trial."

He would have to resist the urge to check whether the recorder was in place in his shirt pocket. Nevertheless, he would not be able to see whether it was switched on. He would simply have to trust the technology.

"Who is the best lawyer?" Martin asked.

"That depends," Wisting said, pulling the frying pan slightly off the heat.

"What does it depend on?"

"Whether you confessed, cooperated and wanted the case to go through the justice system as quietly and smoothly as possible, or whether you denied the charge and wanted to turn it all into a circus."

Martin brought out two plates. "So you wouldn't have let me get away with it?" he asked.

"I would have made sure everything was done properly," Wisting responded, turning the meat one last time.

"Previously, of course, there was a statute of limitations for murder," Martin said, sitting down again. "After twenty-five years a perpetrator could walk free."

Wisting agreed.

"I think that's reasonable," Martin continued. "Everybody changes. It's wrong to punish someone for things they did in a different life. The person who is brought before the court is not the same as the one who committed the crime."

Good arguments existed for having an expiry date for homicide, Wisting thought, but consideration for the murderer was not one of them. He was still searching for the right words to use.

"I can agree with that," he said instead. "Besides, evidence is weakened with the passing of years. Witnesses remember less clearly. The danger of a miscarriage of justice increases when someone is brought to book after such a long time."

Martin got to his feet again. "They're ready," he said, indicating the frying pan.

Wisting lifted the steaks on to their plates.

Martin took out a tin of sweetcorn niblets, opened it and carried it through to the table in the living room, along with two more cans of beer. Wisting cut open the baked potatoes and dropped a dollop of herb butter on each before carrying the plates through. Martin met him before he reached the table, took his plate and sat down with his back to the wall.

"Shall we go hiking tomorrow?" he suggested. "You can see the towers on Grenland Bridge from the summit of Eikedokktoppen. It's only an hour's walk?"

Wisting, happy to go along with this, cut off a slice of steak. The conversation had changed, and his opening had closed down once again.

72

As the excavator rumbled, smoke belched from the engine exhaust before the man at the controls raised the bucket and lowered it on to the grassy embankment. With expert precision, he scraped off the top layer, swung the arm and dumped loose earth on to the lorry's cargo bed.

Line took another sequence of pictures. The man in the driver's cab clamped his cigarette between his lips and swivelled the bucket again.

Huge tripod floodlights were trained on the operative range. Adrian Stiller stood on the sidelines with Nils Hammer, a few local police officers and a couple of men from the roads authority, following each and every movement of the bucket. Line pointed her camera at them, took a photograph and zoomed in so that only Stiller's face was captured in her lens. He lifted his head to her, seemingly aware the lens was directed at him. He looked shattered, as if the investigation had drained him of energy.

She pressed the release button quickly a couple of times before he managed to pull himself together. The result was an authentic portrait. The clenched jaws said something about the gravity of the task he had taken on.

She was grateful to him for allowing her to step behind the cordon, but to be frank, it was no more than fair and proper. He had made use of her and the newspaper in a game of some sort and was obliged to offer something in return.

The digger had removed the top layer of earth in an area approximately five metres long by three metres wide, and she could smell the damp odour of newly turned soil.

Adrian Stiller approached her.

"How deep might she be buried?" Line asked.

"Martin Haugen had access to all the construction machines here at that time," Stiller said. "He could have dug down quite far."

"Do you have enough to charge him, even if you don't find the body?"

Adrian Stiller's eyes searched for her recorder. It was inside her deep jacket pocket and not switched on. "We think so," he said tersely.

"Are you going to go and arrest him at his cabin, right now?"

Stiller took out his packet of Fisherman's Friend lozenges. "Even if we find her here tonight, it's going to take time to establish with absolute certainty that the body is Nadia Krogh," he explained. "That has to be in place first."

"What else do you have on him?" Line asked. "You must have something, something that made you reopen the case in the first place."

The lozenge crunched between Stiller's teeth. "It's important to do things in the right order," he said.

"I won't publish it until you give me the go-ahead," she told him.

Stiller cracked a smile, as if this was an offer he had received from journalists many times before. "Fingerprints," he answered, all the same. "The ransom letters were reexamined, using new technology. Haugen's prints showed up in three places."

"Why didn't you arrest him immediately, then?"

"Because the prints were not on the actual letters but on the newspaper the message was clipped out of. That makes the fingerprints only circumstantial evidence. We wanted to try to get more on him."

"So is that what Dad's doing?" Line demanded. "Are you using him as bait to reel Martin Haugen in?"

"Your father has worked undercover on this for twenty-four years," Stiller replied. "He's never fully believed in his innocence."

Line took some time to digest what Stiller was telling her. "So that means there's a connection between the Krogh kidnapping and the Katharina case?"

"They do at least have a common denominator."

The police radio belonging to one of the officers overseeing the excavation crackled into life. He gave a brief reply, called Stiller over and then pointed along the road, where a large white delivery van was trundling towards them.

"Who's that?" Line queried.

"Crime-scene technicians," Stiller answered, explaining that they would be on standby. "They won't like that big excavator."

Work progressed slowly. The driver dealt with one five-centimetre layer of earth at a time. Now and again he was given orders to stop and a police officer examined any objects that had turned up: roots, twigs and pebbles.

Line photographed the process and uploaded images to the news desk so that they could update the online story.

After half an hour the cargo bed was full and the lorry had driven off. Line remained with Stiller at the edge of the hole, which was now about one metre deep. Torn roots protruded from the smooth walls of earth but, apart from that, there was nothing to be seen.

The police agreed to continue down for another metre before shifting the excavator.

The empty lorry drove forward and work went on. After another half hour it was full again, though still nothing of interest had appeared.

The excavator moved five metres further away and began to scrape off another top layer.

It was now almost midnight. The police officers not involved in overseeing the excavation work were huddled inside a car.

Line felt her phone vibrate in her pocket, an MMS from Daniel Leanger. An outside broadcast van from TV2 was parked at the roadblock while the reporter was in heated discussion with the woman in the patrol car.

The picture had been taken from inside the barrier. Line lifted her head and watched as Daniel's black Audi drew up.

He parked behind Line's car and leapt out to approach her with a beaker of coffee. "Any news?" he asked.

Line accepted the coffee. "Not yet," she said, cupping her hands around the beaker.

Daniel disappeared back to his vehicle and returned with video equipment.

Another load of earth was driven away, and the first lorry took over. The excavator driver lowered the bucket again and lifted more soil. The hand of one of the supervising officers shot up in the air— a stop signal—and he shouted something. He was brimming with an eagerness that seemed very different from any of the emotions he had displayed before.

Line scrabbled to take out her recorder and switched it on as she stepped closer. The excavator shook and shuddered before the engine stopped and silence fell.

"Found something!" was the shout from the gap on the hillside.

73

Wisting dug out his mobile phone while Martin was outside taking a leak. The battery was down to five per cent. Three hours ago he had learned that Stiller had sent sniffer dogs to the E6 at Malvik, but there were no new messages now.

He quickly checked the *VG* Internet pages too. The main story was that police had closed the E18 outside Porsgrunn in connection with their search for Nadia Krogh. Line had written the piece and had obviously been present when the road was blocked. He hurried to switch off his phone again, and filled the cognac glasses.

There was a certain logic in believing that Katharina's body was buried in Trøndelag. In an attempt to make the timeline fit with Martin Haugen as the killer, he had sketched out an inverted course of events: Katharina could have travelled up to see Martin at the construction site and he could have murdered her there. With the starting point as the telephone conversation between them which had ended at 22.14, theoretically, Katharina could have been in Malvik around half past six the next morning, if she drove through the night. This gave Martin a window of thirty minutes before his shift at seven, when his colleagues saw him behind the controls of his excavator. Alternatively, she could have waited until the next day to pay him a visit and arrived there after his shift was over. At any rate, no one had seen her, and witnesses who had eaten dinner with Martin after work gave him even less room for manoeuvre before he tried to call her and began to grow worried. However, what knocked that theory for six was that both the car and the motorbike belonging to Katharina were parked in their garage at home.

Martin Haugen came in again. They had lit a fire in the open fireplace in the living room. Martin added another couple of logs before he sat down.

"Have you never been afraid?" he asked. "In your job, I mean?"

"Mostly I sit in an office these days," Wisting replied. "There's not much there to be afraid of."

"I'm thinking more of when you're coming close to a solution and the murderer knows you're about to expose him. Have you ever been scared of what he might do?"

Wisting shook his head and took a sip of cognac. "Investigations involve more than one person," Wisting answered. "A murderer wouldn't achieve anything by hurting me."

"But do you think a murderer thinks as rationally as that? If he has killed before, surely he might well kill again?"

"I think being a road worker is more dangerous," Wisting said wryly. "Working with big machines and explosive charges and suchlike."

The flames from the fire cast restless shadows over the dark timber walls.

"But there must have been things you haven't shared with the other officers?" Martin continued. "Suspicions you've kept to yourself, or connections only you can see?"

Wisting understood that Martin was exploring the lie of the land, feeling his way forward, in the same way that Wisting had done. He had said so himself. Martin was not someone to turn the other cheek or remain passive—he would go on the offensive.

"The churchyard is full of irreplaceable people," Wisting joked. "I've no intention of taking any work-related secrets with me to the grave."

Martin raised his cognac glass in a toast. "What sort of case are you working on now?" he asked.

"Nothing major," Wisting replied. "I've been busy with a consequence analysis in connection with the new police district."

"What are the consequences?"

"I don't entirely know," Wisting replied. "That's my main point. We don't know how it will work out. Police work has too many variables for it to be possible to say anything with certainty."

Martin refilled Wisting's tumbler. "Why did you become a policeman?" he queried.

"I wanted a demanding, exciting and meaningful line of work," Wisting responded. "Also, I think it had something to do with justice."

"What is justice, though?"

Wisting raised his tumbler to his mouth. This was like the discussions he and Ingrid could have had if she were still living. He enjoyed challenging opinions but restricted himself to what was familiar. Ingrid always saw questions in a larger context. He and Martin had never spoken about such things, and the conversation had an undertone that put him on his guard.

"Everyone being treated equally, and anyone who takes something from someone else being punished for it," he replied.

"Do you think just solutions exist for everything?" Martin went on. "I mean, justice must surely involve finding a solution to satisfy both parties in a conflict."

"In that case it wouldn't be fair to put anyone in prison," Wisting said, in an effort to steer the conversation. "A perpetrator will rarely or never consider that just. I'd prefer to say that justice means everyone gets what they deserve."

"Punishment as just deserts?"

"Call it that if you like."

"But that assumes you're familiar with all aspects of a case?"

"What do you mean?"

Martin raised his eyes to the ceiling, as if searching for the right way to explain. "If a man shoots and kills his wife, then of course he deserves to be punished," he began. "But what if the gun went off by accident? Then perhaps it's punishment enough to carry the guilt for what he has done."

Wisting nodded, wondering whether Martin was about to tell him that either Katharina's or Nadia's death had resulted from an accident. "Accidents are not punished," he replied, neglecting to add that this did not apply if a perpetrator had been careless or reckless. "It has to be an intentional act."

"Then that means you must be aware of all the circumstances of a case?"

"That's what we call investigation," Wisting said sardonically. "Trying to bring the whole truth to light. Only then can we talk about justice."

Martin Haugen went quiet on the other side of the table. Wisting struggled to find the appropriate words to persuade him to open up. However, before he arrived at anything, Martin drained his tumbler of cognac and got to his feet.

"Right," he said, stretching. "If we're going to make it to Eike-dokktoppen tomorrow, it's best we go to bed now."

74

Line moved towards the trench with the others and switched on the recorder to capture the drama swirling in the air. She stood a couple of steps from the edge in case of erosion and craned forward to look down.

The pit was about two metres deep. To begin with, she could see nothing other than soft clay and stones of various sizes. The police were preoccupied with something at the very bottom on one side.

Automatically, Line raised her camera and through the lens was able to see the tip of a boot protruding from the earth wall. The police officers were talking about leather and synthetic materials that did not decompose.

A ladder was propped up and the two crime-scene technicians who had arrived late climbed into the hole. They were not wearing the usual white protective suits normally used by crime-scene examiners but were instead dressed in dark blue overalls with *Police* emblazoned on the back.

Line retreated a few paces to gain some distance. She took several rapid shots and checked the result in the display behind the camera. The images told their own story.

One of the crime-scene technicians had brought a spoon-like tool of the type used by archaeologists. Line stepped forward to the edge again and watched as he began to pick at the earth around the boot while his colleague documented the find with a camera. Soon the entire boot was visible. The shape and style suggested it belonged to a woman.

"It could be just some old rubbish," cautioned one of the police officers. "Something left in the road-fill waste."

No one contradicted him, even though no one around the pit believed that for a second.

A big clump of soil loosened from the earth wall where the technicians were working, uncovering the sole of another boot.

The pair of boots lay less than ten centimetres apart, one a bit further inside the wall, as would be expected if someone were lying with one foot drawn up slightly.

The two technicians discussed how to proceed and agreed to try to pull one of the boots free.

The man with the trowel took hold of the boot and jiggled it loose. A shower of soil spewed out as the first bone appeared, a greyish-brown shaft jutting from the earth.

The crime-scene technician peered down into the boot and showed the contents to his colleague before they turned their attention to the large bone.

"She's lying horizontally, this way," the man with the trowel decided, using his hand to indicate the direction. "We'll have to dig a corridor to get her out."

They scaled the ladder again.

The man in the driver's cab of the excavator discarded a cigarette butt and started the machine again. Following directions, he worked his way down through the layer of earth to the left of the boot.

Line sat in her car with her laptop on her knee, writing a news story describing the discovery of the first human remains. Daniel was walking around with his video camera but was spoken to by one of the police officers, who must have instructed him not to film what was found inside the hole.

Adrian Stiller strode up to the car, opened the passenger door and sat down beside her.

"The family's been notified," he said, with no preamble of any kind. "We can't confirm it's Nadia Krogh we've found, but she's the reason we're here."

Line typed in what he was saying. "Cause of death?" she asked.

"Too early to say anything about that, but the case has always been investigated as a crime."

"Any suspect?"

Adrian Stiller clammed up.

"I wouldn't be doing my job if I didn't ask," Line said. "In the strictest sense, it's a yes/no question. I know the answer, but you can formulate it however you like."

"You can write that I don't wish to comment on that," Stiller told her, gripping the door handle.

"A press statement will be released about the discovery in ten minutes or so," he went on. "If you want to get your story out before then, go ahead."

Thanking him, Line hammered down a few concluding sentences before reading it through. The text was clear—short and concise. She sent it to the news desk with the photograph of the crime-scene technicians on their way down the ladder into the pit and followed this up with a quick phone call to double-check receipt of the story.

By just after three o'clock the hole had been augmented by a channel three metres broad by three metres long and only a thirty-centimetre-thick layer of soil concealed the rest of the remains.

On the road bridge more than a hundred metres to the north a crowd had gathered, mainly from media outlets. In the glow of the streetlamp Line could make out several glinting camera lenses. The police were busy setting up a huge work tent over the discovery site.

Line kept close to Stiller, avoiding being questioned since people

Jørn Lier Horst

could see she was accompanying him, and moved with him behind the canvas.

A large, coarse sieve had been installed down in the original hole, a rectangular wooden box with netting on the base. Every spadeful of earth from the area around the remains was placed in the box and sifted through the rough net in order to sort out larger objects.

Something hit the net, causing the men in the pit to cluster around it. They withdrew a dark object from a lump of earth. Line lifted her camera when she realized what it was. A handbag.

One of the technicians carried it across to a work table that had been set up to examine objects more closely in the light of a desk lamp.

"It's made of PVC," he said, explaining why it had survived more than twenty years in the ground.

Line stood behind the investigators. From between the shoulders of Nils Hammer and Adrian Stiller she could see parts of the bag disintegrate when they began to inspect it. A metal buckle and a strap came loose.

"Can I take a photo?" she asked.

The technician looked up. Probably unaware of the details of this old case, he would not know Nadia had kept her purse in her bag, with the picture of her and her little brother.

Stiller nodded, giving her the go-ahead. The crime-scene technician held up the bag in his blue latex gloves. "Thanks," Line said, lowering the camera.

The technician opened the bag carefully and began to remove the contents, which seemed well preserved: a key ring, lipstick and some little bits and pieces Line could not decipher. That was all. No purse.

Line felt certain this was Nadia's handbag. The description matched. She tried to imagine what might have happened at the time the body was dumped by the side of the road. Her purse had been removed before the handbag was hurled in after her, as in a common assault or robbery.

"Maybe her purse is lying down there too," Stiller said, once work in the pit had resumed.

Line followed every single turn of the spade. Never before had she been so closely involved in police work.

The first bones were revealed. The earth around them was a bit darker than the rest. There were long thigh bones, kneecaps, small bones that must be fingers, and curved ribs. Spindly plant roots twisted and twined through them like a network of nerves. Finally, the skull was unearthed. It looked as if there were cracks in it, and on the right side a fragment seemed to be missing.

The technicians stood deep in discussion, but Line could not catch what they were saying.

"What have you got there?" Stiller asked.

The elder of the two glanced up. "A cranial fracture," he said, while the other documented the injury with his camera.

"Cause of death?" Stiller suggested.

"We'll have to take a closer look when we get everything back to the lab," the technician replied, refusing to draw any conclusions.

They left the skull and moved on to the rest of the body. All the clothes must have rotted away. A dark belt with a rusty buckle was all that was left.

The older crime-scene technician held up an object from the area of the hip bone and transferred it to a brown paper bag. Line wondered whether it could have been something in one of Nadia's trouser pockets and had to zoom in to reveal it as the remnants of a zip fastener.

They also took possession of an earring and a ring before embarking on collecting the bones. They seemed to be sorting them according to which body part they belonged to, starting with the hands.

All the tiny bones forming part of the left hand were dropped into a bag that was marked and stored. Then the bones of the upper and lower arm were placed in the same box before a lid was attached. The left leg was then packed away in the same fashion.

"I've got what I need now," Daniel said. "We won't broadcast moving images of the remains, so there's not much point in me hanging around any longer. I'll go to the hotel and do some editing. What about you?"

"I'll stay a bit longer," Line said.

"It'll be another long day tomorrow," Daniel went on. "We'll have to transmit a new podcast."

Line took the recorder from her pocket and checked how much battery time was left. She would have to charge it soon.

"I'll have to speak to her boyfriend again," she said. "After all, the case takes on a different complexion now she's been found." She followed him to his car and they arranged where to meet the following day.

A police patrol car arrived with pots of coffee and buttered bread rolls. Adrian Stiller called her over and she filled a cardboard beaker before heading back into the tent again.

The two technicians didn't move. They were immersed in dialogue on the right-hand side of what remained of the skeleton.

Adrian Stiller crouched down, squeezing through the tent flaps, with a bottle of water in his hand.

"Coffee's here," he told them, but all at once it struck him that something significant had captured the attention of the two technicians.

"What is it?" he queried.

The older technician looked up. "She has compound fractures," he explained. "In her femur, tibia and arm."

"In addition to the fractured skull," his colleague added.

"What do you make of that?"

The older technician seemed almost unwilling to make any specific deduction. "These are injuries consistent with being hit by a moving vehicle," he said.

"Hit by a vehicle?" Stiller reiterated.

"Of course, it's a natural conclusion, since she's lying here in a ditch."

"There was no road here at that time," Line broke in. "They were still building it."

The technician shrugged. "At any rate, I've only seen injuries like this in connection with road accidents," he said.

Stiller glanced at Line. "You're not to make this public until I've given you the green light," he told her. Line readily agreed.

After the coffee break, the rest of the bones were packed and labelled and hauled up. The two crime-scene technicians then began to fine-sieve the layer of earth on which the skeleton had been lying. They seemed to be concentrating on the head area, and Line assumed they were searching for the other earring. Now and again they stopped and plucked something out of the strainers they were using before throwing away stones too big to pass through the holes.

The missing earring eventually turned up, but the technicians continued their fine-combing of the soil. Occasionally they came across something they kept hold of, but these were too small for Line to identify. It occurred to her that they might be teeth. She spooled back through the photographs she had taken and zoomed in on one of the skull. The jaw was intact and all the teeth seemed to be in place.

"What are you looking for?" she asked, succumbing to curiosity.

The older technician made eye contact with Stiller, as if seeking permission to answer. "Glass fragments," he told her after getting a nod from him.

Line understood. They were trying to support their theory that

Nadia Krogh had been knocked down and killed and were searching for tiny slivers of broken glass retained in her hair or clothing.

"Are you finding any?" she asked.

The technician merely nodded as he continued his work. It was now past six in the morning, and Line was feeling tired. All the tension had drained from her body. The excavation work had little more to offer, but she felt unable to leave the discovery site until the job was finished.

She headed for her car, where she sat behind the wheel and started the engine to heat the interior. Eventually she grew drowsy. Her eyelids slid shut and she fell asleep.

She woke with a start when someone rapped on the side window. It was Adrian Stiller, and the dashboard clock showed 7.38.

Fresh air billowed into the overheated interior when she lowered the window.

"We're finishing up here now," Stiller said. "The road will open again as soon as we're all packed up."

Line glanced across at the tent where the work had taken place. A policeman was busy securing its perimeter with police tape.

"The tent will stay put for a while longer, but to be honest there's not much more to do here apart from fill in the hole," Stiller continued.

"What are you all going to do now?" Line asked.

"We're going to try to catch some sleep," Stiller told her.

It certainly looked as if he needed some, Line thought, more than most of the others here, but she was not so sure he would actually take a break from the investigation.

"And after that?" she queried.

"We'll have an internal run-through to summarize the case," Stiller replied. "But nothing's going to happen until your father gets home."

75

Martin Haugen was first up. Wisting lay in bed listening to him lighting the stove.

The bed creaked when he reached for his mobile phone in his jacket pocket on the chair. Still some power left—three per cent.

A message from Line. popped up: *We've found what we were looking for.* He managed no more than reading that short message before a new text pushed the first one further down the screen: *Looks like our friend was hit by a vehicle.*

These messages had been sent at 3.32 and 5.40 respectively. They had stopped writing about the weather, but the actual messages were in the same simple coded style that really would not fool anyone.

He sent back a question mark to elicit more information. Nils Hammer was still awake. The response came swiftly: *Fractures on arms, legs and skull. Technicians conclude road traffic accident.*

On the other side of the wall he heard Martin rattling the coffee pot.

An accident, in other words, he thought. Was that what Martin had tried to tell him the previous evening, when they'd been talking about justice and receiving just punishment?

What make of car did MH have at that time? he wrote, fully aware he had no need to give instructions to his colleagues at the police station about the next investigative steps. *Speak to the neighbour, Steinar Vassvik, about possible damage to a vehicle,* he added.

Immediately after he pressed Send the display turned black. The phone had run out of power.

Yanking his legs out of the sleeping bag, he sat up in the chilly room. He pulled on his trousers and shirt before pouring water into the basin by the window.

Coffee was ready by the time he walked into the kitchen.

"They're not much good, these beds," Martin commented.

Wisting rubbed his neck and rolled his head in an effort to get rid of a crick. "It's okay for a night or two," he said, with a pained expression, as he helped himself to a cup.

After breakfast they went outside and pulled up the nets. They could see Eikedokktoppen from the boat—a flat mountaintop, with steep slopes down to the lake.

"We'll have to climb up from the back," Martin explained. "The easiest thing is to pack and return to the pickup first, and then follow the path from there."

Their catch was slightly less than the previous day. They rinsed the fish and salted them down while the nets dried in the sun. Afterwards they packed their rucksacks, tidied and swept the floors before Martin locked the cabin door.

Wisting was anxious to go home now. He had considered suggesting they forego the extra hike, but at the same time he had not accomplished what he wanted on the fishing trip. The walk to Eikedokktoppen would provide him with an extra opportunity to coax something out of Martin Haugen.

The bucket of salted fish was heavy and cumbersome to carry through the forest. They took turns but, after a few hundred metres, Wisting set it down and found a branch to hang the bucket from. They hoisted the log on to their shoulders to enable them to carry it between them along the narrow path. Martin went first. Wisting's eyes were fixed on the back of his neck. Within the next twenty-four hours he would be arrested, he thought. The fingerprints on the kidnap letters, together with the discovery of Nadia Krogh's body, would be enough to charge him. A good defence counsel would point the finger at Katharina. She was the one who had left the directions about where the corpse was buried. A lawyer could also claim that Martin knew what she had done, but this was not the same as being an accomplice.

These two days at the cabin had affected him. Working undercover was alien to him and had done something to his self-esteem. In all his years in the police he had endeavoured to be honest, direct and combative in encounters with both colleagues and criminals. His manipulations in regard to Martin troubled him and he was pleased the trip would soon be over.

When they reached the pickup Martin shoved the bucket of fish under the tarpaulin on the flat cargo bed and used straps to tie it down and prevent it from toppling when they started driving.

Wisting's thoughts turned to Nadia Krogh. "Have you always driven a pickup?" he asked.

Martin flipped up the tailgate. "Yes," he answered. "It's really practical. You can carry all sorts of things. I had a couple of off-road motorbikes as a teenager that I used to race. It was great having them on the cargo bed instead of having to tow a trailer."

"Have you ever been in any accidents?"

"That's inevitable," Martin replied. "I drove off the track and broke my collarbone when I was twenty. After that I gave it up."

"I meant in your pickup," Wisting said, walking round to the side of the vehicle. "They seem pretty solid, if anything should happen."

"I've had one accident in the thirty-six years I've had a driving licence," Martin said with a smile.

"I've had two," Wisting said. "Once in a police car during an emergency callout and another time in a little Fiesta. It was a write-off. Since then I've only driven Volvos. They can certainly take a knock."

"These can too," Martin assured him.

"It was my fault both times," Wisting went on, relating how he had crashed at a roundabout in the police patrol car and driven into the rear of another car in the little Fiesta.

"It was the same with me," Martin said. "I drove into the back of a lorry."

"Was that a long time ago?" Wisting asked him.

Martin began walking. "Yes, it was before Katharina went missing," he replied.

A thought crossed Wisting's mind as he took the first steps towards the overgrown path. With every step he took, it grew into a completely self-evident prospect of explaining how Martin Haugen had obtained his alibi.

He tried to reconstruct some of what was in the case documents as he carried on walking. The last phone conversation with Katharina was one of the components of Martin's statement that did not add up. It had lasted for eight minutes and seventeen seconds, with Martin claiming the call was just general before they said good night. Eight minutes was a relatively lengthy phone call. Seen in the light of what they now knew, the conversation had probably been about how Katharina's conscience had been eating away at her and that she intended to hand herself in to the police. It would have been a difficult conversation to have by phone, so Katharina might well have jumped on the motorbike and driven north. They could have met at an agreed spot, and maybe this was when Martin Haugen had reacted with what he had called "inherited primeval instincts" that cannot be controlled. He had gone on the attack. Afterwards he could have concealed the body just as they had done earlier with Nadia, and stowed the motorbike on the cargo bed of the pickup so that he could trundle it into place in the garage when he arrived home.

It was a simple but plausible explanation which, at present, only Wisting could see.

He stumbled on a tree root hidden beneath the brown foliage but regained his footing. It was obvious the path was not much used. Vegetation grew in from both sides and they continually had to avoid bare overhanging branches. In some places they had to walk around fallen trees blocking the path. After a few kilometres they arrived at a fork. The path they took was even narrower and swept up through the landscape. Wisting felt his pulse rate increase and his back become clammy.

Beside a massive oak tree a stream crossed the path. Martin stopped, filled his hand with water and took a drink. Wisting followed suit, and then they continued.

The trip to the summit took an hour, as Martin had predicted. They walked to the edge, where the mountain plunged steeply downwards, to obtain the best view possible. Wisting struggled to find his bearings. The breeze tugged at his trouser legs as he looked out at the vista. He saw the lake where they had rowed and fished, and in the distance he could discern the sea as a darker blue stripe against the pale sky. Apart from that, the forest-clad landscape stretched out in every direction below them.

"There you see Grenland Bridge," Martin said, pointing east.

Wisting could see the two bridge towers projecting like spires. "Were you involved in building that?" he asked.

"Not the bridge, but the tunnel on the north side," Martin told him.

Wisting picked up a stone and threw it over the edge, leaning forward slightly to see it land on the scree below.

"It was my grandfather who brought me up here the first time," Martin said behind him.

Wisting remained standing, with his back turned.

"He said it was a site of historical significance," Martin went on. "The Vikings took their elderly up here, the ones who had become a burden on the community, so that they could sacrifice them.

They also made people who had done irreparable harm and dishonoured their families throw themselves off."

Martin came to stand by his side. "I think it was just something he made up," he said. "There have never been Vikings here, but I remember I was shocked by the story. I was probably only five or six, and that sort of thing can terrify a youngster. I had nightmares about it. The idea that someone could more or less voluntarily throw himself off a precipice was totally inconceivable at that time."

Wisting peered over the edge again. "There are certainly better ways to die," he commented.

"Do you remember what I told you about my ashes?" Martin asked, taking a step back. "This would be an excellent place to scatter them."

There was a disquieting tenor to the whole conversation.

"Write it down," Wisting said, trying to dismiss his seriousness with a smile.

Martin lingered for a while, also with a smile on his face. "What are you going to do when you get home?" he asked.

"Line and Amalie will probably come and visit," Wisting answered, aware of an anxiety that made him step away from the edge. "She's growing up so fast now. She's standing and walking and jabbering away."

His thoughts suddenly turned to Ingrid, who had died whilst working for an aid organization in Zambia.

"She's called after her grandmother, you know," he continued. "Ingrid Amalie, but we only use Amalie. I often think of Ingrid when I see her, and how she didn't live to see her granddaughter. But it's good to know she was where she wanted to be in her life when we lost her," he added, in an attempt to bring the conversation back to Martin. "She was so happy when I spoke to her on the phone for the last time. Delighted at what they had achieved and the possibilities that lay ahead."

Martin was silent. Wisting prepared to ask what he and Katharina had talked about before she had disappeared but did not get that far.

"Katharina was pregnant," Martin told him. His eyes were fixed on the horizon.

"When she disappeared?" Wisting asked, taken aback.

"Long before that," Martin replied. "She lost the baby."

"I didn't know that," Wisting said, adding how sorry he was.

Martin Haugen turned his head the other way. Dark clouds were gathering in the west. "It's going to rain again," he said. "Shall we head back?"

76

Adrian Stiller knew he could sleep, if he had the chance to lie down, but there was no possibility of rest now.

The motor-vehicle records stated that Martin Haugen had driven a Nissan King Cab at the end of the eighties. There had been several owners after him, before the vehicle was deregistered in 1996.

He swung in and parked in front of Steinar Vassvik's house, stepped out of the car and approached the front door. It opened before he had even rung the doorbell, and he recognized Steinar Vassvik from the day he and Wisting had driven past.

Vassvik made no move to invite him in when Stiller introduced himself. "I'm working on old, unsolved cases," he said.

Steinar Vassvik's only response was a brief nod.

"One of the cases we're looking at now is the Katharina case," he went on. "I'm trying to plug some gaps in the old inquiry and wondered if you could help me?"

Another nod of the head, but they still remained standing outside the house. That suited Stiller. He had not intended to stay long.

"What sort of vehicles did Katharina have access to?"

"Isn't that in the file?" Vassvik asked.

"It's my job to verify old information," Stiller replied.

"Can't Martin explain all that?" Vassvik asked, casting a glance at the gravel track opposite them.

"Probably," Stiller said, leafing through some paperwork he had with him. "I've been told she had a Golf and a Kawasaki Z650: is that right?"

Vassvik answered with another brief nod.

"What kind of vehicle did Martin Haugen have at that time?"

The response was rapid. "A pickup. He's always driven a pickup."

"Did Katharina ever use it?" he asked, in an effort to camouflage the information he really sought.

This time Vassvik shook his head.

"Can you recall whether any of the vehicles were damaged in a collision at any time?"

Steinar Vassvik moved his head from side to side thoughtfully. "No," he said, in the end.

"A smashed windscreen, or anything?" Stiller added helpfully.

"There was something," Vassvik came up with eventually. "But it was long before Katharina disappeared."

"What was that?" Stiller queried.

"Martin had driven into a lorry."

Adrian Stiller had to drag additional information out of him.

"He had damaged parts of the bonnet and the right side," Vassvik said. "It was Larsen who fixed it up."

"Larsen?"

Steinar Vassvik gestured in the direction where Stiller had earlier spotted an old vehicle workshop by the roadside. "He's dead now," he added. "But I don't think you'd have found any paperwork for it, if that was what you were looking for. Larsen wasn't very fussy about receipts and that kind of thing."

Stiller envisaged how easy it would have been for Martin Haugen to drive a different car to cover up the damage sustained when he had knocked down Nadia Krogh.

"But you're sure there was substantial damage?" he pressed him.

Before he had dragged out a positive answer, they were interrupted by his phone. Nils Hammer was ringing.

"I had a phone call from the police in Trøndelag," he said brusquely. "The cadaver dog has identified a spot on the hard shoulder, right beside the landslip area."

"I'm coming in," Stiller said, and ended the call.

He thanked Steinar Vassvik as he made for his car. They were closing in on something. Now he was on tenterhooks to know what Wisting had uncovered during the fishing trip.

77

The first light raindrops pattered on the pickup's windscreen when they clambered inside.

"Just in the nick of time," Martin said, turning the ignition.

Wisting leaned forward to look up at the dark sky and narrowly avoided hitting his head on the glass when one of the front wheels bumped into a big pothole.

The pickup jolted forward. Wisting fastened his seatbelt and held tightly to the handle above his window as they lurched along the track.

At last they reached the barrier. Wisting jumped out into the drizzling rain and opened it. Martin passed through and turned out on to the asphalt of the main road before Wisting closed the padlock and hopped back inside.

The tyres turned steadily on the smooth surface. As Martin switched on the car radio, Wisting searched the dashboard for a clock. He discovered it was three o'clock at the very moment the news was announced on the radio.

Martin turned up the volume. Although he was completely unprepared for it, the information made sense to Wisting as soon as he heard it:

"Police sources confirm that human remains were found last night beside the E18 in Porsgrunn which are believed to be of missing Nadia Krogh. The search was initiated after the investigation into the twenty-

six-year-old case was reopened earlier in the week. The E18 was closed all night while the work was carried out . . ."

The newsreader continued speaking about the kidnap case, but the words were lost on Wisting. He took a deep breath. The small compartment felt airless. Now the confrontation would come. A cramping pain pounded his chest, like the onset of a heart attack.

He twisted his head warily to the side. Martin Haugen's demeanour had grown surly and his face wore an obstinate expression.

"They've found her," Wisting said, in an effort to continue the pretence.

Martin did not utter a word. His eyes narrowed and he kept his eyes focused on the road ahead.

Wisting was unsure whether he would be able to keep this up any longer. They had circled around each other for three days, both sensing something lurking beneath the surface. Now the pressure had become too intense.

"You must stop," he said, his throat dry. "Pull in to the verge. We need to talk."

He could not trace any discernible reaction in Martin, apart from the vehicle speeding up.

78

In the course of a few hours, over a million people had read the news story about the remains which had been found, probably belonging to Nadia Krogh. Interest in the story had also caused a meteoric rise in the number of podcast listeners. Almost two hundred thousand had heard the first podcast.

Line had put Amalie to bed and allowed her to take a bottle of warm milk with her. She knew this was a bad habit, but she needed peace and quiet to work.

She linked the recorder to her phone and sat down at her writing desk. "This is an interim podcast while the story develops," she began. "It's just over twenty-four hours since I last spoke to Robert Gran, but a great deal has happened since then. Six hours ago I left the location where police believe they have found the remains of his girlfriend, who went missing in 1987. Now I am going to try to call him."

She dialled the number and heard it ring in her earphones before Robert Gran answered.

"Hi, Robert," Line said, leaving an eloquent pause. "I assume you've heard what happened last night?"

The phone crackled as he took a deep breath and then exhaled slowly. "Yes," he confirmed.

"Has anyone given you official notification?"

"Nobody's told me anything," he replied. "I don't have a part in this, as her parents do. I only know what I've seen on the Internet."

"I was there," Line told him.

"I know that."

"What are your thoughts on it?" Line asked, in the hope of eliciting an emotionally charged response. "Now that she's been found?"

"It's a bit strange. Unreal, in a sense. I've waited for this, for this to happen, but at the same time it's come out of the blue."

He inhaled noisily and continued: "I hope they find out something more. Who did it, and how it happened."

Unable to draw much more out of him, she ended the conversation and rang Liv Hovet for her reaction.

"I was down there having a look this morning," Liv Hovet told her. "It's just down the road from here. It's spooky to think she's been lying there all this time because it implies that the kidnapper must be from around these parts too."

"What do you mean?" Line asked.

"Well, she must have been kidnapped and killed here, since her body was hidden close to where she disappeared."

Line passed no comment on this theory but no longer believed that this was a case of kidnapping. It had been a fabrication to cover up what had taken place and to remove suspicion from her innocent boyfriend.

She wrapped up the conversation and saved the file, together with the other two interviews, to allow Daniel Leanger to start editing them without delay. She then sat down to read out some concluding remarks, without a script but using a few keywords on the notepad in front of her.

"In this episode you heard the kidnappers' demands and how only now, after twenty-six years, Nadia's body has in all likelihood been found. What actually happened? Was this a kidnapping that went wrong, or is the whole Nadia Krogh mystery about something else entirely?

"We, the makers of this podcast, believe we know what occurred and, although the story is bigger than anyone imagined, the solution is simpler. What we know and who we believe to be responsible for Nadia Krogh's death are theories we will explore in the next episode."

She stopped the recorder and sat mulling things over for a while before reading out a new version in which she did not promise any disclosures. She uploaded both versions and left it up to Daniel Leanger and the editors to choose which one to use. Her own preference was the first.

79

"Was it Katharina who ran her over?" Wisting asked.

Slender tree trunks hurtled past on either side of the pickup. Martin did not answer, but Wisting noticed a slight head movement, an almost imperceptible nod.

"You just helped her to conceal the body? Cleared things up?"

The vehicle tilted as they rounded a corner, but Martin did not reduce his speed.

Wisting accepted his silence as confirmation, but this was not something that would register on the hidden recorder in his jacket sleeve.

"Do you remember how I told you that she might have packed her suitcase for going into prison?" Wisting went on, but still received no answer. "I think she wanted to take responsibility for what she had done. For Nadia's death."

He questioned how far he should go in confronting Martin Haugen at this precise moment. No matter what he did or said, Martin was the one in charge. He was the one in the driving seat.

"The code on the kitchen table," he said. "It was a sketch that showed where Nadia Krogh was hidden."

In a sense, Katharina had solved the case for them by leaving that note. Martin could have removed it when he returned home to the empty house twenty-four years ago, but he couldn't touch anything. He himself had sent his neighbour up to the house, to reinforce his alibi, which had also constrained him. Steinar Vassvik would tell the police he had seen a handwritten message on the kitchen table, and it would seem suspicious if it had vanished.

The pickup veered to one side again. Martin did not say anything but simply increased his speed yet another notch.

Wisting peered forward. A long, flat expanse stretched out before them, and a timber lorry was approaching from the other end.

80

"The vehicle's on the move," Hammer reported, his eyes nailed to the computer screen.

The red dot indicating the position of Martin Haugen's pickup was in motion.

"They're on their way home," Adrian Stiller concluded.

Hammer's phone rang. He answered, listened and made an arrangement to have pictures and documents from the dig in Malvik sent over. Then he turned to face the others.

"That was from the police in Trøndelag," he said. "They've found something in the collapsed area of the E6. Bones and other remains, enough to ascertain that they're human."

"Katharina Haugen," Stiller decided, turning to Christine Thiis. "It's time you wrote out an arrest order."

Acquiescing, the police prosecutor disappeared from the room.

"What do we do now?" Hammer asked. "Where should we apprehend him?"

"Somewhere along the road," Stiller replied. "Once he has dropped Wisting off but before he reaches home."

Hammer looked at the screen. "We've got forty minutes or so," he calculated, starting to search for a number on his phone. "We'll need reinforcements. He's probably armed."

Stiller stood with his eyes on the red dot on the computer screen. It was no longer moving. "Do you need to refresh the image or something?" he asked, remembering how the surveillance picture had frozen earlier.

"Not usually," Hammer replied. "The movements are in real time."

Nevertheless, he pressed a key. The onscreen image disappeared for a brief second before reappearing. The red dot was still motionless in the same spot, in the middle of a long stretch of road.

"They've stopped," Hammer said. "Something's happened."

81

The side draught from the massive timber lorry made the pickup sway as the two vehicles passed.

Martin braked hard and swung into a lay-by at the roadside. The vehicle skidded into the gravel on rigid wheels. When it had come to a halt, he turned to face Wisting. "You need to get out," he said.

"Tell me what happened," Wisting insisted.

Martin shook his head.

"No matter what happened, we can resolve things," Wisting continued. "It might look hopeless right now, but that's what my job is—finding a solution to these matters."

Martin leaned forward and rested his head on the steering wheel. He looked resigned for a moment, but then pulled out something concealed beneath his seat. The pistol. It had been in the pickup all the time.

"I want you to get out," he said, cradling the pistol on his lap.

Wisting grabbed hold of the door handle. "I'd like to know what happened first," he said, opening the door a crack.

Martin gulped. "It was my suggestion," he began.

The rest of his explanation came in stops and starts, more or less in words of one syllable, as if he were short of time. "We'd been in Heistad. With friends from work. Katharina was driving. She was pregnant. I suggested we should drive along the new road. It wasn't in use yet. The asphalt had been laid that same day. It was totally black. No road markings. No street lights. I didn't see her at all. Not until her face was on the front windscreen."

"An accident," Wisting said, to soften what had happened. "She was wearing dark clothes. No reflective strips."

"There was an excavator nearby," Martin went on. "After fifteen minutes every trace was gone. The only thing left on the road when we made to leave was her purse, so we took that with us. Everything went smoothly, but then they arrested her boyfriend and Katharina took it into her head to fake a kidnapping."

His words were coming faster now. Everything he had held inside. It was like a dam bursting. He related how he had crashed his pickup to camouflage the damage caused by knocking her down and how everything had affected Katharina. She had lost the baby and slid into a depression. She had wanted to turn herself in and, in the early hours of 10 October 1989, had visited him in an attempt to persuade him to do the same. It had ended in the worst possible way. The flood of words came as confirmation of everything Wisting had already figured out. All they had talked about during the fishing trip had built a foundation for an admission. Martin had been drawn into Katharina's psychological drama until he reached his breaking point. Now he pushed all the blame and responsibility on to her.

"You have to go now," he said, once he had got it all off his chest.

"Let's do this the proper way," Wisting requested.

Martin Haugen lifted the pistol from his lap and flicked his wrist as if to wave Wisting away.

"Out!" he ordered.

82

Adrian Stiller stood with arms crossed and legs straddled, feet planted in the middle of the floor in the cramped CS room. He enjoyed the feeling when everything he had mobilized gradually intensified in pace, as well as the pressure and sense of responsibility for something important.

Hammer placed his mobile phone on the desk in front of him. "He's probably run out of battery power," he said.

Stiller rubbed his eyes. Kaleidoscopic patches flickered on the inside of his eyelids. The red dot was still on the same spot when his gaze returned to the screen.

"Can we send out an unmarked car?" he asked.

Hammer picked up his phone again. "I'll try Telemark," he said. "They're nearest."

"What about the additional manpower?"

"They're assembling down in the garage as we speak."

Stiller listened as Hammer talked to his colleagues in Telemark, explaining the situation and giving them the position of Haugen's vehicle.

"To begin with, all I want is for you to drive past and observe," Hammer concluded.

Stiller wondered whether lack of sleep was playing tricks on him. It looked as if the dot on the screen had moved off again. He forced his eyes shut and opened them again, keeping his eyes fixed on the screen so that he could be certain.

"They're moving again!" he said.

The red marker continued onwards, into Porsgrunn town centre, following the same route Haugen and Wisting had driven when they had travelled to the cabin two days earlier.

There was a tap on the door behind them and Stiller opened it wide. Christine had returned with the arrest order.

"Any news?" she asked.

Stiller pointed at the screen. "They'll be here in half an hour," he told her.

As he said this, the red marker turned to the left and took a different road.

"Where are they going now?" Christine asked, but she received no answer.

"We can't just stand here," Stiller said, grabbing Hammer's arm. "We'll have to go out in the car."

83

Wisting was left standing at the roadside, watching the pickup disappear in a cloud of dust.

It took ninety seconds before a car arrived. Wisting stepped into the middle of the road and waved his arms frantically. The car slowed down before sounding its horn, swerving to one side and driving past.

He produced the police ID from his wallet and tried to stop the next car with his arm outstretched and his palm in the air, as he had learned on his basic police-training course almost thirty-five years ago.

A young woman was behind the wheel. She too reduced her speed and Wisting made eye contact with her through the windscreen. She looked terrified, and he made no further effort to detain her when the car moved out to overtake him.

The next car came from the opposite direction: an old dark-blue Volvo. Wisting got the driver to brake and the car stopped beside him. The driver was a boy in his late teens, with a baseball cap and shoulder-length blond hair. He rolled down the window and scouted around, as if searching for a broken-down car or one that had driven off the road.

Wisting held out his police badge, explaining how urgent the situation was, and that it had to do with a kidnapping case.

"The Krogh case?" the young lad asked.

"What makes you think that?" Wisting queried.

"It's all over the news," the boy explained.

Wisting skirted round the car and jumped in. "What's your name?" he asked.

"Even."

"Well, Even, I'd like you to turn round."

"Turn round?"

"Yes. Did you pass a pickup?"

"Yes, it was driving like a bat out of hell."

"Then I think you should get a move on and turn round," Wisting told him.

The boy turned the steering wheel and made a U-turn. "We're never going to manage to catch up with it," he said.

"I can find out where it is," Wisting said, fastening his seatbelt. "I just need to borrow your phone."

Even reached into the inside pocket of his open leather jacket, pulled out a mobile phone and handed it to Wisting.

84

Stiller was driving. Hammer sat beside him with the tablet on his lap. The red marker was moving through the streets of Porsgrunn town centre, now travelling at a considerably reduced speed.

The mobile phone rang and an unknown number appeared on the dashboard screen. Stiller answered from behind the wheel. The voice that filled the car was remarkably steady.

"It's Wisting."

"Where are you?"

"In a requisitioned car with a borrowed phone," the chief inspector answered. "Where's Haugen? Are you tracking him?"

"He's on the move," Stiller replied, leaving it to Hammer to give an exact position. "What happened to you?"

"My cover's blown," Wisting explained. "I was ordered out of the pickup. He has that gizmo you couldn't find when the electricity was cut off."

Stiller realized he was speaking in riddles to avoid his driver understanding the reference to a gun. "Did he say anything?" he asked.

"Yes," Wisting confirmed. "It all came spilling out."

Stiller took one hand from the steering wheel and raised his clenched fist in a gesture of triumph.

"He's stopped," Hammer said from the passenger seat.

"Where?"

"He's just turned and is now heading in a different direction," Hammer reported.

"Where is he going?" Wisting demanded.

Glancing down at the tablet on Hammer's knee, Stiller followed the red dot, but waited for a moment to be sure before responding. "It looks as if he's on his way to the discovery site."

The phone line crackled. "Where exactly?" Wisting asked.

"The E18," Stiller told him. "Where we dug up Nadia."

85

They kept the phone line open.

Wisting asked the boy behind the wheel to accelerate. "We're going out on the E18," he explained, estimating it would take them eight or nine minutes. He shifted the phone to his other ear. "Do we have any patrol cars in the vicinity?" he asked.

"We're closest," Stiller replied. "Less than six minutes."

"What about Martin Haugen?"

This time Hammer answered: "Two minutes."

They drove on without a word. The young driver pulled out and overtook a taxi.

"Which way?" he asked, as they approached a roundabout.

It dawned on Wisting that they could drive via Herøya and reach the E18 south of the discovery site while Hammer and Stiller closed in from the north. It would probably also be quicker.

"To the right," he ordered, pointing.

A man in a black BMW gave a loud blast of his horn as the young lad squeezed his car in front of him.

"He's getting closer," Hammer said. "Less than half a minute now. Do we have a plan for this?"

Neither Wisting nor Stiller made any response.

Through the phone connection, Wisting could hear the police radio in the other car, with various patrol vehicles reporting their positions, and sirens in the background.

"Two hundred metres away," Hammer announced.

Wisting moved the phone to his other ear again.

"One hundred metres," Hammer continued.

Something was said on the police radio that Wisting could not catch. "He's not stopping!" Hammer exclaimed. "He's driving past."

Stiller swore. His voice was louder on the phone, close to the microphone of the hands-free set.

"What's he up to?" he asked.

"He's driven this route before," Wisting said. "His courage failed him last time. He's going to Hannah and Joachim Krogh's house to tell them what happened to their daughter."

Stiller swore again.

Wisting could hear him banging on the steering wheel. "He's armed and mentally unstable," he reminded them. "Don't we have any units to cut him off?"

"Turning off towards Heistad now," Hammer updated them. "He'll be there in two minutes flat."

Various announcements were broadcast on the police radio. Wisting realized he was in the best position to stop the pickup, but he would not be able to arrive there in time.

86

Wisting was first to get there. It had taken four minutes and eleven seconds.

He directed the driver to move slowly past the grandiose house belonging to the Krogh family. The wrought-iron gate was open and Martin Haugen's grey pickup was parked inside. There was no one to be seen.

He described what he was seeing over the open phone line and asked the young driver to turn and park his car at the kerb fifty metres below the house.

"What shall we do?" he asked.

"Wait for reinforcements," Wisting told him.

The boy nodded, as if the answer was exactly in line with his expectations.

Three minutes later Adrian Stiller and Nils Hammer appeared. Wisting thanked the teenager and opened the door to leave the car.

"You can go now," he said.

"Can't I stay?" the boy asked.

"You can do whatever you like, but don't come any closer than this."

Wisting hopped in beside Hammer and Stiller. Hammer was on the phone providing details to the operative crew when Wisting joined them.

"Her poor parents," Stiller commented. "They should have been spared this."

Wisting made no comment.

"Do you really think he's sitting in there telling them all about it?" Stiller asked.

"With a gun!"

"They're not at home," Hammer said. He lowered his phone and peered up at the house. "They've gone as far away as possible from the media and all the fuss."

Stiller leaned forward to the windscreen. "Is he in there on his own?"

Three uniformed police patrol cars swept into the street. One of them passed the house before drawing to a halt. Three armed officers stepped out, forced their way into the next-door garden and took up position at the rear of the house. The leader of the operation approached the vehicle in which the three investigators were seated.

"We don't want to end up with a situation where he barricades himself in," he said. "Can we phone him and try to talk him out?"

The two detectives in the car turned to Wisting. "I'll have to borrow a phone," he said. Hammer handed him his: Wisting looked up the number and rang it but found it unavailable.

"Shall we go in, then?" the leader asked.

"Check the pickup first," Wisting told him.

Adrian Stiller started the engine and drew a bit closer so that they could more easily follow what was going on. The armed unit's leader gave a few short instructions and four officers moved forward. Two of them covered the others with guns trained on the house, while the other two closed in on the pickup. One cast a rapid glance into the driver's cab before opening the door.

"Empty," he reported over the radio.

"The cargo bed," Wisting suggested.

He caught sight of his fishing rod propped up against a large flowerpot—only the top was visible—with his rucksack beside it. Martin must have removed both.

"He's lying under the tarpaulin," he added.

Fresh instructions were conveyed by radio. The security cordon round the house was maintained as the two police officers walked behind the pickup. One took a couple of steps to one side and directed his weapon at the tailgate as his colleague prepared to open it, with one hand on his pistol holster.

They exchanged brief nods and the tailgate was flipped down.

From the car, Wisting and his fellow-officers could see the soles of a pair of boots. Wisting opened the rear passenger door and stepped out. The policeman who had opened the tailgate had drawn his gun again.

"Come out!" he ordered, but there was no response.

Wisting moved slowly towards them. Pink liquid flowed along the joints of the cargo bed, streaming towards the opening—a mixture of blood and brine.

The policeman took hold of one foot and dragged Martin Haugen closer to the opening. He hunched over him, but soon wheeled round to face the unit leader, gesturing across his throat. Dead.

Wisting stepped forward to confirm Martin Haugen's identity.

The shot had entered his head at the right temple and exited again on the opposite side, shattering the bucket of salted fish.

Stiller arrived alongside him. Wisting turned towards him without uttering a word. He speculated about what kind of person Stiller was, when push came to shove. Whether he was someone who ran away or someone who went on the attack in a threatening situation.

"Did he really confess?" Stiller asked.

Slipping his hand into his jacket sleeve, Wisting unhitched the tiny recorder and handed it to him.

"It's all there," he said, "if your technology has worked."

Stiller took the chip as if it were something rare and precious.

As Wisting turned once again to Martin Haugen's dead body, it crossed his mind that this was not a matter of fight or flight. Martin Haugen believed he had an inherited instinct to resist but, really, he had been on the run for the past twenty-four years. It was all over now.

87

Amalie was sitting on the settee playing with an iPad while Line was curled up with her laptop when Wisting arrived to see them. Both seemed equally engrossed.

"It was Thomas who taught her that," Line said, without looking up from her computer.

Laughing, Wisting whisked Amalie on to his lap, though she still kept a tight grip on the iPad.

"It's probably safer than playing with ballpoint pens," he said with a chuckle.

Line barely looked up from her machine.

"I thought you'd finished writing," Wisting said.

"This is something else," Line explained.

"I listened to the last podcast episode," Wisting told her. "It's a shame there won't be more."

He knew six had been planned but, in the end, there had been only three, and by the time the final episode was released the case had already been solved.

"What are you working on now?" he asked, nodding in the direction of the laptop.

"Family-history research," Line said, glancing up at last. "We do have a Stiller in our family, and I thought maybe we were related to Adrian Stiller, far back on the family tree somewhere. But we're not. A bit of a shame, really," she added with a smile. "Because he's rich and has no heirs."

Wisting returned her smile.

"It seems Stiller isn't his real name, though," Line went on. "None of his relatives is called that. His parents use the surname Palm. They live in South Africa. That's Adrian's name too, but he changed it when he was twenty and returned to Norway to start at police college."

Line turned to face the computer screen again. "But there's something else, something very interesting about him," she added. "His girlfriend disappeared and is presumed dead."

Wisting's eyes widened.

"In South Africa, when he was eighteen," Line continued. "I'm looking into it now. She was never found, and the case remains unsolved. Now, eighteen years later, he's working in the Norwegian Cold Cases Group. Do you think he'd be interested in talking about it in an interview?"

"I don't know him very well," Wisting replied, "but I doubt it. I haven't heard of this story, and it's most likely not something he'd be keen to talk about."

"Is he still in town?"

Wisting nodded. "I'm meeting him later. There's some paperwork to clear up."

Line looked pensively at the screen, where images of English-language newspaper pages were displayed.

"I must find out a bit more before I ask him," she decided.

88

It was time to clear his desk. Wisting sorted out work notes and sheets of scrap paper, some more than twenty years old. There were still unanswered questions about Katharina and Nadia, but now the cases had been closed these less significant mysteries would, regrettably, remain unsolved.

He stood with a note in his hand, reading it several times over before bringing it through to Adrian Stiller's office.

Stiller was also clearing up. He placed ring binders in an empty cardboard box and threw loose sheets of paper in a recycling carton. His pass lay on the corner of the desk, ready to be returned.

He seemed in better shape than he had in recent days. Rested. Wisting's thoughts turned to what Line had told him about his girlfriend, and the motivation he clearly had to work on unsolved cases.

"I know about it," he said, advancing further into the room.

Stiller removed a note peppered with phone numbers from the noticeboard. "What's that?" he asked, turning to face Wisting.

"I know you were the one who wrote the anonymous message to Martin Haugen," Wisting explained, holding up a copy of the four words. *I know about it.*

Stiller broke into a smile. "How did you find out?"

"It can't have been anyone else," Wisting told him. "No one apart from Martin Haugen knew what had happened to Nadia. Besides, I've learned about the way you work."

"How's that?"

"You use provocation as a method and always have a hidden agenda."

Stiller smiled again. "Haugen needed a little push," he said. "To start the ball rolling."

"Was it you I saw outside his house, on the evening of 10 October? On the anniversary of her disappearance?"

"I just wanted to see whether he'd been home and found the note. But it was good fortune that you came, to prevent me from going any further forward. I had no idea about the cameras he had installed."

"But we sent it for analysis," Wisting went on, holding up the note again.

Stiller shook his head. "It was never documented," he said. "I never submitted it. It was only meant to keep him on his toes."

Wisting was unsure whether it was the method itself or having been kept out of the loop that he disliked.

"I've listened to the entire conversation between you and Haugen," Stiller went on. "I'm having it transcribed, but it contains everything the public prosecutor needs to close the case."

Wisting responded with a nod.

"There's just one thing I was wondering," Stiller continued, shutting the flaps on the cardboard box. "It's really a side issue, but that wrapped gift you said her grandmother had brought home from Paris for Nadia. Can we find out what was in it now?"

Wisting smiled. He knew what Stiller was after. There was no present from Paris. It had been a story Wisting had manufactured in an attempt to prick Martin's conscience, to give him a prod in the direction of a confession.

"Words or actions," Stiller added, lifting the cardboard box from the desk. "It's really just a matter of striving to reach a goal."

Wisting looked at the sheet of paper in his hand and folded it in two. "Where are you going now?" he asked. "Do you have a new case?"

"I'm off to Bergen," Stiller replied. "Someone in prison over there wants to tell me how he buried a body seventeen years ago."

Wisting stepped aside as Stiller moved towards the door.

"What about you?" he asked. "Any new, major cases?"

Wisting shook his head. For the first time in ages his desk was completely bare.

JØRN LIER HORST worked as a police officer and head of investigations before becoming a full-time writer, establishing himself as one of the most successful authors to come out of Scandinavia. He writes engaging and intelligent crime novels that offer an uncommonly detailed and realistic insight into the way serious crimes are investigated, as well as how both police and the press work. His books have sold more than three million copies in his native Norway alone, and he is published in forty countries. His literary awards include the Norwegian Booksellers' Prize, the Riverton Prize ("The Golden Revolver"), the Glass Key award, and the prestigious Best Crime Novel in Swedish Translation award from the Swedish Crime Writers' Academy.

About the Author

ANNE BRUCE studied Norwegian and English at the University of Glasgow and now lives on the Isle of Arran, Scotland. She has translated a number of crime novels by Anne Holt and Jørn Lier Horst, including the Petrona Prize–winning *The Caveman* and *When It Grows Dark*, which was longlisted for the CWA International Dagger in 2017.